❦ A ❦
HIDDEN TRUTH

Books by
Judith Miller

www.judithmccoymiller.com

*with Tracie Peterson

HOME TO AMANA

A HIDDEN TRUTH

JUDITH MILLER

BETHANYHOUSE

a division of Baker Publishing Group
Minneapolis, Minnesota

© 2012 by Judith Miller

Published by Bethany House Publishers
11400 Hampshire Avenue South
Bloomington, Minnesota 55438
www.bethanyhouse.com

Bethany House Publishers is a division of
Baker Publishing Group, Grand Rapids, Michigan

Printed in the United States of America

Scripture quotations are from the King James Version of the Bible.

This is a work of fiction. Names, characters, incidents, and dialogues are products of the author's imagination and are not to be construed as real. Any resemblance to actual events or persons, living or dead, is entirely coincidental.

Library of Congress Cataloging-in-Publication Data
Miller, Judith, 1944–
    A hidden truth / Judith Miller.
       p.   cm. — (Home to Amana)
    ISBN 978-0-7642-1000-6 (pbk.)
       1. Young women—Fiction. 2. Family secrets—Fiction. 3. Amana Society—Fiction. I. Title.
    PS3613.C3858H53 2012
    813'.6—dc23   2012013125

Cover design by Lookout Design, Inc.

Author is represented by Books & Such Literary Agency

12   13   14   15   16   17   18   7   6   5   4   3   2   1

To the people of Amana
—for their kindness and inspiration.

Know ye that the Lord he is God:
it is he that hath made us,
and not we ourselves; we are his people,
and the sheep of his pasture.

—PSALM 100:3 KJV

 CHAPTER 1

Saturday, October 29, 1892
Over-the-Rhine District, Cincinnati, Ohio
Dovie Cates

"I won't be going with you."

My breath evaporated in thin, ghostlike whorls as I uttered the words.

The skirt of my black mourning dress whipped in the brisk breeze, and I pressed a gloved hand against the fabric before turning to meet my father's steely gaze.

Never before had I spoken with such authority. But life had changed. And not for the better.

I had questions. Questions that couldn't be answered by my father.

"Dovie Cates, you become more like your mother every day." My father's eyes softened.

His reaction surprised me. I was nothing like my mother. At least not in my mind. We had shared the same thick

7

chestnut-brown hair and hazel eyes, but my mother had been quiet and unassuming, unwilling to speak of her past or consider the future. Traits that were nothing like my own. I fought back tears and the lump that threatened to lodge in my throat. In retrospect, it was likely best Mother hadn't worried about the future, for her life had been shorter than most. A future cut short nearly two months ago when she'd succumbed to the ravages of influenza.

Death had robbed her of a future, and it had robbed me of answers. Answers I'd been seeking. Answers about her past—her life before she'd left Iowa, before she'd met my father, and before I'd been born. Answers about her time in the Amana Colonies.

Father and I progressed along a sidewalk that fronted the narrow brick-and-frame houses built flush with the streets in the Over-the-Rhine district of Cincinnati. Sidewalks mopped or scrubbed clean each day by the German immigrants who lived in the tidy houses with backyard flower and vegetable gardens. Houses similar to the one in which I'd lived all of my twenty-two years.

My father reached inside his coat and withdrew his pipe. "Well, you can't remain in Cincinnati. I've arranged for the sale of the house, and a single young woman with no means of support, alone in the city . . ." His unfinished sentence hung in the wintry air, defying argument.

Hoping to gain his accord, I nodded my agreement. "I don't want to remain in Cincinnati, either."

He slowed his step and cupped his hand around the bowl of his pipe. Holding a match to the bowl, he puffed until the tobacco glowed red and smoke lifted toward the azure sky. "If you don't want to go to Texas with me and you don't plan to remain in Cincinnati, what is it you have in mind?"

There was no telling how my father would react to the idea. Before speaking, I clenched my hands and sent a silent prayer heavenward. "I want to go to Iowa—to the Amana Colonies—and learn of Mother's past."

His jaw went slack and the pipe slipped a notch before he clamped his lips tight around the stem. Confusion clouded his dark eyes, and he shook his head. "Foolishness."

"It isn't!" I argued. "I've given the matter a great deal of thought, and I believe it is an excellent idea."

Could my father not realize how lonely I would be in Texas? While he would be at work during the day and even out of town for short periods of time, I would be left alone in a strange city with nothing to occupy my time, without any friends—and without my mother.

"Tell me, how did you come to such a conclusion?"

"Mother would never tell me about her past—nothing before her marriage to you. Only once did she mention she had lived in the Amana Colonies, but whenever I tried to learn more, she refused to tell me. What can you tell me about her life back then?"

"Not much. And maybe your mother didn't talk about the past because it wasn't of any importance to her." My father blew a ring of smoke into the air.

When I didn't respond, he sighed.

"She did have a cousin, Louise, and they wrote to each other for a number of years." His brows furrowed. "Your mother and this Louise lived in the village known as East Amana, and they were as close as sisters—at least that's what your mother told me. When your grandparents decided to leave Iowa, your mother was forlorn. I was never certain what caused them to leave, but I know it had something to do with your grandfather. I didn't ask a lot of questions."

"Why? Weren't you inquisitive?" A strand of hair escaped, and I tucked it beneath my black bonnet.

A house *Frau* with bucket in hand opened her front door and prepared to scrub the steps leading to the border of sidewalk. She smiled a toothy grin. *"Guten Morgen."*

"Guten Morgen," my father and I replied in unison.

He took another puff from his pipe as we continued onward. "No, I wasn't particularly curious, and your mother never had any desire to discuss the past. Still, I knew her German roots were important to her. When she asked to settle in the Over-the-Rhine district rather than in another section of Cincinnati, I didn't argue. My work kept me away long hours, and I knew that until she learned English, she would be more comfortable among other Germans." He shrugged. "I knew there was no way to change anything that had happened in her past."

His answer surprised me. "Maybe not change it, but perhaps you could have better understood her, if you'd learned of her past." He shook his head as if to disagree, but I didn't stop. "What we learn from the past can help us form the future, don't you think?"

My father arched an eyebrow. "Your youth fills you with grand ideas, Dovie. Wait until you're my age and then see if you feel the same. I'm not worried about the past or the future, but I do care about the present and what I must soon accomplish. My thoughts are upon my new job in Dallas. There is the sale of the house and packing our belongings."

My stomach clenched at the firmness in his voice. I didn't want our conversation to end at an impasse. I didn't want to talk about his new position in Dallas or about selling our family home. I wanted to talk about my mother's past and who she had been before she married him and moved to Ohio.

"Do you know anything else about Mother's cousin Louise? Is she still alive?"

"I have no idea. They quit writing a long time ago, while you were still quite young. I think it was shortly after your grandparents died."

Even if my mother's parents had been alive, I doubted they would be of help. They had both died when I was quite young and prior to my birth. I gathered there had been little contact and few, if any, visits in either direction. Other than my father, there was no one who could provide the information I wanted.

He came to an abrupt halt in front of Krüger's Bakery. After knocking the tobacco from his pipe, he tucked it back into his pocket and nodded toward the door. "Why don't we go inside and have a treat?"

I wasn't certain if he was using the bakery to fend off my questions, but the sweet, yeasty smells of strudel, *Apfelkuchen*, and *Brochen* pulled me toward the bakery door. I stood in front of the counter for several minutes before making my selection and then followed my father to a small corner table. He sat opposite me with his cup of strong coffee and Apfelkuchen while I momentarily savored my own choice—a large frosted *Schnecken* with raisins generously sprinkled into the dough and smelling of warm butter and cinnamon. My mouth watered as I cut a piece with my fork.

After I swallowed the first bite, I looked up at him. "If I could locate Mother's cousin Louise and she agreed, would you allow me to go to Iowa for a visit?" I held my breath, afraid to look across the table as I waited for my father's answer. He appeared thoughtful as he took another sip of coffee. "I would be very lonely in Texas, and you will be busy with your new job." I didn't want to beg, but I'd do so if necessary.

"You are twenty-two years old, Dovie. I don't believe I can stop you from writing a letter. However, you had best be prepared for disappointment."

"But would you agree? If Cousin Louise says I'm welcome to visit, would you give permission?" Before I wrote the letter, I needed the assurance he wouldn't try to stop me once I'd made progress.

"I don't think that will happen. You don't even have a good address. But if she replies before we leave for Texas, I'll grant you permission to make a visit before joining me in Dallas."

I rose from the chair, leaned across the table, and kissed his cheek. "Thank you, Papa."

His lips curved in a melancholy smile. "It's always 'Papa' when you get your way. Am I right?"

I grinned and gave a nod. "I'll send my letter in the morning. If I write her name and East Amana, Iowa, on the envelope, it should arrive without problem, don't you think?"

After wiping his lips, he hiked one shoulder. "Who can say? I don't even know if she still lives in East Amana. There is only one way to find out, and that is to write your letter."

I grasped his hand. "Thank you, Papa. You have made me very happy." From the distant look in his eyes, I knew his decision had come at a price, and my heart constricted. He would be alone in his move to Texas.

He squeezed my hand. "Just remember, this will be for a visit and then you will join me."

A hint of German accented his final words, and I arched my eyebrows in surprise. "What has happened to your perfect English, Papa?"

He grinned. "Sometimes the German accent sneaks back without warning."

Unlike my mother, my father refused to speak German except when required. He prided himself on his excellent command of the English language. On the other hand, I don't think my mother ever felt comfortable speaking English, and her accent had remained thick until the day she died. Though she had been born in this country, my mother had learned little English until after she married Papa.

He pushed back his chair and stood. "Time to go home. There is much to do."

I was pleased he didn't want to linger. If he thought on the matter too much, he might change his mind. Besides, I wanted to get home and write my letter to Cousin Louise. For the first time since my mother's death, the gnawing pain in my heart had lessened a bit.

My father's step slowed as we neared the house. "You shouldn't get your hopes too high. You've had enough sadness these past months. While you're dreaming about being welcomed by distant relatives, you need to remember that it may not happen. Try to keep some good thoughts about coming to Dallas with your papa, too."

We walked up the front steps, and I nodded as we entered the hallway. "I'll do my best." Though I said the words, I doubted I could summon any positive thoughts of life in Texas without the company of my mother or my friends.

I'd been unable to learn much about my mother's past when she was alive, so going to Iowa at this time might be the only opportunity to discover what her life had been like in Amana— and why her family had decided to leave.

I waited until my father went upstairs to his bedroom before I gathered a pen and paper. All afternoon I'd considered what I should say. How did one ask complete strangers if they would agree to have you come for a visit? It lacked proper etiquette. Even if I'd never met them, these were not strangers—they were relatives. "We are united by blood," I whispered.

As I dipped my pen into the bottle of black ink, I prayed that kinship would be enough to open their hearts and their door.

Dear Cousin Louise,

We have never met, so I would like to introduce myself to you. I am Dovie Cates, the daughter of your cousin Barbara. I am sorry to tell you that my mother died from influenza two months ago. If you are reading this letter, you probably still live in the Amana Colonies.

My father tells me that you and Mother corresponded after she left East Amana. I am most eager to meet my mother's relatives. Please don't think me rude, but I would very much like to come to East Amana for a visit. My father is required to move to Dallas, Texas, for his work, and he has agreed that I could come for a visit, should you agree.

It had been several years since I'd written anything of consequence in German, and I studied each word. I didn't want any errors. A mistaken word or phrase could create enough misunderstanding to result in a refusal of my request.

I am a good worker and would be happy to help in any way possible during my stay. My father will soon be required to leave Cincinnati, so I would be grateful for an early reply.

> *Respectfully,*
> *Dovie Cates*

I folded the letter and tucked it into a matching cream-colored linen envelope. My father had been unable to recall the name of Cousin Louise's husband. So although I realized the impropriety, I addressed the letter to Mrs. Louise Richter, East Amana, Iowa, and sealed the contents safely inside.

Still holding the letter in my hand, I bowed my head. "Please grant me this one favor, Lord. You alone know how much it means to me."

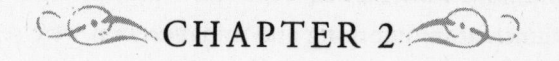

CHAPTER 2

November 1892
East Amana, Iowa
Karlina Richter

"Karlina! The mail wagon is coming. You should hurry and meet Brother Herman outside." I was nineteen years old and had been meeting the mail wagon since my fourteenth birthday, but my mother continued to give me the same instruction each day.

Even with all of the chatter and clanging of pots and pans in our kitchen house, my mother could hear Brother Herman arrive before anyone else. I wasn't sure if it was the clopping horses' hooves on the dirt road, or if she and Brother Herman had some secret signal, but my mother always knew when his wagon was approaching.

With a sweeping gesture, she waved me toward the door. "Take the outgoing mailbag to him, and when you come in, you should begin sorting. He is late again." My mother didn't need a clock to

15

tell her who was early or late. She had a natural instinct for such things. As a young child, I thought she had a small watch tucked in the pocket of her apron or hidden in some other secret place. Her sense of time could prove beneficial or worrisome. Nothing pleased Mother more than people who were on time. And nothing annoyed her more than late arrivals.

As *Küchebaas*, my mother made sure three meals a day and a light lunch at midmorning and midafternoon were served to the nearly forty villagers who lived near our kitchen house. Each meal was served on time, and everyone who worked in Mother's *Küche* soon learned that an interrupted schedule was not to Sister Louise Richter's liking. There were other kitchen houses in our small village, but none that served food as good as my mother's. At least that was my strong belief.

Because the craggy hills surrounding our village had never been considered suitable for growing crops, East Amana was the smallest of the seven villages that comprised the colonies. Though some of my friends said we were the forgotten village, I disagreed and argued we were all equal. When I'd asked my father's opinion, he'd said, *"We are all equal—but some are more equal than others."* Back then I hadn't understood. Now I had gained more insight. Still, it didn't change my love for East or for the sheep we cared for in our village.

Just as the *Grossebruderrat*, the elders charged with making decisions regarding the colonies, determined what work could best be accomplished in each village, they'd long ago decided our Küche should distribute the mail and medicine in East Amana. My mother performed those tasks in the same orderly fashion as she operated the kitchen. A large wooden structure divided into cubbyholes bore the name of each family in the village. Each day, Mother or I sorted the mail and placed it in the proper boxes for pickup. Overseeing the medicine cabinet required far less time than the mail. The medicine chest remained locked, but I knew where to find the key—just in case Mother was gone when someone needed medicine. Of course, the doctor from Main Amana could be summoned for anyone who needed care beyond the basic remedies stocked in our kitchen house.

"I'll have the mail sorted before time for the noonday meal, *Mutter*." I donned my cape and hurried toward the door. A strong breeze captured the thick wool fabric and whipped it away from my body, the cold air biting through my plain blue flannel skirt. Gathering the edge of the cloak, I pulled it tight before I waved to Brother Herman. "Guten Morgen." I looked toward the darkening sky as I called out my greeting. "It is getting colder, *ja?*"

He bobbed his head and leaned down to take the mailbag I offered. "Ja, for sure. Tell Sister Louise she should not put the blame on me for the tardy delivery. The train was late this morning." He grinned and handed me the burlap sack stamped with the word *EAST* on both sides. "Inside you should go, before you catch a cold." He pointed toward the horizon and touched the brim of his hat. "Looks like it could snow this afternoon. *Auf Wiedersehen,* Sister Karlina. And don't forget to give your Mutter my message."

"I'll tell her." Holding the bag tight in my hand, I shivered and glanced toward the sheep barns. Had Father already herded them into the barn? If not, he would likely need help. With the change of weather, his bones would be aching by the time he returned for the noonday meal. I longed to run to the barn and find out, but one look at the sack in my hand and I knew I must go inside.

After hanging my cape on the peg near the door, I stepped into the kitchen. "Brother Herman said I should tell you the train was late, so you should not blame him."

"Ja, ja. Excuses, he always has for me."

I grinned and shook the bag. "There isn't much today. I'll have it sorted and in the boxes in no time." Though my first choice was working with the sheep, I preferred sorting mail to peeling potatoes or cutting noodles. Much to my mother's dismay, the kitchen held no interest for me.

Moving through the envelopes with practiced ease, I sorted and slipped each piece into the appropriate box. As I neared the bottom of the pile, my gaze fell upon a cream-colored envelope addressed to my mother and written in a beautiful script. In the upper left corner was a smaller script bearing the name of the sender. *Dovie Cates.* I searched my mind trying to recollect if I'd ever before heard that name, but I could recall nothing. Surely I would remember such an unusual name.

I shoved the final piece of mail into the Bechmers' mail slot, picked up my mother's letter, and hurried to the kitchen. Stepping close to her side, I tapped the envelope while trying to calm my curiosity. "Who is Dovie Cates?"

My mother's eyebrows dropped low on her forehead. She took the letter from my hand and examined the handwriting. "She's my cousin Barbara's daughter." Her complexion paled and she hesitated a moment before she shoved the letter into her apron pocket. "I'll read it later."

My excitement plummeted like a deflated balloon. "Later? But there's time before the meal must be served."

"I think I am a better judge of how much time is needed." She straightened her shoulders and jutted her chin. "The letter will wait. Hungry stomachs will not."

Though I wanted to ask if I could read the letter while she continued with her chores, I bit back the request. Seeing the determined look in her eye, I knew the roasted pork, sauerkraut, and boiled potatoes would come first.

For all of us.

A short time later the men, women, and children entered the dining hall. Our parlor and bedrooms were on the upper floor of the house, while the large kitchen and dining hall encompassed the lower floor. The men took their positions at tables on one side of the room, and the women and children gathered at tables along the other side. Once prayers for the meal had been offered, everyone took their seat on the wooden benches along each side of the tables. Wood scraped on wood as everyone settled. Everyone except the kitchen workers who remained busy filling pitchers and bowls until the meal had been completed. Only then would my mother and the other workers eat.

I glanced at my father several times throughout dinner. He shifted his weight, as though sitting on the bench was causing his bones to ache. When the junior girls who were learning kitchen work began to serve our dessert of stewed apples and raisins, I managed to signal him. Once the parting prayers had been uttered and most of the others had departed, my father approached.

"You are worried about the sheep?" A faint smile curved his lips.

I nodded. "Did you get them to the barn, or do you need me to help you?" Since my father's health had worsened, I'd been assisting him more and more with the sheep. And although the work wasn't really proper for a young woman in our society, I had been around the animals since I was a young girl and had inherited my father's love for tending sheep. A fact that hadn't escaped my mother. I wasn't certain if she'd turned a blind eye to my time in the barns because I was such poor help in the Küche or because of my father's declining health. To me, the reason didn't matter. I was simply pleased she didn't object.

"Ja. They are fine." His gaze settled on the tables filled with dirty dishes. "You were hoping to get out of helping wash dishes?"

"*Nein*. It's not my week for dishwashing." I stepped closer. "Mutter received a letter today—from Dovie Cates." I waited, hoping he'd supply me with additional information, but he didn't respond.

"Was there anything else in the mail?"

I shook my head, disappointed by his lack of interest. "Mutter said she is the daughter of her cousin Barbara."

"I suppose that is right. I knew Barbara had a daughter, but I didn't remember her name. What did she say in her letter?"

My excitement mounted. Perhaps he was more interested than I'd thought. "Mutter hasn't opened the letter yet. She said she'd wait until after we finished the noonday meal."

He grinned. "And you are hoping that I will hurry her along with reading the letter. I am right?"

Seldom could I hide such feelings from my father. In my younger years he said he knew me better than I knew myself—and he probably still did. "You are right." I grasped his arm and he flinched. "I'm sorry, *Vater*. Your bones are aching more than usual today?"

"Ja. But don't say anything to your Mutter. She will only worry. Come. Let's see what we can find out about this letter from your Mutter's relatives."

I followed behind. Better to let him take the lead. My Mutter would be quicker to answer Vater's questions than my own. He stood in the kitchen doorway and waited until Mother finished talking to the other women. "You have a few minutes for me, Louise?"

Mother turned and her eyes softened when she looked at my father. "I knew when you walked in the door that you would need some medicine." She reached into her skirt pocket and withdrew a packet of powders Dr. Zimmer, the physician in Main Amana, had prescribed. "Sit down at the table and I'll bring you water."

He didn't argue. My father may have been interested in the contents of Dovie Cates's letter, but right now his pain exceeded his curiosity. Moments later I was sitting beside him when my mother returned with the water. She arched her brows. "If your Vater doesn't need your help, you can go upstairs and dust the furniture."

My father dumped the packet of powder into the glass, stirred, and swallowed the mixture in one gulp. He swiped the back of his hand across his lips. "We thought you would want to share your letter with us." He glanced at me. "Isn't that right, Karlina?"

"Ja. I told Vater about your letter from Cousin Barbara's daughter."

My mother slapped the pocket of her apron, and the envelope crackled against her palm. "*Ach.* I already forgot about the letter, but that one—she is always putting her nose into the business of others." My mother tapped her nose and looked at me. I thought she might refuse to open the letter now, but she winked and withdrew the letter from her pocket. "Let's see what Dovie has to say." Sliding the tip of her finger beneath the seal, she opened the envelope and withdrew several sheets of stationery that matched the creamy envelope.

My mother unfolded the pages, her eyes rapidly moving back and forth as she read the first page. Father sat quietly while I fidgeted, hoping she would soon say something. When she placed the first page face down on the table and continued to the second page without a word, I could stand it no longer. "She has pretty handwriting, ja?"

A silent nod was my mother's only response. My father patted my hand. "Patience is a virtue, child. Your mother will talk to us once she has finished reading."

I did my best to heed my father's words, but I now wished I'd taken a seat alongside my mother, where I might have been able to read over her shoulder. Instead, I intently watched her features change as she read. On the first page she had appeared sad, but now her face reflected surprise, and as she finished, I saw worry in her eyes.

My father waited a moment. "Bad news?"

"Cousin Barbara is dead. Influenza. About two months ago." Sadness tugged at my mother's lips.

No doubt she was also recalling the deaths of my twin brothers.

Whenever someone in the villages died of pneumonia or influenza, a sad longing returned to my mother's eyes. For all of us it
rekindled memories of what their lives might have been.

Mother cleared her throat and swallowed. "Barbara was never
blessed with good health."

My father reached across and patted my mother's hand. "Barbara's suffering is over and she is in a better place—she is with
the Lord."

"Ja, I know. And I will see her again one day. Still, it is hard
to know she is gone from this earth." She gathered the pages and
put them in order. "Her daughter wants to come here for a visit."

My father's jaw went slack, and he picked up the letter. "Maybe
she doesn't understand German so well and confused her message to you."

"Her German is very *gut*. There is no mistake. She says her
father's work requires that they move to Texas. She wants to come
here and visit with us while he goes and finds a house for them."

Mother startled when I clapped my hands together. "That
would be wonderful! How old is she? It would be like having a
sister here in the house with me."

Pans clattered in the kitchen and my mother frowned. "I am
thinking she is twenty-one or twenty-two—maybe twenty-three.
For sure, she is a year or two older than you."

"Please tell her she can come, Mutter."

My father continued to read while my mother ignored me and
stared at him. When he finally finished the letter, he nodded.
"You are right. Her German is gut."

With a sigh, my mother tucked the pages into the envelope.
"What do you think about her coming for a visit? What should
I write and tell her?"

"Oh please, Vater. Say yes. Surely she should be able to come
and meet us."

My father folded his hands together. "To be honest, it is confusing. After all these years it is strange that her daughter would want to visit the colonies. I do not understand why she would seek you out. Barbara hadn't written for years."

"You know it was the circumstances. . . ."

"Ja, ja. I know, but it is odd she would wish to come here rather than go with her Vater. And odd that he is willing to be separated from his daughter so soon after his wife has died."

"Who can say why he is willing. Maybe he thinks she will bear the loss of her mother more easily." My mother tucked the envelope back into her pocket.

"We don't need to decide right now. We will pray about it, and then you can write to her."

His response dampened my spirits as much as stepping into the Iowa River in the middle of winter. Though I had no idea what Dovie might be like, the thought of having a girl near my own age living in our house pleased me a great deal. And learning about the outside world intrigued me, as well. Unlike those living in Main, Homestead, and South, there was no train station in East. When there was a need for the train to stop here, we would hang a red flag from the pole—and that didn't happen often. Visitors were rare in our village. We could count on seeing them at lambing season and during the annual sheep shearing. Otherwise, there was little to bring others to East.

My father stood, a signal for all of us to return to our work. Remembering my mother's mention of dusting, I looked toward the door leading outdoors. "Would you like me to go to the barn and see to fresh water for the sheep?"

When he hesitated, my mother waved. "Go on. The dusting can wait until you get back, and your father needs to rest. Just make sure the furniture is dusted before the evening meal."

I pecked a kiss on my mother's cheek. Going to water the sheep didn't please me as much as if I'd heard my parents agree that Dovie could come for a visit, but it far surpassed dusting furniture.

Grabbing my cloak, I hurried outside before my mother could change her mind. The clouds that had earlier settled on the horizon finally moved overhead, and pellets of sleet stung my cheeks as I hurried down the street and onto the dirt path leading to the sheep barn. Most of the sheep had come inside, but a few stood beneath the protective roof along the side of the barn. A small door remained open to permit them entry when they finally decided they wanted more shelter than the roof provided. As I walked inside, several of the animals instinctively came to me.

Though I had to agree God created animals that could be considered more intelligent than sheep, I also didn't forget the Bible references to his people as sheep. I ran my fingers through the thick wool of a ewe as I continued toward the door leading to the sheep standing outside in the sleet. I called to them. Recognizing my voice, they ambled toward the door and came into the warmth. Their need to be tended and cared for wasn't much different than my own. Sometimes they strayed and needed the shepherd's crook to bring them back into the fold. Was that what Dovie hoped for? Tender care that would bring her into the fold?

I picked up a large bucket, and as I walked to the pump, I prayed my parents would agree to let Dovie come and visit us.

CHAPTER 3

The sound of my mother's footsteps echoed on the stairs leading to our upstairs parlor. Even though the time for evening prayer meeting had not yet arrived, darkness draped the evening sky. Mother opened the door and stepped inside as my father pushed up from his chair.

He greeted her with a kiss on the cheek. "I received word from the elders that they have decided upon a young man to help me with the sheep. He'll arrive in the morning."

My mother stopped short and her smile faded. "Tomorrow? I could use more notice than one night, George." She *tsk*ed and shook her head. "Karlina and I will need to prepare the spare bedroom when we return from prayer meeting," she said, glancing at me.

Her features softened as my father grasped the back of the chair for support. "I am sorry for my gruff response. You need help caring for the sheep, and I've prayed the elders would send someone. Now that the Lord has answered my prayers, I am still complaining."

My father's lips curved into his familiar smile. "I know you are tired, Louise. I will help Karlina when we return home."

Mother shooed him with a dismissive wave. "Ach! I will not have my husband cleaning house. What would people think!"

My father chuckled. "Who cares what they think? Besides, they know only what you tell them."

My stomach bound in knots. There would undoubtedly be many changes with the arrival of this new worker. "But what about Dovie? That was going to be her room."

Both of my parents turned and looked at me, but it was my mother who answered. "You can share your room with her. She won't be here long, and sharing a room is not such a bad thing."

She was likely correct on that account. My twin brothers had shared the room that would now be assigned to the new shepherd, and they had enjoyed being together. When the two of them died of pneumonia, my mother closed off the room and used it only when needed for an occasional visitor. I was twelve when the twins died, and I still missed the sound of their laughter. Because I had never fallen ill, a twist of guilt continued to nag me from time to time. I never wanted to forget my brothers, but it had become easier to ward off such thoughts in recent years.

"Your mother is right. The room is needed for the young man."

"Ja. I understand and I will be pleased to share my room." It had taken several days for my parents to reach their decision and write a letter inviting Dovie to visit us. Mutter had expressed more misgivings than Vater, but she had finally agreed that she could not refuse Dovie's request. I didn't want to do or say anything that would cause them to regret the invitation. Besides, Dovie wouldn't arrive until spring. There would be ample time to rearrange my room for her visit.

"Who is this new shepherd? Is he from South or West Amana?" Smaller flocks of Shropshire sheep were pastured in those other two villages, but only in East was a flock of great magnitude maintained. Our combined flocks had increased to nearly fifteen hundred sheep, but my father was the overseer of just the operation in East. As the size of our flock increased, my father's responsibilities had grown in equal measure. I couldn't deny his need for an assistant manager, though I hoped he wouldn't hand over any of my tasks to the new shepherd.

Since the death of my brothers and with my father's diminishing health, he had granted me more responsibility with the sheep. Of course, the fact that my mother didn't complain when I was away from the kitchen had proved to be important, as well.

Shrugging into his heavy jacket, my father arched a brow. "His name is Anton Becker. He is from High Amana, and he's twenty-three years old."

"High? There are no sheep in High. Is he a shepherd?"

"I have told you what you need to know about the young man. He is the choice of the elders, and I will trust their decision." My father opened the door. "You should do the same."

"Ja, Vater. I will do my best." I said the words, but during our brief walk to prayer meeting at the Wentlers' house, I wasn't so sure I'd be happy with the elders' decision, especially if this new shepherd was a farm laborer or basket weaver who had no experience with sheep. How could he possibly be considered a good choice?

While the neighbors who attended our nightly meetings offered prayers of thanks for the help that would be arriving in the morning, I questioned God's decision and adopted a wait-and-see attitude.

When Anton Becker arrived at the barn the following morning, I greeted him with as much excitement as I could muster.

He glanced around the barn as though he'd arrived in a strange land. And to him, it likely was.

I took pity upon him when his weak attempt at a smile fell short. "We are pleased you were selected to come and help us, Brother Anton." I stepped forward. "I am Karlina Richter; my father is the overseer of the sheep here in East."

He yanked his cap from his head and a shock of dark hair fell across his forehead. "Pleased to meet you," he murmured as he continued his examination of the enclosure. "I was told to come straight to the barn and that Brother George Richter would give me my instructions."

"Where are your belongings? Did you take them to the house?"

"*Nein*. Brother Kortig, one of our elders from High, brought me. He said he would take my trunk to the house and then return and talk to your Vater. Is he here?"

I shook my head. "His health is not gut this morning, and he returned home for a short time. I'm sure Brother Kortig will have no trouble finding him."

He raked his fingers through his hair. Clearly, he was uncomfortable.

"Have you worked with sheep before, Brother Anton?"

"*Nein*, but this was the elders' decision."

"Ja. So my Vater told me."

He leaned his tall frame against one of the support beams, careful to avoid contact with any of the sheep. "What else did he tell you?"

"Only your name and that you live in High."

"*Lived* in High. For now I live in East." The wariness in his eyes diminished. "So that is all you know about me?"

"Was there something more my Vater should have told me?"

"Nein." He pushed away from the beam and straightened his shoulders. "I think I should go up to the house and meet your

Vater. Brother Kortig would not like it if he knew I was alone with a girl in the barn." He turned up his collar and donned his cap. "Probably your Vater would not like it so much, either."

I grinned. "You will like my Vater. He is a kind man and a gut teacher." When he continued toward the door without a response, I followed him for a few steps. "You should take the path up to the road and turn left. Ours is the kitchen house on the corner."

He strode out of the barn and followed the path without a backward glance. Shivering, I hurried after him and closed the door. It was good my father was a patient man, for Anton Becker would need much instruction.

And the instructions could begin with how to close the barn door.

While I entered the amounts of feed usage into the record book, my thoughts remained on Anton and why he had been the elders' choice. They hadn't based their decision upon his ability. And what had he meant when he'd said, *"For now I live in East"*? Was he planning to be here for only a short time? It made no sense to teach him how to work with the sheep if he would be leaving in the near future. Without warning, the answer came to me. *He's in East for his year of separation.* The reason was as clear as an Iowa sky on a starry night. The elders had chosen Anton because he had recently become engaged to a girl in High. He would spend his year of separation in East and then return to High and marry the girl.

There could be no other reasonable answer. And yet the thought annoyed me. Not because I cared if Anton Becker married— though I pitied the girl who would marry a man who did not know how to close a door behind him. Instead, I was irritated because we would spend the next year teaching him to care for sheep and then he would depart as quickly as he'd arrived. Strictly speaking, he'd be of little use at all during his time in East. Didn't the elders realize my father needed someone who would learn to love shepherding, someone who had a desire to spend their life caring for sheep, and someone who enjoyed the peacefulness of a rolling pasture on a spring day?

Someone like me.

Except the "someone" had to be a man.

I had finished my entries when the barn door opened and a gust of cold wind rushed in ahead of my father and Anton. If my father had misgivings about the elders' decision, they remained well hidden. "Anton tells me the two of you have met." My father didn't wait for an answer. "Brother Kortig has departed for High, so I thought it would be gut to bring Anton down to the barn and tell him a little about our sheep and what will be expected of him each day." He turned his attention to the young man. "My daughter knows as much about these sheep as I do, and they respond to her more quickly than anyone else. There's much you can learn from her."

I wanted to tell Anton his first lesson would be about closing doors, but I didn't want to cause him embarrassment on his first day in our village. "I am here much of the time, so if you have questions, you can always ask me."

My father pulled his coat tight around his neck. "The most important thing you must learn is this: No flock will be quiet and pleasant without the frequent attention of a kind, quiet shepherd. They are, by nature, easily handled by a shepherd who will give them gut care, and the only way you will learn proper management is to handle the stock. In other words, the best way to learn is by doing."

I wasn't certain if Anton was bored or frightened, but his interest appeared to be elsewhere as my father continued to explain what would be expected of him. When my father hesitated for a moment, Anton interrupted. "I probably won't remember everything you're telling me, so why don't I begin learning by doing. Didn't you say that was the best way to learn?"

I didn't miss the twinkle in my father's eye as he pointed to the floor. "Since you're in a hurry to begin, you can start with mucking out the barn. We also have several sheds that provide shelter for the animals. Once you've finished in here, you can work on those. I'm going to return to the house, but Karlina can point them out to you once you've finished in here."

Once my father departed, Anton picked up a shovel. "I am thinking I should not have been in such a hurry."

"Ja. Sometimes it pays to remain silent and listen. But with your early start, you will have plenty of time to finish before the evening meal." I tried to withhold a chuckle, but to no avail. Anton's knuckles turned white as he grasped the shovel, and the flash of anger in his eyes both surprised and frightened me. "I'm sorry, I shouldn't have laughed."

He didn't accept my apology. He didn't say a word. Instead, he clamped his jaw so tight that the tendons in his neck stood out like garter snakes. I set to work scooping the corn and oats in equal measure. I thought it easier to prepare the mixture in advance, and had planned to explain the process to Anton. But after observing him for a few moments I decided to wait for a time when he was in better humor.

I had neared the barn door, prepared to return home, when Anton called my name. I turned and he stood leaning on the shovel. "I'm sorry for the way I acted. I am told I have a problem with my temper."

"And do you?"

This time he chuckled. "I think you already know the answer to that question, but I am hoping to improve."

"Then I shall pray that you do so. And thank you for your apology."

CHAPTER 4

Dovie

I peered out the window, my heartbeat matching the chugging rhythm of the train. Since our departure, I'd noted each change in the passing landscape. From the bustle of cities to the rolling plains, the ride had provided glorious panoramic views. Now, as we approached our destination, fear overshadowed my earlier excitement. A lump the size of a summer melon rested in the pit of my stomach.

"What if they haven't received my second letter?"

"What?" My father turned and looked at me, his eyebrows arched high on his forehead.

"Cousin Louise. What if she hasn't received my letter? If they aren't expecting me, what do you think will happen?"

My father raised one shoulder and let it drop in an exaggerated shrug. "I don't know. They might tell you that you can stay, or they may tell you that they are unable to accommodate you right now. In that case, you'll get on the train with me tomorrow and come to Dallas." He withdrew his pocket watch and checked the time. "You'll have your answer in an hour or so." He lifted my chin with the tip of his index finger. "There's no reason to worry, Dovie. It's not as if you'd be stranded with no place to go. Besides, I'd rather you were going to Texas with me than going to an unfamiliar place and visiting strangers."

His words bore a sting that disturbed me. Throughout my childhood, he'd been gone for weeks at a time, due to his work, so his desire to now keep me close at hand seemed odd and out of character for the man I knew. Perhaps the finality of my mother's death had seeped into his bones and he feared being alone. No matter the reason, his reaction pained me.

"But you said I could visit them." I disliked the fact that he continued to refer to my mother's relatives as strangers, but I didn't mention that again.

"I did, but that doesn't mean it's my choice. We have only each other, Dovie, and I had hoped . . ."

His voice faded, but I didn't miss the tiny glint of expectation in his eyes. He wanted me to change my mind and go with him. But I couldn't. Not when we'd come this far. I needed this time with Mother's family—if they would have me.

We fell into a lingering silence as my thoughts returned to Cousin Louise's recent letter. I'd been touched by her words of condolence and her kind invitation to visit. All except her final notation suggesting spring as the best time for my arrival.

Delaying my visit until spring was impossible. And I doubted my response would be delivered to her before we departed Cincinnati. I should have mentioned that Father was expected in Texas before Christmas, but I hadn't, and I couldn't change a letter that had already been mailed.

A conductor passed through the aisle. "Amana! Main Amana!"

He continued to announce the next stop in a clear, crisp voice. As the train slowed and then came to a jarring halt, I knotted my hands together and prayed I'd be greeted by welcoming hearts.

My father held out his hand and helped me down the final step from the train. Smoke curled from the depot chimney as a cold, brisk wind cut across the flat expanse of farmland. "Not much warmer than the weather we left in Cincinnati."

A tall, raw-boned man wearing work pants and a long-sleeved shirt motioned to a corner where coals glowed red in a wood-burning stove. "Best seat in the house is that bench right over there in front of the stove. Waiting for the next train?"

My father shook his head. "No. We need transportation to East Amana. Do you know who can help me with those arrangements?" He posed the question in perfect German.

The man grinned and pointed toward the door on the opposite side of the station. "My wagon is outside. That's why I am here."

My excitement mounted. If Cousin Louise sent someone to pick us up, she must have received my reply. I couldn't believe my good fortune. "Are you Louise Richter's husband?"

He momentarily appeared pleased that I, too, spoke German, but then his brows drew close together as if he hadn't understood. "Nein. I am Brother Joseph Ackermann. You were expecting Brother George?"

"I . . . I don't know."

My father stepped between us and briefly explained the circumstances of our arrival. "I suppose we could stop at the hotel before going to the Richters' home, and I could register and leave my bags."

"Ja, whatever pleases you is fine with me. The two of you can decide while I put your belongings in the wagon." Without waiting for an answer, he lifted a bag under each arm and held one in each hand. Tall and lanky, Brother Ackermann was certainly strong.

He stepped around my father and met my gaze. "So you are going to stay and visit with Brother George and Sister Louise. I think you will like them, and their daughter, Karlina, too. I am guessing you are about the same age. That girl is gut with the sheep. I never saw anything like it. Girls are usually in the Küche, but not Karlina." He chuckled. "That one has a mind of her own. Is gut she lives in East."

I didn't know what he'd meant by that final remark, but I didn't ask. I was certain I'd soon learn why it was good to live in East. Besides, I was more surprised to learn about Karlina. And curious why Cousin Louise hadn't mentioned her daughter. Had it been an oversight, or had she decided that piece of news would further encourage my visit? Perhaps she hoped I wouldn't come.

"Come along, Dovie."

As my father grasped my elbow, I pushed aside my troubled thoughts of Cousin Louise and the contents of her letter. After all, she'd said I could come for a visit. Perhaps not at this time, but once she heard the circumstances, surely she would understand. I climbed into the wagon and pulled my collar tight around my neck, thankful for both my scarf and gloves.

The driver released the wagon brake and slapped the reins against the horses' rumps. The pair of horses lumbered away from the depot and soon traversed a wooden bridge that crossed a canal. My father gestured to a large redbrick building to our right. "What's produced at the mill?"

"That's our woolen mill." Brother Ackermann nodded to the left. "And that's the brewery over there."

My gaze shifted from one side of the street to the other as we passed through the village that, in some respects, reminded me of Over-the-Rhine. Perhaps it was the tidiness of the brick and wooden houses. Or perhaps it was the dormant flower gardens and fruit trees that would bloom in the spring. Yet I thought the naked grapevines clinging to trellises on the sides of their homes and the unpainted wood houses weathering in the changing climate quite strange. And there weren't any women carrying their shopping baskets to market, children playing in the streets and yards, or vendors hawking wares from their wagons or at corner stands. I realized the weather likely would keep some inside, but it seemed odd to see so few people. In fact, most of the well-maintained houses with their gable roofs and nine-over-six windows appeared empty of inhabitants.

"Where is everyone?" I'd done my best to withhold my questions, as the driver didn't appear eager to converse. Yet I wasn't accustomed to the lack of activity, and my curiosity got the best of me.

The driver glanced in my direction. "Like me, they are at work." He pointed to the smoke rising from the woolen mill. "We are mostly self-reliant in our villages, with little need of anything from the outside world. All of the people who live here contribute their skills and work for the good of all."

My father didn't appear surprised by the driver's comments, so I wondered if my mother had told him more about her former life than he'd shared with me. Then again, perhaps he was tired, cold, and more concerned about his trip to Texas than life in Amana. Without direction from the driver, or so it appeared to me, the horses slowed their pace and came to a halt outside a wooden structure that was considerably larger than the other houses we had passed.

In one fluid motion, the lanky driver set the brake and jumped down. "This is the hotel. What bags do I take inside?"

Had it been warmer, I would have remained in the wagon, but the cold dictated otherwise. My father grabbed one of his cases and pointed to the other one he would take to Texas. He had forwarded his large trunks on to Dallas, and I wondered if they would be waiting when he arrived or if the few personal items from our house would be lost for all time. I didn't want to believe that the delicate glass bowl or the fluted vase that had come with my relatives from Germany would end up in the hands of some stranger who couldn't appreciate their beauty or significance.

Once inside, I held my gloved hands in front of the wood-burning stove in the lobby while my father signed his name in the guest book and received a key to his room. He spoke to the man behind the desk for a few moments and then motioned to me. "Come along, Dovie."

"Don't you want to take your suitcases to your room? I can wait."

"No need," he said. "They'll be delivered upstairs for me. Besides, it's better we get over to East before it becomes too busy."

Busy? My father was making no sense. He pointed to the door, and I frowned. "I see no reason to rush. Nothing seems very busy around here," I whispered.

"I am told your cousin Louise is in charge of a kitchen where these people eat their meals. As suppertime draws closer, she will have little time to talk to us." He took hold of my arm and helped me into the wagon. "At least that's what the man inside told me."

My father's response left me with more questions than answers. How could everyone eat at Cousin Louise's house? That didn't seem possible. Once Brother Ackermann had taken his seat beside my father, I leaned forward. "Do you take your meals at the home of my cousin Louise?"

He chuckled and shook his head. "Nein. I live in this village—Main Amana—not in East."

I nudged my father's arm. "There, you see? I am thinking the clerk misunderstood your question."

"Your cousin will explain our eating arrangements, but the clerk in the hotel wanted you to understand that when mealtime approaches, all of the kitchen houses are very busy. The Richter Küche is no different."

I didn't exactly understand, but he'd clamped his lips tight, as though he didn't intend to elaborate any further.

Brother Ackermann urged the horses along the hard-packed dirt road that wound past several large unpainted barns and then directed the animals eastward until all signs of the village disappeared behind us. The three of us traveled in silence while I continued to observe the passing terrain. Instead of the level farmland I'd seen on our approach by train, the wagon carried us toward an undulating landscape with rocky outcroppings. And though I knew little of farming, this land didn't appear suitable for producing crops.

Despite the fact that the driver kept his eyes on the road and his head tucked low, I decided to venture a question. "Is this land a part of the colonies?"

He gave me a sideward glance and nodded. "Ja. There are twenty-six thousand acres in all." When I gasped at the figure, he chuckled. "Some is in timber and swamp, but much of it is cultivated for farming, and we use about four thousand acres for grazing our animals." He pointed toward the houses slowly coming into view. "In East the sheep are plentiful, and they graze well on land that isn't good for farming. God directed us to Iowa, and we are most thankful. This land we own is gut for our large crops of grain as well as our vegetable gardens; it provides us with timber for building our houses and fueling our fires. There are hills and valleys that are gut for grazing animals, and there are creeks and a river to provide the water we need. God has been gut to our people."

"But *you* own none of it," my father said. His comment caused Brother Ackermann to turn and stare at him.

"Ja, that is right. But I am satisfied. For me, to be content is more important than any possessions, Mr. Cates. Each man must decide for himself." His lips curved in a broad smile. "And I am free to leave if I should become unhappy. Nothing holds me to this place, except my desire to be here."

Smoke rose from the chimneys like welcoming signals, and I longed for the comfort of a fire to warm my hands and feet. As we entered the far end of the village, I hoped we'd soon stop in front of one of the houses. This village appeared smaller than the one we'd left, but it was of little consequence to me. "Does Cousin Louise live in one of these houses?"

"A little further. Her house is at the end of the street. If you walk up to the cemetery, you can look down into the valley and see much of our land, especially in winter, when the trees are completely bare and there is little to block the view."

I wasn't sure I wanted to visit the cemetery, but I thanked him for the information. Moments later our wagon came to a stop in front of a two-story brick house.

"Here we are." The driver looked in our direction before he set the brake and jumped down. "I think I will go inside with you and warm myself before heading back. A cup of hot coffee should help." Without asking, he unloaded my bags and strode toward the door.

I'd longed for this moment to arrive. But now that we were here, I couldn't move from the hard wooden seat. I sat there, frozen in place. Brother Ackermann glanced over his shoulder and motioned for us to follow.

My father stood beside the wagon, offering his outstretched hand. "Come along, Dovie. It's too cold to sit outside."

CHAPTER 5

"I brought your company from the train station, Sister Louise."
The wagon driver turned and shouted to his left as he placed my
bags near the kitchen door and then strode across the room. He
gestured for my father and me to follow.

I wanted to call after him and tell him Cousin Louise wasn't
expecting me, but it was too late. And unlike me, he appeared
confident I would be welcome. A short, stout woman with gray-
ing hair and a kind face appeared in the doorway. Her blue-eyed
gaze brushed over my father before resting on me. She took several
short-legged strides across the dining room and rested one hand
on a large white apron that protected a dark calico dress.

Long wood tables and benches filled the room, an aisle separat-
ing them into two distinct sections. Though aligned in a coor-
dinated fashion, the sight of so many benches and tables in one
room appeared strange to me. I couldn't help but wonder how
many people ate their meals in this room.

"Dovie?" The woman's brows dipped low on her forehead as she continued to study me. "You look like Cousin Barbara." She strained forward. "I wasn't expecting you." She looked at my father. "Either of you. At least not now. I wrote a letter. I said spring would be best for a visit." Confusion clouded her eyes. "Ja, spring is the time I said you should come." She glanced toward the window as if to assure herself that spring hadn't somehow slipped around the corner while she'd been busy in the other room. "It is still winter."

I forced a smile. "I received your letter. And I wrote back, but . . ."

Before I could finish, Sister Louise motioned to the wagon driver. "There is a pot of hot coffee in the Küche, Brother Joseph. Please help yourself." The driver grinned and ambled toward the other room. Once he'd disappeared, Cousin Louise returned her attention to my father and me. "I did not receive another letter." She waved her hand in a circular gesture. "Yet here you are. Strange that you have arrived before your letter, ja?"

I gave my father a sideways glance. He had offered to mail my letter on his way to work. Had he? Instead of affirming the missive had been posted, he avoided my gaze.

"No matter." A generous smile curved her lips. "I am Louise. Your Mutter's cousin. Even if I am surprised to see you in the winter, it is gut to have you in our home."

My father stepped forward. "I am Nelson Cates—Dovie's father."

"Ja. Barbara wrote me when she married you." Cousin Louise tipped her head to one side as if examining my father's every feature. "And for a few years after, too." She ran a finger beneath the wide cotton strap of her apron. "Strange that the two of you arrived before Dovie's letter. Makes no gut sense." Cousin Louise's comment hung there like a sagging clothesline.

I wasn't sure how to answer and was thankful when my father finally cleared his throat. "I find you can't always depend upon the mail, and I do understand you weren't expecting Dovie until spring. However, what with my work, I had little choice. If her visit isn't convenient, she can accompany me to Dallas. It won't create any problem for me—or for her."

My father's comment caused me to once again wonder if he'd mailed my letter. I didn't want to believe he would give me permission but then sabotage my plans. I stared at him, unable to erase the distasteful thought from my mind. His eyes didn't reveal guilt—but they didn't reveal innocence, either. I might never learn the truth, but during the coming days I planned to keep a lookout for my letter.

"Nein! Her visit isn't a problem, only a surprise. I thought spring would be better because of the weather, and I thought you would want to be at home for Christmas. But you are most welcome in our home, Dovie."

The warmth in Cousin Louise's voice swept over me like a rain-freshened breeze, and I realized the lump that had taken up residence in my stomach had disappeared. Though I didn't know what lay in store for me, I no longer feared being rejected. Finally I would discover something of my mother's past.

Cousin Louise's eyes shifted to my father. "And you are welcome, as well. We will soon be serving the evening meal, but you can go upstairs to the parlor and rest until then. Once I've finished my work, we will visit." She hesitated for a moment. "Or after prayer meeting."

My father took a backward step and pointed to the heavy wooden door. "No, but thank you for the offer. I'm going back to the hotel with Mr. Ackermann. I have an early train to catch in the morning."

Cousin Louise tightened her lips into a thin seam and shrugged. "I can tell you my food is better than what they serve at the hotel."

"For sure, she is right about that." Brother Ackermann stood in the doorway holding a cup of coffee and leaning against the doorjamb. "If I lived in East, this is where I'd want to eat my meals." He chuckled before downing the last of his coffee. "You want me to take those upstairs, Sister Louise?" The driver gestured toward my trunk and suitcase.

"Ja, that would be gut, Brother Joseph." She returned her attention to my father. "And how should we contact you while you are in Texas, Mr. Cates?"

My father withdrew an envelope from his inside pocket and handed it to Cousin Louise. "Inside, you'll find the address of the company where I work. Once I've located a place to live, I'll send the address to Dovie. And to you." The final words seemed to pain him. He turned to me. "Unless you've changed your mind."

I crossed the distance between us and hugged him. The familiar scent of pipe tobacco and wool greeted me. "I haven't changed my mind. I'll be fine, Father." I leaned back and looked into his eyes. "I'll write as soon as I have your new address."

"*Our* new address." He brushed the back of his fingers along my cheek. "Together, we'll enjoy spring in Texas."

Since Mother's death, I had noticed changes in my father, but his recent sorrow and desire to keep me close continued to catch me by surprise. Never before had he appeared so forlorn and hopeless. I could see it in his eyes, hear it in his voice. A chapter of his life had come to an end, and he didn't want to move on. At least not alone.

I held his hand as we walked to the front door. He pulled me close, and I kissed his cheek. "You'll be so busy you won't have time to miss me, Papa."

"Or maybe you'll be so unhappy in Iowa that you'll decide to join me in Texas for Christmas." When I kissed his other cheek, he whispered into my ear, "Just remember that I'll be here until six o'clock tomorrow morning. You have until then to change your decision."

Once my father and the driver departed, Cousin Louise waved me toward the other room. "Come with me to the kitchen. I will introduce you to all the sisters who work here." When my forehead creased in a frown, she smiled. "We address each other as 'Sister' or 'Brother' here in the colonies. We all consider ourselves brothers and sisters in Christ."

"I see. And will I be your sister, as well?"

My question seemed to momentarily baffle Cousin Louise. "The other sisters will likely address you as such since you are staying with us and we're not accustomed to outsiders visiting, but it is our faith that binds us as sisters and brothers, not simply being present in the village." When I didn't acknowledge the remark, she continued. "During harvest or shearing, the elders will sometimes be required to hire outsiders to help with the work in our villages. Those hired workers are not addressed as 'Sister' or 'Brother' because they aren't members of our faith."

"But my mother was your sister as well as your cousin," I said.

Cousin Louise chuckled. "Ja. And I loved her very much." Her laughter was like sunshine on a dreary day, and I followed her as she strode into the kitchen. Though I doubted I would remember all of their names, Cousin Louise introduced me to the other women, who were busy stirring pots, chopping vegetables, or slicing thick pieces of meat. Just like her, they wore dark dresses, large aprons, and small black caps. I wasn't sure what to think of the plain attire. At least my dress wasn't much different from theirs.

I leaned to one side and whispered in Cousin Louise's ear. "Are they all in mourning, too?"

"Nein. We always wear modest clothing of dark colors." A grin as bright as a summer morning curved her lips. "There are Amish settled to the south of our villages. They come here to purchase goods from time to time. I'm told they believe our clothing is quite fancy." She pointed to the white-dotted design in her charcoal gray dress. "To them, I suppose it is. They purchase only plain dark cloth—nothing with design. Each of us must follow what we believe to be the right path for our lives."

I wasn't certain when or where I might find the correct path for my life, but from all appearances, the ladies working in Cousin Louise's kitchen had found theirs. While laughing and visiting with one another, they stirred, peeled, and cooked with purpose and determination. To see such joy and friendship permitted me a glimpse into the life my mother had left behind many years ago. She'd had few friends during our years in Over-the-Rhine, and seeing these women now caused me to realize how lonely she must have been.

"My mother was happy here?" I hadn't planned to quiz Cousin Louise, but the question slipped out before I could stop it.

Her eyes glistened and she gave a slight nod. "Ja. She was happy."

Before Cousin Louise could elaborate any further, the back door burst open and a girl, who appeared to be a few years younger than I, bolted into the room. Arms extended, she scuttled across the room to warm herself near the stove. After an exaggerated shiver, she glanced in my direction. Her ice-blue eyes sparkled as she adjusted a black gauzy cap over her thick brown hair. Her mouth dropped open, and she lifted her mittened fingers to her parted lips. From her surprised reaction, I could see that visitors were uncommon in the colonies, just as Cousin Louise had earlier mentioned.

"Karlina! How many times must I tell you there is no rushing through the kitchen when we are cooking! Too many accidents can happen."

A sheepish grin spread across the girl's face. She grasped her mother around the waist and kissed her cheeks. "I am sorry, Mutter. Now will you introduce me to our guest?"

Cousin Louise extended her hand to me, and I stepped closer. "Karlina, this is Dovie, my cousin Barbara's daughter."

"Dovie? But you weren't supposed to come until spring." She removed her thick mittens and unfastened her heavy wool cape. "My room isn't prepared."

Heat flooded my cheeks. My unexpected arrival was proving to be inconvenient for everyone. "Perhaps I can help?" I could think of nothing else that might ease the uncomfortable situation my appearance had created. "I'm quite good at cleaning and arranging furniture."

Karlina unfastened her cape and hung it on a nearby hook. "Ja, we can do it together. I'm happy you are here, Dovie. Just surprised." Looking toward her mother, she arched her brows. "We have time before supper, ja?" Her full lips curved into a broad smile that produced deep dimples in each of her rosy cheeks.

Cousin Louise chuckled. "If you use your time to work instead of to talk, you can accomplish much before we eat." She waved toward the other room. "Karlina will help you learn our ways, Dovie."

"Learn our ways." I wasn't certain exactly what all that would include, but from the little I'd observed so far, I had much to learn.

CHAPTER 6

Karlina

My excitement mounted as we climbed the steps to the room I would share with Dovie. She possessed an air of sophistication that I had noticed among the visitors I'd occasionally seen at the train station in Main Amana. Yet never before had I visited with anyone from the outside world. And realizing that I would have Dovie all to myself every evening filled me with more joy than I had thought possible. Though her German dialect was a little different from our own, I had no problem understanding her—and soon she would understand us with greater ease, too. For a brief time, most new arrivals to the colonies had difficulty with our mixture of dialects. Even from village to village there were slight differences in our language, for the immigrants who had established our original settlement of Ebenezer in New York had gathered from several German provinces, as well as Alsace-Lorraine and a small number from Switzerland. Our dialect had evolved and changed, becoming a mixture of those original languages.

If she remained in East long enough, Dovie's proper German might even change a bit. I didn't know her very well just yet, but I already liked her and hoped she would remain with us for quite some time. Though Mother had warned me Dovie wouldn't be here for long, I couldn't help but recollect that my mother was sometimes wrong. I hoped this would be one of those times.

While we rearranged the furniture to make room for Dovie's belongings, I answered her questions and asked some of my own. She wanted to know about life in the colonies, and I wanted to know about life outside. I was awed by her description of a forty-three-foot-high fountain in Cincinnati—a gift from the citizens of Munich—and her freedom to visit parks, museums, and libraries. I laughed when she told me about the wienerwurst man who carried a large tin full of sausages and strolled through the streets and parks each day, selling them to eager customers. And though I tried my best, I couldn't picture the churches with colored-glass windows and steeples that rose toward heaven—so unlike our own plain meetinghouses that were free of adornment. We even called them meeting halls rather than churches in order to maintain a feeling of simplicity.

Pushing my dresses closer together in the wardrobe, I made space for Dovie's gowns. I looked over my shoulder. "We have nothing like that in the colonies."

"No churches?"

"Oh ja, we have meeting halls, but not like the ones you are talking about. Unless you knew it was our meeting hall, you wouldn't guess it is where we worship. Our meeting halls are much like our people—very plain and free from adornment."

Dovie stared at me, her forehead wrinkled in disbelief. "I can't imagine such a church. The only ones I've ever seen have been quite beautiful. Is this because you can't afford the additional costs?"

"Nein. It is because our people believe we should keep our

thoughts upon the Lord when we worship, not be distracted by beautiful decorations or adornment."

"I suppose there is soundness to that idea, but I think it would be difficult for me to become accustomed to such a change." She reached into her trunk and withdrew several dresses, all in dark colors. I was momentarily surprised, but then remembered that she was in mourning.

She unfolded one of the dresses and shook out the wrinkles. "With all of my dark dresses, I won't be quickly mistaken for a visitor."

I didn't disagree, but whether she donned a dark-colored dress or one of bright red, everyone in East would know that she was an outsider, for we all knew one another.

She dug deeper inside the trunk, removed a framed picture, and held it out to me. "This is a picture of my mother and father, taken two years ago."

I stared at the photograph of a tall man with his hand resting on the shoulder of an attractive woman who was wearing a white waist with ruffles at the neck. "You look a great deal like your Mutter."

Dovie traced her finger around the frame. "That's what everyone says, but I think my mother was much prettier than I am."

"Maybe, but no person can take credit for their outward appearance—that is God-given. Some of the most beautiful people I know are not lovely on the outside, but their inner beauty shines so bright that I consider them beautiful."

"Do you really believe people look only at inward beauty?"

"Nein. But I believe the world would be a better place if we could love and accept one another. Don't you agree?"

Dovie placed the photograph on the small bedside table. "I do, but I think you would find the practice much more difficult to apply outside of the colonies."

I shrugged. "I have never been anywhere else, but you may be right. Sometimes it's hard to love others, even here in the colonies." She chuckled. "I try my best, but sometimes I don't do so gut." She snapped open a sheet and tucked it around the mattress. "My patience has been sorely tried since our new shepherd recently arrived."

Dovie caught the corner of the pale blue quilt and spread it into place. "What's wrong with the shepherd?"

"I had hoped he would come to us with experience and be gut help. Instead, he knows nothing of sheep or their care and must be taught everything."

"At least he will learn the way your father prefers the work done. I remember my father talking about a man who came to work for his company, and this man wanted to do things the way he'd learned in his old job. Father said it was harder to change that man's old ways than to start with a new worker."

There was certainly truth in what Dovie had said. Perhaps I shouldn't be so disappointed over Anton's lack of ability. Besides, it had permitted me more time in the barns. "Do you like animals and being outdoors?" I plopped down on the bed.

"I've never had a pet, but one of my friends had a dog that I liked very much. As for the outdoors, I enjoy growing flowers, and I always helped my mother with the small vegetable garden she planted in our backyard each year." Dovie touched her fingers to the tiny stitches that formed a tulip pattern on the blue coverlet. "This coverlet is beautiful. The stitches so tiny and perfect. Did you make it?"

I shivered and shook my head. "Nein. My sewing and cooking skills are very poor. Instead, I enjoy working with the sheep and being outdoors as much as possible." I shrugged my shoulders. "A big disappointment to my Mutter but a great help to my Vater. And right now, he is the one who needs the most help."

A bell rang in the distance, and I jumped up from the bed. "That is the bell that lets us know we should prepare for supper. You will soon learn about the bells. They help us know when to depart for work, when to return for the noonday meal, when to go back to work, when to go to meeting—when to go everyplace we need to go." I took her hand. "The men and women eat at separate tables, so you should sit beside me." I noted the flicker of fear in her eyes and squeezed her hand. "You will be fine. Just do what I do."

Dovie forced a smile, but the fear remained in her eyes.

I preceded her down the steps and into the kitchen. "Do you need our help, Mutter?"

In spite of the freezing wind that whistled through the trees, perspiration dotted my mother's forehead. She wrapped her apron around the handle of a kettle and moved it to the worktable. "Not today. Dovie is our guest. You take her to the dining room and explain our customs."

Dovie inched forward. "I am happy to help, Cousin Louise."

Worry creased my mother's forehead. She took pride in serving meals on time. To stop and visit or give directions to a novice in her kitchen would cause undesired delay. Reaching for a ladle, she spooned a thick stew into one of the large tureens. "Thank you, Dovie, but not this evening. Perhaps tomorrow. You go into the dining room with Karlina."

If my mother's refusal pained Dovie, she kept it well hidden and followed me into the other room, where we stood and waited until everyone had entered. The men stood at their tables, the women and children at theirs. Prayers were offered before we took our seats.

While Sister Marta filled and carried bowls to our table, Dovie leaned close to me. "Where is the shepherd you spoke of earlier?" I placed my index finger to my lips and gave a slight shake of my head. Dovie grinned and poked my side with her elbow. "Do tell me. I want to see which one he is."

Sister Bertha cleared her throat and sent a disapproving look in our direction. Instead of remaining silent, Dovie smiled and arched forward. "Hello. I'm Dovie Cates. My mother grew up here in East Amana. Perhaps you knew her—Barbara Cates. Her name was Lange before she married, Barbara Lange."

Sister Bertha's frown deepened. "I understand you are a guest, but we speak only when necessary during our meals."

Dovie's jaw snapped together, and her lips tightened until they curled inward and disappeared. I reached beneath the table and gripped Dovie's hand. She squeezed in return, and in that moment, we sealed our friendship.

For the remainder of the meal, Dovie watched the ladies at our table. If one of them took a second helping, she took a second helping; if one of them salted their food, she salted her food; if one of them held up a glass for more water, she did the same. She made certain she did nothing that would produce any cause for criticism. When we'd finished our stewed apples, we stood to be dismissed with prayer.

The moment the prayer ended, I leaned and whispered into Dovie's ear, "Anton is the tall one with the dark hair." Just then Anton turned and saw both of us staring at him. He grinned and raised his hand in a slight wave. "Ach! He saw us looking at him." I grabbed Dovie's hand and pulled her toward the stairs. "Quit looking at him!"

"Why? He's quite handsome and he waved at you. That means he likes you."

"I don't want him to think we are talking about him. He waved because he saw us staring at him, and he didn't know what else to do." I could feel the heat rising in my cheeks. If Anton thought we were discussing him, he'd be sure to ask me when I met him in the barn tomorrow. And what would I say if he did? *Dovie wanted to see the shepherd who doesn't know how to handle the sheep.* Or, *Dovie thinks you are quite handsome and that you must like me since you waved at us.*

"You're wrong. I could tell from the way he smiled and waved that he cares for you."

I pinned Dovie with a stern look. "Anton is here to work with the sheep. I am not yet certain, but I believe he is here for his year of separation." While keeping my voice low, I continued walking her toward the stairs. "I do know he is a man with a temper, and that does not make for a gut husband. Besides, in the colonies, we do not think marriage is necessary for us to enjoy an abundant life."

Dovie stopped midstep and turned to face me. A deep V had formed between her eyes. "What does all of *that* mean?"

Reaching around Dovie, I pushed down on the heavy metal latch and opened the door to my room. After a quick glance toward the stairs, I nudged her forward. "Let's go inside." Who could say when Anton might bound up the stairs. Over the last few days, he'd begun visiting with my father in our parlor after supper and walking with our family to prayer meeting each night. I wouldn't want him to overhear our conversation.

Once the door closed behind us, I sighed with relief. "What part do you want me to explain?"

"About separation and abundant single lives—all of it. There are lots of married people here, aren't there?"

"Ja, that is true. But we believe that if a person can remain single, it is better."

Dovie's frown deepened. "But why? What makes it better?"

"You have more time. When you are not working, your time can be devoted to worshiping the Lord rather than caring for your family."

"But the Bible says man needs a—"

I held up my hand. "I know what the Bible says about man needing a helpmeet. Our elders permit marriage. But to make sure the couple is sincere in their wish to wed one another, they go through a year of separation. Usually the man is sent to another village, and the couple can see each other only when time permits. Which isn't very often."

"I find the idea of separation quite odd. We believe the courting period helps a man and woman discover whether they are suited for marriage to each other. How can that occur if they are separated?"

I shrugged my shoulders. "I do not make the rules, and I cannot speak with authority on the subject of separation, but the practice seems to work here. My Mutter says it is a time of learning to trust your heart and a time of learning to trust the person you plan to marry."

"I suppose the idea has some merit, though I'm still not convinced." Dovie dropped onto the edge of the bed. "And you believe Anton is betrothed to someone in another village and has come to East for his year of separation. Is that right?"

I nodded and quickly enumerated my reasons.

"Why don't you ask him? Or ask your father."

"To ask a single man such a question is not proper. And if I ask my father, he may gather the wrong idea and think it wise to keep me away from Anton. And that would mean keeping me away from the sheep. Other than helping with the animals, I have no interest in Anton Becker and who he will marry."

Dovie grinned and shook her head. "I'm not sure I believe you."

I would let Dovie think whatever she wanted. The only interest I had in the new shepherd was teaching him to properly care for our sheep.

CHAPTER 7

December 1892
Dovie

I awakened to the sound of creaking floorboards in the room next to us. Cousin Louise invariably managed to hit every one of them as she prepared to greet each new day. Karlina said there was no need for the morning bells with her mother in the house, and I tended to agree.

Since my arrival, I hadn't discovered much about my mother's past, but I had learned that back in 1842, after receiving a word from the Lord, the first members of the Community of True Inspiration sailed from Europe, where they had been persecuted for their religious beliefs. I heard about the places they had lived in Europe and how they worked to establish their first villages near Buffalo, New York. I also learned that as the outside world encroached upon them, their religious leader, known as a *Werkzeug*, received another word from the Lord that the people should leave and settle elsewhere. In 1855 the group began a slow migration to their present location in Iowa.

In addition to teaching me the history of the Inspirationists, Cousin Louise and the other ladies had been quick to instruct me in a variety of kitchen tasks. I'd also met Anton, the new shepherd, and even though Karlina denied any feelings of significance between the two of them, I remained convinced that I had detected more than a working friendship. Whenever I broached the subject of Anton, Karlina brushed aside my questions and talked about some problem with the sheep.

In much the same manner, Cousin Louise brushed aside my questions about my mother and her family's departure from the Amana Colonies. I didn't want to annoy Cousin Louise with my persistence, but I had come here with questions, and I didn't want to leave until I had answers. A sense of urgency nudged me, for I needed those answers before my father sent for me to join him in Texas.

Thus far, there had been no word from him, but as the days passed, my concern mounted that he would write and expect me to join him. I continued to watch for mail from him, and I also watched for the second letter I'd written to Cousin Louise prior to our departure from Cincinnati. Thus far, it hadn't arrived. Either my father had failed to post the letter, or it had been lost somewhere along the way. Although I didn't want to think my father had intentionally deceived me, I now tended to believe he had never mailed the letter.

I buttoned my dress as Karlina quietly recited her morning prayers. I'd become accustomed to hearing her pray in the morning and evening. Each evening after she finished her nighttime prayers, Karlina would explain anything I hadn't understood during the day. On one of my first nights with her, I had questioned her practice of praying while washing and dressing in the morning and while undressing at night. She had smiled as she detailed lessons from the *Kinderstimme*, a book used to teach children the practice of virtue and their duty to God, to fellow members, and toward themselves. I'd listened intently to a few of the rules Karlina had memorized. Most sounded like things my mother had taught me as a child: Direct your eyes ever and only upon Jesus, your beginning, aim, and goal; do not elevate yourself because of a few good deeds, for thereby you rob God of the honor; and guard yourself against the misuse of the name of God or of Jesus; do not use either in vain or from habit. Just like Karlina, Mother had memorized, remembered, and taught them to me. Though I had been unaware until now, my mother had shared some of her life in Amana with me. I wasn't certain why, but the realization gave me a feeling of hope.

The two of us walked downstairs together, and Karlina donned her heavy cape while I slipped into my wool coat and buttoned it tight around my neck. Gathering the two water buckets, I followed her outdoors.

"I'll see you at breakfast," she called as I walked to the water pump and she strode toward the barn with her chin tucked tight against her chest.

"And I will be much warmer than you on this cold morning." My words transformed into puffs of white vapor and disappeared as quickly as ice on a summer day. If I moved quickly, I could have the buckets filled and return inside to warm my hands before the bread wagon arrived. I'd almost finished when I heard the bell in the distance, which meant Berndt Lehmann, the young man who worked at the bakery, was arriving at the Fuchs' kitchen house.

I topped off the final bucket, and walking carefully to avoid spillage, returned to the warmth of the kitchen. "Here you are, Cousin Louise. I know the ladies will be happy if the coffee is ready when they arrive."

"Ja, for sure they like that. And they work better, too." After grinding the coffee beans, she dipped water into both of the large enamel coffee boilers while I warmed my hands near the stove.

The moment I heard the jingle of the bread wagon outside our Küche, I turned away from the stove and hurried to the door.

"Guten Morgen, Dovie."

"Good morning, Berndt."

When I'd first met Berndt, I'd requested he address me as Dovie. He said he would agree if I would reciprocate. I wasn't certain Cousin Louise would approve of the familiar form of greeting we'd adopted, but I didn't ask.

He jumped down from the wagon and walked to the rear of the enclosed wagon. "I have your bread and the coffee cakes for Sunday breakfast." He opened the door of the wagon. The contents had been neatly organized and the orders arranged by kitchen house.

I watched as he moved the rectangular metal container that held the stacked coffee cakes. I extended my hand to accept the container, which had been designed and made by the village tinsmith. "The coffee cake makes everyone happy to see Sunday morning arrive."

"But Sunday mornings are not so happy for me."

I arched my brows. "And why is that? Doesn't your father bake enough coffee cake that you may have some?"

He laughed and pushed his hat further back on his head. A wave of sandy hair dropped across his forehead. "Oh, he makes sure there is always plenty for the Schneider Küche. But on Sundays I don't get to make deliveries, and that means I don't get to see you."

Berndt's comment both surprised and pleased me, for meeting the bread wagon each morning had quickly become the best part of my day. In spite of the cold, undeniable warmth blossomed and spread across my cheeks. Under any other circumstance, I would have worried. But today anyone who saw me would attribute my rosy complexion to the freezing temperatures.

"I wish I could figure out some way my family would be reassigned to eat in Sister Louise's Küche."

"That would be very nice, but I don't think it will happen." Berndt's family lived much closer to the Schneiders' Küche, and the location of your house determined where you took your meals.

"I'm afraid you are right, but still it would be nice if I could see you more than when I make the bread deliveries." He reached inside the wagon and removed a large tray lined with loaves of bread. "Why don't you take the bread. The tray isn't as heavy as the container of coffee cakes."

Berndt was handing me the bread tray when the back door slammed with a loud bang. I twisted to look over my shoulder. Sister Louise stood on the porch, her hands cupped to her lips. "What is taking so long? Is Brother Berndt baking the bread in his wagon?"

"Nein! But if it would make you happy, I will see if I can put a stove in the wagon to keep the bread warm for you, Sister Louise." Brother Berndt's laughter echoed in the crisp morning air as he strode to the back door, carrying the metal container in one hand while cradling extra loaves of bread in his arm.

Sister Louise remained at the door and held it open. "You spend too much time talking, Brother Berndt. I do not think your Vater knows that you could return to the bakery a half hour earlier each morning if you didn't waste time visiting."

Berndt set the container on the table while I started removing the coffee cakes. "But you are the last delivery of the day, Sister Louise. I have been up half the night baking for you, and instead of offering me a cup of coffee, you criticize me for being friendly."

"Ach! You are not fooling me." Sister Louise flapped her dish towel in the air. "It is your Vater who has been baking half the night. And if it is coffee you want, you know how to help yourself." Berndt didn't wait for another offer. He picked up a cup and filled it to the brim while Sister Louise examined the coffee cakes.

"The cakes look gut. Tell your Vater I send my thanks."

"What about the bread? Does it look gut, as well?"

Sister Louise picked up one of the crusty loaves and gave a nod. "Ja. I never have complaints about anything your Vater bakes."

Berndt grinned. "I bake the bread by myself every Saturday so Vater can bake the cakes. I thank you for your compliment, and it is my great pleasure to please you, Sister Louise."

"Ja, well it is proper you help your Vater as much as possible."

Berndt took a sip of his coffee. "You must always have the final word—just like my Mutter."

I expected to hear Sister Louise protest, but instead she headed into the dining hall to give some of the junior girls instruction. Berndt lifted the empty container from the table.

"Thank you for your help, Berndt."

"Since I don't deliver bread to the Küche on Sunday, maybe I will see you sitting across the aisle from me in the meeting hall instead."

I shook my head. "I'll be helping in the kitchen tomorrow so that Sister Marta can attend church instead." I didn't consider myself as skilled as the women who worked in the kitchen, so I had felt a sense of pride when Cousin Louise asked me to oversee the junior helpers on Sunday mornings. She said it would give Sister Marta an opportunity to attend Sunday meeting. I would have liked to attend myself, but helping in the kitchen would be of greater benefit to the community. "It is one way I can express my appreciation to Cousin Louise and the other women for their kindness to me. And a way of showing that I am willing to serve God and other members of the community."

"I see you have been learning some of our beliefs."

"I am trying. Karlina has been helping me."

"I would be pleased to act as your teacher if you would like to ask me questions when I deliver the bread." He hesitated a moment. "Or maybe you would like to go ice skating tomorrow afternoon?"

Skating sounded wonderful, but I wasn't sure if Cousin Louise would approve. "I couldn't go without permission."

The back door opened and two of the kitchen workers bustled inside. "For sure, it is going to snow before evening," one of them said as she removed her heavy cloak.

Just then Sister Louise strode back into the kitchen. "Are you still here, Berndt? You are crowding the kitchen and keeping us from getting breakfast cooked. If you don't move along, you'll be late for your own breakfast." She rested her hands on her hips. "I don't know any Küchebaas who tolerates stragglers wandering into their dining hall—especially Sister Frieda."

Berndt pulled his coat collar high around his neck. Before he moved away from my side, he tipped his head a little closer. "I'll come over tomorrow afternoon and see if I can gain Sister Louise's permission to take you skating."

I didn't answer, but my heart quickened at his suggestion.

Later that morning after the breakfast dishes had been washed, the pots scrubbed, and the kitchen and dining hall floors swept, Cousin Louise sat down and began to make a list for her purchases at the general store. "May I come with you to the store?"

She looked up. "If there is something you need, I will put it on the list."

"Nothing I need, but with Christmas not far off, I thought I might see if I could find a gift for Karlina." My father had given me a small sum of money before we'd left Cincinnati. "Pin money," he'd called it—to be used for incidentals while we were apart. I wouldn't be able to buy anything extravagant, but I doubted I'd find anything in the general store that would match the expensive selections available at Mabley and Carew, Rollman's, or Alms and Doepke, three of the large department stores in Cincinnati where Mother and I had occasionally shopped.

"Gifts are not necessary, but if it pleases you to come with me, you may come along." Cousin Louise folded the piece of paper and tucked it into her skirt pocket. She gestured toward the pegs on the far wall. "You will need your coat. It is much colder than it looks."

I quickly retrieved my coat and also grabbed Cousin Louise's cloak at the same time. "And you will need this to keep you warm." I giggled and handed her the heavy garment.

"Ja, you are right." She stood and turned to Sister Marta. "Please make sure the coffee, bread, and jam are ready by midmorning. I hope I will be back by then, but who can say for sure."

Except on Sundays, the workers returned to the dining hall for a light lunch that was served between breakfast and the noonday meal. The same happened between the noonday meal and supper. The practice surprised me, but Cousin Louise explained that hard work required energy, and the extra sustenance provided the workers with necessary stamina. It also created extra work in the Küche, but nobody appeared to mind—it was as customary as the other three meals served each day.

Sister Marta's brows knit together in a frown. "I take care of it every day. Why would today be any different?"

Cousin Louise patted her friend's arm. "And you do a wonderful job. I don't know what I would do without your help."

The compliment was like a soothing balm and immediately erased the frown from Sister Marta's face. It hadn't taken long for me to see that Cousin Louise knew how to manage every woman in her kitchen. Some needed compliments, some needed to share their problems, and others enjoyed laughter. Whatever the need, Cousin Louise adapted and helped. And today I planned to seek her help. I hoped to use our time together to gain some answers about my mother.

On several occasions I'd broached the subject, but Cousin Louise's answers had always been guarded—at least they'd seemed that way to me. Each time I attempted to dig deeper into the past, she changed the subject or sent me to the other side of the kitchen to help cut noodles or peel potatoes. But on our way to and from the store, we would have uninterrupted time together, and I planned to use that time to full advantage.

We'd gone only a few steps beyond the porch when I asked my first question. I didn't want to waste precious time. "Tell me about my mother, Cousin Louise. I want to know what she was like when she lived here, and why her family left."

Pulling her hood tight around her head, she glanced in my direction. "I know you miss your Mutter, but digging into her past will not bring her back. I am sure she told you everything she thought was important for you to know. She loved you very much."

"How do you know that?"

She *tsk*ed and shook her head. "Because mothers love their children and because she wrote to me after you were born. She was delighted to have a daughter of her own."

"And my father? Did she write about him, too?"

Cousin Louise hesitated. "Not so much. But you must remember that I did not know your Vater."

She hadn't known me, either, but I didn't want to say that or it might stop her from telling me more. "What else did she tell you?"

"At first she wrote about her move to Covington, Kentucky, with your *Oma* and *Opa*, and then later about getting married and moving across the river to Zinzinatti."

I smiled at her pronunciation. "Did she say she liked it there?"

Cousin Louise's hard-soled shoes clacked on the board sidewalk. "I don't think she ever felt as at home as she did in the colonies, but she was happy your Vater agreed to live in that place she called Over-the-Rhine. In one of her letters she said there were many German immigrants. That pleased her, I think."

"Maybe it pleased her a little, but I don't think she was ever completely happy. There were many days when I couldn't convince her to leave the house. Most of the time, she appeared melancholy, but she wouldn't tell me why. Vater said it was because she never was very healthy, but I think she may have regretted marrying my father and having me."

"Nein." She stopped and turned to me. "You should never think such a thing. Your Mutter loved you, and your birth gave her great joy. I am sure you miss her very much." She patted my arm with her gloved hand. "I can tell you that your Vater was right about your Mutter's health. She was a sickly girl and she always tired easily." Bowing her head against the cold breeze, she strode toward the store with a determined step.

Our conversation had ended, and I didn't know any more than when we'd walked out of the Küche. How would I ever learn about my mother's past if Cousin Louise refused to talk to me?

# CHAPTER 8

Karlina

Over the past weeks, Anton had settled into our home, but I still hadn't detected any signs that he enjoyed working with the sheep. I considered the sheep to be an extension of our family, but Anton viewed them merely as work. I thought it a privilege to care for them, but he viewed it a punishment. He'd never said these things to me, but when I was in his presence, I sensed he'd developed little, if any, fondness for shepherding.

Both my father and I had been patient in our teaching—my father more so than I, for I couldn't understand anyone who didn't enjoy caring for animals. But Anton avoided the sheep whenever possible. At least that was how it seemed to me. He grumbled when required to go to the pasture and watch over the sheep. He much preferred the idea of keeping them in the barn all winter. Except when the ground turned exceedingly wet or during winter snows, my father pastured the sheep. Years of shepherding had convinced him that fresh-air foraging provided the best care for the animals. Closed inside the barns, they developed more sickness. Fresh air, fresh water, proper food, and a loving shepherd—those were the things necessary for raising good sheep, at least that was my father's belief. Right now the sheep might be receiving fresh air, water, and good food, but I didn't believe they were being tended by a loving shepherd.

I'd done my best to offer kindness and gentle instruction, but Anton was different from the other men in our village. Instead of being cheerful and pleasant, most of the time he appeared quiet and withdrawn or angry and sullen. Only when he spoke to me about his inventions did I see a glimmer in his eyes and hear excitement in his voice.

Even on Sundays the animals needed care, which was another matter that annoyed Anton. When we'd returned from meeting a few minutes ago, he'd started toward the stairs, and my father called to him.

"Ja?"

"Are you forgetting the sheep?"

His features tightened into a frown. "I would like to, but it seems there is always someone to remind me."

I was surprised when my father chuckled. "All of us need reminders, Anton. I'm here to remind you when you forget the sheep just as my aching body reminds me that I must slow down. Our hungry friends who come to this dining hall every day are a reminder that meals must be prepared. And the ringing bell in the tower keeps all of us on schedule. You see? We all must pay heed and be thankful for the reminders in our life."

Anton didn't appear convinced. He trod to the kitchen, the soles of his shoes slapping the wooden floor with an angry beat.

Drawing close to my father, I sat down next to him. "I can go and take care of the sheep, Vater. You know I do not mind. And Anton does not want to go."

"All the more reason he should do it. One day he will learn to serve with a cheerful heart. Until then, he will make himself miserable."

"And the sheep, Vater. They sense his anger and frustration when he is around them. Have you not noticed that they are not as calm as they used to be?"

"I was a shepherd before you were born, child. I understand that the sheep do better with a shepherd who tends them with a pleasant spirit. Let me worry about Anton. You should know that I won't let any harm come to the sheep." He pushed up from his chair and slowly straightened his body. "If it will ease your worrying, you can go down to the barn and check on the sheep, but wait a few more minutes. Give Anton time to complete his work before you go down there. I am going upstairs for a rest."

My eyes remained fastened upon my father as he hobbled across the room. His once-broad shoulders now hunched forward, and his long-legged stride had been replaced by a limping gait. He didn't need to speak of his pain—the changes in his carriage and posture spoke for him.

I'd been watching the clock with great intensity when the kitchen door opened and someone entered. Thinking it was Anton, I jumped up and hurried toward him. My heart thudded an angry beat as I mentally prepared what I would say to him. He couldn't have possibly completed his tasks so quickly.

I charged toward the kitchen but stopped short as I crossed the threshold. "Brother Berndt!" It was all I could manage at the moment. Once my racing heart had recovered, I attempted a smile. "What are you doing here?"

"I thought you and Dovie might want to go over to the pond

for some ice skating this afternoon. I can build a fire, but we don't have to stay too long if you're afraid of getting cold."

"Me? Cold? I stay out with the sheep half of the winter. Remember?"

"Ja, but Dovie might not be so used to the cold weather."

Dovie hadn't mentioned ice skating, and I didn't even know she'd met Berndt. She hadn't mentioned him, but then it dawned on me. She'd likely met him when he delivered the bread each morning. Still, it seemed odd he would suddenly appear and ask to go skating. He'd never before invited me, so Dovie had seemingly captured his interest. Still, without knowing how she might feel, I didn't want to agree.

"What brings you here, Brother Berndt?" I hadn't heard my mother's footsteps and startled when she spoke. "You have begun to deliver bread on Sundays?" Her eyebrows arched as she awaited his answer.

"I was thinking it would be a gut afternoon for ice skating. I thought Karlina and Dovie might want to join me." He touched his hand to the metal skates slung over his shoulder.

My mother removed a coffee cup from the shelf. "I think Dovie is resting. She took charge of the Küche for me while we were at meeting this morning. She can go if you go, also, Karlina. You can ask her if she wants to go with you, but I will be surprised if she has ice skates." My mother lifted the coffeepot from the back of the stove and filled her cup as I turned and hurried upstairs.

I hoped Dovie wouldn't want to go—at least not now. I needed to check on the sheep, and I knew my mother wouldn't give permission for Dovie to go alone with Berndt. When I opened the door to the bedroom, Dovie startled. She was sitting at the small desk and quickly placed her arm over something. I didn't know if she was writing a letter, but I was surprised she would hide it from me. It appeared she had more secrets than just Berndt. The thought troubled me, but I forced a smile.

"Berndt, the young man who delivers the bread each morning, is downstairs." I knew the explanation wasn't necessary, but if she wanted to pretend, I could do the same. "He asked if you would like to go ice skating. He included me in the invitation, but only to be polite—and to gain Mother's approval."

"Oh yes! I was going to tell you that he'd mentioned going this afternoon, but then I forgot. In truth, I didn't expect him to appear." She fidgeted in her chair. "Besides, I didn't bring ice skates."

My curiosity continued to build as she scooted to one side as if to keep secret whatever she'd been doing. What was she concealing? "Mutter says you can go if I go along, but first I need to check the sheep. Who knows? Maybe Anton would like to join us."

She grinned and pointed her finger in my direction. "I knew you cared for him."

"I don't care for him any more than any other man in the community. He is my brother in the Lord, nothing more."

"And maybe one day your husband, too! Who can say?"

I sighed and shook my head. "I only suggested asking Anton because I thought it would be rude to exclude him."

Anton wasn't the type of man I would ever want for a husband. I had promised to pray for him and had kept my promise. Since then, I hadn't observed much change in him. In fact, I hadn't observed anything that made me think he even wanted to change. Who would want a husband like Anton Becker? Certainly not me.

Dovie giggled. "I'm not so sure I believe you."

"Do you want to go to the pond or not? I can probably borrow ice skates from one of the girls who live nearby."

Dovie glanced toward the desk. "That seems like a lot of trouble. Maybe Berndt should come back in an hour—after you and Anton finish tending to the sheep."

Perhaps I'd misjudged and she hadn't expected Berndt. Either that, or she feared I'd see whatever she was hiding. I backed toward the door. "I'll go down and tell him. And you can go on with whatever you're concealing on the desk." I walked out before she could reply. I didn't want to cause an argument, but I couldn't resist letting her know she hadn't been as sly as she'd thought.

When I entered the kitchen, Berndt stretched to look behind me. Once he realized I'd returned alone, his smile disappeared. "Dovie doesn't want to go skating?"

"She'd like to go, but it would be better if we could meet you after I tend to the sheep. You go ahead and we'll meet you at the pond when I've finished."

He shrugged and nodded. I didn't miss the disappointment in his eyes. "Tell her I will have a warm fire ready by the time you get there."

On my way to the barn, I decided I would invite Anton to join us for ice skating. Working with the sheep could be a lonely task, and since coming to our village, he'd had few opportunities to form friendships with any of the young men. An afternoon of skating and an opportunity to visit with Berndt might improve his attitude. The idea pleased me and I quickened my step, but my excitement plummeted when I entered the barn.

One look and I knew Anton had accomplished little, if anything. From the odor and appearance, it was obvious he hadn't mucked the barn. And he'd closed the sheep doors and all of the vents. He'd been told that sheep need good ventilation, even in cold weather. I surmised from the bleating that the sheep weren't any happier than I. What had he been doing for the last hour, and why was the barn closed up tighter than a drum?

"Anton! Are you in here?" In the dim light, I saw his hat slowly rise above one of the wood partitions used during lambing sea-son. When he didn't say anything, I ran the length of the barn. A knot of fear formed deep in the pit of my stomach. Had one of the sheep knocked him over and injured him? Had he been lying out here with a broken bone, or was he bleeding? In those brief moments, I envisioned all sorts of tragic farm accidents that could have rendered him helpless. Panting when I arrived at the stall, I leaned forward to catch my breath. "Are you hurt? What happened?"

He appeared bewildered by my concern. "All is well."

His calm reply surprised me. How could nothing be wrong? The barn was closed and none of his work had been completed. He shuffled one foot, and I saw the corner of a tablet of paper that he'd been trying to push under the straw. I stepped around him, leaned down, and picked up the pad of paper, and handed it to him.

"You've been sitting back here drawing while the sheep are wandering in this foul barn? And why is everything closed? They should be outdoors. My Vater and I have told you that the sheep doors and the vents should be open if they are inside. They become too warm without fresh air."

"And then they become sick. I know. You repeat your orders every day. I am tired of hearing the same things over and over." He kicked the bottom slat of the enclosure. "It is too cold in here with the doors open."

I took a backward step, astonished by his bad behavior. I had expected an apology. Instead, he'd responded with anger. Remain-ing calm, I pointed to the closed doors leading into the side shel-ter that we used to release the sheep. Those doors were seldom closed. "If you would do what you've been told, I wouldn't have to repeat the same instructions. And if you are cold, you should wear another sweater under your coat. It is not gut for the sheep to become overheated. You can take care of yourself, but they are helpless. You are their shepherd. They need your care, but instead you draw pictures and ignore their needs."

His face turned deep red, and the vein in the side of his neck pulsed. He shoved the tablet toward me and thrust his finger atop the drawing. "*This* is to help the sheep. It is a way to bring fresh water into the barn for them. Does that sound like someone who doesn't care about them?" His jaw twitched.

I stared at the drawing and recalled a Scripture I'd learned years ago. *Wherefore, my beloved brethren, let every man be swift to hear, slow to speak, slow to wrath: For the wrath of man worketh not the righteousness of God.* I opened my mouth to quote the verses from the book of James, but something deep inside stopped me. To make an issue of his anger at this time would only make matters worse.

"Having fresh water flow into the barn would be a gut thing, Anton, but maybe you should first make sure the sheep have clean straw and fresh air. After that you can work on your inventions."

His jaw relaxed and his eyes softened. "So you think this could work?"

"You are the inventor. My Vater would be a better judge of whether it would work. You should show him the drawing and explain how you would plan such a system." I gestured toward the other end of the barn. "Right now, we must get busy and clean the barn."

He didn't argue, and for that I was pleased. Later I would mention his anger, but for now we would clean the barn. I sighed. There would be no time for ice skating today.

CHAPTER 9

I didn't know who had been more disappointed regarding the skating incident, Berndt or Dovie. I had expressed my regret, but Anton did nothing more than mumble a quick one-word apology. Later he'd told me he believed his time was better used perfecting his invention than ice skating. In turn, I told him he should sometimes consider others. He nodded, but I wasn't certain he'd taken my comment to heart. I hoped the joy of the Christmas season might soften his behavior.

The days leading to Christmas were always busy in the colonies. Since only the bakery and the kitchen houses had ovens, the women took turns going to the bakery to bake their Christmas cookies. Each woman prepared her own dough in the kitchen house and took it to the bakery on her assigned date. On cookie-baking days, Berndt's father, Brother Erich, would build the fire a little higher so that once the bread was done, there would be enough heat remaining for one or two women to complete their cookies.

Each year Brother Erich prepared a list setting out the time and day for each woman to come and bake. Most of the time, the women were happy with the schedule, but occasionally there would be complaints. As with most things, there was always someone who felt slighted, someone who feared that another woman would receive fifteen extra minutes in the bakery. At such times Brother Erich became a diplomat of sorts, explaining that women with larger families required more time in the bakery. His cajoling usually worked, but when he had a problem he couldn't solve, my mother would offer a little time for baking in our kitchen. Though it wasn't the most convenient arrangement, Mutter somehow made it work. I was always happy when one of the neighbors baked in our kitchen, for it meant I would receive a few samples.

Today we would mix the dough for our Christmas cookies. And though working in the kitchen was not something I wanted to do all of the time, baking Christmas cookies was more fun than work.

"You need first to mix the sugar into the butter, Karlina. And then you can add the eggs—one by one. Don't try to hurry and add them all at once. And make sure the sugar and butter are nice and creamy before you add the eggs."

I grinned at Dovie, who had taken her place beside me. Dipping a large measuring cup into the sugar, she filled the metal container and lifted it out. Using a table knife, she leveled the sugar and poured it into the bowl. "We will need to take turns stirring. My arm gets tired. And Mutter says the cookies are not gut unless the dough has been mixed properly."

"Ja, that is right. And you should remember that you are the one who is always wanting the butter cookies, Karlina."

I giggled. "I know, Mutter. They are my favorite."

"They are your favorite because you like to use the cookie

cutters." My mother's flour handprints decorated the front of her long, dark apron.

"We need to remember to take the cookie cutters to the bakery tomorrow."

My mother shook her head. "Nein. This year we will be baking here."

Her reply surprised me. We could complete our baking much more quickly at the bakery, and Mother hadn't mentioned we wouldn't be going there. In fact, I'd been teasing Dovie about seeing Berndt when we went to do our Christmas baking.

I stopped stirring. "But why?"

She pointed to the cookie batter. "Keep stirring." Once the wooden spoon was moving again, she gave a pleased nod. "Because the bakery will be very busy, and I told Brother Erich I would be willing to bake here."

"Are the other Küchebaases baking in their Küches?"

"I cannot say if they are or not. And what they are doing is not important to us as long as we are able to bake our cookies. If it frees time in the bakery, I am pleased to help."

"It will take longer to bake them here."

"And what do you have to do that is so important that you can't take a little extra time to make cookies? Tomorrow we can put up the Christmas pyramid and the other decorations while we are baking the cookies. With three of us, we can keep a close watch so none of them burn." She gave me one of her smiles that said she was pleased, but I didn't understand why we'd be baking at home when our name had been on Brother Erich's list for tomorrow afternoon.

Once we were alone in the kitchen, I nudged Dovie and handed her the wooden spoon. "When Berndt brings the bread tomorrow, you should ask him who is taking our place baking cookies at the bakery."

"No. He will think that I am asking because I was hoping to spend time with him."

I added flour to the buttery mixture while Dovie stirred. "Well, weren't you?"

"Perhaps, but he doesn't need to know."

"Then the next time I see him, I'll tell him you had been hoping to see him at the bakery, but for some reason we were removed from the list."

Dovie lifted the spoon from the bowl and pointed it in my direction. "Don't you do it, Karlina." A glob of batter dropped from the spoon and plopped into the bowl.

"Keep stirring, Dovie." My mother entered the room and smiled as she pointed her finger at the bowl. "Your cookies are not going to turn out well if the dough isn't mixed."

We worked at a feverish pace and had completed mixing several batches of dough by the time the kitchen workers returned to begin supper. I made my escape to the sheep barn, though I felt a little guilty for leaving Dovie behind. After mixing all that cookie dough, I doubted she was excited to help with the supper preparations.

The reason our family name was removed from the baking schedule was never discovered. At least not by me. Dovie said she never asked Berndt about the matter, and when I had a chance to inquire several days later, he denied any knowledge of the baking schedule. Since I could find no reason to doubt him, I decided I was making a mountain out of a molehill. There were more important things requiring my attention. Christmas would soon arrive and I hadn't yet decided upon a gift for Dovie.

I'd asked her a few questions about Christmas in Cincinnati, and she'd spoken of beautiful decorations in the city and commented that her family had continued to use a Christmas pyramid, but I wondered if our simple fare would disappoint her. We owned one of the prettiest Christmas pyramids in East. It was three tiers high with carved carolers on the first tier, farm animals on the second, and angels blowing their trumpets on the third. When lit, heat from the six candles surrounding the base of the pyramid would cause the propeller on top to turn. I thought there could be nothing as lovely as our pyramid. But Dovie lived in a big city where her father could have purchased something even better. Being without both of her parents during the holiday would be difficult, and I wanted to somehow make it special. But how? Then I remembered something else she'd told me, and I hurried upstairs to find my mother.

I peeked in the parlor and into her bedroom, but when I heard a noise in Anton's room, I hurried down the hall. "Here you are!"

"Ja, changing the sheets. Where did you think I would be?"

"Maybe in the kitchen." I was much more familiar with schedules in the sheep barn and pastures than with my mother's routine. "I was thinking about Christmas."

My mother glanced over her shoulder. "And I was thinking about all the laundry that must be carried out to the washhouse."

I chuckled. "I will carry the laundry to the washhouse, Mutter. But first I want to tell you about my Christmas idea." While she finished the bed and tossed the sheets into the woven laundry basket, I hastily explained my plan.

"I think it would be fine, but you must do it on your own. I will not have time to help. And hiding part of your secret is going to be difficult."

My mother was right. I hadn't worked out all of the details. I lifted the basket and followed her downstairs. "What if I remain at home on Sunday morning and Dovie goes with you to meeting? That would give me time alone in the Küche."

My mother's forehead creased into deep ridges as she considered my suggestion. "I don't know, Karlina. Dovie will not be here much longer, and she has agreed to help in the kitchen on Sunday mornings. It will seem strange to her if I change the plan, don't you think?"

"Let me take care of convincing Dovie. She has already expressed interest, and I can tell her I want her to attend meeting one time before she must leave."

My mother signaled for me to go. "Hurry, now. I have much to do, and you should already be at the barn filling out the record books."

When Sunday arrived, I didn't know who was more excited, Dovie or me. She had accepted my explanation with delight. Of course, neither of us truly knew when she might leave for Texas, so she didn't want to miss an opportunity to visit at least one meeting. There had been only one letter from her father since his departure, and it hadn't sounded as though he would send for her right away. Thus far he'd been unable to locate a home for them. He'd given her the address of the hotel where he'd rented a room, and she'd recently mailed him a letter and a Christmas card she'd purchased at the general store. So far there had been no Christmas greetings from him.

If that bothered Dovie, she hadn't revealed it to me. Still, I wanted to make Christmas special for her. The minute my parents, Dovie, and Anton departed for church, I set to work. This would be my only opportunity—I didn't have time for failure.

One of the two junior girls who helped on Sunday morning wrinkled her nose as they entered the kitchen. "Why are *you* here?" She stretched sideways and looked into the dining hall.

"You won't find Dovie in the other room, so you best get to

work." I signaled for both of them to begin their tasks. "Mutter left your instructions on the table."

"And what will you be doing while we're busy preparing the meal?"

"I'm going to be making special Christmas candy for Dovie, but you must promise not to tell." Both of the girls giggled and covered their mouths. I rested my hands on my hips. "What is so funny?"

Mary, the older of the two, shook her head. "N-n-nothing. We've just never seen you cook anything before."

"No need to worry. I'll be working at this end of the Küche. The rest is yours." I knew they would seize every opportunity to watch my techniques. Of course, we all knew I had none. "And don't mention this to anyone. It is to be a surprise."

Mary nodded. "I'm sure it will be." She remained at her table but eyed me as I gathered my ingredients. "What kind of candy are you making, Sister Karlina?"

"*Marzipankartoffeln.* Have you made them before?"

Both girls nodded their heads. "Ja. Making the marzipan potatoes is easy. But I hope you have already shelled the almonds. Shelling and chopping the almonds will take more time than you have this morning."

My mother had already warned me about shelling the almonds, and I went to the general store after she gave me permission to make the candy. I used some of my time in the barn to shell the nuts. After telling Anton of my surprise for Dovie, he helped with the project, and when we had finished, I helped him clean the barn. I was certain he had come out ahead on that exchange.

I didn't tell anyone, but I had used the coffee grinder to chop the nuts. I'd been careful to wipe away any remnants from the device when I finished last night. One of the men told Mother that the coffee had tasted extra good this morning. I held my breath and waited. But when she merely thanked him, I was certain she hadn't noticed anything was amiss.

"Do you think I have enough?" I held out the bag of chopped nuts. I'd begun with a large bag, but once they were chopped, it didn't seem like much.

Both girls stepped closer and looked into the sack. Antje shook her head. "You won't make much candy with that."

Mary agreed and pointed to a wood bowl and pestle. "You need to make the nuts finer. They are chopped, but for the marzipan, they need to be ground like flour." She grinned at me. "You should be thankful you have nothing to cook, or you would never finish."

I could see they were taking great delight in my lack of ability, but I was determined to make the best candy possible. Besides, I didn't need much. This was a gift for Dovie, not the entire village. My hand and arm ached by the time Antje and Mary declared the nuts fine enough for mixing with the sugar, flavoring, and egg white.

"Be careful you don't add too much liquid at once, Karlina. You don't have enough almonds to thicken the paste."

As the time passed, the girls took pity on me and I was thankful for their help. Both of them checked the mixture and declared it a good consistency to form the Marzipan into the shape of small potatoes. While I rolled them, Mary drew near and gave a nod of approval. "They look gut. You have the cocoa and cinnamon mixed so you can coat them?"

"Nein. I will do that once I've finished rolling them."

She reached for the metal container of cocoa. "I will mix it for you. The candy needs a little time to dry before everyone returns to the kitchen."

I thanked her, and while I finished rolling the mixture into oblong potato shapes, she pushed them around in the cocoa mixture until they were covered. "You need to dust some of the cocoa off so they look like real potatoes."

Once I had finished rolling the shapes, I followed Mary's example, and when I was done, my candy looked as good as any I'd ever eaten. I admired them with more than a little pride and then looked at the two girls. "They are gut, ja?"

"To taste tells the real truth," Mary said. She eyed the candy and then traced her finger above each one as she counted.

"We wouldn't want Dovie to get sick from eating too many," Antje said, drawing closer. "I think we should taste them and see if they are gut enough to give as a present."

A nod of my head was all they needed before each one bit into a piece. "It is perfect," Mary declared.

"It is." The surprise in Antje's voice affirmed that they were telling the truth.

A warmth of satisfaction washed over me. Soon I'd be ready for Christmas.

CHAPTER 10

Christmas Eve
Dovie

When supper had been eaten, the dishes washed, and all of the women departed for the day, Cousin Louise and Cousin George instructed Karlina, Anton, and me to go to our rooms.

"I'll tell you when you may come out," Cousin Louise said. "And no peeking, Karlina."

While Karlina and I went into our bedroom, Anton went off by himself. "I do feel sorry for him. It doesn't seem right that he can't be with his family for Christmas." I knew my opinion didn't matter to anyone. I was an outsider and didn't understand many of the decisions made by the elders. But I did know that even being surrounded by another family wasn't the same as being with one's own, and Anton and I had that in common this Christmas. I swallowed hard as memories of past Christmases pushed to the forefront of my mind.

Karlina sat down on the edge of her bed. "I feel sad for Anton, as well. I asked my Vater why he couldn't go home for at least a couple days, but he told me I should not question the decision of the elders. They believe he will do better if he remains away from his own village for a longer time."

Taking a position on the edge of my own bed, I met Karlina's gaze. "What has he done that is so bad?"

Karlina shrugged. "He says he has a bad temper and the elders had warned him that he would need to leave his village if he did not learn self-control. He didn't tell me what he did; he just said that he didn't heed their warning." She clasped her hands together. "And it is true that he has difficulty controlling his temper."

She spoke with an authority that allowed fear to enter my mind. I leaned forward and grasped her hands. "Has he lost his temper with you?"

"He has spoken in anger, and I have seen evidence that he lacks control, but I know he is working hard to conquer his shortcomings. I do think he is doing better, but it is likely the elders have judged him correctly." She straightened and withdrew her hands. "Please don't think harshly of him. We all have faults, and he is working to correct his. But he has been sent to work in a place that isn't familiar or to his liking."

"I would think the elders would have chosen to send him to work where he could most easily adjust. Even to me it is obvious he doesn't like working with the sheep."

"There is much he can learn from working with the sheep. When they finally begin to trust and follow him, the elders will likely send him home."

I chuckled. "So the sheep can judge good character?"

"Ja!" Karlina bobbed her head. "Much better than most humans, I think."

We could hear noises in the parlor, and even though this wouldn't be the same as Christmas Eve in my own home, my anticipation increased along with Karlina's. I hoped that she would like my gift. In that moment I realized I had nothing to give Anton.

"Karlina, I have no gift for Anton. What can I do?"

"A gift is not necessary. He will not expect anything from you." She grinned. "I doubt he has thought of gifts for us."

"But you have a gift for him, don't you?" I hoped she would say no, but she nodded her head, and my heart plummeted. "What will I do?"

She clapped her hands together. "I know! He wants to learn English." She jumped up and went to the desk and pulled out a piece of paper. "Write down that you will give him English lessons so long as he is a gut student and doesn't become angry when corrected."

"The English lessons are a wonderful idea, but I am not going to say he has to study and remain calm."

"You may be sorry if you don't."

I laughed and nodded. "Then I will tell him at our first lesson."

"Agreed. Now hurry or we will be called to the parlor before you finish."

I composed the note, slipped it into an envelope, and carefully penned Anton's name on the outside. I was blotting the ink as Cousin Louise called to us.

When we stepped into the hall, I noticed she'd closed the door to the parlor. "First, we must go downstairs to the kitchen and have our cookies and coffee; then we will come upstairs to the parlor."

I tucked the envelope into my pocket and hoped I could place it with the other gifts once we returned upstairs. While Karlina and I arranged cookies on one of the large china platters, Cousin Louise lifted the coffeepot from the back of the stove and filled cups with the steaming dark liquid. We had gathered around a small table in the kitchen to eat our cookies when the door burst open and Pelznickel tromped into the room, carrying his burlap bag and leaning on a long walking stick.

Karlina had told me that each year Brother Herman dressed as grizzled old Pelznickel and came to the houses in East. Once he arrived, he decided if we had been bad or good throughout the year. The gift he retrieved from his bag revealed his decision. I'd never had a visit from Pelznickel, but I'd heard some of my friends in Cincinnati talk about such visits. Standing in front of Anton, he reached into his bag and withdrew a small sack. After pondering his decision for a minute or two, he handed it to Anton along with a similar one to both Karlina and me.

Ringing a brass sleigh bell that had been fastened to the leather belt that surrounded his worn fur coat, he bellowed a laugh. "No switches or coal for anyone this year." He reached down and helped himself to several cookies, waved them in the air, and tromped to the door. "Merry Christmas!"

We returned his Christmas greeting while Anton opened the small paper sack. His mouth gaped open when he looked inside the bag. "An orange and some pieces of hard candy. The first time I haven't received switches in many years."

Brother George grinned. "Then this indeed is a gut Christmas for you. Maybe Pelznickel knows that you have been studying the Scriptures and have learned that 'A wrathful man stirreth up strife: but he that is slow to anger appeaseth strife.'"

Anton closed the paper sack. "I learned that Scripture many years ago, Brother George."

"Ja, but now you are putting it into practice. That is the key. To learn the Scriptures is one thing, but to practice them in our daily life is another. That is what we all must try to do." He stood and squeezed Anton's shoulder. "Even Pelznickel understands that you are trying to do better. Come, let's go up to the parlor and see if there are any gifts to be opened."

When Cousin Louise opened the parlor door, it wasn't the gifts that captured my attention, but the lone stocking that hung above the fireplace. From the bright smile on Karlina's lips, I knew she was responsible. Tears threatened as I recalled telling her of the tradition my parents had begun when I was a small child. I never imagined that she would hang a stocking for me. While Cousin George lit the candles on the pyramid, she removed the oddly shaped stocking from the mantel and handed it to me.

"Merry Christmas, Dovie." Karlina placed her hand on the stocking. "As you can see, I do not knit very well, and I must admit that I made this stocking when I was only thirteen years old. Mutter declared it unusable. It has been tucked away in my drawer ever since. But after hearing of your tradition, I think I found a good use for it."

I stood and kissed her cheek. "Merry Christmas to you, Karlina. It is a very special stocking that I shall treasure."

Anton choked back a laugh. "I think Karlina handles wool better when it is still on the sheep."

Even Karlina laughed at his joke, but then she said, "Reach inside and find what I made for you."

I sat down, placed the misshapen object on my lap, withdrew several small packets, and unwrapped one. "You made candy, Karlina?" I looked to Cousin Louise for affirmation.

"Ja, she did it on Sunday while we were at meeting."

Anton leaned toward me and held out his hand. "Maybe you should let me taste it to make sure it is fit to eat."

"And maybe you should keep your hands to yourself. That is Dovie's gift." Karlina lifted a package from the mantel and handed it to him. She smiled. "But this one is for you."

Anton unwrapped his candy and popped a piece into his mouth. "Umm. It is not very gut, Dovie. I think you should give yours to me. I will eat it for you and save you the misery."

Laughter filled the room, and the sound created an uneasy mixture of joy and sadness deep within. It seemed wrong to enjoy myself this first Christmas after my mother's death. I wondered if my father had someone to laugh with on this cold winter evening. Forcing the thought from my mind, I handed out my gifts to each of them and watched with anticipation as the three of them unrolled the scrolls of paper and Anton opened his envelope.

"This is beautiful, Dovie." Karlina's eyebrows rose in surprise. "Is this what you were hiding at the desk when I came up to the bedroom?"

I nodded. "I was afraid you had seen it."

From the surprised look on her face, I knew that Karlina hadn't discovered what I'd been creating. I'd chosen a different verse of Scripture for each family member, and using the calligraphy skills I'd been taught in school, I had painstakingly penned the verse onto thick linen paper. I'd written the verses in German, of course, and had even sketched a small sheep on the one I made for Karlina.

"Nein, but I did think you were keeping a secret from me."

"Only a Christmas secret. And I will put them in frames for you, but there wasn't time enough to do that earlier."

Cousin Louise clucked her tongue. "You do not need to do more, Dovie. This is quite beautiful, and George can make us frames for them, can't you, husband?"

He nodded his head. "Ja, and I will be pleased to have something useful to do when my bones are aching and I'm unable to tend the sheep."

Anton waved his envelope toward me. "I cannot read this. It is not written in German."

I smiled and gave a nod. "It says that if you would like, I will teach you some English while I am here. Karlina said you are interested in learning."

"To speak, ja, but even if you remained for the rest of your life, I do not think you would have enough time to teach me to read and write another language."

"Then I will spend some time each day teaching you to speak English, and we shall not worry with reading or writing."

Anton tucked the piece of paper back into the envelope. "Thank you, Dovie. This pleases me very much."

I exchanged a secret smile with Karlina. Her suggestion had been perfect. In truth, he appeared much more pleased with the promise of English lessons than with the shepherd's crook Brother George and Cousin Louise had given him.

We had nearly finished opening our gifts when Cousin Louise lifted a package from beside her chair. "This is from your Vater, Dovie. It arrived the other day, but I saved it for Christmas."

My heart tightened at the sight of my father's handwriting. He hadn't forgotten. All of them watched as I opened the box. A smaller box lay nestled inside the larger one, and an envelope rested below. I'd been eager for news from my father, but the sight of his letter brought both joy and uneasiness. What if he sent for me before I learned more about my mother?

Karlina drew closer. "Do you have any idea what it might be?"

Hoping to temper my unsettling thoughts, I forced a smile. "No, but soon we shall all know." I untied the string, peeled away the brown paper, and opened the box. Inside lay a gold locket engraved with my initials. I lifted it from the bed of black velvet and clicked the latch. My breath caught when it flipped open and revealed a tiny picture of my mother. I traced my finger over the likeness, longing to once more feel the softness of her skin or hear the sweetness of her voice.

"It's beautiful," Karlina whispered. "Is that an early picture of your Mutter?"

I swallowed back my tears. "Yes. The picture was taken on their wedding day." I handed the locket to Cousin Louise and watched as she examined the picture.

A tear formed in her eye as she handed it back to me. "I loved your Mutter deeply. She was like a sister to me, and I know you miss her." She clasped my hand. "After our twins died I spent many hours on my knees asking God to fill the empty spot in my heart with His love. I hope you have been doing the same, Dovie." She cleared her throat and pointed to the letter. "Maybe you would like to go and read your letter while George and Karlina show Anton the best way to use his new shepherd's crook."

I nodded. "Yes, I think that's a good idea." I hesitated a moment and then grasped her hand. "And one day soon I hope you will be willing to share more about my mother."

I stood and hurried from the room before she could deny my request.

Once inside the bedroom, I opened the envelope. My father's letter spoke of his new position and that he'd been spending long hours at work. He didn't reveal if that was by choice or if the extra hours were required by the company, but I guessed it was more by his choice. He said he missed me, but he didn't sound as lonely as I'd expected—likely because he'd been filling his days with work so he couldn't think about missing Mother. He'd also included additional money for any necessities I might need. I continued reading and then turned the final page, where he had added a postscript.

You will recall that I agreed to post your second letter to Louise and George. However, upon arriving in Texas, I discovered it in the jacket pocket of my blue suit. Please accept my apology, and please tell Louise and George that I beg their forgiveness for my oversight.

The added brief notation solved the mystery of my letter to Cousin Louise, but I wasn't certain the missing letter had been an oversight.

I glanced up when Karlina poked her head around the bedroom doorway. "Are you done? Mutter said I shouldn't bother you if you were still reading your letter."

Smiling, I waved her forward. "Yes, I'm finished."

"I know I am being selfish, but I hope your Vater did not say he wants you to come to Texas." Her blue eyes were a near match for the walls in the Amana houses and the meeting hall. When I'd commented on the sameness of the color, Karlina told me all walls were painted with whitewash that was lightly tinted with blue pigment. "It is the only color we use. When we all have the same thing, there is no jealousy." She'd made the statement with authority, and I had no reason to doubt her, for I'd quickly learned that equality was of great importance to the colonists.

I folded the letter and tucked it into the envelope. "My father says that he has not yet found a suitable place for us to live. It seems he has been quite busy working long hours, but there is a lady who has agreed to help him locate a small house. There is no assurance if or when he might find such a place, but I am hoping that I will be here until spring."

"You must stay until the lambs are born. It is the very best time of the year. Just wait and see—you will love East during the springtime."

I didn't doubt Karlina's words, for I had already discovered much to love about East and the people who lived here. Within the confines of the small village I felt somehow connected to both the past and my future. A feeling I could not explain, but one that kindled a desire to remain among my mother's people.

CHAPTER 11

January 1893

Since the change in his delivery route, my time with Berndt had been brief. I missed his easy manner and our friendly chats. When he made the bread delivery on Christmas Eve morning, I had given him a small package with Christmas cookies we baked. They seemed a silly gift for a baker's son, but Karlina said he would like them. She had been correct. Berndt had appeared most pleased but also embarrassed because he had nothing to give me. I had laughed and told him I would take ice skating lessons in exchange, and he readily agreed.

Today I hoped he could make good on his gift. Yesterday Cousin Louise granted us permission to go ice skating at the pond this afternoon, and Karlina had already borrowed a pair of ice skates for me. While Karlina finished dressing, I hurried down the stairs and raced into the kitchen. If I wasn't downstairs when he arrived,

Cousin Louise would meet the bread wagon, and I'd have no opportunity to invite Berndt to join us.

Cousin Louise looked up from the stove. "Why are you running? There is a problem?"

I came to an abrupt halt and straightened my shoulders. "No. I was afraid I would be late."

"Late?" She rubbed my shoulder and smiled. "It is gut you want to help, Dovie, but you do not need to be the first one in the kitchen every morning. You are a visitor, and even though we encourage hard work in the villages, you should not be working more than those who live here."

Outside, the clang of the bread wagon's bell reverberated in the frozen morning silence. My attention shifted toward the door. So did Cousin Louise's. I turned toward the pegs near the back door with my hand extended toward my coat. "I'll go and meet the wagon."

Cousin Louise's blue eyes sparkled with an understanding glint. "So that is why you have been coming down here so early—you don't want to miss seeing Berndt." She folded her arms across her waist and nodded. "Go on and get the bread, but remember that he does not have time for visiting."

Not wanting to miss even a moment, I hurried outside and waited for Berndt, my heart pounding so hard I thought it might bounce out of my chest. I strained to see the familiar wave of his cap, for even on the coldest days he would yank it from his head and swing it in greeting. Dancing from foot to foot to keep warm, I smiled and waved in return as he approached.

"Guten Morgen, Dovie!" He pulled back on the reins and brought the horses to a stop. Clouds of vapor rose from the animals' nostrils, and though they shimmied as Berndt jumped down from the wagon, they didn't attempt to move. "It is gut to see you. What a bright smile on this cold morning." He pulled his cap back onto his head.

I tried to control my excitement, but I could hardly keep from jumping up and down. "I have a surprise."

Together we walked to the rear of the bread wagon. "And what is your surprise?"

"We are going ice skating today. Me, Karlina, and Anton. I hope you will come with us. Cousin Louise agreed Karlina and I can go."

Instead of the excitement I'd expected, he frowned. "I think the ice could be weak at the pond. It might not be safe."

I rubbed my arms. "It is very cold. I don't think Cousin Louise would give permission if she thought—"

"I am sure she would not, but Cousin Louise does not have a way to know if the ice is solid, does she? The weather was very cold, but then it turned warmer, and it has remained above freezing for many days during the last two weeks. Such changes in the weather can make for dangerous ice." He placed his gloved hand on the wagon door. "Some years it is safe to skate in November. Other years the ice can be too thin in January or February." He pushed down on the lever and opened the doors. "Besides, I cannot go with you today."

My shoulders drooped. "But why? You said you would give me skating lessons."

He leaned closer. "And I very much look forward to giving you those lessons. But not when there might be thin ice. And not when I must go and help cut timber after the noonday meal. Much help is needed to keep a gut supply throughout the winter. You should tell Anton that if he is not busy with the sheep, he should come and help us. The more men who help, the more wood for our fires, ja?"

I forced a smile and nodded. "I don't know if Anton can help. Cousin George may have work for him."

If Anton agreed to cut lumber, Karlina, who had been doing her best to make Anton feel welcome in East, might decide we should wait to go skating. And that was the last thing I wanted. Besides, how much wood could be needed in one winter? If Berndt thought the ice wasn't thick enough for skating, the village shouldn't require as much wood, should it? And I'd seen the men going out into the timbers and returning with the large horse-drawn wagons filled with heavy uncut logs. Surely cutting more wood wasn't necessary today. They had the remainder of the winter to chop down trees.

Berndt withdrew a large bread-laden tray from the wagon. "I know there may be other work for him, but we can use his help if he is not needed otherwise. If he is able, he should meet us at the Fuchs' kitchen house after lunch. You will tell him, ja?"

I couldn't be certain what Anton would choose to do. After spending so much time with the sheep, he might enjoy working with the men. "I'll tell Karlina to speak to him when she goes down to the barn this morning."

He grinned. "*Danke*. And once the freezing weather returns, I will take you skating. I promise."

"I look forward to the day when you will keep your promise." I lifted the tray from his arms. "But do not be surprised if I find time to go before then."

His dark eyes clouded, but I turned and strode back to the kitchen before he could utter any more warnings. What I had hoped would be a sweet afternoon with Berndt had already turned sour.

Cousin Louise opened the door for me, and I placed the tray on the worktable. She drew near and quickly inspected the bread. "There is something I must say to you, Dovie." Concern clouded her eyes as she met my gaze. "It is better that you think of Berndt as no more than an acquaintance—a fleeting friend. He is a nice young man, and I am afraid he may begin to think of you as more than a friend." She inhaled a deep breath. "If he is interested in more than friendship, he will be deeply hurt when you depart for Texas." She arched her brows. "It is not fair to give him hope for something that can never be. Do you understand?"

My jaw dropped. She thought I had been encouraging Berndt's attentions, acting in a flirtatious manner with no thought for the future. No consideration of how my actions might affect both him and me. She obviously didn't realize that Berndt had been the one who'd initiated our friendship. I had merely responded to his kindness. Granted, I now enjoyed his company more than that of anyone other than Karlina, but I hadn't been flirtatious—not in the least. Of late, I had given consideration to my future both in Amana and in Texas, but those thoughts had not included Berndt. After all, we didn't know each other very well, so why would she make such comments?

As Cousin Louise continued her warning, what had happened suddenly became clear. "You told his father to change the bread route," I whispered.

"Ja, I did. I could see in Berndt's eyes that he was already caring too much for you. What I did was not to hurt you or to hurt him, Dovie. It was to save both of you from disappointment and pain." She reached out and put her arm around my shoulder. "Your Vater left you in my protection, and I must do all that I can to make sure nothing bad will happen to you while you are with us." She released my shoulder. "Now, we must get busy before we fall behind with our work. The other women will soon be here."

There was no need to say anything. I didn't doubt her good intentions, or the fact that she wanted to protect me. But I was old enough to protect myself—and so was Berndt. Was it so terrible to want to enjoy the company of another person?

The clanging of pots and pans drew me from my thoughts, and I quietly set about my breakfast duties. I fried sausages, peeled potatoes, and sliced bread. I filled dishes with strawberry preserves and rhubarb jam, and I fetched coffee when needed. Yet throughout the remainder of the morning, I continued to dwell upon Cousin Louise's remarks.

"Why so quiet this morning?" Sister Marta stood beside me rolling dumplings that would be dropped into the beef broth for the noonday soup. "Other than a greeting when we arrived, you have said nothing to any of us. Are you not feeling well?"

I forced a feeble smile. "I am fine."

"I think you are missing your Mutter. It is normal to be sad after a death, but you must remember that your Mutter would want you to be happy and to serve Christ with a joyful heart." She balanced another dumpling on the growing pile.

"I'm sure you're right, Sister Marta." She finished rolling the last of the mixture and carried the large bowl to the stove. Her gesture was kind, but I didn't want to hear that I should serve Christ with a joyful heart. I wanted to hear that Berndt could go ice skating with me. Ugly as it would seem to Sister Marta, that was the truth.

It wasn't until the bell rang to announce the noonday meal that I realized I'd forgotten to tell Karlina or Anton about the wood cutting. I hurried to fill the remaining serving bowls while watching for Karlina. Moments later, the back door burst open, and Karlina removed her cape and hurried toward me, a smile splitting her face.

"Anton is going with us. He was most pleased for the invitation." She rubbed her hands together and held them close to the stove. "I think he is beginning to like it here."

"I don't know why you worry about his happiness so much, Karlina. Are you beginning to care for him?" I winked and gave her a little shove with my hip.

"Nein! A contented shepherd makes for contented sheep. That is why I want him to be happy living here."

I giggled. "So it is only the sheep you worry about? I'm not so sure I believe you."

"I will admit that I am liking him more than when he first arrived. He has softened a little and is trying to do what he is told. The sheep are more at ease with him now, so that is a gut sign."

"Always the sheep," I said.

"Karlina! You need to go to the dining room and quit interfering with our work." Waving her wooden spoon, Sister Marta shooed Karlina toward the other room.

I grasped her arm as she stepped away from the stove. "There is something I forgot to tell you."

"Karlina!" Wrinkles as deep as a rugged canyon creased Cousin Louise's face. "Listen to what Sister Marta has told you and go into the dining hall. You know better than to visit in the Küche during mealtime."

"Tell me later," Karlina whispered. Skirting between the women, she stopped only long enough to say, "I'm sorry, Mutter."

This afternoon I was helping to keep the bowls and platters filled, so there would be no chance to tell her about Berndt until after the meal. I watched the table where Karlina was seated. The moment the bowl of potatoes emptied, I hurried to the table with a refill. The aroma of succulent roasted pork wafted toward me as I bent forward. My stomach growled and Karlina covered her mouth with a napkin to hide her laughter.

I leaned close to her ear. "We need to talk as soon as the after-meal prayer is recited."

Sister Bertha cleared her throat with a noisy growl. When I glanced in her direction, the old sister shot me a look of extreme disapproval. I had kept my voice at a whisper, but even that annoyed her. I backed away from the table. With any luck, Sister Marta would agree to serve Sister Bertha's table for the remainder of the meal.

When I returned to the kitchen, Cousin Louise pointed to the worktable, where some of the other women sat eating. "I fixed you a plate. The junior girls will keep a watch if anything is needed."

I sat beside Cousin Louise, thankful to be away from Sister Bertha's disapproving looks and thankful for the warm food that would stop the growl in my stomach. Because I was eager for the meal to end, it seemed to go on forever. Cousin Marta, determined to cheer me, did her best to draw me into the idle chatter around the worktable—something the women enjoyed in the kitchen but was frowned upon in the dining hall.

When I heard the scraping of chairs and the murmured prayer that followed the meal, I jumped to my feet and carried my dirty plate to the sink. Before I turned around, Karlina was at my side.

Taking hold of her wrist, I pulled her to a far corner of the room. "There is something I forgot to tell you this morning before you went down to the barn." Watching that none of the other women would draw close and overhear, I told her Berndt would not be coming with us. Karlina frowned and I shook my head. "But that is not all of it. He said Anton should come and help the men cut timber if he is not busy today. Berndt said he should come to the Fuchs' Küche after the noonday meal."

"But we are going skating." Karlina wrung her hands together while the other women scurried about the kitchen with a determination that resembled a swarm of worker bees. "You forgot to tell him or me. It was an honest mistake. I'm sure there are more than enough men to help cut timber." She grinned and clasped my hand. "There's no harm done."

I sighed with relief. "Will you tell Anton?"

Karlina shrugged. "There's no reason. Berndt will think Vater had chores for Anton to complete. As soon as you finish here, come to the barn and meet us. I have already taken your skates down there."

A sense of relief washed over me as I trudged through the frozen, snow-dusted grass toward the sheep barn an hour later. Karlina's response had eased my conscience. But when I thought of Berndt, a sense of regret remained. I had truly wanted him by my side today.

Karlina and Anton sat near one of the doors, skates slung across their shoulders. Anton jumped to his feet the minute I entered. He frowned and impatience shone in his eyes. "What took so long?"

A spark of anger flared in my chest, and I returned his frown. "There is much work that goes into preparing meals in the Küche and much that must be cleaned afterward, as well. I do more than sit here with the sheep all day."

His eyes turned dark. "You think all I do is sit in the barn?"

Karlina stepped between us. "We all work hard, but now we are going to have a few hours of fun. Don't spoil our afternoon with arguing." She tugged on Anton's sleeve. "Come. Let's go to the pond."

She shot a pleading look in my direction, and I gave a nod. "You're right." Overhead the sun shone bright, and all signs of the early morning frost had disappeared. I glanced toward the sky and recalled Berndt's warning. "Berndt said the ice might be weak in places."

"I will check to see how it looks when we get there, but I think it will be fine." Anton leaned around Karlina and met my gaze. "I thought Berndt was coming with us. Is he busy baking more bread?" He chuckled.

"What is funny about baking bread? You eat it at every meal and should be thankful there are good bakers in the village."

Karlina sighed. "Must the two of you argue about everything?"

Anton tipped the brim of his cap. "I am sorry, Dovie. Baking bread is honorable work. I shouldn't have laughed. But you still haven't told me. Where is Berndt?"

I glanced at Karlina. "He had to go and help cut timber this afternoon."

"Ach! Getting up in the middle of the night to bake bread and then cutting timber all afternoon, there is no rest for him."

"And no skating," I said.

The three of us approached an area along one side of the pond where ashes and the remains of burned logs were circled by large rocks and some thick logs. While Karlina and I collected pieces of wood and tossed them into the fire pit, Anton continued toward the pond to examine the ice.

After walking out onto the ice in several places, he trudged toward us and flashed a smile. "It is gut and thick at this end, but I am not so sure once you get closer to the middle. I think we shouldn't go beyond that line of trees." He pointed to a spot about midway down the length of the pond. He looked at both of us. "You see where I mean."

"Ja, we can see the row of trees." Karlina lifted her gloved hand and pointed to the spot. "Over there."

We strapped on our skates while Anton started the fire. Karlina and I held hands as we made our way onto the ice. It had been many years since I had skated, and I'd never been good at the winter sport.

"It will go better if you glide instead of taking those short, choppy steps." Karlina showed me by moving her feet in an exaggerated smooth movement.

I wrinkled my nose. "If I thought I could glide without falling, I would glide."

Anton joined us on the ice and soon turned and began to skate backward. He held out his hands to me. "Hold my hands and try to glide. I won't let you fall."

I glanced at Karlina, and she gave a nod. "Go ahead. You need to become sure of yourself, and then it will be easy."

While Anton helped to steady me, Karlina skated in a circle around us and shouted words of encouragement. She applauded when Anton let loose of my hands and I managed to glide for a short distance before returning to my short, jerky steps. Anton immediately grabbed my hands and forced me back to the earlier glide. Though it took a while until I felt more at ease, I took off on my own sometime later.

Karlina and Anton were soon skating side by side, the two of them in perfect symmetry as they created figure eights or turned to skate backward and then forward. Unlike my clunky movements as I continued down the pond, they had an elegance all their own. My gaze shifted and I caught sight of a young man sitting near the fire. I squinted into the bright sunlight. It almost looked like Berndt.

But it couldn't be. He was cutting timber.

Anton skated past me, waving his arm toward the man. He cupped his hands to his mouth. "Berndt! Come and join us. I am glad to see you. Dovie can use your help out here." Moments later, with expert precision, Anton came to a stop at the edge of the ice.

Soon Karlina skated past me, but when I tried to glide along behind her, I lost my footing and dropped to the ice. After one failed attempt, I gained my footing and returned to my clunky hitch-step style.

I watched Berndt push up from the log. Taking long strides, he walked toward Anton. Shoulders straight and lips sealed in a tight angry line, he strode to the pond's edge. "Is this how you help others in our village?"

Anton smiled. "Ja, I have been helping Dovie all afternoon. She is doing much better with her skating."

Their voices echoed in the silence of the cold winter afternoon.

"I am not talking about Dovie and her skating. I am talking about cutting firewood to keep our people warm on cold winter days." His voice cracked with anger. "Instead of working alongside the other men in the village, you are out here having fun with the girls. What kind of man shuns his duty toward the community?"

My stomach clenched and fear gripped my heart. Like a bird learning to fly, I fluttered my arms to maintain my balance and drew close to Karlina. I clutched her arm.

The veins in Anton's neck were stretched taut.

My fear swelled to new heights. I opened my mouth, but the words stuck in my throat. Anton pulled back his arm. I strained to reach him, but my effort failed.

With one swift, decisive motion, he landed a hard fist in Berndt's midsection.

CHAPTER 12

I watched in horror as the two men fell in a heap on the ground. Berndt held a definite advantage since Anton hadn't removed his ice skates. On the other hand, Anton stood a head taller than Berndt and was every bit as muscular. Karlina and I cried for the two of them to stop as Berndt pulled Anton back to his feet. Neither listened to our shouted pleas, so while fists continued to fly, Karlina removed her skates.

With the fearlessness of a mountain lion, Karlina forced her way between the two men. Anton hoisted his fist in the air, but at the sight of Karlina, he dropped his arm.

"Both of you stop!" Karlina's shout cracked through the air like a buggy whip.

Rage contorted their faces as both of them took a backward step. A button from Anton's coat lay on the ground, and a ripped seam in Berndt's jacket would need stitching. Leaning to one side and peering around me, Berndt balled one hand into a fist and extended his arm toward Anton. "I should have given you more of this!"

I took a sidestep to block his view of Anton. "Stop it, Berndt! What are you thinking? I can't believe you would do this."

He glared at me. "Why are you criticizing me? He threw the first punch. I only protected myself. It's Anton who doesn't know how to conduct himself."

Karlina stepped around Anton, who had now removed his skates and appeared ready to begin another round of fighting. "Berndt! This isn't Anton's fault. He didn't know about cutting timber this afternoon. Dovie forgot to pass the message to me before I left after breakfast. By the time she told me, it was too late for Anton to join you, so I didn't bother to tell him."

"You just decided not to tell me?" Anton's eyebrows shot high on his forehead, and disbelief shone in his eyes.

Karlina nodded. "Ja. The men would have already left for the woods, and—"

"Did you decide I could not find my way to the woods?" Once again the vein in Anton's neck tightened like a thick rope.

"Well, they move about, and you're not familiar with East and where the men do their cutting. I'm not certain, either."

"Well, I'm sure your father could have given me some idea. Now I appear to be lazy and unwilling to help where needed." He glowered at Berndt. "When word of this gets out, I will never be accepted."

"And do you think this fighting helps? I doubt the elders would be pleased to hear there were fists flying this afternoon." She turned toward Berndt. "And who are you to decide what work any man in this village should do? You're not a farm *baas* who sends the men out to work each day."

My lips quivered, and I fought to hold back tears. "This is my fault. I owe all of you an apology."

Anton pointed at Berndt. "No. This is his fault. Berndt is the one who came here with his head set for a fight."

Berndt clenched his fists. "That's not true. I saw Brother George when we came through town with the last load of logs. We talked for a few minutes, and he told me the three of you had come down here skating." He looked in my direction. "I was worried. I told Dovie the ice might be weak, and I wanted to be sure you were all safe."

"Ja? So you see we are safe and then you decide to fight with me?" Anton's lips curled in anger.

Karlina and I formed a barrier between the two men. They were acting like schoolboys, each one trying to best the other. "Would you please let me talk?" I said. "If you are still determined to fight once I explain, then I will step out of the way, and you can knock each other senseless."

My final comment captured their attention, and the two of them silently listened while I explained the mishap. "I now realize we should have told you, Anton. You should have had the right to make your own choice." I turned toward Berndt. "And you should not have jumped to conclusions without first knowing the truth." I took a deep breath. "I take full blame for creating the misunderstanding, but I do not take blame for the injuries you inflicted upon each other." I shook my head. "The two of you must decide how this will end."

Karlina grasped Anton's arm as she looked back and forth between the two men. "For anyone else to know what has happened here will serve no gut purpose. Would it not be better if the two of you apologized and we all agreed that this was a grave mistake? I, too, am at fault. Not one of us can say we acted in a manner that would please our heavenly Father."

Anton extended his hand to Berndt. "I am sorry that I hit you. I sometimes think with my fists instead of my head, and it causes me no end of trouble. I hope you will forgive me for my poor behavior and lack of brotherly love."

Berndt took a tentative step forward and shook Anton's hand. "And I ask that you forgive me for my unkind words. I spoke in anger, knowing that my comments would cause a fight." He bowed his head toward Karlina and me. "I also ask that both of you forgive me. My jealous nature has ruined your afternoon."

Karlina's lips curved in a feeble smile. "Then we are all agreed that nothing shall be said to anyone else?"

The four of us bobbed our heads in unanimous agreement. Given our options, we'd made the best decision for all of us. At least that was our hope.

❖

All night I tossed in my bed like a ship pitching in an angry storm. Though I was usually out of bed before the first morning bell, I didn't rise until ten minutes after the second bell had chimed. Even then, I didn't move with any speed, and I was late going downstairs. As I entered the kitchen, Cousin Louise returned inside carrying the oversized bread-laden tray. A whoosh of cold air skittered across the floor before she closed the door. She settled the tray on the worktable and hurried to the stove.

"When I said I wanted you and Berndt to become only casual friends, I did not mean you should quit meeting the bread wagon, Dovie." Her teeth chattered as she added more wood to the fire.

"I am sorry, Cousin Louise. I will be sure to be on time tomorrow morning." I had expected her to be pleased that I'd missed seeing Berndt but decided she disliked the cold more than she feared Berndt and me talking to each other. Besides, how much could we talk now that she'd made certain his schedule had changed?

"I need a little help upstairs this afternoon, but then you may do as you like for the remainder of the day. Perhaps you and Karlina can go skating again. She said you fell only one time yesterday. A few more afternoons, and you will be skating as gut as the rest of the young people."

"Instead, maybe you and I could visit this afternoon. I would enjoy hearing some stories about my mother. You said she was happy here, and it would give me pleasure to hear of her child-hood."

A glimmer of wariness clouded Cousin Louise's eyes. "We will see. I have much work to do. Besides, there is little of interest that I can tell you."

I poured the coffee beans into the grinder and began to turn the handle. "Anything will interest me. What is it you think I am looking to hear, Cousin Louise?"

"I don't know, child, but my hours with your Mutter were spent playing games, picking grapes, learning to knit and crochet, and memorizing Bible verses and our guide for daily living. You can learn as much about her childhood by observing life in the village as I can tell you."

"But surely you know what made her happy and the things she liked—things that others might not have enjoyed."

Cousin Louise shook her head. "We all enjoyed the same things, Dovie. Our lives in the colonies are similar. We took pleasure in our dollhouses and the tiny furniture our grandfathers and fathers made for us. We laughed when we went wading in the pond dur-ing the heat of summer." She wiped her hands on her apron. "You desire to know your mother's innermost thoughts, but only she could have told you those things. And we stopped writing letters a long time ago, when you were still a child."

The other kitchen workers arrived, and Cousin Louise hurried away to give instructions—and to get away from me. At least that was what I believed. I was sure she could tell me much more about my mother—if only she would.

After the noonday meal, I followed Cousin Louise upstairs and helped dust the parlor while she worked in the bedrooms. I waited and hoped she would mention my mother, but she didn't. Instead, she dismissed me with a cheery smile. "You should go and practice your ice skating."

I hesitated in the doorway. "Why did you and my mother quit writing to each other?"

"Your Mutter stopped answering my letters." She picked up the broom and dust rag and walked by me. "I need to finish cleaning."

I couldn't imagine why my mother would suddenly cease corresponding with her cousin, but to say anything further appeared to be useless. I would bide my time a little longer and continue to hope my father wouldn't send for me. I lifted my coat from the hook, buttoned it tight around my neck, and pulled on my mittens. Perhaps Karlina would join me at the pond. I picked my way down the slope and entered the barn through the smaller door.

"Is anyone in here?" The smell of hay and damp wool permeated the air. I walked a little further into the barn. "Karlina? Anton?"

"Over here, Dovie." Karlina's voice trailed from the far side of the barn. I walked in that direction but couldn't spot her. I was about to call out again when she stood up. "We're working on Anton's watering invention. Come and see."

I approached the spot where the two of them were working. "Anton thinks we can manage to bring fresh water into the barn by using his new method."

"Ja, but first I must get the water to flow properly through the tubing and inside. There is much to figure out."

I did my best to appear interested and listened while he explained a bit about the process, but when he went to look for another container, I stooped down beside Karlina. "Would you like to go skating with me? I am done with my work, and your Mutter has given her permission."

Karlina glanced toward Anton. "I promised to help him with this, but I will go tomorrow if you like."

I stood up and took a backward step. "Maybe I will go and try a little by myself. Are the skates down here?"

Karlina jumped to her feet. "I don't know if that's such a gut idea. Do you think it is smart to go by yourself? You might fall and if you are hurt . . ." Her voice trailed off as if to let me imagine the consequences.

"I don't plan to fall down. If I'm not back by the time the bell rings, you should come and look for me." Worry glimmered in Karlina's dark eyes and I smiled. "I promise to come by the barn before I return to the house. That way you will know I am safe." Anton returned with a large tub and placed it on the ground. "And I will expect to see this wonderful watering machine when I return."

"Ja, well you can expect whatever you want, but it will take more than a few hours to finish my work with this."

All three sets of ice skates hung on nails pounded into a board near the door. "I'll get the skates and be back in a little while."

Anton looked up from his drawing. "Don't go beyond the line of trees that I showed you yesterday."

"I promise to be careful." I hesitated a moment. "Maybe we should try another English lesson tonight?"

Anton grinned. "After prayer meeting would be gut, ja?"

I bobbed my head, waved, and hurried toward the ice skates. I grabbed the pair Karlina had borrowed from her friend and slung them across my shoulder as if I'd been going skating for years. Disappointment assailed me the moment I turned toward the pond. To go skating alone wouldn't be much fun. If I managed to skate with any grace, there would be no one to cheer for me. Then again, should I fall down, no one would see me. Yesterday I had felt less than ladylike when I landed on the ice with my legs akimbo. And no doubt I'd looked like a chicken flapping its wings when I'd attempted to get up, but Karlina's encouraging words had boosted my confidence.

Yet expecting Karlina to be free at my every whim was unreasonable. This was her home and she must complete her chores. I must remember, as a visitor, that I should be more sensitive to the work schedules of the entire family, including Cousin Louise. To press anyone too much might result in my early departure for Texas.

Instead of disappointment, I should be pleased that Anton wanted to attempt another English lesson this evening. Since Christmas, I had met with him twice. Karlina had joined us both times, and although we'd all had fun, Anton hadn't learned much English. Tonight I would discover how much he remembered from our previous lessons.

I sat down on one of the fat logs near the pile of ashes that had provided warmth yesterday afternoon. There would be no fire today. Another reason I wouldn't be here long. After strapping the skates over my shoes, I picked my way onto the ice.

"Glide," I whispered. "No clunky steps. Push and glide. Push and glide." I said the words over and over as I skated as far as the row of trees and inhaled a huge lungful of the crisp air. Continuing onward, I made a giant circle, never once returning to my clunky hitch step. Proud of my accomplishment, I shouted to the wind, "Look at me! I can skate."

"Ja, is gut!"

Too quickly, I turned toward the approving shout. My skates betrayed me and forced my legs into a scissorlike position. Seconds later I was sprawled on the ice like one of the marionettes I'd seen performing at Washington Park in Cincinnati years ago.

Using my hands, I turned toward the man who had caused my fall. Already I could feel the cold working its way through my wool coat. He finished strapping on his skates and raced toward me with the precision of someone who had been born with metal runners on his feet.

"My apology to you. You are German?" He arched his brows.

His German bore a different accent, one that I couldn't distinguish. I nodded. "German and English. Do you speak English?"

He shrugged his shoulders and shook his head. "I will help you to stand." He continued to speak in German. He circled behind me, and before I could object, he placed his hands under my arms and lifted me to my feet in one quick motion. He kept his arms around me until I steadied myself, and then he returned to stand in front of me.

"I am sorry you fall. My fault." He looked me up and down as though he'd encountered some strange new species. "Where you live?"

Carefully, I lifted my arm and pointed toward the village. "East Amana."

He stared at me for a long moment before he shook his head. "Nein." He pointed to my head, and then touched the sleeve of my coat. "Not Amana."

I had no way of knowing how much German he could understand, so I answered as simply as possible. "I am visiting my family."

He smiled and nodded. A hank of black hair fell onto his forehead, and he tucked it under his woolen cap. "I am Jakub Sedlacek." He tapped his gloved hand on his chest.

"I am Dovie Cates."

"Doovie Cates. I am happy to know you." Moving his hand from his chest, he pointed toward an easterly stand of trees in the distance. "I live on farm. My family is Czech. You know Czech?"

I shook my head. So that was the difference in his accent. I knew I'd heard it before. A group of Czech people lived in Over-the-Rhine, but most of them spoke German as well as their native tongue. As a young girl, one of my friends had been Czechoslovakian, but she had learned more English and German than I had learned Czech. I doubted I could remember any of the language.

He held out his hand. "You want skate some more?"

Without thinking, I accepted his hand and pushed into a glide. In Cincinnati, skating with a complete stranger would have been unacceptable. But out here in the middle of the countryside on an obscure pond, it didn't seem to matter that I'd never before met this young man. We were simply two people enjoying the company of each other.

"At our farm are my mother, father, grandmother, and sister. You come and meet them?"

"I don't think my family would like that. They worry if I am gone too long." I didn't want to hurt his feelings, but I couldn't possibly go to his home.

He dropped my hand and made a wide circle around me as I continued to skate. "You no need to be afraid. We are gut people. Not like Amana, but still gut. We are Catholic. We work hard. Sometimes I help with Amana sheep."

"You help with the sheep?" His final comment captured my interest more than anything else he'd said.

He pretended to be holding something in each hand, and he moved his arms together and apart in a rapid motion. "With the shearing." He rubbed his hand down his arm. "Taking off the wool."

"Yes. I understand." I skated closer. "Do you know George Richter and Karlina, his daughter?"

His blue eyes shone with delight as he nodded with enthusiasm. "Ja. The shepherd in charge and his daughter. Very nice, very nice."

I patted my chest. "My family."

He arched his brows. "Ja? You daughter, too?"

"Nein. Cousin."

His eyes registered confusion. I wasn't certain he understood how I was connected, but at least he understood I was related to the shepherd in East Amana. And the fact that he sometimes worked for Brother George provided me with a greater sense of ease. When he reached for my hand, I readily accepted.

"I bring my sister for meet you tomorrow. You like that?"

I found his enthusiasm contagious. "Yes, I would like that very much. What is her name?"

"Sophia. She laughs a lot—happy all the time. Gut heart." He turned backward and skated facing me. "You want to try?" He drew a half circle in the air. "Backward skate? You try?"

"Not yet. Maybe when I become steadier."

"Maybe tomorrow. Sophia can show you."

We'd been skating for a half hour when I pointed to the side of the pond. "I must go now." I'd already been gone longer than I'd intended, and I didn't want Karlina to worry.

Jakub didn't argue. He skated alongside me and held my arm while I sat on the log. When I reached for one of the leather straps, he covered my hand and moved it to the side. "I do for you." He removed his gloves and quickly unbuckled the skates, removed them from my shoes, and handed them to me.

"Thank you, Jakub."

He looked up at me, his eyes sparkling with pleasure as the sunlight danced off his black hair. "You welcome, Doovie. What time tomorrow?" He pointed to the sun.

"One o'clock?" I held up one finger. He gave a firm nod, pushed to his feet, and flew across the pond, his skates creating a whooshing sound as the blades cut into the ice. He waved when he reached the other side.

I waved and turned toward the barn, my heart feeling lighter than it had since my mother's death. Odd that a stranger had been the cause of such a joyous afternoon. I hadn't gone far when I caught sight of someone in a distant stand of trees. I waved, but the figure bolted and disappeared.

Probably Anton, I decided. And he likely didn't want me to know that he'd come to check on me. I exhaled a quick sigh of relief, pleased I'd headed home before he saw me skating with Jakub.

While Karlina prepared coffee after prayer service, Anton and I sat on wooden stools near one of the worktables. I wondered if he would mention watching me at the pond, but when he didn't bring up ice skating, I began our lesson. Scooting to the edge of the stool, I pointed to my mouth. "Look at my lips so you can see how to form the words and then repeat after me."

He nodded his head and stared at my mouth.

"I laughed with him." I motioned for Anton to repeat the sentence.

"I lahvfd vidt him."

"Good!"

"Gut!"

Both Karlina and I giggled. "You did not need to repeat when I said "good." I was telling you that you had done a good job." I pointed to my lips. "We will go far."

Anton straightened his shoulders. "Ve vill goh fahr."

When I clapped my approval, Anton beamed.

We continued the lessons until Cousin Louise finally called for us to come upstairs and prepare for bed. "You did very well tonight, Anton. Each day you should repeat what you learned this evening. I think you are an excellent student."

His chest swelled. "Danke."

"You are welcome," I said, pleased with the success of his lesson.

Tonight I had seen a different Anton. This evening I had observed a young man that I liked very much. Little wonder Karlina found him attractive, even if she hadn't yet admitted it to me—or to herself.

CHAPTER 13

Over the past three weeks, I'd met Jakub and his sister at the pond on several occasions. Our times together were always filled with laughter, and their joyful nature rejuvenated my spirit. Although they'd become increasingly insistent that I visit their home and meet the rest of their family, I'd resisted. Meeting them at the pond was one thing, but going to their home was another. To explain skating with strangers at the pond would be easy enough. Leaving the boundaries of East Amana without permission—well, that would be an entirely different matter.

Both Jakub and Sophia appeared hurt by my refusal, and though I tried to explain, I wasn't sure either of them completely understood. Jakub had thought his solution quite perfect. "You need to tell Shepherd Richter you come visit the Sedlacek farm. He knows me. It will be fine."

When I explained that Cousin George would never approve

such an idea, Jakub had appeared confused. "You are not Amana girl. Should not be a problem."

Our discussion went round and round until I finally called a halt to the idea and explained that I was a guest of the Amana people and must follow their rules. Jakub didn't argue further, but when we parted, he grinned. "I think one day you will change your mind."

I merely waved and continued toward home. With Karlina busy helping with the sheep, logging all the records on the feed and care of the animals, and helping Anton with his invention, my afternoons had become increasingly lonely, but to take such a risk would be far too foolish.

This morning I walked into the kitchen with less than an enthusiastic heart, for I knew my afternoon would be spent alone again. Cousin Louise considered me a visitor. As such, she had decided I should not work as many hours as the other women. I appreciated her thoughtfulness, but being alone with nothing to do wasn't what I wanted or needed. During some of my afternoons, I wrote to my father, but I had heard nothing from him since Christmas.

I decided he must be traveling, too busy, or too tired to write to me. When I checked the mail each morning, my emotions would shift like the wind. I wanted to receive a letter, but I didn't want my father to send for me—not yet.

"Good morning, Cousin Louise." The sound of the bread wagon's bell jingled, and I continued toward the door.

"Guten Morgen, Dovie." She poured water into the large coffee boiler as she greeted me. "Thank you for filling the bucket." She pointed to the metal pail. Of late, I'd been going out to fill a bucket of water in the morning so there was no delay in starting the coffee.

I didn't bother buttoning my coat. I wouldn't be outdoors for long. My visits with Berndt had become increasingly shorter due to Sister Fuch's complaints if he arrived even a few minutes later than expected.

He jumped down from the wagon and rubbed his hands together. He smiled as I walked toward him. "I think it is a gut day for ice skating, don't you?"

I shrugged my shoulders. "I don't think today is much different from yesterday or last week."

He stepped closer. "But I can go with you today. We have finished cutting timber, so once I finish the deliveries, my afternoons are my own."

Excitement pumped through my veins. Unable to withhold my enthusiasm, I clapped my hands together. "I have been so lonely during the afternoons. Your news cheers me more than you know."

We walked to the rear of the wagon, and he withdrew the large tray of bread. "I think it would be better if we would meet outside of town, and then we can walk together. Two o'clock?"

"Two o'clock is good. I'll be there." I didn't ask why we would meet outside of town. I already knew. There would be disapproval if we were seen together. And if someone saw us, they might curtail our afternoon of fun. I didn't want to risk that possibility, and I was pleased Berndt felt the same.

Throughout the morning, my excitement mounted. When I returned to the kitchen to fill the bowls with cottage cheese during the noonday meal, Cousin Louise touched my arm. "You need to quit rushing, Dovie. All morning you have been scurrying around the kitchen like a barn cat chasing a mouse."

"I am sorry, Cousin Louise. I'll slow down." I refilled the bowls and waited while she cleaned the edge of each dish.

"Would you like to come with me today? We will be quilting at Sister Fuch's this afternoon." She handed me one of the bowls.

"It will give you an opportunity to see how your mother quilted with us when she was a young woman."

My stomach lurched. "Today?"

"Ja. After we have cleaned the kitchen, we will go." She nodded toward the dining room. "I would ask Karlina, but she would only say no. I am guessing she has already told you she isn't fond of sewing." Cousin Louise smiled. "Sometimes I don't think she is fond of people, either. Only the sheep." She stepped around me with the other bowl of cottage cheese. "Come. We need to take these to the tables."

She had assumed I'd be delighted to go with her. And most days I would have. "Why today?" I whispered as I returned to the dining room. Unfortunately, my whisper hadn't been quiet enough, for Sister Bertha held her index finger to her lips and shushed me before I'd even had a chance to set the bowl in front of her.

I turned my head to keep from scowling at her. The woman had no patience, but today I couldn't worry over Sister Bertha and her desire for total silence. I needed to think what I was going to do. Most days we finished cleaning in the kitchen by one o'clock. That meant we would depart for the Fuchs' kitchen house before I was scheduled to meet Berndt. There was no way I could send word to him. What would he think if I didn't show up? But what would Cousin Louise think if I declined her invitation?

Some of these women had known my mother. They could tell me about her. I wanted to meet them and hear what they would tell me. Besides, after all the questions I'd asked Cousin Louise, I simply couldn't refuse to go with her. I stood and bowed my head while the others offered the after-dinner prayer, my thoughts on Berndt rather than supplications to the Lord.

I startled when Cousin Louise touched my arm. "Do you have a sewing kit, Dovie?"

"Yes. It belonged to my mother."

"Gut. Why don't you go upstairs and get it. You can bring it with you and help with the quilting. I am sure your mother taught you, ja?"

I smiled. "Yes. I have an Amana-style quilt that we made together. It is with the belongings we shipped to Texas."

She appeared pleased. I wasn't sure if she was happy that I knew how to quilt or that Mother had taught me something of her Amana heritage. I hurried upstairs to find the sewing kit. I'd unpacked my belongings, and the few things I didn't often need had been placed in a bottom drawer of Karlina's wardrobe.

Kneeling on the multicolored wool carpet that covered the wood floor, I opened the drawer and dug to the bottom. In the midst of my excavation, a thought flashed through my mind, and I rocked back on my heels in a prayer-like posture. Karlina! She could leave the barn and go meet Berndt. There were many excuses she could use. I doubted either Anton or her father would question her, but Karlina was clever—she would think of something if need be.

After pushing aside my silver dresser set, which appeared out of place in these stark surroundings, my fingers grazed the sewing kit. My hand trembled as I pulled it from the drawer. I needed to hurry downstairs and speak to Karlina. One hard shove and the drawer closed. I flew out the door and down the steps.

"Dovie. Again you are racing around like a hungry barn cat. There is no need to run."

I bobbed my head. "I'm sorry, Cousin Louise." I scanned the room, my heart thrumming in my chest. "Where is Karlina? The kitchen?"

"Nein. She has already gone to the barn. She said two of the sheep are not well and she needed to get back and check on them."

Cousin Louise turned toward the kitchen with a towering stack of dishes balanced in her arms. "That Karlina worries over the sheep more than most parents worry over their children."

For a moment I was certain my heart would quit beating. How could this happen? I'd been so sure I'd come up with a plan that would work. I continued to glance around the dining room. There were still lots of people in the hall. Maybe Cousin Louise was wrong. Maybe Karlina hadn't yet left. When I didn't see her, I looked toward the men's tables.

I didn't want to ask Anton, but I would. Or at least I'd ask him to tell Karlina of my plight. Surely she would go and talk to Berndt once she'd heard my problem. But Anton was nowhere to be seen, either. No doubt he'd left with Cousin George and Karlina. I dropped to one of the wood benches and covered my face.

"You are sick?"

I looked up and was met by Sister Bertha's probing eyes. "I am fine." I forced a feeble smile and stood. The old sister looked at me as if she didn't believe me.

"If you are fine you would not sit holding your head." She mimicked my earlier position. "But if you say you are fine, I will not argue." She scuttled off, muttering something about young people, but I didn't listen. I was too worried what Berndt was going to think.

I tucked my chin against the cold wind as Cousin Louise and I walked to the Fuchs' kitchen. "The sun fooled me. I thought it would be warmer this afternoon." She drew her cloak tighter around her body. "I am glad we don't have far to go. And you should be glad you did not go ice skating this afternoon."

I snapped my head in her direction. I hadn't said anything about going ice skating. Had she simply guessed that I had plans to go, or had she overheard me talking to Berndt? Was that why I'd been invited to go with her today?

My curiosity got the best of me. "How did you know I was going skating?"

"I did not know. It was no more than a comment." Cousin

Louise stared at me for a moment. "Did you plan to go skating? You should have told me." She shivered. "No. It is too cold to skate. It is much better you will be quilting with me."

She was probably right. It was colder than I'd thought, as well. Still, it didn't change the fact that Berndt would soon be standing in the frigid wind waiting for me. I hoped he wouldn't wait for long. After all these weeks, I would learn more about my mother, yet I couldn't fully take pleasure in the occasion.

"Here we are." Cousin Louise guided me toward the steps of the kitchen house. Like the Richter kitchen house, the Fuchs' house was larger than the others in the neighborhood. The two houses were similar, except the room Cousin Louise used for the mail and medical supplies had been set up as a quilting room in the Fuchs' kitchen house. In addition, the quilting room was larger. I soon discovered every bit of the additional space was needed to accommodate the women who arrived and gathered around the quilting frame.

When the other ladies opened their sewing kits and removed their needles, I did the same. An older woman, her face lined with wrinkles, carefully threaded her needle. "I am Sister Ann. Sister Louise tells me you are Barbara Lange's daughter."

All eyes turned in my direction. "That's right. Did you know her?"

"Ja. She lived in East. If you live in East, you know everyone who lives here." She chuckled and gestured to Cousin Louise. "Did you not tell her we are the smallest of the villages?"

Cousin Louise poked her needle into the fabric. "She knows we are the smallest."

"And the best," Sister Ann said. "But I do not think Sister Louise would tell you that." Several other women joined her raspy laughter.

"It is not gut to compare ourselves with others, so I did not tell her East is the best village." She peeked from beneath hooded eyes. "Even if it is the truth."

The room filled with laughter. Sister Ann giggled until tears rolled down her wrinkled cheeks. I laughed, too. Not because I understood their joke, but because it was impossible to remain straight-faced when surrounded by such mirth.

Sister Ann was considerably older than the other women, so I doubted she had been a close friend of my mother. But when the room quieted a little, I drew closer to her. "Were you one of my mother's schoolteachers, Sister Ann?"

She tucked her handkerchief into the pocket of her apron. Several of the other women chuckled. "Nein. The schoolteachers in our villages are men. Only when they are little and in *Kinderschule* do women care for the children—while their Mutters are working in the gardens or kitchen houses." She held her needle in the air. "And sometimes the Omas help teach them to knit and crochet. It's gut for everyone to be busy. And the little ones like learning from the Omas."

"Because they spoil them," one of the women retorted.

"Nein, because they are patient when they teach," another put in.

I leaned toward Sister Ann. "So you cared for my mother when she was a little girl? In the Kinderschule or teaching her to knit, maybe?"

"Nein. I was only telling you I could not have been her schoolteacher, and I did not work in the Kinderschule." She gave me a pointed look. "And when your Mutter was a little girl, I was too young to be an Oma."

Seeing the deep lines that furrowed her face and her blue-veined hands, I wasn't certain that final comment was completely correct.

She glanced up from the line of fine stitches she'd completed. "Before your Mutter worked in the Richter kitchen house, she worked in the gardens, and that is where we became acquainted. I was the *Gartebaas*." She nodded toward Cousin Louise. "Like Sister Louise is the Küchebaas. You understand?"

I nodded. "You were in charge of one of the big gardens."

"Ja. And your Mutter came to work for me when she was maybe fourteen." She shrugged one shoulder. "I can't remember for sure how old she was, but it was after she finished her schooling. Then she came and worked in the garden for me." Her brow furrowed as if she was trying to recall those long-ago days. "Sister Barbara was a gut worker. She liked to be in the garden, but later she went to work for Sister Ruth in the *Küchehaas*." She pointed her needle toward Cousin Louise. "Sister Louise's Mutter."

Cousin Louise chuckled. "And you never forgave her, because Barbara was such a gut worker. It still makes you unhappy to think about it."

"Ja, well, I had no say in the matter. The gut workers get shifted around, and the lazy ones stay with me forever."

"You are still the Gartebaas?"

She frowned and shot me a challenging look. "You think I am too old to work in the garden?"

"N-no." I shook my head so hard I wondered if my brain might rattle.

Her eyes softened. "That is gut, because I can work longer hours than most of these younger ones." She grinned and smoothed her palm across the pale blue fabric.

It was clear I'd struck a tender nerve with Sister Ann. I didn't want to repeat that error. "It's nice to hear my mother was a good worker. Thank you for telling me."

"Just like these other sisters, Barbara liked the onion harvest when she was here."

Several of the women chimed their agreement. "Onion harvest is still a fun time," Cousin Louise said. She gave me a sidelong glance.

"For two or three weeks in the summertime, almost everyone helps with the onion harvest. Wagonloads of onions are brought to the village, and we spread them out for trimming and sorting."

While she continued to stitch, Cousin Louise explained the process. And though it didn't sound like fun to me, I could see the women's excitement swell as she told how they gathered in groups of twenty or more to complete the task. I didn't understand their enthusiasm, but if I stayed long enough, perhaps I could experience the onion harvest for myself. Then I might understand their excitement.

"For me, it is the best time of year," Sister Ann said.

One of the other women laughed. "That is because you get to boss everyone. Not just the garden workers."

Sister Ann readily agreed. "Ja, and I am gut at being the baas. I have the most experience, so it is a gut job for me." She gestured toward me. "You should not just sit there. Let us see how well you can stitch."

I had threaded my needle, but I feared I might not meet the standards of these women. When I hesitated, Cousin Louise nudged my arm. "Go on. Your stitches cannot be any worse than some we have seen in the past."

Unlike the pieced quilts used by others, Amana quilt tops were one piece of fabric, usually a soft pastel shade. A pattern was traced onto the fabric before a layer of wool and another plain piece of fabric were stacked underneath. The three layers were then mounted onto the quilting frame and stitched together following the pattern lines. I poked my needle into the fabric, and as I made my first stitches, I could sense the women looking in my direction and examining my handiwork.

When no one shouted for me to stop, I continued sewing. For a moment I wondered if the layer of wool between the quilted fabric came from the sheep in Brother George's barn. Even though it was doubtful, I liked the idea. There were not enough sheep in the colonies to supply all of the wool needed in the woolen mill, so much of the wool was purchased from outsiders—that is what Karlina had told me.

The woman who had introduced herself as Sister Margaret said, "You quilt as well as your mother. We were friends many years ago when I worked in the Richter Küchehaas."

When I asked what she recalled the most about my mother, Sister Margaret thought for a moment. "She loved spice cake, and she would always ask Sister Ruth for any leftovers to take home with her."

The comment tugged at my heart. For as long as I could remember, my mother had baked a spice cake at least once a month. "What about the rest of you? Can you tell me any stories about my mother? Or other things she enjoyed?"

"Oh, I remember that she got in big trouble one time when we were in school," Sister Elsa remarked. "Your Mutter loved to read, and she wanted something different than the same history book all the time. We used the history book for history, reading, and for any other class Brother Erich could think of. Your Mutter thought that if he could not find the history books, we would get some new ones."

I was enjoying this story, for I had never thought of my mother as brave enough to do anything against the rules.

"She hid them." Sister Elsa looked down at the quilt and pulled her threaded needle through the fabric. "Actually we both hid them, but when Brother Erich threatened to make everyone do extra schoolwork, your Mutter took the blame. She had to clean the schoolroom for an entire month, but at least Brother Erich didn't tell your Oma and Opa." She had a faraway look in her eyes. "Ja, your Mutter loved to read. Any book she could find, she would read. Even the farm magazines. Did she keep reading books after she left East?"

"Yes. She loved books. She would read to me every night, and my father would take us to visit the big library in Cincinnati, where we would borrow books."

"I am glad she married and was happy," Sister Elsa said. "When she left East, I thought she would never be happy again. She was so in love. I remember how she cried and cried about leaving Brother Er—"

"Sister Martha! I brought some leftover *Kuchen* that we can enjoy later."

"No need to shout, Louise." Sister Fuch directed a confused look at Cousin Louise. "You handed me the cake when you arrived. I know I am to serve it to the women."

"Is it a spice cake?" Sister Elsa smiled at me.

"Nein. It is plum cake." Cousin Louise turned to Sister Dorothea, who was seated beside her. "You and Sister Barbara were friends, Dorothea. Tell Dovie what you remember."

Sister Dorothea was a sprite of a woman with sparkling eyes and a quick smile. "I remember how much Sister Barbara loved to go to the river." She motioned to Cousin Louise. "Do you recall the day we went down there and my brother almost drowned?"

Cousin Louise nodded. "He would have drowned if John Mueller hadn't pulled him out by his shirt. That gave us all a scare for sure."

The stories continued, most of them about the antics they had all enjoyed as young people, but Cousin Louise made certain Sister Elsa didn't have another opportunity to mention my mother and the man she'd had to leave behind.

While the women talked and stitched, I listened, but my thoughts returned to the schoolteacher, Brother Erich. Had that been the man my mother loved? I thought the teacher must have been much older than my mother, but it could be possible. My own father was ten years older than my mother. Perhaps she preferred older men.

I knew Cousin Louise wouldn't answer my questions about Brother Erich, but maybe I could find someone who would.

The next morning I walked outside to meet the bread wagon, uncertain how Berndt would greet me. I waved as he drew near and was pleased to see a smile on his face.

The moment he was close enough to hear me, I called, "Good morning!"

"Guten Morgen!" He jumped down from the wagon and stepped close. "I was worried you might be sick. Something important kept you away yesterday?"

I heaved a sigh of relief. "Yes, something very important." I quickly explained what had happened. "I'm sorry you had to stand outside in the cold weather." I glanced toward the kitchen house, knowing that if I was outside too long, Cousin Louise would scold us. "Can you go this afternoon?"

Berndt winked, and I could feel the heat begin to rise in my cheeks. For once, I was thankful for the cold weather. He wouldn't see the effect he'd had on me.

"Ja, I can go. I will meet you by the stand of trees near the edge of town. Two o'clock?"

"Two o'clock. I promise I will be there this time."

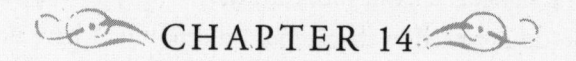# CHAPTER 14

February 1893
Karlina

I snuggled between the sheets and pulled the quilt tight beneath my chin. *"Psst."* I waited only a second. *"Psst.* Are you awake, Dovie?"

The bedcovers rustled and Dovie giggled. "Yes. If I had been asleep, that hissing sound of yours would have wakened me."

"It was not that loud." We giggled together and a brief silence grew between us before I told her what was bothering me—why I wasn't able to sleep. "I think my Mutter knows that sometimes you have been meeting Berndt."

In the shadows I could see Dovie's form as she pushed to a sitting position and rested her back on the headboard. "Why? What has she said? Tell me."

"She asked if I knew what you've been doing in the afternoons."

"And what did you tell her?"

I could hear the growing panic in Dovie's voice. "I—"

"You didn't tell her I've been with Berndt, did you? Because I don't spend every afternoon with him."

"No, I didn't say you were with him." Shifting to my side, I bent my elbow and rested my head in my hand. "I told her I was in the sheep barn in the afternoons and I could not say with certainty where you went after you finished your work in the Küche."

Dovie sighed. "Thank you, Karlina."

"You do not need to thank me. I did not lie. I have not seen you and Berndt together." The defensive words rushed from my lips, as though I felt I had to prove I'd been truthful. "I know only the few things you have told me, but I never *saw* you with him."

"Did she ask anything more?"

"She said she was going to talk to my Vater and see if I could go with you some afternoons when it is not so busy. She is worried about you, Dovie. She believes you are worrying too much about the past instead of planning your future."

"I don't want her to worry about me. The only thing I have wanted is to learn about my mother's past. And now that I'm here, I still can't get the answers I want."

"Did Berndt gain any information about Brother Erich, the schoolteacher?"

Two weeks had passed before Dovie told me about Sister Elsa's comment at the quilting bee. Instead of asking me or my Mutter, she had asked Berndt about Brother Erich. He'd never heard of the man but said he would see what he could discover.

"Yes, but I don't think he was the cause of my mother's unhappiness. From what Berndt told me, Brother Erich was round as a toad with bulging eyes, and he died before my mother left East Amana."

I was glad Dovie had asked Berndt to conduct the investigation, for if I'd ever heard of Brother Erich, I couldn't remember. And Dovie likely believed my Mutter wouldn't give a direct answer about the schoolteacher. And I agreed.

"Is that all?" I wasn't sure what else Berndt could have discovered, but I wanted all the details.

"What else could there be? Sister Elsa wouldn't have been making a reference to Brother Erich if he was already dead when my mother and her family left the colonies. Other than asking Sister Elsa, I don't know how I can find out." Dovie was silent for a moment. "Maybe that's what I should do."

The muscles in my neck stiffened. "What?"

"Go and talk to Sister Elsa. Do you think she would tell your Mutter? Maybe we could come up with some reason for me to go and speak to her about something else, and then I could ask her. What do you think? Help me plan some reason to approach her."

Dovie's excitement bubbled across the short distance between our beds, but my chest tightened. If I became involved in some scheme to obtain information from Sister Elsa, my Mutter would be most unhappy with me. And I knew she would eventually discover any part I played in Dovie's plan.

"I don't think that is such a gut idea. All of the sisters talk among themselves, and Sister Elsa would surely tell my Mutter you'd been asking questions."

"But what harm would it do? I don't understand why everything must be such a secret."

"I am not so sure there are secrets. I think it is only that my Mutter wants you to quit dwelling on the past. Why does it matter if your Mutter was sad when she left the colonies? She made a happy life in Cincinnati, ja?"

"That's just it, Karlina. I'm not sure my mother was ever completely happy."

"But you cannot change that, so what gut does it do to keep on with this digging into her early years?" My stomach tightened into a knot. "Dovie, why can't you just enjoy being here with us?"

"I do, but I . . ."

Her voice quivered, and I sat up in bed. "Are you crying? Please don't cry."

She sniffled. "I don't believe my mother was ever truly happy. I know she loved me. But I think if she had been given the choice between living here or with my father and me, she would have chosen life in Amana." Her voice cracked as she uttered the final words.

"You torture yourself with these thoughts. Let me speak to my Mutter and see if she will reveal anything. But please don't speak to Sister Elsa. She is a sweet lady, and I do not want trouble to brew between her and my Mutter."

My offer satisfied her, and I thought she'd drifted off to sleep.

Suddenly she spoke. "What about you and Anton? I know he cares for you. I see the way he watches when you are in the same room with him."

"You see things that are not there, Dovie, but we have become gut friends. Since the trouble with Berndt, I have seen great changes in him. Not once have I seen him lose his temper. He is more patient, and the sheep will even follow him out to the pasture now without problem."

Dovie chuckled. "If the sheep like him, then I am sure you will think he is wonderful."

"It is true that being gut with the sheep is important to me, but I am pleased that he has gained control of his temper. And it has made him happier, too. After his fight with Berndt, we talked for a long time. He said he never wanted to hit another person, and he needed to find a way to control his anger." Lying there in the darkness, I recalled how sad and defeated Anton had looked that day. The inability to control his temper plagued him, and he'd begged me to help him find some way to overcome his failings.

The wood slats beneath Dovie's mattress creaked. "What did you tell him?"

"That I did not think he would be successful unless he looked to God for help. I told him that I had kept my promise and had been praying for him every day, but he needed to pray for himself every day, too—to ask God to give him the strength to overcome his weaknesses."

A narrow shaft of winter moonlight danced across Dovie's face. "Did he agree?"

"Ja. He asked me to pray with him each morning when we go down to the barn before breakfast. It is how we begin each day." I smiled in the darkness, pleased that we'd developed this habit. I believed the practice had drawn me closer to God, too. "I also suggested that he recite a passage of Scripture if he felt his anger begin to take hold."

"And did he also think that was a good idea?"

Dovie sounded as though she didn't believe Anton would ever consider doing such a thing. "Ja. He even asked me what I would recommend."

"Really?"

"Ja. And I told him I thought the shepherd's psalm would have a calming effect."

Dovie giggled. "He should have known you would suggest the twenty-third Psalm. I am glad you have been able to help him."

"It is God who has helped him, not me."

"Yes, but you pointed the way. My mother used to tell me that there are times in our lives when we need people to point us in the right direction. That's what you did for Anton." She was still for a moment. "And no matter what you say, I think he is in love with you."

I didn't respond. If I let myself think about love, it would make my friendship with Anton uncomfortable, and I didn't want that to happen.

The following morning before I'd had time to say my morning prayers, Dovie reminded me of my promise.

"I will speak to Mutter, but I want it to be at the right time. It is better that I approach her when we will have no interruptions and I don't have to hurry back to work." I saw the look of exasperation on Dovie's face, but I didn't let it dissuade me. "I know her better than you. Please let me do this my way."

"Just don't take too long. Each day I worry there will be a letter from my father telling me he will soon arrive to escort me to Texas."

"Ja, I understand. I will do my very best." When Dovie hurried out the door to meet the bread wagon, I sighed with relief.

While I finished dressing, I considered when I might find the proper time to speak with Mutter. In the kitchen she was surrounded by the other sisters, and when we were in the parlor, either my Vater or Anton was around. Maybe on the way home from prayer service this evening. There wouldn't be enough time for a full discussion on our short walk home, but if I gained Mutter's interest, she would make certain we had time by ourselves to finish the talk. With my plan decided, I made my bed and walked downstairs, feeling much relieved.

I hummed a tune as Anton and I walked to the barn. He nudged my arm and grinned. "You are happy this morning."

"Ja. It is a gut morning. Lots of sunshine, and I get to see if you have learned to keep the records the way I taught you."

Over the past weeks I'd been showing Anton how we entered the detailed records for each of the sheep. Records regarding their feed, illnesses, and treatments; the amount of wool each one produced at shearing time; and the number of lambs born to each of the ewes. There was more time to teach him before lambing and shearing seasons began; and though he wasn't fond of the record keeping, my Vater believed it was the duty of a good shepherd to maintain records. If Anton later went to work shepherding in another village, the knowledge would prove useful. My Vater said many farmers maintained only the production records for their sheep, but he thought that idea foolish.

Anton grunted. "My time would be of better use developing an invention than writing numbers in those ledger books."

His comment troubled me. "If that is what you think, then I suppose you should tell it to the elders instead of me. I cannot change what work you will do." Just when I thought he had begun to like working with the sheep, he made an occasional comment that caused me to believe otherwise.

"Do not take offense so easily. Even your Vater has said that the record keeping is tiresome. If I make any remark about disliking something in the barn, you act as though I have insulted you." He pulled open the barn door and stepped to the side.

The musty smell of hay wafted toward me as I walked inside. "You're right, Anton. I am sorry. Even I don't always consider the record keeping a pleasant task."

After he opened the side doors, the sheep proceeded to amble outside while Anton set to work mucking the barns. The ground was dry enough that he could take them out to the pasture once he'd finished his work inside.

My eyes grew tired as I went through the figures and recalculated the amounts of grain we had used and what remained. Unlike most shepherds, we didn't have to worry about the grain. Our farms produced enough to supplement the sheep, as well as all of our other livestock. Still, my Vater wanted accurate records.

"I'm through in the barn. I'm going to take the sheep to those hills that overlook the pond." Anton drew near and looked over my shoulder. "Have you found any mistakes?"

When I turned my head to answer him, our lips were only inches apart. A shiver coursed through me. I knew I should back away, but the look in his eyes locked me in place. My throat constricted and my mouth turned as dry as wool batting. He closed the short distance between us and gently kissed my lips. My insides quivered at the sensation, and when I opened my eyes, he took a backward step.

"I am sorry, Karlina. Please don't be angry with me, but I have longed to do that for far too long."

I stared at him in disbelief. "You have?"

He tipped his head to one side. "You mean you cannot see that I care for you?"

I inhaled a deep breath. Dovie had been right. "I knew you cared for me as a friend, but I didn't know you cared for me as . . . as . . ." I didn't even know how to finish the sentence.

He grinned. "As more than a friend?"

I bobbed my head.

"Then let me assure you that I care for you much more than any friend. You have become an important part of my life, Karlina. We will talk more later. If I don't take the sheep out to pasture now, your Vater will wonder what has become of them."

Long after he had departed, the touch of Anton's kiss lingered on my lips.

Each time I looked his way, Anton grinned at me, and I wondered if my mother or father would soon become suspicious. On the way to prayer meeting, I whispered to him that he should stop.

"I will try," he whispered. "But I cannot promise."

He didn't do well keeping his word. I caught him looking at me and smiling several times when he should have had his head bowed. Before we departed the meeting, I chastised him about his behavior.

"How do you know I didn't have my head bowed? You wouldn't have seen me if you'd been praying."

I nodded. "You are right." I glanced to see if anyone was nearby. "On the way home, I need to speak privately to my Mutter. Would you walk with Vater and draw him into a discussion about the sheep?"

He grinned. "I would rather walk with you, but I'll do as you ask."

"Danke, Anton."

He winked and my heart fluttered.

My Mutter approached with my cloak draped over her arm. "Come along, Karlina."

As we stepped outside, I heard Anton ask my Vater when he thought the first lambs would be born.

I looped my hand into the crook of my Mutter's arm. "I am concerned about Dovie. She has told me some things that grieve her—matters regarding her Mutter. Yet she doesn't believe she will ever discover the truth."

My Mutter's jaw went slack. "What are these things that grieve her?"

Holding tight to her arm, I leaned a bit closer. By the time we arrived home, I had repeated all of what Dovie had told me.

Once we entered the kitchen, my Mutter turned to my Vater. "You and Anton go upstairs. Karlina and I will make coffee and bring it to you."

"And maybe some of the cake?" My Vater grinned and pointed to the leftover Kuchen on the worktable.

My Mutter waved him toward the other room. "Ja, and some cake, too."

The moment the men left the room, my Mutter motioned me to a stool near the worktable. She questioned me at length, nodding and frowning as I answered her questions.

"She told me these things before, and I thought I had convinced her she was mistaken. It is not gut that she believes her Mutter was unhappy. I will pray about this and see what the Lord reveals to me."

I would be praying, as well. I didn't want Dovie taking matters into her own hands.

# CHAPTER 15

Dovie

I didn't say another word to Karlina. She had told me that her mother planned to pray and I must be patient. But each day it became more difficult. For more than a week, I had been watching Cousin Louise with eager eyes, hoping for some sign that she was ready to give me a glimpse into my mother's past. I believed she could lay my questions to rest, but only if she and God came to a mutual understanding. An understanding that agreed with my desires.

After we completed cleaning the kitchen, Cousin Louise dismissed the sisters. "Go home until time to prepare for supper. Dovie will help me prepare the midday refreshment. I am guessing you all have work waiting at home for you."

Cousin Louise's comment wasn't unusual. Often it took only two people to prepare the midmorning and midafternoon refreshments. The only part that surprised me was that I had been selected to help her. Normally I didn't work in the kitchen after the noon-day meal had been served.

The women called their good-byes as they scurried out the back door. From the kitchen window, I stood watch as their garments flapped in the blustery February wind. Gathering their cloaks tight, the women bowed their heads against the cold air and strode off in several different directions.

"I hope you did not have plans for this afternoon, Dovie." Cousin Louise stood in the kitchen doorway.

I turned away from the window and smiled. "No. Nothing important." More and more often, Berndt had been required to help at the sawmill during the afternoons, so our time together had become less frequent. We had not arranged to meet today. My only plan had been to answer my father's recent letter.

"Let's go upstairs and sit in the parlor, where it is more comfortable. I want to talk to you a little, and there are some things I will show you."

My heart quickened. Finally Cousin Louise was going to talk to me about my mother. It took everything in my power to keep from racing up the steps. By the time we entered the parlor, my anticipation was bubbling like a pot of water on a hot stove.

"Go in and sit down. I must get something from the bedroom."

I tapped my foot, my impatience increasing with each passing moment. When I heard Cousin Louise's footsteps, I folded my hands and leaned forward. "What do you have to show me?"

"First we will talk." She lowered herself onto the chair opposite me. "Karlina tells me you hold on to the belief that your mother was unhappy."

"I know what you have told me, but I still believe she would have given up everything in Cincinnati in exchange for a life here."

Cousin Louise shook her head. "It is true your Mutter was very sad when your grandfather decided they would move to the outside." She inhaled a deep breath. "Like most people, your Mutter was unhappy sometimes and happy at other times."

"You weren't around her, Cousin Louise. She was mostly sad, and whenever I would question her about her life in the colonies, she would only shake her head and tell me that the past was gone and could never be changed. Then she would refuse to discuss it any further."

"Ja, well, that is true, but I believe you have drawn far too much from her words and her refusal to talk about her early years. I am hoping that these will set your heart at rest and you will finally realize how much your Mutter loved you." She withdrew a small packet of letters from her pocket. "These are letters written to me by your Mutter. After you have read them, I do not think you will ever question her love for you again." She placed the letters on the table beside me.

My mother's neat script flowed across the face of envelopes that had yellowed a bit with age. "Thank you, Cousin Louise."

She nodded. "I am going downstairs. You remain up here and read the letters carefully. I think your mind will be set to rest after you finish reading them."

I waited until I heard her footsteps on the stairs before I reached inside the first envelope. Doing as Cousin Louise had instructed, I carefully read each letter. When I finished, I leaned back in the chair. Disappointment washed over me. There were lengthy gaps of time between the letters. The first letter contained news of my mother's upcoming marriage and my father's promise to find them a home in the Over-the-Rhine district of Cincinnati. The next told of their small wedding and setting up their little apartment. There were a few that told of life in Cincinnati and that her marriage and the move from Covington to the other side of the river had been like moving to a new world. The only remark about Amana in all of the letters had been in one where she'd written *The change from living in my father's house to making a new home with Nelson is as great as when my family left East Amana and moved to Kentucky.* There was nothing in these letters that Cousin Louise hadn't already told me.

I rested my head against the back of the chair. How did she think these few letters would answer my questions? There was nothing that revealed why my mother had longed to remain in the colonies even though her parents had decided to leave. Maybe if I probed for an answer about why my grandparents left, I would discover something further. Still, I doubted whether Cousin Louise would tell me much more. She'd said these letters should set my mind at rest.

After tucking each letter into the proper envelope, I wandered downstairs. Bowls of preserves and apple butter sat on the tables. In the kitchen, Cousin Louise was cutting thick slices of dark bread to serve with afternoon coffee.

She glanced up. "You feel better now, ja?"

I shook my head. "The letters say little more than you had already told me."

Her brows dipped low, and the sharp knife remained poised above the loaf of bread. "But they are her own words, written in her hand. You now know what I told you is true."

I forced a feeble smile. "I never believed you were telling me untruths, Cousin Louise, but I think there is more to my mother's story, much that remains unspoken. Those are things I want to know."

She turned her gaze back to the bread and lowered her knife against the hard crust. "I am sorry you are disappointed, Dovie. I am praying that God will give you peace about your mother's past so that you may step into the future."

Her words were enough to tell me that I need inquire no further. "If you don't need my help, I think I'll go for a walk."

"It's cold and windy, but if you wish to take a walk, I can finish here by myself." She smiled and waved me toward the door.

I grabbed my coat from the peg, and as soon as all the buttons were fastened and I'd pulled on my gloves, I hurried out the door. In truth, I thought Cousin Louise was probably pleased that I had asked to leave. With me gone, she didn't have to worry about more questions. Taking the same route I'd used on many other days, I unconsciously walked toward the edge of town and glanced toward the stand of trees where I had met Berndt on so many occasions. Silly as it seemed, I rather expected to see him standing there, but the only movement among the trees was a lone rabbit foraging for something to nibble upon.

An echo of voices drifted from the pond, and I wondered who might be skating this afternoon. Perhaps Jakub and his sister. I hadn't seen them in some time. Jakub had waved from a distance one day when I'd been skating with Berndt but had disappeared almost the moment I caught sight of him. Since then, neither he nor Sophia had been at the pond when Berndt and I were there.

In spite of the cold, a bright afternoon sun shone on the ice, and I cupped my hand above my eyes to gain a better view. The two figures on the ice had their backs turned to me but then whirled in unison, and I recognized Jakub and Sophia. I lifted my arm and waved wildly in their direction.

"Ahoj!" The two of them called as they skated toward the edge of the pond.

"Guten Tag!" I hurried toward them, wishing I'd brought my skates. "It is good to see you. Where have you been?" I asked slowly. "You are never here when I come skating." Jakub had understood some of my German before—at least when I didn't talk too rapidly.

Jakub pointed to a tree and moved his arms back and forth. "Cutting. For at home, to keep warm." He pointed to the dancing flames. He had started a fire in the same place Berndt and I made our fires.

I nodded my understanding. It seemed everyone was busy cutting wood in order to keep warm throughout the winter. "You have been doing well?"

He nodded and pointed to the fat log that we used as a seat. While Sophia circled on the ice, he sat down beside me. "A little sickness. My *matka* and *babička*." When I frowned, he chuckled and said, "Mutter and Oma."

"Ah, your Mutter and Oma have been ill."

He held his index finger and thumb a short distance apart. "A little. Better now." He pointed to my feet. "No skates?"

I shook my head. "Just walking today. No skating."

He pointed toward East Amana. "Where is the man you skate with?"

"Berndt? He had to work this afternoon." I didn't know if Berndt was cutting wood, working at the sawmill, or sweeping the bakery, but I made the same motions Jakub had made earlier.

He laughed and nodded. "You come here again and skate?"

I hitched a shoulder. "Maybe, but not until next week."

"What day? Sophia and I will come, too."

I thought for a moment. Berndt was always busy on Thursdays. That should be a good day. "Thursday?"

He nodded as Sophia returned to the edge of the pond and joined us. She leaned down to unfasten her skates. "Time to go, Jakub." She looked up at me, her eyes sparkling. "Come meet our matka?" She reached over and grasped my hand.

I glanced back toward the village. There was no reason to hurry back. Cousin Louise wasn't going to answer my questions, and I wasn't expected to help prepare the evening meal.

"Come have some *káva*." She pretended to lift a cup to her lips.

Jakub had removed his skates while Sophia talked, and when I hesitated, he motioned for me to come along. "Come and meet." He smiled. "You will like."

I knew that going to the home of strangers would be frowned upon, and going by myself would be considered unacceptable behavior. Yet who would know? Cousin Louise was accustomed to my being gone during the afternoons. Karlina and Anton were busy working, as was Berndt. The prospect of sharing coffee with this inviting family sounded far more enjoyable than returning to the kitchen house.

"Danke. I will come with you."

Jakub's eyes widened with surprise, but his smile was bright enough to light a dreary day. I walked between the two of them, enjoying their laughter as they joked with each other. Their house was farther than I'd expected. When we arrived, I knew I couldn't stay for long. To be late returning for the evening meal would require more answers than I would want to give.

As we entered the house, the smell of baking sweets encircled me like welcoming arms. I lifted my nose and inhaled the yeasty sweet aroma. My mouth watered and I gazed around the kitchen. Two women sat at the table. One was bent and gray-haired, her face lined with wrinkles as deep as the grooves in Cousin Louise's wooden cutting board. Her lips curved in a toothless grin and she motioned to the chair beside her. When I didn't move, she patted the seat of the chair.

"She wants you to sit down," Jakub said. He took my hand and gently tugged me toward the chair. "Babička, this is Dovie." Her toothless grin widened.

I nodded and wished her "good afternoon" in German. Whether she understood or not, I didn't know, but she bobbed her head. Strands of gray hair danced around her weathered forehead until she lifted a blue-veined hand and swiped them away.

Jakub turned to the younger of the two women. "And this is my matka." Her dark hair bore streaks of gray, and I guessed her to be near the same age as Cousin Louise. Her eyes were as dark as coal and sparkled when she smiled. She pointed to the empty chair.

I sat down, uncertain what to do or say. Before I could worry for long, Sophia had placed a cup and saucer in front of me and then filled my cup with coffee. Jakub's mother said something to Sophia that I couldn't understand while Jakub pulled a chair close and poured coffee for his mother, grandmother, and finally for himself.

Sophia placed a platter in the center of the table and small plates and forks in front of us.

"*Kolaches*. You will like," Jakub said. He rubbed his stomach. "Very good."

Jakub's mother lifted the platter and offered it to me. I was afraid I would be late getting home, but I couldn't refuse. I smiled my thanks and lifted one of the sweet rolls from the plate. A dollop of cherry filling sat nestled in the center of the pastry. I cut off a bite, lifted the fork to my mouth, and bit into the soft texture. The delightful consistency of the tender dough and sweet filling was as good as any pastry I'd ever tasted in Krüger's Bakery.

I looked at Jakub's mother and pointed to the pastry. "Wonderful. Very good." I wished I could speak in their language so that she would understand.

She nodded and pointed to Jakub's grandmother. I turned toward his grandmother and repeated my praise. The older woman nodded and smiled, then helped herself to one of the kolaches. After taking a bite, she grinned and motioned for me to take another. I hadn't yet finished the first. I shook my head, and she frowned.

I motioned toward the door. "I must go home soon."

After Jakub explained, she wiped her hands on her napkin and got up from the table. Soon she returned with a cloth napkin, wrapped two of the kolaches inside, and pointed to me. "She wants to give you those to take home with you," Jakub said.

Her eyes gleamed with pleasure. I couldn't refuse. A short time later, I bid them all good-bye and thanked them for the coffee and kolaches. Jakub grabbed his coat when I neared the door.

Jamming his arms into the sleeves, he quickly fastened the buttons. "I will walk with you. To make sure you are safe."

He turned to explain to his mother, who nodded and waved to me. Sophia and the other two women were deep in conversation when we walked out the door. "They are very nice, Jakub. Thank you for inviting me." I grinned and tapped the napkin. "And for the kolaches."

He laughed. "I was sure you would like them."

We walked in silence until we neared the pond. "I'll go the rest of the way by myself. I am fine."

He didn't argue. "You come for sure next Thursday?"

"Yes. And I'll bring the napkin back." I grasped his hand. "Thank you, Jakub. I had a nice time."

"Bring your skates," he called as I walked to the other side of the pond.

"I will!" I waved and continued toward the kitchen house, my heart much lighter than when I'd departed. Nothing had changed. I still knew nothing about my mother, but while I had been with Jakub and his family, none of it seemed to matter. As I sat around the table in their tiny kitchen, I had completely forgotten about my mother's past, and it had felt good. Maybe Cousin Louise was right. Maybe I did need to forget the past and move into the future.

I gasped when the clock in the watchtower chimed. It was the first bell, the one telling the workers supper would soon be served. I began to run and soon caught sight of the barn. As I came across the rise, Karlina, Anton, and Cousin George appeared.

I jammed the napkin into my coat pocket and held my hand

near the opening. I didn't want to risk the possibility of the napkin protruding, for that would cause a flurry of questions. Karlina was the first to spot me. She waved and shouted my name, and then all three of them came to a halt. Panting, I ran toward them while holding my hand over my pocket.

Karlina leaned to one side and looked at my hand as I came to a stop beside her. "What's wrong with your hand?"

"Nothing. I had a small ache in my side." I pushed my hand tighter against my side.

Cousin George continued walking. "Come or we will be late to supper. It would not be gut for all of my wife's family to be late entering the Küche."

I sighed with relief, thankful any further conversation regarding my hand had been avoided.

As we entered the village, Cousin George glanced over his shoulder. "Where have you been this afternoon, Dovie?"

My relief evaporated like snow on a spring day. "I went for a walk down by the pond. I had Cousin Louise's permission."

"You were skating?"

"No. I didn't take skates with me."

"Once the weather begins to warm up, you must not go skating by yourself. The ice will become weak, and you could have an accident." Cousin George pointed toward the sky. "I do not think we need to worry about melting ice right away. Looks like snow clouds in the distance."

Though I had no knowledge of snow clouds, I murmured my agreement and hoped we would arrive back at the Küche before Cousin George would ask any more questions about my whereabouts. I didn't want to tell an outright lie.

CHAPTER 16

While thoughts of my mother's past had been nonexistent during the time I'd been with Jakub and his family, the nagging questions returned once we arrived back at the kitchen house.

Cousin Louise arched her brows when I walked inside with Karlina, Anton, and Cousin George. "You have been at the barn all afternoon?"

"I went for a walk down to the pond. You said I could go. Remember?" I glanced at Cousin George, who had stepped closer and was listening to our exchange.

"Ja. But when you came in with the others, I thought you had been at the barn. You did not get too cold being outdoors for so long?"

"No. Someone had been skating earlier, and they left a small fire burning near the pond. I added a little wood and was able to warm my hands." I hoped my story sounded believable. Most of what I'd said was true.

Brother George removed his coat. "Is not gut that people go off and do not put out the fire. That is a bad way of doing things."

I swallowed hard. "It was almost out. I stirred it a little to keep the embers going and added some twigs to keep it hot."

Brother George appeared somewhat appeased. "And you made certain the fire was out before you left the pond?"

"Yes." I couldn't meet his eyes when I answered.

It had been Jakub who had put out the fire, but there was no doubt it was out before we left and when we returned after leaving his house, as well. But because I didn't want to find myself on a train to Texas, I didn't add any of those facts.

Snow began to fall after supper, and Anton and Karlina suggested the possibility of going sled riding the following afternoon. I agreed it would be fun, but they were far more excited by the prospect than I was. Karlina could deny that she had feelings for Anton, but I knew better. I wondered if Cousin Louise had observed the change in her daughter's behavior when Anton was around, for she seemed to notice everything else.

After Karlina recited her prayers, she settled into her bed. "You didn't appear excited to go sledding tomorrow. Do you want me to ask Berndt to come along? Would that make you happier?"

The hog-hair mattress shifted beneath me as I turned. "You can ask him, but I think he will have to work. His father is keeping him busy most every day." I hesitated only a moment. "I am guessing because of your mother."

"What do you mean?" Though I could distinguish no more than the outline of her body in the darkness, I didn't miss the hurt in Karlina's voice.

"I think she knows we were meeting in the afternoons and told his father."

The bedclothes rustled and Karlina's feet hit the floor. She crossed the short distance between our beds and sat down on the edge of the mattress. "I did not tell her you had been meeting Berndt. Is that what you think?"

"No. But I think she somehow found out. Someone could have seen us at the pond and told her."

Karlina reached for my hand. "I think she would have told me, but she hasn't said a word. Just because Berndt must do chores in the afternoon, it does not mean—"

"Not long ago he was able to meet me most every afternoon. Suddenly he could not. Does that not seem strange to you?"

"Nein. In the winter there are extra jobs to be done. Timber needs to be cut, and ice must be harvested from the river. Everyone who has time is expected to help with those chores."

"Perhaps you are right." Karlina started to release my hand, but I grabbed a tight hold. "Did your mother tell you about our conversation today?"

"Ja. After prayer meeting. She said the letters did not satisfy you."

"Those letters said nothing more than what she'd already told me. I don't know why she thought they would help." I hitched up in the bed. "Did she say anything else?"

"Only that she's praying you will forget the past. Do not push her too far, Dovie. I do not want her to suggest that you go and join your father in Texas." She squeezed my hand. "I like having you here."

As Karlina returned to her bed, I rolled to my side and plumped the feather pillow. I didn't want to anger Cousin Louise, but my heart longed for knowledge that would connect to my mother's past. Even I didn't understand my need to gain this knowledge, but I wouldn't be satisfied until I learned the truth.

I smiled in the darkness. "I like being here, too, Karlina. And I won't push too much."

Unless I have to. I stared into the darkness and asked God's forgiveness for the lies I'd told earlier in the day. I also asked that He guide me to the truth so that I could find peace. I thought it was the least He could do, since I had to live the rest of my life without a mother. I would see if He agreed.

A light snow fell throughout the night, and by morning there were at least three inches on the ground. Karlina peeked out the window and clapped her hands. "When you go to the bread wagon, tell Berndt we are going sledding this afternoon. Tell him I am inviting him to join us," Karlina said as I prepared to go downstairs.

I stepped to the window and peered outside. "Maybe the wagon won't be able to make it through this snow."

"He will make it. The kitchen houses must have their bread, milk, and meat. You can be sure that the wagon boxes were prepared with runners last night." Karlina chuckled. "The horses will be pulling a bread sleigh instead of a bread wagon."

"In that case, I'd better hurry." I pushed down on the heavy metal latch and opened the bedroom door. After passing through the parlor and outer hallway, I bounded down the steps. The familiar jingle of the bread wagon announced its approach as I stepped over the threshold into the kitchen.

"Berndt will bring it inside, Dovie. The snow is deep, and he will be wearing his boots. When the snow is deep, he is used to bringing the orders inside."

Just as Cousin Louise predicted, Berndt arrived at the back door. He stomped his boots on the porch, and I hurried to open the door. "Guten Morgen." He placed the bread trays on the worktable and removed his cap. "Did you ask for all this snow, Sister Louise?"

"Nein. You can be sure it was not me." Cousin Louise studied the bread trays, obviously making sure she'd gotten her full order.

"What about you, Sister Dovie? Are you the one to blame for

the snowfall?" He turned his back toward Cousin Louise and winked at me.

"Maybe." I could feel heat slowly climbing up my cheeks. "Karlina and I decided it would be fun to go sledding this afternoon, and sure enough, we awakened to all this snow." I fastened my gaze on him, hoping that he would understand what I was trying to tell him.

"Ja, well then I will have to blame the two of you that I had to put the runners on the wagon." He grinned and nodded. "I hope you will have fun this afternoon. I like the big hill beyond the cemetery when I go sledding, but you can be sure Karlina knows all the gut spots."

He arched his brows as if asking where he would find us. At least I hoped that was what it meant, so I gave a slight nod and said, "She told me that was where we were going." In truth, Karlina hadn't mentioned our sledding destination, but I was certain I could convince her.

"You'd better be on your way, Berndt. Otherwise, Sister Fuch will think you are stuck in a snowdrift along the way. She will send the men out looking for you. If that happened and you were discovered loitering in my kitchen, I would never hear the end of it." Cousin Louise waved him toward the door.

Berndt tugged his cap onto his head and grinned. "I don't think you need to worry. Sister Fuch prefers to place the blame on me when things go wrong with her bread deliveries." He strode toward the door. "Auf Wiedersehen."

"Was that Berndt?" Karlina came into the kitchen and shot a questioning look in my direction.

"Since the snow hasn't yet been shoveled off the walkway, Berndt carried the bread inside for us." I picked up the small bowls of rhubarb jelly and nodded toward the dining room. Karlina followed me to a far table. "I think he will meet us at the hill near the cemetery. We couldn't talk alone because your mother was in the kitchen."

"Karlina, you are keeping Dovie from her work." Cousin Louise rounded the doorway and stepped into the dining room. She gestured toward the back door. "We will need milk."

Karlina's shoulders sagged. "You want me to go to the cellar and get it for you?"

"Ja, and hurry. We do not have time to waste. Be sure to put on your boots."

Karlina scurried toward the kitchen and I followed her a few moments later. Soon the other women arrived, all of them stomping their feet on the back porch and commenting on the weather as they entered the kitchen. Most brought their knitting or mending with them, declaring they wouldn't go home until after the evening meal.

"I think that is wise. We may get even more snow during the day," Cousin Louise said. "We will have a gut time visiting in between serving times."

Once the cleaning had been completed after the morning meal, I approached Cousin Louise. "I thought I would dust the upstairs rooms this morning while you visit with the others."

On any other day, I would have taken the opportunity to seek out one of the women and try to gain personal information regarding my mother. But today I wanted to go sledding. And I didn't want Cousin Louise to have any excuse for denying our request.

Cousin Louise removed her apron and hung it near the doorway. "That is not necessary. There are other times when we can dust the upstairs rooms." She studied me for a moment. "Unless that is what you would prefer."

"It is. Thank you."

"I don't think anyone has ever before thanked me for such a thing, but you are welcome. You need not come downstairs to help with the midmorning meal." She chuckled. "I have more than enough help for that."

Cleaning cloth in hand, I worked my way through the parlor, the bedroom I shared with Karlina, and Anton's room. Only the bedroom shared by Cousin Louise and Cousin George remained. I would still have time to write a letter to my father before the noonday preparations began. This bedroom was a bit larger than the others, but not by much. There were two single beds, two small tables, and a large wardrobe. Soon after arriving, I'd learned that only single beds were used in the colonies, a fact I thought strange, since my parents had shared a bed. I didn't ask why, for I feared the answer might embarrass either me or the person I asked. Perhaps the elders thought it a better and more economical use of time and materials to make only one size bed and one size mattress, but I wasn't certain.

As I drew near the table in the far corner, my gaze fell upon a sizable packet of envelopes that looked similar to the ones Cousin Louise had received from my mother. They were tied with a string and turned facedown on the table. My heart hammered a rapid beat, and my stomach tightened into a knot. I reached for the packet and turned it over. My mouth went dry as I stared at my mother's familiar handwriting. I ran the pad of my thumb along the edge of the envelopes. There were far more letters here than Cousin Louise had shown to me.

What was in these letters, and why hadn't she given me all of them to read? Instinctively, I glanced over my shoulder as I pulled one of the envelopes from beneath the string.

With quivering fingers I removed the letter. While keeping a sharp ear for approaching footsteps, I scanned the pages. This letter had been written when I turned five years old. Mother wrote about our visit to the department store to purchase a new dress for my birthday gift that year. Without reading her description, I could still vividly recall that day and the beautiful pale blue dress with lace trim. Never had I felt as lovely as when I'd modeled that dress for my father. His reaction had meant as much to me as the dress itself. Other than that, there was nothing more than an account of the weather, my mother's progress on a quilt, and several questions regarding the health and welfare of Cousin Louise and her family. I tucked the letter back inside the envelope.

One by one, I continued reading the letters. Most of them contained nothing that I did not already know about my mother. Resignation that I would never discover anything new assailed me. After one more letter, I would quit reading. As I had with each of the previous missives, I carefully unfolded the pages and scanned the contents. The date at the top of the page reflected this letter had been written only a short time after my mother and her family departed East Amana. On the second page of the letter, I stopped and reread the passage.

When you are able, please tell E that I continue to miss him and that my heart is broken. Nothing can change what happened. I know he, too, regrets our failure to act in good time. Still, I will always be thankful I had the opportunity to love him, and I hope he feels the same.

If I had forced matters further and fought to remain in East, it would have created an irreconcilable breach with my parents. I know the advice of the elders was sound, but I had hoped they would convince Father to remain in the colonies. But all of that is now in the past.

As for the situation with the baby, I know E's mother was not eager for the added responsibility, but I was helpless in the situation. I am thankful for her willingness to step in and take my place. I know she will be good to the child. Please keep me posted about the baby's progress as you are able.

I must close for now. Please write soon.

Your loving cousin,
Barbara

I gasped and clutched my chest. A *baby*. And who was this E that my mother claimed to love? My thoughts raced as I tried to make sense of the letter's contents. Surely this was the man Sister Elsa had alluded to while we were quilting at Sister Fuch's. But who was he? And whose baby was she inquiring after? I attempted to swallow but felt as though a noose had tightened around my neck. Had my mother given birth to a child before she left the colonies? Was E the father? Had the disgrace caused her parents to take my mother and leave?

My breath turned shallow as I considered the possibilities. I willed my hands to cease quivering and returned the letter to the envelope. Then I reached for the stack. There were many other letters. Perhaps one of them would tell me more.

At the sound of footsteps on the stairway, my heartbeat quickened. After returning the packet to the table, I rushed from the bedroom and into the parlor. I grabbed my cleaning rag, and for the second time that morning, I dusted the grandfather clock.

My heart was pounding so hard, I was sure Cousin Louise could hear it when she entered the room. Her eyes shone with concern as she looked at me and then glanced down the hallway. "There is something I need to take care of in the bedroom." Moments later, she returned to the parlor. "You have already dusted in the bedrooms, ja?"

"Yes." The look in her eyes told me she knew I'd been in there—and that she was troubled. Hoping to ease her concern, I forced a smile. I didn't want her to question me further. "I'll be downstairs as soon as I finish dusting in here."

"Gut. Soon it will be time to start the noonday meal." She trod from the room, her footfalls slow and heavy as she returned downstairs.

Once I was certain Cousin Louise would not hear me, I returned to the bedroom and opened the door. I fastened my gaze on the table. The packet of letters had disappeared. There would be no opportunity to read the remaining letters, and now I was left with more questions than answers.

CHAPTER 17

Karlina

Dovie's lack of enthusiasm baffled me. When I'd departed that morning, she had been excited about the possibility of going sledding. But for some reason, her earlier fervor had disappeared. Convincing Father that he should permit both Anton and me the privilege of going off to play in the snow for an entire afternoon had not been easy, but we worked hard and completed our tasks before the noonday meal. After complimenting us on our fine work, my father willingly granted his permission.

A light snow began to fall as we walked out of the kitchen. The sleds stood leaning against the fence, the runners waxed and gleaming in the afternoon sun. Anton walked ahead of us to retrieve the largest one. As we followed, I looped my gloved hand through Dovie's arm. "What is wrong with you? I thought you were looking forward to this afternoon. Now you are as sour as Sister Bertha."

She smiled at the reference to the old sister who constantly shushed us during meals. "Even with lots of practice, I don't think anyone could match Sister Bertha." She reached for the smaller sled.

The snow crunched beneath our feet as the three of us trod toward the hill beyond the cemetery, Anton on one side of me and Dovie on the other.

Leaning forward to see around me, Anton gestured toward the hill. "Is Berndt going to meet us?"

Dovie appeared distracted, and I nudged her arm.

"I think he's coming, but I'm not sure. I told him we would be sledding, but I don't know if his father will have other work for him this afternoon."

Anton arched his brows at me, and I shrugged. Dovie obviously had no interest in talking, and though she continued to pull the smaller sled behind her, I wondered if she had lost all interest in our outing.

I reached for her free hand. "You didn't tell me what is bothering you." I squeezed, and her thick knitted mitten squished beneath my fingers. "I have known you long enough to realize when something is not right. Did you receive a letter from your Vater?"

"No. He hasn't written for some time now."

"So that is why you are unhappy? You expected a letter today, and it did not arrive?"

She shook her head. "I know he is busy. When we parted, I understood I wouldn't hear from him often. Most men don't enjoy letter writing like women."

"Ja, but I am sure he likes to receive your letters. You have been faithful to write to him every week."

I waited to see if Dovie would offer some other reason for her change of mood, but she remained quiet. Twice more I prodded her for a possible reason, but she offered nothing.

Soon the whooshing blades of our sleds cut through the snow

and echoed in the cold wintry silence. I hoped that once we reached our destination, Dovie's excitement would return. The sun reflected off the whiteness that surrounded us, and I squinted as I gazed toward the rolling hill.

"Someone is waving. It looks like it might be Berndt up there!" Dovie nodded. "It probably is."

My concern shifted to irritation. "I thought you would be happy to see him. Is there nothing that will cheer you?"

Her lips curved into a wavering smile. "I'm sorry. We'll have lots of fun." She picked up her pace and chattered about the beauty of the snow, but I didn't miss the strain in her voice. Each word was forced and artificial, totally unnatural.

"I thought I had misunderstood your message this morning." With a smile as broad as a barn door, Berndt ran toward us. "It's almost two o'clock." He pointed to a spot not far off. "I got a fire started."

"We couldn't leave until Dovie finished in the kitchen," I said. "But we're glad you waited." I nudged Dovie's arm. "Aren't we, Dovie?"

"What?" She bore that same distracted look again. "Oh yes. I'm glad it snowed."

Berndt appeared confused by her answer, and so was I. Still, he smiled at her and motioned to his sled. "Ready to go down the hill?"

She shook her head. "I think I'll warm myself by the fire. The rest of you can go ahead."

"Why don't you and Anton try your sleds?" I suggested. "By the time you come back up the hill, we'll be ready to give it a try."

Berndt's disappointment was evident to me, although Dovie didn't appear to notice. Or if she did, she chose to ignore his feelings. Side by side, we walked toward the fire while the men got onto the sleds. Berndt had surrounded the glowing wood with thick logs, and I wondered if he'd brought them from home. If so, his father wouldn't be pleased to discover their woodpile had diminished in size.

Dovie sat down on one of the logs, and I lowered myself to the space beside her. I waited for a moment while she stared into the fire. Finally I could stand the silence no longer. "Either you tell me what is wrong or we might as well return home. This isn't any fun at all!"

"I'm sorry, Karlina."

"I don't want an apology; I want to know what is wrong!" Perhaps my irritation would shake her loose.

She clutched her hands together and turned her head toward me. "Promise you won't say anything to your mother."

"I promise. Now, what is it?" I clenched my jaw and waited.

"Do you know anyone in East named Erich?"

"Oh, ja, there are three—maybe four, I think." I thought for a moment. "No. Just three. Erich Heinimann is now living in West."

She edged closer. "How old is he?"

"I do not know. I think maybe he is a little older than my Vater. Why?"

Dovie didn't bother to answer before continuing with another question. "What about the other Erichs? How old are they? Do they still live in East?"

She leaned toward me as though my answer would make some great difference in her life, yet I couldn't imagine why she'd suddenly developed this powerful interest in men named Erich.

I inhaled a deep, cold breath of air. "Well, there's Erich Wiesler. He is six or seven years old." I scrunched my brow and attempted to remember. "Maybe he is eight."

She waved at me as if swatting a pesky fly. "He doesn't matter. Who else?"

I wanted to tell her Erich Wiesler mattered a great deal to his family and friends, but Dovie's impatience grew more intense. "There are two others. One is a little younger than me. Berndt knows him."

When I mentioned asking him, she shook her head. "No. He doesn't matter, either. What about the final one?"

"There is Berndt's father. His name is Erich. He is older than my Mutter, but not by too many years, I don't think. Berndt could tell us how old he is." I looked toward the hill and cupped my hands to my mouth, but before I could call out to Berndt, Dovie grabbed my arm.

"No! Don't ask him. It does not matter." She jumped to her feet. "Don't tell anyone I asked you about this. You promised." Her jaw settled in a tight line, and her lips opened only a slit as she hurled the command. I didn't miss the panic in her voice or the fear that shone in her eyes.

I took her arm. "Please, Dovie. Sit down." I tugged a little more, and she lowered her weight onto the log. "I do not know what all of this is about. I would like you to tell me, but I cannot force you." She opened her mouth to interrupt, but I held up my hand. "I promised I would not say anything, and I will not." Wrapping my arm around her shoulder, I said, "I hope you know that you can trust me with your secrets."

I felt her shoulders relax beneath my hand. Perhaps I had helped, but I couldn't be certain. When Anton and Berndt returned to the top of the hill, they waved for us to join them. I was surprised when Dovie jumped to her feet and hurried to Berndt's side.

She sat on one sled, and I settled on the other. I glanced over at her as Anton and Berndt prepared to shove off and jump behind us. She smiled, but I could see it was a forced gesture. For the rest of the afternoon, we went up and down the hill, three of us taking great pleasure in the pastime while Dovie only pretended to have fun.

❖

Although I didn't think Berndt or Anton had noticed the difference in Dovie's behavior, Berndt appeared at the barn the following day. Anton and I were working on a new apparatus he thought would be helpful when the lambs were born in a few months. Berndt strode across the barn and stooped down beside us. He stared at the contraption and scratched his head.

"Exactly what is that?"

Anton looked up from his work. "This is going to help us to feed the lambs if the ewes have multiple births or do not have enough milk." Anton lifted the tub in which he'd cut holes and was attaching hoses. "At least that is my plan. Karlina hopes there will be no need to use it, and so do I. She says it is best if the mothers can feed their babies without the need of our help."

Berndt studied the apparatus before asking several questions. "You're quite gut at thinking up new ideas." Berndt tapped his finger to his head. "Very smart."

Anton glanced back down at the tub. "Danke, Berndt. It is nice of you to say so. Are you not working this afternoon?"

"Ja. I must go and cut wood in a little while. The barn is on my way, and I wanted to talk to Karlina for a minute." Berndt looked at Anton. "About Dovie. I want to talk to her about Dovie."

Anton chuckled. "Ja, well I think you need to ask Karlina. For sure, I do not answer for her."

He nodded. "But if Karlina says she will speak to me, you do not mind? I don't want there to be any more problems between us."

"There will be no more problems between us, Berndt." Anton reached for a piece of hose, inserted it into the bucket, and then looked at me. "I would like to keep working on my feeding machine, so maybe the two of you could go to another part of the barn to have your talk, ja?"

"I think we could do that." I smiled at Anton before I stood and walked alongside Berndt to a nearby stall. A breeze cut through the open door of the barn, and the familiar smell of hay and damp wool filled my nostrils as I turned toward Berndt. "You want to talk about Dovie. What is it you want to know?"

He pulled off his hat and scratched his head. "She acted very odd yesterday. Several times I asked her what was wrong, but she continued to tell me that nothing was the matter and she was having a good time. But I could see that she wasn't. And her mind was somewhere else." He rolled his cap and shoved it into his pocket. "Did she say anything to you? Have I done something to make her angry? All night I tried to think of anything I'd done or said that might be improper, but I could think of nothing."

What could I say to him? I had no answers. "She didn't act like herself yesterday, but I do not think it had anything to do with you. Although she didn't mention anything, I wonder if she was feeling unwell yesterday. You should not worry yourself, Berndt."

"That is what I tell myself, but it is hard when you care for someone like I care for Dovie."

My throat caught at his declaration. "Have you told her that you care for her?"

Berndt pulled his hat from his pocket and wrung it between his hands. "A little. I think she knows, but I must be careful. To fall in love with a girl from the outside presents more problems than even I know how to handle." He leaned against the wooden slats of the stall. "Do you think Dovie intends to remain in the colonies?"

"She has never, not once, mentioned staying here for gut. I know that she is not eager to leave just yet, but her father is in Texas, and each day I think a letter will arrive telling her she should come and join him." I placed my palm on my chest. "I do not want you to end up being hurt when she goes to Texas."

He bobbed his head. "Ja, I know. My Vater has told me the same thing. He does not want me to spend my free time with her."

"And my Mutter has warned Dovie, as well. I think they fear you both will suffer if you should care for each other as more than friends."

He dug the toe of his boot into the straw. "It is too late for that, Karlina. How does a man stop himself from caring for someone? It is like trying to catch rain when there is a hole in the bucket. Impossible."

Pain shone in his eyes, and my heart ached for him. "Then you must look to the Lord for help and guidance, for I have no answers for you."

He unfurled his cap and pulled it onto his head. "Before we parted yesterday, Dovie asked me some questions about my family. Do you know why she would ask about them?"

I folded my arms and met his steady gaze. "What kind of questions?"

"She wanted to know if I had ever lived with my Oma and Opa."

"And what did you tell her?"

"I told her ja, that we all lived in the same house until they died. Right after I told her is when she said she wanted to go home. When we got back to the house and I asked her if we could go skating on Saturday afternoon, she said she would be busy."

My thoughts swirled like a blizzard in winter. I didn't know what to make of Dovie's questions to Berndt. I didn't know of any reason she couldn't go skating on Saturday. Worst of all, I didn't know how to help him.

"Will you talk to her, see if you can find out something for me? Tell her that I want to see her and I care for her?"

I swallowed hard. "I don't know if that's wise. Your Vater and my Mutter have both—"

"Please. Just speak to her, and if she says she doesn't want to spend time with me, I will not bother her again."

Though I wasn't certain I was making the right decision, I agreed.

Berndt started for the door, stopped, and turned. "There was one more thing Dovie asked me."

I took a step forward. "What was that?"

"She wanted to know where Sister Elsa lives."

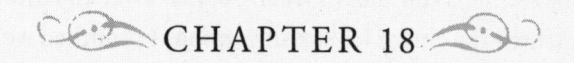

CHAPTER 18

March 1893
Dovie

More than a month had passed since I'd read the letters in Cousin Louise's room, but my questions still remained unanswered. Berndt had told me where Sister Elsa lived, but finding the time and opportunity to speak to her alone had proved a challenge.

A close watch on Sister Fuch's Küche finally reaped the benefit I had hoped for. Each afternoon I had waited out of sight as some of the sisters filed out of the Küche to go home for an hour or two after the noonday meal. Unfortunately, Sister Elsa hadn't been among those who departed to complete personal chores during the afternoon. Not until today.

I smiled at the sight of her, pleased I hadn't given up my vigil. Once she bid the other sisters good-bye and turned the corner, I hurried along the wooden sidewalk. Taking long strides, I soon closed the gap. "Guten Tag, Sister Elsa." She stopped short and wheeled around on her heel. "I hope I didn't startle you."

She clasped her lightweight cloak against the late March breeze. "Only a little." She smiled and pointed toward the cloudless blue sky. "Is gut weather we have now. Springtime is my favorite, and it is approaching."

The warmer weather had been welcomed by most everyone. Everyone except Jakub and his sister, Sophia. Over and over Jakub had lamented the end of ice skating season. I promised we could continue to meet at the pond, but I knew he'd be like the other men—busy preparing and planting the fields. Springtime afternoons would not grant the freedom winter had permitted, and I would see less of him.

"I like this time of year, too."

Sister Elsa darted a glance to the empty space behind me. "You are alone?" Her voice bore a cautious tone.

"Yes. But just like you, this is my free time away from the Küche." Hoping to set her at ease, I smiled and drew closer. "I wanted to ask you about something you said when I came to Sister Fuch's house when we were quilting."

Her features settled in a deep frown. I didn't know if she was trying to recall the event or if my question annoyed her. When she didn't reply, I decided to continue. "You said my mother, Sister Barbara, was very unhappy when she left here. I think you said she was in love with someone named Erich? Is that right?"

"If you have questions about Sister Barbara, you should talk to Sister Louise. She is the best one to tell you anything you want to know." She stopped in front of a sandstone house—the one I had learned was her residence. Turning toward me, she crossed her index and middle fingers. "Sister Louise and Sister Barbara were as close as blood sisters." She bobbed her head. "Ja, Sister Louise can answer your questions better than I."

I thanked her and turned toward home. There was no need to push for anything more. Sister Elsa's lips were sealed, and I had a strong suspicion Cousin Louise was the one who had sealed them.

A robin sang a warbling announcement of spring's anticipated arrival. All around me I saw evidence of new life. Barren trees had formed new buds, and before long, fruit trees would blossom and early blooming flowers would add a splash of color near the weathered wooden sidewalks. The hills and valleys had already sprouted a new, lush green carpet, where the sheep and cattle would graze. At any other time, the splendor of God's creation would have caused my heart to sing. But after Sister Elsa's unhelpful response, I found it impossible to take pleasure in my surroundings.

Whether I wanted to put the past behind me or not, Cousin Louise had determined to set my sights upon the future. Surely the conclusion I had drawn from the letter was correct. Otherwise Cousin Louise would not be working so hard to keep the truth from me. I returned to the Küche, my thoughts a mixture of determination and surrender. I didn't want to concede defeat, yet it appeared that any further efforts would fail. With the ability of a talented chess player, Cousin Louise had executed plans to block my every move.

"There you are! And just in time to help. I didn't know where you went." Cousin Louise motioned for me to hang my jacket and come to the worktable. "Karlina said she thought you had gone down to the pond, but Sister Bertha said you'd gone in the other direction."

Her unasked question hung between us like a morning fog. "It is a beautiful day so I went for a walk to see if any of the flowers had begun to bloom in the village." Though my answer was not entirely true, I had been looking at the blooming foliage as I walked to Sister Fuch's Küche and on my way home, as well.

"I am glad you have returned. You remember I told you about dying Easter eggs for the children?"

I nodded. Last week Cousin Louise had explained that each Küchebaas dyed Easter eggs and baked Easter cookies for the children who ate in her Küche. These were special tasks that appeared to please Cousin Louise. She had explained that we would dye the eggs between church services on Good Friday because there was less meal preparation on that day.

"Tomorrow we will dye the eggs, but today we will boil them." She glanced toward the window. "I hope the weather stays warm for Easter. It is so early this year that it would not surprise me to wake up to snow." She shook her head as if the snow had already begun to fall.

I arched my brows. With such warm weather today and Easter arriving on Sunday, I doubted we would need to worry about snow, but I kept my opinion to myself. "Would you like me to go to the cellar and bring up the crocks?"

"Ja. And I will fill the pots so we can boil the eggs." We had been saving the yellow and red onion skins since the first of the year. Cousin Louise said they provided good dye for the hard-boiled eggs, but we would also use some of the dye from the woolen mill for brighter colors. I had been looking forward to the event since I'd first learned of the unusual methods for preparing the Easter eggs. But egg dying wouldn't begin until tomorrow.

She pointed to the side table. "I have mixed up one batch of cookie dough. We can bake cookies this afternoon and dye eggs tomorrow when the other sisters are here to help."

"I thought Karlina wanted to help with the cookies. Should I go down to the barn and tell her we're going to bake?"

"Nein. One of the ewes dropped triplets, and Karlina is needed at the barn."

"Dropped?" I pictured babies falling from their mother's arms.

Cousin Louise looked at me as though I'd grown two heads. "Ja, dropped. Gave birth to triplets."

I slapped my palm on my forehead. How silly of me. Of course! I hiked a shoulder. "I grew up in the city, Cousin Louise. I am not accustomed to farm language."

"Well, it is time you learned, since the ewes will be *dropping* their lambs from now until the end of April. When we finish, you should go to the barn and see them." She lifted a kettle of water onto the stove. "Lambing and shearing seasons are the times when visitors come to East. Everyone wants to come and see the lambs or watch the shearers' skills. And who can blame them? Those are gut times of the year. But right now we need to prepare the eggs." She motioned to the door. "Hurry to the cellar and we'll get started."

Boiling the eggs had been a fairly quick and simple process. Once we finished, Cousin Louise removed cookie cutters from one of the cabinets and spread them across the worktable. I traced my fingers over the familiar tin shapes. Large and small rabbits, a squirrel, chicken, lamb, a large sheep, cow, and a pig. "These are like the cookie cutters my Mother and I used to make our sugar cookies. I still have them. They're packed in one of the trunks my father sent to Texas."

Cousin Louise broke off a fat chunk of dough, sifted a light dusting of flour on the worktable, and flattened the dough into a circle. "Ja, I am sure Barbara kept the cookie cutters that belonged to your Oma. She loved baking cookies." Using her rolling pin, Cousin Louise manipulated the dough until it met her requirements for the perfect thickness. She rested a hand on her hip and surveyed the flattened mixture. "That looks gut. You can begin to cut the shapes and place them on the cookie sheets."

Together, Cousin Louise and I rolled, cut, and baked the cookies, filling the air with a sweet vanilla scent. By the time the men arrived for their midafternoon respite, they were sniffing the air like children. "You should not be thinking it is cookies you will be eating," Cousin Louise announced when they looked toward the kitchen with anticipation. "The Easter cookies are for the children, and there are no extras." A chorus of groans could be heard from one end of the dining hall to the other. Cousin Louise laughed at their antics before she pointed to the tables. "You will have to settle for bread and jam with your coffee. We have much to accomplish before Easter."

When Cousin Louise returned to the kitchen a short time later, she instructed me to place the cooled cookies in large crocks. "We will need the space to begin supper preparations. The other sisters will be returning soon."

We had placed the last batch of cookies into a crock when Sister Bertha entered the kitchen. She glanced around the room, her attention settling on the crocks of cookies. "I would have stayed and helped with the Easter cookies, Sister Louise. Why didn't you tell me you were going to bake today? We usually bake the Easter cookies on Good Friday. Why the change this year?" Sister Bertha frowned at me, as though my visit had given rise to the irregularity.

Cousin Louise didn't look up from her work. Instead, she continued to shape and align several rows of sausage patties. "This is not the first time we have baked before Good Friday. We have more children in the Küche this year, and I needed to adjust the schedule so we would have enough time to dye all of the eggs on Good Friday. There would not be time enough to do both in one day." Cousin Louise nodded toward the sink. "But I would be happy for some help washing the dirty bowls and baking pans."

Sister Bertha promptly set to work scrubbing. "I hope the eggs will not be dyed when I arrive tomorrow. You know I enjoy the Easter preparations."

Cousin Louise stepped closer to Sister Bertha. "I will make certain there are plenty of eggs for you to dye tomorrow after first church service."

On Good Friday there would be three services—a fact I'd learned from Karlina. In order to give added thanks to the Lord, holidays in the colonies were celebrated with extra services. In addition, Cousin Louise had explained, Good Friday was a day of fasting, when only bread and water would be consumed. With no meals to prepare, there would be ample time for dying eggs.

Cousin Louise wiggled her index finger for me to draw close. "I am sure you are tired after all the baking, Dovie. You do not need to help with supper, but I would be pleased if you could sort the mail." Her shoulders slumped. "If I do not have it sorted by supper, there will be complaints."

No doubt she was even wearier than I. However, I could be gone from the kitchen, and she could not. "I will be happy to do so, Cousin Louise. And thank you for the opportunity to bake cookies with you."

The afternoon had been pleasant. On several occasions I'd considered asking a question or two, but decided it wouldn't be fruitful. Besides, I was sure it would ruin this special time with Cousin Louise. I scattered the mail across the large oak table, and before I had a chance to place any of the envelopes in their proper cubbyholes, my gaze fell upon a letter bearing my father's distinctive script. The sight of his familiar handwriting was enough to send my heart into a rapid thump that rang in my ears. I longed to hear from him, but with each letter I worried he would expect me to leave the colonies and join him in Texas. I tucked the letter into my pocket and finished sorting the mail.

Once I'd completed the task, I stopped at the kitchen door. "I'm going upstairs until time for supper."

Cousin Louise smiled and waved me toward the stairs. I moved in a slow and methodical fashion, my fingers touching the letter inside my pocket as I ascended the steps. Inside the bedroom Karlina and I shared, I opened the envelope and removed the contents. Once again my father had enclosed extra money for my needs. I had written and told him that Cousin Louise refused his previous monetary offering and there was no need to send additional funds. Did it give him some sort of comfort to send the money? Or perhaps he felt a moral obligation? Who could say? I would again attempt to give the money to Cousin Louise. Perhaps this time she would consider giving it to the elders.

I tucked the money into my skirt pocket and settled on the side of the bed. After scanning the first page I moved on to the second, looking for any indication that my father desired an immediate reunion. It was near the end of the second page that I stopped and reread the passage.

> *I have met a lovely woman since coming to Dallas. I think you will like her very much. She is eager to meet you, but since I must continue to work long hours and you have indicated a desire to remain in Iowa a while longer, I trust you will be pleased to receive my agreement. I would, however, wish to hear from Louise and George that they are willing for you to continue as their guest.*

A lovely woman? Mother had been dead for less than a year and my father had met a *lovely* woman? Tears threatened and I pressed my fingertips to my mouth. I didn't want to cry.

What was it Mrs. Lowenstein, our landlady in Cincinnati, had told me shortly after Mother's death? *"Women grieve, but men replace. Your father will remarry quickly, so you better find a man and make a life of your own."* I had thought her foolish—and I'd said so—but it appeared Mrs. Lowenstein had been correct. Maybe if I had gone to Texas with him, this wouldn't have happened. Father wouldn't have been so lonely. I returned downstairs to join the others for supper. If my father decided to marry this woman, I had only myself to blame.

Dying Easter eggs didn't hold the same anticipation for me as it had yesterday. My father's letter had cast a shadow over the experience. Cousin Louise stepped to my side and handed me a piece of string. "Tie it around the egg, and when you drop it into the tinted water, it will create a design."

Carefully, I wrapped the string in various directions before I dropped it into the water. When I lifted the egg from the onion-skin-tinted water bath, it was a lovely honey color. After the egg dried, I removed the string and viewed the unique pattern that remained on the shell. While I continued dying string eggs, Karlina used a stylus of beeswax to write names or draw designs on the eggs before dipping them into the water.

Sister Bertha had taken charge of the dyes from the woolen factory. Pots of water had been set to boil, while glue from the woodshop was mixed with dye in a smaller pan. The smaller pan was balanced on the large pot of boiling water and had to be stirred until it bubbled. "It will thicken as it cools," Sister Bertha said with an air of authority. She had commandeered several of the other women and set them to stirring the various pots of red, blue, and green dye.

When the pans of dye had cooled, Cousin Louise picked up an egg and motioned for me to join her. Carefully, she rolled the egg in the jelled substance and lifted it for me to see. The color held fast and the egg turned a brilliant red.

"It's beautiful."

"It is the use of our dyes and the way we mix it with the glue.

The combination makes the colors more vivid than any other Easter eggs you will ever see." She smiled. "You try." She handed me an egg, but I shook my head. "What is the matter with you? Yesterday you were in gut spirits and excited about the egg dying, but today you seem like a different girl. Something has happened that I do not know about?"

I told Cousin Louise about the letter from my father, but I didn't mention the lovely lady he'd met—only that he was busy working. "He asked if you would write and tell him whether it would be an imposition to have me remain a while longer."

"And you are worried that I will tell him you must leave?" She patted my shoulder. "We told him you were welcome to stay with us until he was settled. That has not changed." She rolled another egg in the blue dye. "I will write him this evening. Now that we have settled your worries, I want you to enjoy dying eggs, ja?"

I picked up an egg and rolled it in my hand. "I'll do my best, Cousin Louise."

When I didn't smile, she pressed closer. "This is a time of year when we reflect on the sacrifice of our Lord—His death on the cross to give us the gift of eternal life." She hesitated a moment. "This time of year brings sadness as well as joy. We are sad the Lord was required to suffer for us, yet joyful He rose from the dead, and we will be with Him in heaven one day. I am sure your Mutter taught you all of these things." I didn't miss the question in her voice.

I nodded my head. "Yes. We went to church. Not every day like here, but we went on Sundays. I have learned about Jesus."

The corners of her mouth lifted in a broad smile. "That is gut. Since you are going to remain in the colonies a while longer, I could ask your Vater if he would like you to attend services with us. I think George could persuade the elders it would be wise. Would be gut for your heart. Would you like that?"

I nodded. "I came here to learn about my mother's past, and I think taking part in church services will help me learn more about her."

Cousin Louise's smile faded a little. I didn't think my answer was exactly what she'd expected—or wanted.

CHAPTER 19

April 1893
Karlina

After the first set of triplets arrived, lambing season began in earnest. Several ewes gave birth to twins the following week, and then another set of triplets was born. In addition, there were numerous single births and all were healthy. We didn't normally have this many multiple births so early in the season, and I wondered if it was a sign there would be even more arriving later. I hoped not, for single lambs had a much greater chance of survival.

My father looked up as I entered the barn. "Another set of twins early this morning," he told me. "We are having quite a year." He pointed to a distant stall and grinned. "They are over there."

I hurried to take a peek at the newborn lambs. The lambs and their mother appeared healthy and content. "They look gut. No problems with the birth?"

"Nein. The mother needed no assistance." He shook his head.

"It will not be the same with this one." I walked across the barn to where my father had positioned himself beside a laboring ewe. "Anton! You need to come over here and help so you will know how to do this in the future."

"I am working with the feeding machine."

My father had been pleased with Anton's invention to feed lambs that couldn't be nursed by their mothers. The machine had already been put to good use this spring, and after a bit of encouragement, the lambs had taken to suckling from the device. But now it seemed Anton wanted to work only with feeding the lambs in order to perfect his invention. And while I thought his idea praiseworthy, there was much more for him to learn and other tasks that needed his attention. And his response to my father had been both disrespectful and disobedient.

"Leave the feeding machine and come here. Now!" My father craned his neck to see if Anton was on his way.

I wanted Anton to hurry up before my father lost patience. My father was not a man who shouted angry words of frustration, but when pushed to his limit, he would mete out punishment appropriate to the misdeed. I feared he would assign Anton tasks that would keep him away from his inventions if he did not heed my father's direction.

Only a few moments passed before Anton strode toward us. "I was helping that small lamb that was born yesterday. It is having some trouble learning to use the feeding station." He rounded the end of the stall. "With two sets of triplets, it has been a big help."

My father waved him forward. "It has helped, but there is more to learn than feeding the lambs, Anton. Right now, this ewe is having some trouble and may need help. I want you to watch so that you can assist in the future." The ewe was lying on her side with her head turned in the air. "She's been straining for over an hour, and I'm going to check her to find out the problem. Come over here and kneel down beside me."

My father covered his right hand and forearm with a thick coating of lard, spoke softly to the ewe, and then inserted his hand into the ewe's birth canal. "The lamb's legs are back rather than in the forward position. When this happens, you must cup the lamb's hooves in your palm and bring them forward. If the lamb is small, it can be pulled with one leg back. If it is normal size, both legs need to be forward."

Anton looked back and forth between my father and the wide-eyed ewe. "But what if you cannot bring both legs forward?" I didn't miss the tremor in his voice, nor did my father.

"First, you remain calm so that the animal does not sense any fear. Then you slip a soft rope onto the legs, like this." My father picked up a piece of soft rope that he had fitted with loops at both ends and slipped them onto the lamb's front legs. "It's necessary to push the head back far enough so that the legs can be drawn forward." My father performed the task with such quickness and ease that he'd completed the task as he finished the explanation. He removed the loops from the lamb's legs and stood up.

Anton appeared relieved that he hadn't been required to help. "I don't know if I could do that, Brother George."

"You will be amazed at the things you can do. When you feel unprepared for a task, you should repeat the Bible verse in Philippians that says, 'I can do all things through Christ which strengtheneth me.'"

Anton nodded, but I didn't think he appeared convinced. "That is a gut verse, Brother George, but if I must help one of these ewes give birth, I would like to have you, as well as the Lord, by my side."

My father chuckled. "You will receive more training before you are left alone to help any ewes in distress. But I cannot be with you all the time, so instead of worrying with your inventions during the lambing season, you need to use your time to learn more about the sheep and their care. That way you will gain the needed confidence."

When Anton looked toward the feeding station at the other side of the barn, I wondered if he'd truly heard my father's admonition. "So we are done here?"

"We need to make certain the mother claims her newborn and that the lamb nurses. If she hasn't nursed within a half hour, we'll give them some encouragement and put them in one of the closed stalls so they can bond. For now, we'll keep our distance and watch them. You can do that while I go and wash up."

Anton remained near the stall, but the ewe and her newborn lamb didn't hold his attention. Instead, he peered longingly toward the feeding machine. I closed the distance between us. "You would be wise to keep your focus over here," I whispered. "My father is a kind man, but he expects you to follow his orders. I'll go over and see if the feeding machine is working properly."

"Thank you, Karlina."

I glanced over my shoulder and sighed when I saw him watching me. I motioned for him to turn back to the ewe and then continued across the barn. I was surprised by Anton's concern over the invention. It had been working quite well, and there was no need for him to hover over the lambs while they nursed.

I smiled at the two lambs suckling at the machine. They had quickly accepted nursing from the bucket of goats' milk that was attached to tubes and nipples. Both of the lambs were thriving, but they had been the strongest from each set of triplets. Instead of removing the smallest lamb from the ewe, my father would take the strongest. "The little ones need their mother's milk the most," he had told me when I questioned the practice. "The larger ones will survive if we hand-feed them with goats' milk."

Because my father was careful with breeding and the amount

of food the ewes received, we didn't have as many triplets as some sheep farms, but we seldom lost any of the triplets. When I was young, I had hoped every ewe would have triplets. But after learning of the difficulties for both the lambs and the ewe, I changed my mind.

I loved lambing season. The new life among the sheep matched the arrival of spring and the time of rebirth throughout all of nature. This was the time of year when joy bubbled inside me like a rippling stream. Along with their mothers, the firstborn lambs were already frolicking in the pasture near the barn. Soon we would take them to more distant pastures, but for now they remained under close supervision, where predators could more easily be kept at bay.

The lambs had completed their feeding, and I was preparing to take them outside when I heard a woman's voice drift from the other side of the barn. Squinting my eyes, I strained to gain a better view. The woman was talking to Anton. I saw him shake his head. She grasped his arm, tipped her head back, and giggled. Who was this woman, and why didn't Anton move away from her? Though her appearance was that of an Amana woman, her forward behavior caused me to think otherwise. A flame ignited deep inside me as she continued her possessive hold on his arm.

Keeping to the shadows, I tiptoed across the hay-strewn floor until I was close enough to hear. Then I positioned myself behind one of the thick support beams. Eavesdropping wasn't proper, but hanging on to a man's arm was inappropriate. Besides, I simply could not stop myself. When the woman glanced over her shoulder, I captured a glimpse of her profile. She looked to be close to my own age and quite pretty. Jealousy now fanned the flame that had ignited in my heart.

Anton had professed he cared for me, so why did he continue to talk to this young woman? I peeked around the edge of the beam. She smiled up at him, and my stomach clenched. "I know you still care for me, but you need not worry. I won't tell my brother—or anyone else." She released his arm and brushed his cheek with her fingers. "Not until you're ready."

I gasped. As I turned away, my arm struck a pitchfork and it crashed to the floor. Both Anton and his friend pivoted toward me. I wanted to flee from their presence, but my feet remained planted like a couple of deep-rooted trees.

Anton extended his hand toward me. "Karlina! Come and meet Violet."

My gaze shifted from his face to hers. Her lips curved in a frozen smile as she took a step toward me. "Guten Tag, Karlina. I am Violet Nagel—from High. I am a dear friend of Anton's." She had once again wrapped her fingers around his arm.

"Ja, so I can see."

Anton pulled free of her grasp and walked toward me. "Violet and I grew up together. Her family lived down the street from mine. She has a brother, Frank. He is my age."

Violet hurried after him. "Anton and I are even better friends than he was with my brother." She looked up and batted her eyelashes at him.

"How did you manage to come to East for a visit with Anton?"

Traveling from village to village was unusual. There were only a few times each year when residents might travel to another village. And when those trips took place, it wouldn't be a young woman traveling by herself. Seeing Violet alone in the barn and learning she'd traveled from High both annoyed and fascinated me.

"My Vater is with me. He needed to go to Main to see Dr. Zimmer. I asked to come along so we could stop in East and see Anton."

"I am sorry your Vater is ill. He is waiting in the buggy for you?" I was surprised an ill man would be traveling such a distance.

Usually our doctors would travel to care for someone who needed medical attention.

"My Vater is the doctor in High. He needed to discuss a medical matter and borrow some medical instruments from Dr. Zimmer." She nudged Anton. "Which means I can come along when he returns the items to Dr. Zimmer. Won't that be nice?"

Anton shot a look at me. "You should not come because of me, Violet. We are very busy with the sheep."

"Not too busy for a few minutes with those you care about, I hope."

Anton ran his index finger beneath his collar. "I care about all the people in High, but that does not mean I have time to visit with them. You know that much depends upon how well I am able to adapt to my work here in East."

"That's one of the reasons I wanted to stop and visit with you. I feared you might hold me responsible for your banishment to this . . . this . . . place." She sniffed and curled her lip as though he'd been exiled to the most horrible location on earth. "I wanted to assure you that my feelings run deep and this was none of my doing. I defended you."

Discomfort replaced my earlier interest. Violet's comments had taken a much more personal turn. They bore a flavor that made me think Anton's affections for me had been nothing more than pretense. I'd heard enough to believe that more than friendship existed between Violet and him. "If you will excuse me, I need to see to the lambs. Thank you for introducing me to your dear friend, Anton."

He stepped forward and blocked my path. "You do not need to go. The lambs are fine. Besides, I am sure Violet would enjoy learning more about the sheep."

We both looked at him as though he'd lost his senses, but it was Violet who spoke first. "I am sure that if I have any questions, you would be the best one to answer."

"I believe you're correct, Violet." I gestured for Anton to step aside. When he didn't immediately move, I gave him a look that said, *You'd better get out of my way.*

He shuffled one step to the right, leaving me only a narrow space. As I squeezed past him, he leaned close to my ear. "I want to speak to you later. This is not what you think."

I didn't acknowledge the remark, for I knew my eyes and ears had not deceived me.

On the way home from prayer meeting while my mother and father were engaged in conversation, Anton drew near. "I want to explain about Violet."

"There is nothing to explain. She is your dear friend from High."

"She is not a *dear* friend—she is an *old* friend."

I arched my brows. "She is my age, I would guess."

"Ach! I did not mean she is old in years. I have known her since we were children, so we have been gut friends a long time."

I shrugged. "You told me that earlier. I don't know why you feel you must continue to explain. It makes no difference to me."

"It makes a difference or you would not be acting cold toward me. You think that there is something more than friendship between us, but I am telling you there is not."

"Really?" I gave him a sidelong glance. "I think it is Violet who needs your explanation, not me. From what I heard, she believes there is a great deal more than friendship."

"Then she is wrong."

"Tell me, Anton, did you kiss her on the cheek and tell her that you think she is wonderful? Did you whisper the same sweet words to her that you have said to me?" I hissed the words at him, careful to keep my voice low so that my parents would not hear.

"I think Violet hoped that one day we would be more than friends, but I did not encourage her. No matter what anyone in High says, I never encouraged her."

I wondered at his final comment. Why would others in High think he cared for Violet if he'd never given any indication? A lump rose in my throat and tears threatened. I blinked hard and squeezed my lips into a thin line. I would not cry!

But I would guard my heart.

CHAPTER 20

Dovie

Ever since I'd read some of the letters my mother had written to Cousin Louise, I'd struggled to comprehend the contents. How I wished I could have read all of them. I was sure there was more I would have discovered. Over and over I recalled what had been written. I also contemplated what had not been written but only intimated.

As I considered the contents of those missives, I arrived at only one conclusion: Berndt Lehmann was my half brother. Berndt was the child my mother had mentioned in her letter, the child that Erich's parents had begrudgingly agreed to care for, the child she had left behind.

My stomach roiled at the thought. That was the real reason Cousin Louise and Berndt's father wanted to keep us apart. They didn't want me to find out. Worse yet, they didn't want us to fall in love with each other. It all made perfect sense, yet it made no sense at all. Could my mother have given birth to a child and left him behind? Had she hidden the child's birth from my father? Was that why she'd told him so little about her life in Amana? She feared he might discover the child born out of wedlock?

There was so much I wanted to know. Did Brother Erich's wife know about my mother? Did Berndt think she was his mother? To ask him such a question would be impossible, yet I wanted to know. And had my grandparents' decision to leave the colonies been based upon feelings of disgrace? I knew little of how such a situation would have been handled in the village, yet there surely must have been talk. All the ladies in the Küche must have known. Were they forbidden by the elders to speak of such matters?

Perhaps I would soon learn, since tomorrow I was going to attend Sunday meeting with the rest of the family. Cousin George had gained the accord of the elders. Because I would be remaining in the colonies for a prolonged period of time, and because I had expressed a desire to attend meetings, the elders decided I should be encouraged to do so.

As usual, Sister Bertha was the first to arrive at the kitchen this morning. Cousin Louise smiled and greeted her. "I am glad you are here early, Sister Bertha. Pour a cup of coffee. We need to talk."

A fleeting look of suspicion crossed Sister Bertha's weathered face, but she removed a cup from the shelf, wrapped the corner of her apron around the handle of the coffeepot, and poured herself a cup of the steaming brew. She carried the brimming cup to the worktable and pulled out one of the tall stools.

"So what do we need to discuss? You need help planning the spring menu?"

I had learned that the weekly menus remained the same through-out each season. Every Monday we served the same meals through the winter. Every Tuesday we served the same meals, and so on. A change in the menus occurred only when we moved from one season to the next. In winter, the fruits and vegetables we canned or dried were served. In spring and summer, the abundant fresh produce from the kitchen gardens graced the tables. The spring menu didn't need to be planned, but Sister Bertha liked to feel she contributed to such decisions. At least that's what Cousin Louise had told me.

"Nein. We don't need to worry about menus, Sister Bertha." Cousin Louise had settled on a stool across the worktable. "I am going to need your help in the Küche on Sundays."

The older woman arched her bushy gray eyebrows. *"Ich?"*

"Ja, you. The elders have decided it would be gut if Dovie attended Sunday meeting while she is here. It will help her learn more about our ways. For now, Brother George and I thought she could attend every other Sunday. That way she could still help in the kitchen when not at services. Since you have worked on Sundays in the past, I naturally thought of you."

Sister Bertha exhaled a deep sigh. "Why not ask Sister Marta to return to Sunday mornings? It was her job before Sister Dovie arrived. I do not like to miss Sunday meeting." She shook her head and frowned.

Cousin Louise nodded. "Well, I will not force you, but Sister Marta has not been well these past weeks, and I don't think she should take charge any longer. I thought of you because you are the most capable and have more Küche skills than the younger women."

Sister Bertha's frown faded as Cousin Louise showered her with praise. "For sure, I would not want Sister Marta's health to suffer. It is true that I have excellent skills in the kitchen. The elders should have assigned me my own Küche long ago." Her eyes shone with sadness as she uttered the sorrowful lament.

Cousin Louise seized the opportunity. "Then this will be your chance to be the Küchebaas every other Sunday morning. When

I return from meeting, you can continue to be in charge, if you'd like." The older woman stared into her coffee cup, obviously weighing the idea. When she didn't reply, Cousin Louise leaned across the worktable. "You are well versed in the Scriptures and testimonies of our leaders, but Sister Dovie has received limited religious training."

Sister Bertha lifted her head and looked at me. "It is true you need to be learning the Bible and studying to lead a good and useful life." She turned her attention to Cousin Louise. "And it is true that, because of my age, I have had more years of training than the rest of you. So I have decided I am the best choice to fill the position."

"Thank you, Sister Bertha. It will be gut to have your help on Sundays." Cousin Louise pushed up from her stool.

The older sister stretched her neck and tipped her head like a rooster preparing to crow. "Help? I will not be helping. I will be in charge." She lifted her cup and took a swallow. After placing the cup on the table, she looked in my direction. "You wish to thank me?"

Knowing a show of gratitude was expected, I bobbed my head. "Thank you for your willingness to serve, Sister Bertha. I appreciate your sacrifice."

"You are welcome. I know the Lord is pleased that I am going to give you the opportunity to worship." She picked up her cup and carried it to the sink.

As the other sisters arrived, Cousin Louise drew close to me and winked. "Sister Bertha would deny that she is sometimes filled with pride, but today I think her pride is a benefit to the three of us—and to the Lord, if such a thing is possible." She chuckled as she picked up a knife and began to slice the bread.

The following morning I donned one of my dark mourning dresses and added one of Karlina's dark shoulder shawls with a long point in the back. This would be different from the meeting I had attended as a guest at Christmastime. Today I would attend in order to learn more about my mother's faith.

"Turn around and let me make certain the point is in the center." Karlina arranged it at the shoulders and gave the point a slight tug. "It is gut. Now cross the points in front and hold them, and I will tie the apron around your waist."

I did as she told me and then turned for her approval. She nodded and handed me one of her caps made of fine black gauze and trimmed with a row of black tatted edging. Black satin ribbons hung from each side of the cap and were long enough to tie beneath my chin. I brushed my hand down the front of the crisp black apron. "This is very different from the clothing worn to church in Cincinnati. There some of the ladies wear hats decorated with flowers and feathers. Some of the decorations are so large that you can't see around them. And always the ladies wear fancy dresses. Only the women who cannot afford better would wear unadorned clothing to church."

Karlina bobbed her head. "Here it is the opposite. Years ago, before our relatives left Germany and came to this country, they rebelled against the worldliness of the church. It was back then that the women chose to wear simple dark clothing and refrain from dressing in elaborate clothing or wearing fancy hats." She placed a gauze cap over her shiny brown hair. The black ribbons hung loose on either side of her chin. "We are taught that such adornment can lead to vanity."

"Having attended a few of the large churches in Cincinnati, I think there is probably some truth in that belief. My mother always said Easter Sunday was more a fashion show than a time of worship."

Together we walked downstairs, where Sister Bertha had taken full charge of the kitchen. When Cousin Louise tried to help her with breakfast preparations, the older sister had sent her away. When I attempted to help clean up after breakfast, she'd told me she didn't need my help. She had, however, made good use of the two junior girls who were assigned to work on Sunday mornings. They were scurrying from kitchen to dining room like mice on a sinking ship.

Sister Bertha walked to the foot of the stairs and gave a nod of approval as she passed by Karlina and me. "Make sure you are not late—late to meeting is not acceptable."

Karlina frowned at the older woman, and once Sister Bertha returned to the kitchen, Karlina leaned close to my ear. "She acts like she is the only person who knows the rules. I feel sorry for the girls who must stay and work with her. From now on, I think they will dread Sunday morning in the Küche."

As soon as Karlina's parents and Anton joined us, we departed. Since my arrival, both Karlina and Cousin Louise had explained snippets of church history and practices to me. I was glad for that, as it would help me to feel more at ease today and in the weeks to come.

We were approaching the meetinghouse when Cousin Louise motioned Karlina and me forward. "We will be attending the second meeting, but Karlina will attend third meeting with you, so you won't be alone, Dovie."

I hoped Karlina didn't mind, for I realized that she normally attended second gathering. Cousin Louise had explained that there were three congregations, and members were assigned by their age and spiritual state. The first meeting was for the older and most pious members. They met in a small room in the meetinghouse. Most of those assigned to the second gathering were middle-aged, and they met at the same time, but in a different assembly room. The third group consisted of children over the age of seven and the young married people. Since I wasn't yet versed in the faith, I was assigned to third church.

Karlina squeezed my hand. "I am pleased to attend with you. The others will know that I'm there to sit with you, and that I have not been demoted because of bad behavior."

I had learned that the elders could promote members from one group to another, or move members further back in the room as a sign of increasing piety. On the other hand, elders could also demote members to a lower church or move them to a bench closer to the front as a sign of diminished piety. Because of my status, I would be sitting near the front in the third meeting—and so would Karlina.

We entered through the door assigned to the women, and Karlina led the way to the proper meeting room, where we took our place in the front row on the women's side. "Thank you for your willingness to sit in front with me," I whispered.

She nodded and smiled, but kept her eyes straight ahead. Feet shuffled and benches creaked as the boys and girls and the men and women shuffled into the room from their respective doors. Soon the elders walked to the front of the room and took their seats on the long bench. One of the elders read Scripture from the Bible, and another read and instructed from the testimonies of former church leaders. I did my best to listen to what was being said, but my eyes tended to wander and compare the starkness of the interior to the church we had attended in Cincinnati. Here there was nothing but the unadorned glass windows, pale blue walls, bare pine floors, and benches that had been crafted of solid wood with no thought of comfort in their construction.

When the service ended, I was thankful to leave behind the hard wooden bench. Karlina held my arm as we exited the church. "We will wait for Mutter and Vater. Sometimes first and second gathering is a little longer." She smiled. "I think this service is shorter because some of the children can't sit still for long."

Karlina waved to Anton. As he strolled toward us, Karlina told me that he had been assigned to third church when he'd come from High, but he had since advanced to a position further back. "I think he will soon be promoted to second gathering."

He glanced at the clear blue sky as he came alongside Karlina. "With such beautiful weather, I am thinking there will be a lot of visitors to see the lambs this afternoon."

"I am sure you are hoping Violet will return to see you." Karlina's voice was as cold as winter's first frost.

I looked back and forth between them and wished I could escape before the conversation turned more personal. Karlina and I had discussed Violet's visit to the barn earlier in the month. Karlina had told me Anton refused to admit he and Violet were anything more than friends. A claim Karlina didn't choose to believe. When I'd suggested she might be drawing an incorrect conclusion, she'd become angry with me. We agreed we wouldn't discuss the matter further, so I was surprised when she mentioned Violet in front of me.

Anton squared his shoulders and shook his head. "You are making something out of nothing, Karlina. I am not going to argue with you. Whether or not Violet comes to see the lambs is of no importance to me." He moved away from the tree. "Please tell your Mutter and Vater that I have gone back to the house." He turned and strode away before Karlina could say anything to detain him.

"He isn't fooling me one bit. He is in love with Violet, and I am sure she is part of the reason he was sent to East."

I folded my arms across my waist. "You became unhappy with me the last time we talked about Violet and Anton so we agreed we would not discuss them anymore."

"Ja, I know what we agreed." She frowned at Anton's back as he retreated from the churchyard. "And I know I am right about him."

I nudged her arm and gestured toward the women's door. "Who is the woman talking to your mother?"

"That is Sister Anna, Berndt's mother. Have you never met her? I thought she was present when you went to the quilting at Sister Fuch's."

"No, she wasn't there. I have never met her." First and second gatherings had finished, and men and women were exiting their respective doors.

"Come. I will introduce you. She's very shy but nice. She works at the Kinderschule."

My hands turned clammy at the idea of meeting the woman everyone referred to as Berndt's mother. A part of me wanted to meet her, yet another part remained hesitant. Karlina grasped my hand and pulled me forward. Before I could protest, I was standing in front of Cousin Louise and Sister Anna.

Cousin Louise smiled and held out her hand. "This is Dovie, my cousin Barbara's daughter."

Sister Anna leaned toward me. "I am pleased to meet you. Berndt has spoken of you."

I wanted to know what Berndt had told her, but I refrained from asking. "I am pleased to meet you, as well."

Cousin Louise took my arm. "Everything went gut for you in meeting?"

"Yes. I didn't lose my voice when it was my turn to read Scripture." The evening before I had expressed fear that the words would get stuck in my throat and I wouldn't be able to speak.

"I told you the Lord would be with you."

"Guten Tag, Sister Dovie." All three of us looked up as Berndt came to a halt beside his mother, who frowned and then nodded toward Cousin Louise. "Guten Tag, Sister Louise." He turned to me. "You have met my Mutter, ja?"

I nodded. "Cousin Louise introduced us."

His lips curved in a broad smile, but his mother didn't appear quite so pleased. "Your Vater is waiting for you, Berndt."

He nodded. "Today will be a gut day for viewing all the lambs, don't you think?"

I wasn't certain to whom he was speaking, but neither Cousin Louise nor his mother replied, so I spoke. "Anton says he thinks there will be a lot of visitors today."

"Berndt." His mother pursed her lips and glanced toward where the men had gathered.

He waved and hurried away, but not before I saw the look in his eyes. He wanted me to meet him when he came to see the lambs today. But now that I had discovered we were related, I needed to do exactly what Cousin Louise and Berndt's father had wanted all along—stay far away from him.

But could I?

My stomach clenched, and I knew the answer. Not when he might be the best possible link to discovering the truth.

# CHAPTER 21

Berndt had appeared on Sunday afternoon, but not alone. Sister Anna had accompanied him. When I saw her at his side, I decided Cousin Louise and his mother had joined forces to assure his time with me would be limited to bread deliveries, so I had remained at a distance.

As soon as I heard the bread wagon's jangling bells the following day, I hurried outside. Berndt jumped down from the wagon and rushed to my side. "I am sorry we could not spend time together yesterday. My Mutter never wants to come and see the lambs, but she was determined to come with me yesterday."

"You don't need to apologize, Berndt. I think your parents and Cousin Louise have all agreed we should not spend time together."

"Ja, my Mutter and Vater say it is not wise for me to keep company with you—that if I want to take a wife, I should decide upon a gut Amana girl."

A roar of condemnation sounded in my ears. Because I was not an *Amana girl*, had they labeled me as less than good? Was I considered no more than a pariah to be shunned by the *good* people? My mind told me my thoughts were an exaggeration of the truth, but my heart squeezed in a tight knot. I was an outsider and therefore an undesirable mate for any man in the colonies. It didn't matter that my mother had once been one of them—I was not. And why did it matter, anyway? I had not come here with any aspirations of becoming one of them. I'd come with only one goal in mind: to discover the truth about my mother and the reasons her family left East so many years ago.

I inhaled and tried to calm down. "I did not know that being my friend would create so many concerns for everyone, but I do not want to be the cause of trouble for you. I understand you need to follow your parents' wishes."

He motioned for me to follow him to the rear of the wagon. "I do not need my parents to tell me who can be my friend. I am no longer a little boy, but a man—old enough to choose a woman to love and marry, if I want."

"You may be old enough, but the elders will decide if you've made the proper choice. And from what I have learned, they can withhold their approval, so you need to be careful with your choice." I reached forward to take the bread tray from him. "I only wish I could reassure your mother and Cousin Louise that they need not worry about us. That we are friends—and we will never be anything more."

Berndt's head snapped as though I'd slapped him. His dark eyes seared me like burning coals. "Is that how you feel about me? That I am no more to you than Anton or any of the other young men who live here?"

I swallowed hard and looked away. He was much more to me than any other person in East, but I dared not reveal that truth.

I couldn't tell him we shared the same mother—not until I was positive. "We are dear friends. I didn't mean to lump you together with all of the other young men in the colonies. I am sorry if my words stung. It wasn't my intent." I didn't mention that his earlier words about a good Amana girl had been every bit as hurtful to me.

"And you are still willing to meet me sometimes?" Hope flickered in his dark eyes. "We will be careful so there is no talk. I am sure we can trust Karlina and Anton to help us if need be."

I didn't want to involve Karlina or Anton, but I did want to leave the door open for future visits with Berndt. If I was going to unravel the truth, I'd need him to ask some questions—questions only his father and Sister Anna could answer, because Cousin Louise had become a closed book.

"I don't know how or when we'll meet, since you need to take extra care, but I'll leave those decisions to you."

Berndt removed his cap and waved it toward the back porch. "Guten Morgen, Sister Louise."

"Did you forget that you are here to deliver bread?" Cousin Louise stood on the porch, her hands resting on her ample hips.

"Nein, I did not forget, Sister Louise. Your order is ready." He pointed to the tray I was holding in my arms. He turned his head and kept his voice low. "I will meet you at the pond tomorrow afternoon, ja?"

"Yes," I whispered. I kept my eyes on the bread tray as I approached the porch. I didn't want Cousin Louise to ask any questions.

The following afternoon, I headed off for the pond with questions arranging themselves in my head like one of Cousin Louise's grocery lists. I'd need to be careful. If I flooded Berndt with too many personal questions, he'd become suspicious. Though

I wanted to sit him down and quiz him like a schoolmaster, I knew that would be impossible. I already knew he didn't have any brothers or sisters—Karlina had answered that question. Perhaps I would begin by asking him how long his parents had been married. And if I was fortunate, his answer would lead to a discussion that might tell me much more than expected.

After the noonday meal, I waited until the women had begun to wash the dishes before I approached Cousin Louise. "It's a beautiful day. I think I'll go for a walk if you don't need me." I held my breath and waited. I hadn't considered what I would do if she wanted me to dust the upstairs bedrooms or sort the afternoon mail.

She looked up and smiled. "You go and enjoy yourself. For sure, it is a pretty day the Lord has given us."

I grabbed my bonnet and hurried out the back door before she could change her mind. I didn't need to go far to see and smell the beauty of spring. Crabapple and pear trees heavy with scented blooms and flower gardens lush with bright colors filled the air with their sweet perfume. I inhaled deeply and picked up my pace as I approached the pastures surrounding the barn.

Some of the lambs were outside with the mother ewes, and I stopped to watch as they frolicked after each other. Like children playing follow-the-leader, they climbed onto fallen tree branches and large rocks, then jumped down and chased through the lush grass.

Over and over again they repeated the routine. Instead of playing with the others, one of the small lambs stood on its mother's back and proceeded to survey the area like a night watchman. I giggled as I took in the sight. No wonder Karlina took such pleasure in her work. No matter how difficult life might be, the lambs provided an endearing sight. Soon the ewes would be sheared, and I hoped to witness that event. Karlina said the sheep shearing always drew a crowd of people.

I saw Anton in the distance, his shepherd's crook in his hand as he led the sheep a bit further. From what I'd observed, he appeared to be enjoying his work with the sheep, although he still talked about his inventions far more than the sheep. And I'd observed a look of distaste when Karlina had mentioned the shearing and the fact that he would need to learn the process. I couldn't blame him if he was uneasy about tackling a job that likely required great skill and patience.

I waved but couldn't tell if he'd seen me. He appeared engrossed in keeping the sheep together. No doubt he worried he might lose one or two, though Karlina said Helmut, the furry black-and-white sheep dog, kept a sharp eye for stragglers as well as wolves and wild dogs. When Karlina had first spoken of wolves and wild dogs, I'd turned fearful of venturing across the fields, but she said they were more interested in stray sheep than in humans. And since I'd never seen evidence of any wild animals, I'd pushed aside my fear. Yet as I walked toward the pond I wondered if they posed a special threat to the tiny lambs that chased after each other unaware there might be hidden danger nearby. A chill coursed down my arms, and I tightened my lightweight shawl, but it didn't ease my apprehension.

"I'm being silly," I muttered and lowered my head against the stiff breeze. I had hoped to see Berndt sitting by the pond when I arrived, but he was nowhere in sight. I settled on one of the logs near the fire pit we had used during the cold of winter and waited. With the snap of each twig or crack of a branch, I jumped and turned, sure I would see him approach. I'd been waiting for what seemed at least an hour when I heard a noise from the opposite direction. I trained my eyes across the pond, prepared to run should a wolf or some other wild animal emerge.

Moments later a figure appeared, and I stood to gain a better view. Jakub! I hadn't seen him for some time. He waved and came running toward me at a gallop. I looked over my shoulder to make certain I didn't see Berndt in the distance. I'd never spoken to him about Jakub or his family. I knew he wouldn't approve of my visits to their home. I squinted and continued to watch the road, hoping to catch sight of his sister, Sophia. Should Berndt arrive, it would be better if Jakub's sister was with him. Being seen alone with a young man would be frowned upon—not only by Berndt, but by everyone else in the village.

Jakub came to a jarring halt a few steps in front of me. Perspiration dotted his forehead, and ruddy streaks highlighted his cheekbones. He bent forward, gasping for breath.

"You didn't need to run. I saw you coming and waved."

Strands of black hair fell across his forehead. "I saw, but I was afraid you might leave. I need to speak to you." He wrung his hands together and glanced toward the hillock he'd just crossed.

"What's wrong? Where's Sophia?"

"She's sick. Everyone is sick. Can you come? We need help."

Though it shamed me, I suddenly wanted to turn and run the opposite direction. I'd had enough of illness in the past year. "What kind of sickness?" The thought of walking into a houseful of ill people caused my stomach to flip upside down. I clamped my lower lip between my teeth while I attempted to come up with a solution—a solution that didn't include my going to Jakub's house. "There's a doctor in Main Amana. You can go there. I'm certain he'll come and help."

"My father says no doctor. We don't have money to pay." He continued to wring his hands. "Besides, my father doesn't trust doctors."

"If he doesn't trust a doctor, he surely won't trust someone like me. I don't know anything about medicine and healing." I took a small backward step, hoping Jakub would realize I wasn't what his family needed. "I'm sure the doctor would understand if you can't afford to pay." In truth, I had no idea what the doctor would tell him, but I knew I was not capable of giving medical advice.

He shook his head. "A few years ago we had a doctor for my little sister. She died, and now my father says doctors are no better than butchers."

What would his father think of me if I tried to help and one of them should die? I shivered at the thought.

Jakub reached forward and grasped my hand. "Please come with me, Dovie. I'm very frightened and don't know what to do."

I glanced over my shoulder. Where was Berndt? "I was supposed to meet someone this afternoon. I shouldn't leave."

He dropped his hold on my hand. "I thought you were a friend to my family, Dovie. Friends help each other."

I wasn't certain what bothered me more: the pain reflected in his eyes or the sadness in his voice. My callous words and indifference had wounded him, and rightfully so. His family had treated me with warmth and kindness, yet I was unwilling to offer help in their time of need. Shame washed over me.

"You're right, Jakub. Friends do help each other. Forgive me." I extended my hand. "I don't know what I can do, but I'll try."

Relief spread across his face and he once again grasped my hand. "*Děkuji. Děkuji.* You make me so happy." His stirring words of thanks touched my heart. All signs of his earlier sadness had vanished. "Come!"

He tugged on my hand and I followed, still not knowing if I had made the correct decision, but I couldn't walk away without trying to lend aid to Jakub and his family. Once he'd secured my agreement, he held fast to my hand and hurried up the sloping hillock. We'd gone only a short distance when the toe of my shoe caught beneath a jagged rock and sent me plummeting to my knees. I yelped in pain as one knee hit a sharp corner of the outcropping.

Jakub knelt at my side, his eyes flecked with fear. "You broke a bone?"

The sharp rock had caused a rip in my skirt, and I rubbed my fingers across the frayed fabric. "I don't think so." I motioned for him to turn around, and I lifted my skirt. Blood trickled from my knee, so I pulled a handkerchief from my pocket and dabbed the blood. A bluish discoloration had already begun to form around the cut and scrapes that continued to ooze blood.

I folded the handkerchief into a triangle and tied it around my leg for protection before I worked my leg back and forth. Nothing was broken, but that didn't stop pain from shooting through my knee when I attempted to stand. "You can turn around. I think I'll need you to help me up." I brushed the dirt from my skirt— I'd worry about the tear later.

Jakub leaned forward and helped me to my feet. Hesitating for a moment, I gained my footing but rested heavily on his arm as we finished the upward climb to the road. I sighed when we arrived at the dirt path, for I knew I must walk more than a quarter of a mile before we would reach his house. I hobbled at a slow pace, and though I knew Jakub wanted to rush me along, he remained patient. When I finally caught sight of the frame structure, I picked up my pace just a little. Once there, I could sit down and rest my leg.

Jakub pushed down on the metal door latch and shoved against the heavy wood door. "It is me, Jakub. I brought Dovie to help us."

I squinted against the darkness that shrouded the room. Heavy coverings draped the windows obstructing the afternoon sunlight. While trying to remember the layout of the furniture, I picked my way across the room. Had Jakub not caught my arm, I would have tripped on the narrow bed that had been moved into the kitchen. "I think I need to stay in one place until my eyes adjust to the darkness."

"We moved my grandmother in here. The kitchen is warmer and she gets chilled. When I try to cover her, she says the blankets are too heavy, so I decided to move her bed." He sighed. "I'm sorry it is so dark, but the light bothers Sophia."

"It's fine. I just needed a little time for my eyes to adjust." I hoped my smile would reassure him, but after one look around the kitchen and into the parlor, I wasn't sure I would give hope to anyone. Truth be told, I wanted to back out of the kitchen and run in the opposite direction. The familiar odor of sickness permeated the house, and memories of my mother's final illness flooded my thoughts like an unleashed storm.

Jakub touched my arm. "Do you think this is influenza?"

"Maybe," I whispered. "I'm not a doctor." I leaned down and gently touched his grandmother's forehead. "Bring me a basin of water. She needs some cool compresses to help bring down the fever." I kneeled beside his grandmother and stroked her hand. After he placed the basin on the floor beside me, I soaked a cloth and placed it across her forehead. A moan escaped her lips, and my heart squeezed at the pitiful sound of the small, helpless woman. Her unkempt gray hair splayed across the pillow, and purplish-blue veins protruded across her forehead and down the sides of her thin face. She might be too weak to fight off this illness. The thought skittered through my mind as I stood and moved to Sophia's bedside.

The young woman stared up at me with fever-glazed eyes. Her skin was hot to the touch. She placed a single finger on her parched lips, and I signaled for Jakub to bring a cup of water. I looked over at the makeshift bed next to Sophia, where Jakub's mother was sleeping fitfully. I placed my hand against her cheek. At least she didn't feel as feverish as the other two women.

As Jakub approached with the cup, I returned to Sophia's side and placed an arm under her shoulders. She drank only a few sips before her head lolled to the side and her eyes closed. I handed the cup to Jakub and lowered her back to her pillow.

Jakub crouched beside me. "My father must be feeling better. He is not in the house."

My spirits lifted. "Maybe he realized a doctor is needed and he's gone to fetch Dr. Zimmer."

He shook his head. "If he is feeling better, he went out to work in the fields. I told you he does not trust doctors."

I couldn't believe that Jakub's father would leave his sick family alone and go out to work in the fields. Who would do such a thing? Was it more important to till the soil than tend to one's ill wife and family? I frowned. "Surely he wouldn't leave his family in this condition and go out to plow fields."

Jakub pointed toward the door. "If we don't plant, there are no crops. If there are no crops, we have nothing to eat and no money to pay for our land. Nothing is supplied for us like it is for the people in Amana. Sick or not, we must work."

"The people of Amana work very hard, too, Jakub. No one gives them anything, but they have more people to depend upon during their time of need." For some reason, I felt called to defend my mother's people and their way of life.

"I know, but when you have only your small family and everyone is sick . . ." His voice broke and I saw the fear that lurked in his eyes. "It is hard." He bowed his head. "And if my father has gone to plow the field, then it is because he must provide food for his family."

I had been too quick to judge. Who was I to decide what or how this family should behave during a time of illness and need? "I'm sorry, Jakub. I should not have been critical of your father's decision, but I hope you will stay with your family and do what you can to bring down their fevers. I can ask Karlina if there is something she can recommend. We have a medicine cabinet in the kitchen house."

Jakub grasped my hand. "You would do that?" His eyes opened wide and glimmered with a ray of hope.

"I'll ask, but I don't promise she will know what to do. My mother had influenza, and the doctor gave her some medicine, but I don't know what it was." I hesitated a moment. "It didn't help except to relieve the coughing." I glanced at his mother, who was the only one who I'd heard cough. "Do they all cough?"

"More my mother than the others. My father coughed a lot for several days." Jakub stood and walked to the window. "Maybe I should go and see if he is in the field. He may have become weak."

I didn't want him to go in search of his father and leave me here to care for his family. There was no telling when he might return, and I needed to get back to the Küche before I was missed. I stood and brushed a strand of hair from my forehead. "I'll go with you. I need to get back home. I promise to ask Karlina to help. Maybe we can come tomorrow and bring some medicine." His eyes brightened and he nodded. "You should make sure to keep cool compresses on their heads if they have a fever."

We walked to the door, and he grasped my hand. "You come with me to see if we find my father before you go—please." His beseeching tone melted my resolve to return home, and I followed him to the adjacent fields.

Jakub had been correct about his father. He was walking behind two large draft horses that were pulling a plow and tilling the soil. When he saw Jakub, he waved and called to him. From this distance, his father looked the picture of health. When Jakub ran ahead of me, I picked up my pace and followed on his heels, thankful the ache in my leg had subsided.

The older man doffed his wide-brimmed hat and greeted me as I approached. His skin appeared sallow and he leaned heavily on the plow as he spoke to Jakub. I understood only a word or two, and while they talked, I surveyed the tilled acreage. Numerous birds fluttered overhead, surveying the upturned earth for a worm or tasty bug. A large blackbird dipped down, snatched a morsel with its beak, and took to the air.

I was looking skyward when Jakub stepped close and touched my arm. "My father is feeling much better. He says if you can bring us any medicine that would help, he would be grateful. But no doctor." Jakub glanced toward his father. "My father believes God will heal the rest of the family just as he has been healed, but he thinks medicine would be good to help ease their discomfort."

My eyes shifted from Jakub to his father, who was closely watching me. I nodded and smiled at him. "I will do my best," I called to him before leaning a little closer to Jakub. "I must go back now."

"I'll walk you to the pond."

Although I argued he should go back to the house and care for his relatives, he insisted upon escorting me. Guilt nagged me as he remained close to my side, and I hurried as fast as my feet would carry me. The sooner we arrived at the pond, the sooner he would return home and care for Sophia, his mother, and his grandmother. We were picking our way down the rocky hillock where I'd fallen earlier when I noticed movement beyond the pond. I shaded my eyes with one hand to gain a better view. Was that Berndt?

My foot slipped and Jakub grabbed me around the waist and held me close. When I tried to pull away, his cheeks turned crimson and he released his hold. "I thought you were going to fall. I didn't mean . . . forgive me . . . I was trying to help."

I forced a smile but kept my eyes focused upon the distant figure, now certain it was Berndt. "Thank you, Jakub. I know you didn't want me to fall. I'm fine now."

The moment we arrived at the pond, I insisted he return home. When he didn't argue, I sighed with relief. Once I was on the other side of the pond, I hiked my skirt and ran toward the house. Though my leg once again ached, I needed to get home. I was sure Cousin Louise would question me about the tear in my skirt. That could be easily enough explained.

Answering questions about Jakub would not be so easily answered. And I was certain Berndt would soon quiz me.

CHAPTER 22

Karlina

I softly clapped my hands and herded the lambs toward the feeding machine that Anton had set up at the far end of the barn. The enclosed area provided them with a secure corner in which to feed. Just as the other lambs had learned to seek their mothers at feeding time, these lambs had quickly discovered this was the place where they would receive their milk. I smiled as they romped toward the feeding station with the energy and enthusiasm of hungry children. They were nudging one another in an effort to find their respective places when the door of the barn opened and a shaft of sunlight fell across the lambs' woolly fleece. Anton had gone to the far pasture with the other sheep, and I hadn't expected him to return for at least another hour.

"You're back ahead of—Berndt!" I stepped away from the lambs and closed the gate to the feeding area. "I'm surprised to see you here. I thought Anton had returned early."

Berndt strode toward me, his hands shoved deep inside his pockets. "I was over by the pond, but I didn't see Anton. He probably moved to one of the far pastures." He mashed his lips together in a hard line.

"It's a beautiful day. It appears you have the afternoon to yourself. Why are you looking so unhappy?"

He picked up a long piece of straw and rolled it back and forth between his finger and thumb. "I'm not supposed to be by myself." He sighed and then pitched the piece of straw to the floor. "What do you know about that Czech fellow, Jakub, and Dovie?"

I felt as though Berndt was setting a trap of sorts. The idea annoyed me. "Not a lot more than you do. You've met Jakub at the pond when we've been skating. He has come over to help with shearing for the past few years. He's a hard worker and very polite. I'm not sure why you are linking him with Dovie." I turned and walked back to the feeding area to check on the lambs. Berndt stayed close on my heels, and when I stopped, he nearly pushed me into the gate.

"Does Dovie talk about him?"

There had been a few times when Dovie and I had mentioned Jakub after meeting him while ice skating at the pond. But lately Dovie hadn't said much about Jakub or anyone else. I hadn't considered it before now, but our evening visits had become less specific and more condensed. "She hasn't mentioned him since winter, when he would be at the pond skating sometimes." I turned to face him. "Why are you asking questions about Jakub?"

Berndt raked his fingers through his thick hair. "Because I was supposed to meet her this afternoon—over by the pond." He hesitated a moment and looked toward the lambs. "My father insisted I go to the mill and pick up the order of flour before I could leave for the rest of the afternoon, which meant I was late getting to the pond." He inhaled a deep breath, pursed his lips, and then exhaled in a giant whoosh. "Dovie wasn't there. I didn't know if she'd been there and left or if she was late, too."

"So did you wait?"

"Ja, I waited for a long time, but finally I decided I'd better head for home."

"And you never saw her?"

He shook his head. "Nein. I had started walking toward home, but on the way I kept feeling the need to look over my shoulder. I was a good distance from the pond when I turned for the third time, and then I saw her." He bowed his head. "She was with Jakub Sedlacek."

I was doing my best to understand, but I couldn't figure out how Dovie could have suddenly appeared with Jakub when Berndt had been watching for her at the pond. "Where did you see them? You turned around, and Jakub and Dovie suddenly appeared out of nowhere?"

He bobbed his head. "Ja! That's exactly what happened. I couldn't believe my eyes. One minute there is nothing, and the next minute I see two figures coming over the rise and down the hill. I stopped and watched because it looked like it might be Dovie, but I told myself it could not be. She wouldn't go beyond the boundaries of our land."

"I do not think it was her." I motioned toward the lambs. "I need to see to them."

Berndt followed behind me. "I was wrong—and so are you. It was Dovie. I am positive. And Jakub held her in his arms."

"What?" I spun on my heel and stiffened. "Now I know you are mistaken. You saw someone else. Never would she behave in such a manner." I wanted to order Berndt out of the barn for making such an accusation. How dare he!

"I know what I saw, Karlina. I care for Dovie. I didn't want to believe it, either. But I am telling you the truth. I think maybe she saw me, too, but she didn't acknowledge me. You should speak to her when you are alone this evening. Ask her where she was this afternoon. See what she tells you." He stepped away from the feeding stall. "It will soon be suppertime. I must go home."

The utter sadness in his voice tugged at my heart. "I will do my best to find out where she was today, but maybe this is a reminder of what you've been told by your Vater."

He shrugged his shoulder. "We will see. I will hope there is some gut explanation for what I saw." His voice cracked, and he turned and hurried away.

No doubt my mother would believe God had sent Berndt a warning. Right now I didn't know what to think. I didn't want to believe Dovie had permitted Jakub to take liberties with her. I also didn't want to think Jakub would force his affections on a woman. He seemed a nice young man, always courteous and kind. Still, I didn't know him well.

The lambs had completed their feeding, and I decided to head to the house a little early. I might get there before Dovie. If she'd seen Berndt, she would likely return at a slow pace in order to avoid meeting up with him.

Sister Marta was outside at the water pump when I neared the house and I waved to her. "Is Dovie inside, Sister Marta?"

She placed a large metal bucket beneath the pump and shook her head. "Not unless she has been upstairs in her room all afternoon. I haven't seen her since we finished the noonday meal." After priming the pump, she filled the bucket and commenced telling me about one of the junior girls who had dropped an entire bowl of eggs all over the floor earlier in the day. "What a mess we had." She chuckled as she lifted and pushed down on the pump handle one final time. As she hoisted the bucket, she glanced toward the street. "Dovie's coming down the sidewalk right now." With the bucket handle tightly clasped in her hand, Sister Marta headed back inside.

I waited for a moment and then waved to Dovie. She offered a halfhearted wave in return and her usual smile didn't appear. As she drew closer, I noticed the dirt stains and tear in her skirt. My hands trembled. Perhaps Jakub had attacked her. I rushed forward and wrapped her in an embrace.

"Are you all right?"

Dovie gently released herself from my hold and stared at me as though she thought I'd suddenly gone mad. "Why wouldn't I be?"

I pointed at her skirt. "Look at you. Your skirt is torn and dirty, and your hair is loose and tangled. What happened?"

She swiped a hand down the front of her black skirt. "I fell on a jagged rock and made a mess of my skirt. I think I can stitch it well enough to keep it from fraying any further. And with an apron over top, no one will notice the skirt has been mended." She lifted several strands of hair and tucked them behind her ear. "The wind has been blowing, and my hair came loose on the walk home."

"Where did you go?"

Her eyes opened wide. I hadn't intended to sound so harsh, but I needed to know what had happened and if she was trying to protect Jakub.

"I went to the pond." She flicked at a splotch of dirt.

"Is that where you fell down?"

She drew her lower lip between her teeth. "Not too far from there. I don't have time to explain before supper, but we can talk before you leave for prayer meeting. I need to wash up before the bell rings."

I stood there and watched her run indoors. For a moment I considered following her upstairs, but I knew I must wait.

❖

The minute we'd finished the evening meal, I motioned Dovie to follow me upstairs. When we arrived in the parlor, I waved her toward the bedroom. "My Vater might come up to read his Bible before prayer service. Let's go in the bedroom."

Once inside, I closed the door and sat down on my bed. Dovie sat down opposite me and folded her hands in her lap. "First you must promise you won't say anything about what I am going to tell you."

"I'm not sure I can do that. What if it needs to be told?"

Determination shone in her eyes. "I promise that you are the only one who needs to know, but I must be able to trust you."

I wasn't sure I was doing the right thing, but if I didn't agree, she would never tell me what had happened during her outing. "I promise," I whispered.

"Good." Her lips curved in a satisfied smile. "I went to the pond today. I was supposed to meet Berndt."

"I know."

She frowned. "How did you know? I didn't tell anyone."

"He told me, but it doesn't matter. Go ahead with your story."

My interruption had distracted her, but she soon regained her momentum. "Berndt never did show up, but while I was waiting, Jakub appeared. He came down to the pond and begged me to come back to his house. His family is sick, and he wanted me to help."

I stared in disbelief as she told me that she had gone to Jakub's house. "I cannot believe you would do such a thing. You are joking with me, ja?"

"No, I'm not joking. They are very ill and need help. Isn't that what Christians do? Help each other? Jakub begged me to go with him. How could I refuse?"

"Ach! I cannot believe you would be so foolish as to go alone with a stranger to his house. What were you thinking, Dovie? Do you not realize what could have happened?" I stopped and covered my mouth. "Did he hurt you? Is that how your skirt got torn?"

"Karlina! How could you even think such a thing about Jakub? He is a very nice young man, and he did nothing except seek help for his sick family."

As I listened to her indictment, a flame of anger rose in my chest. "You should not be condemning me. You are the one who is in the wrong. You went off of our property with a man you barely know. And Berndt saw the two of you embracing."

Dovie's mouth dropped open. "I thought I saw him when I was coming back down to the pond, but he was nowhere in sight on my way home."

"So you admit the two of you were embracing?"

"No! I lost my footing, and Jakub took hold of me to keep me from rolling down the hill. Since I had fallen on my way to his house and ripped my skirt, he was trying to protect me—nothing more. And if Berndt cares so much about me, he would have been at the pond on time and none of this would have happened."

I needed to harness my anger. If we continued down this path, nothing would be resolved. "Let's not place blame on anyone. Berndt's father needed him to go to the mill and pick up flour. Berndt has work he must perform whether it interferes with his personal plans with you or not. And he couldn't tell his father he was going to meet you, could he?"

Dovie shook her head. "No, but you must try to see this from my side, Karlina. I couldn't tell Jakub that I wouldn't help him when I was doing nothing else but sitting at the pond. I think you would have done the same thing had you been in my place."

I wanted to tell her she was wrong. That I would have followed the rules and never gone off our land with an outsider, but I couldn't. Truth be told, I didn't know what I would have done. "You must not go back there, Dovie. It isn't wise. Mutter and

Vater would be very unhappy if they knew you went to Jakub's house."

Dovie inhaled a deep breath. "They need medicine, and I need you to go with me to help them. We can go tomorrow afternoon."

"What?" The high-pitched squeak echoed in the room. "I cannot do that. Please don't ask me."

"But I *am* asking you. They need our help. I promised Jakub we would bring some medicine from the supply cabinet. Please say you'll help. Jakub's father is doing better, but Sophia, his mother, and his grandmother are very sick. I think it's influenza."

"Influenza?" I clasped a hand to my chest. "What if we should contract the illness and bring it back to the village? The effects could be horrible. I do not think my Mutter would understand if I intentionally took such a risk. My brothers died of pneumonia, and if something happened, she would—"

"My mother died of influenza, and neither my father nor I got sick. And you didn't become ill when your brothers contracted pneumonia. Just because we go and help them doesn't mean we'll get sick." She leaned forward and gathered my hands in hers. "Giving them medicine is the right thing to do, Karlina. Is it not what the Bible teaches us to do? Are the rules about not going off the land more important than people who need help?"

"I do not know." I withdrew my hands from her clasp and leaned back. "I have never been faced with such a decision." I rocked back and forth on the edge of the bed. "In order to help you, I must disobey my parents and the church. This goes against everything I have been taught."

"Not everything, Karlina. You have learned God's Word. Tell me that what I am asking you to do is not in the Bible." Dovie pinned me with a hard stare.

"To help the sick and needy is a directive from the Bible, but to obey your parents is also an instruction I should follow. I am torn." I bowed my head and stared at the pine floor. "I will pray and seek God's answer."

"What if you don't have an answer by tomorrow? They could die."

I lifted my head and met her beseeching gaze. "Even with our help, they may die, Dovie. Their future is in God's hands, not ours."

"But sometimes God wants our help. He expects us to be His hands, don't you think?"

My stomach knotted. Dovie could present a better argument than anyone I'd ever met. But my answer needed to come from God—not Dovie Cates, for I would have much to explain should any of us become ill. "I must pray and seek God's answer. Unless I believe it is God's will for me to go to the Sedlacek farm, I will not go with you." I wrung my hands together, and for the first time I wished Dovie hadn't come to our village. If anything happened, I might never again gain my mother's trust.

All during prayer meeting, I prayed about the problem Dovie had dumped in my lap. I prayed the Sedlacek family would get well without my help—that a miracle would heal all of them during the night and that Jakub would be waiting at the pond to tell Dovie she need not come to their house. I prayed for wisdom to do the correct thing and for God to direct my path. On the way home, I prayed Dovie would accept whatever decision the Lord placed on my heart. When I went to bed, I prayed God would provide a clear answer so that I would act in a manner that would please Him.

And I also prayed God would answer all of my prayers by morning.

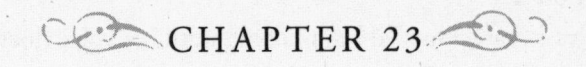

CHAPTER 23

Dovie

I did my very best to refrain from mentioning Jakub and his family, but when morning arrived and Karlina recited her morning prayers, I couldn't help but watch and wait—hoping that God had told her to help the Sedlaceks. She finished her prayers and when she turned, I was staring at her. I didn't miss the worry that shone in her eyes before she looked away. I hadn't intended to cause her greater distress; I merely longed to hear that she had received a directive from above.

When she continued to avoid me, I stood and straightened my skirt. I had mended the tear and brushed the remains of dirt from the garment last evening. "My skirt looks almost as good as new, don't you think?"

Karlina eyed the garment. "Almost, but not gut enough that it won't be noticed. You should put your apron on before the others arrive." The bell on the bread wagon jangled in the distance, and she looked toward the window. "There is Berndt. You'd better hurry."

I didn't want to hurry. I didn't want to see Berndt at all. I worried he might ask me if I'd been with Jakub, or he might attempt to trick me into admitting I had gone to the Sedlacek farm. Maybe if I waited upstairs long enough, Cousin Louise would go out and get the bread.

At least that's what I'd been hoping until her voice floated up the stairs. "Hurry, Dovie. The bread wagon will soon be here, and I am grinding coffee."

I started toward the bedroom door. "We can talk later." When Karlina didn't reply, I glanced over my shoulder. She was kneeling beside her bed, head bowed, hands folded, and eyes closed. She'd already recited her morning prayers, so I knew she must be pleading with God for an answer to my request. My prayers this morning hadn't been near as long as hers. I was depending on the fact that God knew and understood the importance of this mission. But just to be sure, I uttered another soulful plea as I trudged down the stairs. Slowly I crossed the distance, still dreading my meeting with Berndt.

I stepped across the threshold and leaned against the doorjamb. "Guten Morgen, Cousin Louise."

"Guten Morgen." She smiled and gestured toward the door. "I think Berndt has arrived."

Berndt had already climbed down from the wagon and had opened the rear doors. The smell of the freshly baked bread greeted me like a warm embrace, and I took a deep breath.

"Guten Morgen, Dovie." Berndt's voice bore an unfamiliar tone—more formal than usual. "You were not at the pond when I arrived yesterday. Where did you go?"

Instead of meeting his intense stare, I kept my focus on the bread trays inside the wagon. "You weren't there when I arrived, either." He quickly explained what Karlina had already told me. I wanted to grab the bread trays and flee inside, but his broad hands remained clamped along the edge of the pans. "Cousin Louise is waiting for the bread."

"And I am waiting for an answer. Where did you go?"

Finally I met his hard look. "I went for a walk up along the hillside. Too late, I realized that I had gone beyond the Amana boundaries. But good fortune prevailed, and Jakub Sedlacek appeared and led me back to the pond." He remained silent, his eyes dark and brooding. "You remember Jakub, don't you? He and his sister skated at the pond this winter. And he helps Cousin George with the shearing sometimes. At least that's what Karlina told me when we first met him."

I was rambling like a fool, but he continued to stare. He didn't blink, not even once. "I think he helps during lambing sometimes, too. Cousin George says he is a good worker and a nice young man."

"And what about you, Dovie? Do you think he is a nice young man?"

"Y-yes, of course I do. He was most courteous, and I was thankful for his help."

"And did you enjoy his embrace?" He leaned forward an inch or two. "Did he kiss you while you were up there on the hillside with him?"

Anger fired deep inside me. How dare he say such a thing! I backed away from him and squared my shoulders into a rigid line. "What kind of woman do you take me for, Berndt? Do you think so little of me that you would accuse me of unseemly behavior with a near stranger? If so, why do you care what I do with my free time?" Hands clenched into tight fists, I stared at him and waited for his reply. My searing words proved strong enough that he finally blinked.

"I asked because I saw you on the hillside with Jakub." He tapped his index finger alongside his right eye. "He had his arms around you, and it didn't appear you were trying to run away from him."

I had clamped my teeth so hard that my jaw ached. "You're right. I wasn't trying to run away. I slipped on a rock, and if Jakub hadn't assisted me, I might have fallen and broken a bone. In your mind, I suppose that would have been a better outcome."

"I do not think it would be gut for you to break a bone, but I do think you should have remained within the boundaries of our land. I told you our land didn't go beyond the hill. If you hadn't climbed up there, none of this would have happened."

"And if you had arrived on time, I wouldn't have gone wandering. But neither of us can change what is in the past." I glanced toward the house. "I need to take the bread inside before Cousin Louise comes looking for me."

When I reached for the tray, he covered my hand. "Will you meet me this afternoon? I promise to be on time."

I shook my head. "I can't, Berndt. I promised Karlina I would spend the afternoon with her."

He pulled his cap from his pocket and yanked the bill low over his eyes. "I have forgiven you, but you are still angry."

"I cannot tell you that I am not hurt by your accusations, but I forgive you. Still, I cannot change my plans with Karlina." I lifted the tray from the wagon.

"Then later in the week?"

"Perhaps. Let's wait and see before we make plans. It is better if we are both sure we will be free before we set another time and day."

His lips drooped. "I think you are maybe still a little angry. Maybe you will be pleased to have my company on a day when Karlina is busy in the barn. Soon they will be shearing the sheep, and she will be needed at the barn all day."

I nodded and smiled, for I needed to be careful. I wanted him to understand I was no longer angry, but I didn't want to give him a definite answer until I knew how things would go with the Sedlacek family. If Berndt should again see me leaving the boundaries of the Amana land, he might decide to say something to the elders. If that happened, they would no doubt elect to put me on a train bound for Texas. They would not want to be responsible for a young woman who did not follow the rules.

Karlina didn't say anything to me before she left for the barn after breakfast, so I waited for some sign when she returned for the noonday meal, but she passed by me as if I were invisible. It was my day to serve, and each time I entered the dining room with fresh bowls or platters of food, I watched to see if she might look in my direction. When she didn't, my spirit flagged. Without her, I wouldn't be much help to the Sedlaceks. She knew much more about treating sick animals and people than I did. But if she hadn't received a nudge from the Lord, I was certain she wouldn't help.

I dreaded carrying such bad news to Jakub. Shoulders sagging, I leaned against the sink and tried to gather my thoughts. What would I say to him?

After the meal was over and the parting prayer was being recited, I hurried to the kitchen and poured some beef broth into a small crock. Even if Karlina wouldn't go with me, I wanted to take some broth to Jakub's family. After I filled the crock, I wrapped it in a towel and placed it near the side door. Shortly after I returned to the kitchen, Karlina stepped across the threshold.

"Mutter, if you do not need Dovie's help this afternoon, I thought we would take a walk. It's a beautiful afternoon, and I could show her some of the distant pastures."

Cousin Louise's eyebrows knit together. "Not too distant. You know your Vater was talking last night about the wild dogs causing problems again. Now that the lambs are born, they have become bolder."

Karlina tipped her head to the side. "Ja, Mutter. I am aware of the dogs. I work with the sheep all the time."

"I know, but it is better that I warn you." She picked up an armful of dirty plates and carried them to Sister Marta, who was intently scrubbing the dishes and dropping them into the rinse water. "A gut reminder will keep you more alert."

"You are right, Mutter. And I'll be sure to take along a thick walking stick for protection."

Her mother nodded her approval. "Both of you should take one. Two is better than one." Her forehead wrinkled, as if considering her comment. "Well, most of the time two is better than one, but not in childbirth, for sure."

"Sister Louise!" Sister Bertha spun on her heel and glowered at Cousin Louise. "We do not talk about such things."

"Ach! We are all women. There is nothing shameful about what I said, but if you wish to take it before the elders, I cannot stop you."

Clearly flustered, Sister Bertha wiped her wet hands on the corner of her apron. "I did not say I was going to speak to the elders. I only said childbirth was not a topic we should discuss openly."

Sister Marta picked up a towel and began to dry the dishes. "You worry too much about the little things, Sister Bertha."

While the women continued their lively discussion, Karlina stepped close to her mother's side. "We will sort the mail before we leave."

Her mother patted her arm. "Danke, Karlina. You are a gut girl."

Karlina waved me toward the small adjacent room and motioned to the mailbag sitting on the table. "You sort the mail while I see what medicine is in the cabinet. I hope I can find something that might help Jakub's family."

Until she'd actually mentioned Jakub's family, I'd been holding my emotions in check. But once she said she was going to look for medicine, I couldn't contain myself. I spun her around and pulled her close. "Oh, thank you, thank you! This means so much to me, to Jakub, to his family."

Karlina pushed against my shoulders. "You're squeezing the breath out of me, Dovie. And you need to keep your voice down. Sister Bertha has big ears, remember?"

I released my hold on her. "I'm sorry," I whispered. "But I'm glad the Lord answered our prayers. Did you receive some special sign?"

She gave me a sideways glance. "Nein. I'm still not sure this is what I am supposed to be doing, but I told the Lord that if everything worked so that we could go to the farm without interference, I would take it as a sign He wanted me to help."

I pointed to the crock I had placed near the door. "That's broth to take to them. Even if you decided against going with me, I knew I must do something."

Karlina didn't comment. Instead, she pointed to the mail pouch. "You need to begin sorting."

I poured the mail onto the table and sorted as quickly as my hands would move. "So far, things are going well. I'll keep praying that nothing will stop us from helping the Sedlaceks."

Karlina fished in the drawer and retrieved a key for the medicine cabinet. I continued to sort the mail, quickly shoving the envelopes into the proper cubbyholes. From time to time, I darted a glance toward Karlina as she searched through the bandages, bottles of medicine, and instruments. I silently gave thanks as she stuffed several items into a cloth bag. She completed her task and moved to my side. As soon as we finished the mail, she nodded toward the side door.

"We'll go out this way." She tucked the cloth bag beneath her cloak and pushed down on the metal hasp.

"Wait. Shouldn't we take some wine to them? I remember the doctor instructed me to give my mother small sips of wine."

Karlina nodded. "I have some in the bag. You'll need to carry the crock of broth. I hope you have an answer prepared if someone should stop us and ask questions."

Though I hadn't even thought to prepare a response, I forced my lips into a smile and hoped it would be enough to reassure Karlina. While doing my best to balance the crock, I maintained a careful watch on the bulge beneath Karlina's cloak. I didn't want her bag to fall to the ground on our way. "Thank you, Karlina. I am so happy you decided to help."

"We haven't arrived yet. The Lord may stop us before we get there. If so, don't argue with me, for I will not change my mind." She gave me a hard look. "Are we in agreement?"

I didn't want to agree, but I did. There really was no choice. If I hadn't, she would have turned around and gone home right then. I couldn't let that happen. "I think Jakub will be watching for us. He was very worried when I left yesterday."

"I hope he remains hidden. The last thing we need is for him to stand on the ridge waving to us. If someone sees us or him, we're going to have no end of trouble on our hands." She shook her head. "I don't know why I agreed to do this." When we neared the outlying edge of the village, Karlina withdrew the cloth bag from beneath her cape and held it by the drawstring.

"How were you holding the bag in place?"

"It wasn't difficult. I placed the drawstring over my shoulder and held the bag beneath my arm."

"You're just full of good ideas, aren't you?" I'd almost said "sneaky" ideas, but I knew Karlina wouldn't be pleased by such a comment.

"We can't be gone too long. No matter how sick they are, we need to get back before anyone comes looking for us. On the way back, I think we should circle through the far pasture just in case Berndt or Anton should decide to come and find us."

I didn't argue. I thought it a good idea. "Anton is doing much better with the sheep, isn't he?"

Karlina nodded. "Ja. He is very pleased about the feeding machine. It works very well. He better controls his temper, too. I think he is content for now."

"Just for now?" I grinned and nudged her. "I think he will be happy to remain in East. By the time the summer is over, I think he will be asking your father if he can marry you."

Her face turned crimson and she looked away. "You are always thinking about love."

"When a man looks at a woman the way Anton looks at you, it is impossible to ignore. I am sure your father sees it, as well." We began our hike up the hillside, and I pointed to the outcropping. "Be careful. That's where I fell yesterday."

Had it been only yesterday? It seemed so long ago since I'd made the trek up this hill with Jakub by my side. I hoped that his family had fared well during the night. As we continued on, my mind wandered back to my mother's final illness. Nighttime had always been the most frightening, both for her and for me. Everything always seemed worse during the night.

"I am glad Jakub isn't anywhere in sight."

Karlina's comment interrupted my thoughts and brought me back to the present. Looking up, I scoured the top of the hillock. We were almost at the top when I caught sight of a plaid jacket. "There's Jakub over behind that stand of trees. I'm sure he's seen us and is waiting."

"Don't call to him," Karlina hissed. "There's an echo from up here. Anyone below would hear."

I nodded. As long as she remained and helped, I wouldn't object to any of Karlina's directives. She could command and I would obey. When we reached the top of the hill, I stopped long enough to catch my breath, but Karlina continued to march onward.

She waved me forward. "I'm tired, too, but there isn't time to waste. You can rest once we get to the house."

Before I could reply, Jakub stepped out from behind the trees. His lips curved into a broad smile as he loped toward us. "I have been praying you would come. I was watching the meadow beyond the pond." He stopped in the middle of the road, but Karlina stepped around him and continued toward the house. Jakub turned and hurried alongside her. "When I didn't see you, I was afraid my prayer had not been answered. Just as I was about to give up, I saw you come from the far side and circle around." His smile widened. "And I gave thanks to God."

Continuing her rapid pace, Karlina glanced toward Jakub. "Did you see anyone else down there while you were watching for us?"

He shook his head. "Coming around the far side takes longer."

Karlina narrowed her eyes. "I know that, Jakub, but I also know we were less likely to be seen."

All three of us were breathing hard when we arrived at the front door. Karlina stopped. "Where is your Vater?"

Jakub waved his hat toward the distant field. "Out there, tilling the ground." As if sensing her concern, he said, "Only the women are inside. Sophia remains the same, but my mother and grandmother are a little better." He pushed down on the latch and pushed the door open. "Should I wait out here, or do you want me to come inside to help?"

"I don't know where anything is. At least until I see how they're doing, you had better come in with me. You, too, Dovie. I'll need your help if they're as bad as you say."

Both Mrs. Sedlacek and Jakub's grandmother appeared somewhat better. Jakub's grandmother even offered a weak toothless smile when we entered the room. Her gray hair was in a state of disarray, and I was glad she had no mirror nearby. She would have been sorely embarrassed by her appearance. Mrs. Sedlacek sat beside her on a sagging horsehair sofa. Though their health had improved, their lack of strength was apparent.

"I've brought some medicine and broth that I hope will help you feel better, Mrs. Sedlacek." Karlina drew closer to Jakub's mother. The older woman appeared confused, and Karlina motioned to Jakub. "You need to tell them what I am saying about the medicine and diet."

"Since both your mother and grandmother are doing better, they should try to keep up their strength with broth and small portions of wine. We brought some along with us. They should also drink barley water, and if you can make a thin gruel, that will help. Do they have a sore throat or cough?"

Jakub spoke to his mother and then turned back to Karlina. "A little bit sore throat, but no more cough."

"You should have them simmer one teacupful of vinegar, half a teacupful of honey, and one teaspoonful of cayenne. That will help the sore throat." She removed several bottles from the burlap bag and then walked to Sophia's side. She dropped to her knees beside the girl and felt her forehead. "She is far too warm. Bring me some cool water, Jakub."

I drew closer to Karlina. "Should I heat some of the throat medicine for them while you examine Sophia?"

Karlina nodded while she continued to check Sophia. The girl murmured and Karlina leaned closer, but I moved away and began mixing the vinegar, honey, and cayenne. Jakub's grandmother watched me with wary eyes. From the way she was watching me, I wondered if she would drink the medicine once I'd finished, but I had to hope Jakub would persuade her if I could not.

The front door closed with a bang and water sloshed over the sides of the bucket as Jakub hurried to Karlina's side. She motioned toward the floor, and he placed the pail beside her. After removing several cloths from the bag, she dipped them in the water, and then placed them across Sophia's forehead, behind her neck, and at the bottom of her feet.

Once the throat medicine had simmered, I set it on the table to cool and returned to where Sophia lay motionless. Karlina stood and pulled Jakub aside. "She isn't doing well at all. I think you should have a doctor for her. If this is influenza, she could die. Does your father understand?"

Jakub nodded. "He will not have a doctor."

"Is it because of the money? Dr. Zimmer would come and treat her without pay. I'm certain he would. Besides, any money he receives goes into our community funds, not to him." Karlina touched Sophia's head and looked at Jakub with imploring eyes. "Sheep shearing begins next week. I know my Vater will need your help. You can use some of that money." The desperation in her voice frightened me, and I stooped down beside her.

I tipped my head until my lips almost touched her ear. "She will live, won't she?"

Karlina turned to me, but she didn't answer. "She is in God's hands."

Jakub reached forward and grasped Karlina's hand. "Is that all you can do for her?"

"I am going to give you some quinine. You must give this to her three times a day. I truly don't know if it will help, but I don't know what else to give you. Try to have her drink the broth and a little wine, if she will." She pointed to the mixture I'd simmered on the stove. "Have your grandmother and mother take a teaspoonful of that medicine for their sore throats. They need to continue to rest."

Karlina tucked the bottles into her bag and motioned for me to follow her to the door. "We need to go."

Jakub rushed ahead of us to block our departure. "But you'll come back tomorrow, won't you?"

Karlina hesitated. "I will pray and see if the Lord leads me to come back, Jakub. I am going against my Vater and the church by coming here. I cannot promise I will return. You should let the doctor come and see her."

He shook his head. "That will not happen. I told Dovie. He does not trust doctors." I touched his arm, and he sidestepped away from the door. "Is there nothing else I can do?"

"Pray, Jakub. That is the most important thing. We must all pray."

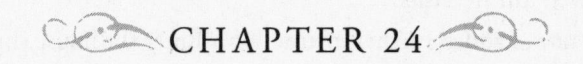

CHAPTER 24

Karlina

Though we had taken the longer path back toward town, there would be more than enough time for me to stop at the barn before we returned home. I didn't want to admit it to Dovie, but I had grown to care for Anton, and it was close enough to supper-time that he should be back from the pasture. As we crossed the meadow, I lowered the bag from beneath my lightweight cloak.

"You take what's left in the medicine bag back to the house. I'm going to stop at the barn before I return." When I held it out to Dovie, she backed away as though I had tried to hand her a poisonous snake.

"What if someone sees me getting into the medicine cabinet? I could never explain."

She was correct, of course. It wouldn't be good if that should happen. "Take it upstairs and put it under my bed. It will be safe there. I can take care of it later."

Apparently that had been enough to relieve Dovie's concern. While I held the empty crock, she took the bag and tucked it inside her jacket. With the added bulk, her coat protruded on one side. If anyone saw her, the bulge would likely give rise to questions. I didn't mention that fact. No need to cause further alarm, but I would advise her to wear a cloak in the future—if there were future visits.

For now, I added further instruction. "Enter the house through the side door. That way you can avoid my Mutter and the other women. If you go through the kitchen, they will want to chat with you. I wouldn't want the bag to slip and fall while you're in their presence." She nodded toward the crock. "Besides, they would want to know why you had one of the crocks. You should put it under the sorting table and return it to the kitchen later this evening."

Dovie beamed at me. "You think of everything, Karlina. That's a wonderful plan."

When we neared the barn, she veered to the right and I turned toward the left. I kept my gaze settled on her until the barn blocked her from my sight. As I pushed open the barn door, I wondered why it had been closed on such a beautiful day. With only a light breeze and moderate temperatures, the barn should have been open for better ventilation. Over and over, I'd explained to Anton that the barn needed to remain cool for the sheep. Some days I thought he had learned a great deal but on others, I wondered if he recalled anything Vater and I had taught him.

When his mind became occupied with some new invention, he seemed unable to concentrate his energy on anything else. Yet he had promised my father that until we completed the shearing, he would refrain from further inventions. In turn, my father explained that he would have time to dream of new inventions while he was outdoors caring for the sheep during the summer. He wouldn't be able to turn his drawings into tangible form while out in the pastures, but my father's encouragement had proved to be a significant incentive to Anton.

The sweet smell of hay floated on the breeze. Most visitors thought the smells inside a barn unappealing, but nothing comforted me as much as entering the giant structure and inhaling the familiar scents. Once inside, I stooped down beside one of the pens, where a young lamb nuzzled her mother while another stood on the ewe's back for a better view of the surroundings. For several moments I ran my fingers through the lamb's lightweight layers of woolly fleece.

As I grabbed hold of a wood slat and prepared to rise from my crouched position, voices drifted from the other side of the barn. I recognized Anton's clear baritone, but the other voice was higher, probably a soprano, and most definitely a woman. Except during lambing or shearing, women were seldom anywhere near the barn. Guilt tugged at me. I should reveal myself. Instead, I remained paralyzed, hidden behind the sheep pen.

The woman was speaking, and I struggled to hear. "My father said that if you have learned to control your temper, he will not argue against our marriage when you return to High."

Violet! She had returned—likely her father had gone to Main either to borrow or to return another medical book or instrument and she'd taken advantage of the opportunity. My thoughts took wing, and I wondered how often she had been meeting with Anton. Had he been sending her letters to tell her of his schedule? I frowned at the thought. Surely not. He wouldn't have taken such a chance. The mail was sent and delivered through the Küche. He wouldn't want me to discover he was writing to Violet. Then again, instead of leaving his letters on the sorting table, he could have dropped them into the outgoing mailbag, and no one would ever know.

My stomach tightened at the thought. Would Anton do such a

thing? Was he in love with Violet? My feelings for him had blossomed over the past months, and only last week, he had declared his love for me. How could a man care for two women at the same time?

Anton murmured a reply, but I heard only a few words. Unfortunately, one of the words was *love* and the others were *return to High*.

Only a few hours ago, I had deflected Dovie's remarks about Anton's love for me because I wasn't prepared to share his declaration with her, or with anyone, for that matter. But I had believed his words of love. How foolish I had been. How thankful I was that I hadn't told Dovie. Having to go back and tell her it had all been a lie would have been horrid.

"Anton, you're teasing me, but I am pleased to see you are feeling so good-natured." Violet's high-pitched voice drifted across the barn and took my breath away. I felt as though I'd inhaled a lungful of ammonia. Anton had told me they were no more than friends, yet Violet's words and actions were those of a woman who was far more than a friend.

I wasn't watching when one of the lambs drew near and nuzzled my hand. The surprise of the lamb's cold, wet nose on my hand caused me to yelp. Shifting, I clasped a hand to my mouth, lost my balance, and landed on my backside.

"What was that?" Violet screeched. "Who's in here? Show yourself."

"It was nothing, Violet. Probably one of the sheep moving around in the pens, but I think your Vater will be returning. It would be wise to wait outside for him. I do not think he would be pleased to find us alone inside the barn."

Finally Anton had spoken loud enough for me to hear him. And what I heard caused my stomach to lurch. They would be heading in my direction. I needed to show myself or find a hiding place.

Better yet, I would go back outside and pretend to be entering the barn as they departed. That way I could question him at length regarding Violet, and he wouldn't know I had been listening in on his conversation. I told myself I hadn't truly been eavesdropping, for I'd been unable to hear most of Anton's remarks.

Slowly, I moved into a crawling position and began my retreat. With each forward movement of my knee, my skirt pulled downward and I had to release the fabric. I finally lifted the skirt so that it puddled around me and provided my legs with the necessary freedom to crawl out of the barn. My heart quickened at the sound of their approaching footsteps. They would soon round the corner and spot me. I hurried my movements and had almost arrived at the door when a long shadow fell across my path.

I swallowed hard, not wanting to look up and see my father staring down at me. What would I say when he asked why I was crawling around the barn like a toddler? I remained frozen on all fours as I waited to hear my father's voice.

"Have you lost something?"

I sat back on my heels and stared up into the eyes of a man I didn't immediately recognize. Not until I heard Violet squeal at her father did I realize who had discovered me. I peered into the watery blue eyes of a tall, angular man dressed in a dark suit. Dr. Nagel had come looking for his daughter and had caught me crawling across the barn floor.

"Karlina! Did you fall? Are you injured?" Though his voice was strong and clear, the straw muffled Anton's footsteps as he ran toward me.

I didn't have time to answer before he was kneeling at my side. When I looked up, I was met by two piercing stares. Anton's dark eyes revealed concern, but suspicion lurked in Violet's.

"I-I am fine," I croaked.

Anton grasped my elbow as I attempted to stand, but the toe

of my shoe caught on my hem. I stumbled and he grabbed me around the waist.

Violet exhaled a disgusted noise. "Surely you could think of a more original way to gain a man's attention. I'm surprised you didn't—"

"Violet Nagel!" Her father's reprimand stopped her midsentence. "Your words are unkind, uncharitable, and embarrassing. An apology is in order." Violet glared at me. "And I expect to see and hear a pleasant manner while you apologize."

Her look softened a modicum, but there was no friendliness in her demeanor. "If what I said was untrue, I apologize."

Her qualified apology didn't deserve an acceptance, but I didn't want to prolong her stay or endure any questions from her father. "Your apology is accepted."

Violet folded her arms across her waist. "And I think it would be most appropriate if you apologized for eavesdropping on a private conversation." She looked at her father with her lips curled in a wicked smile. "Sister Karlina was on the floor of the barn eavesdropping on my conversation with Brother Anton. I'm sure you don't consider that proper behavior for Sister Karlina, do you?"

Her father looked back and forth between Violet and me. His eyes clouded and his lips tightened into a thin seam. Clearly he didn't want to be drawn into the midst of a disagreement between two women.

"We need to be on our way, Violet. And you need not worry yourself about the inappropriate behavior of anyone else. You were inside the barn without a proper chaperone. We discussed this before we left home, and you promised you would remain in plain sight while you were in Anton's company. Do you recall that conversation?"

Violet's eyes widened, and she inhaled a deep breath. "Please, Vater. There is no need to talk about this in front of a stranger."

She sidestepped around me and hastened to her father's side. She stopped long enough to glance over her shoulder. "Auf Wieder-sehen, Brother Anton."

Anton tipped his head. "Auf Wiedersehen, Sister Violet, Brother Nagel."

Brother Nagel bid us both good-day before he walked away. I was thankful Violet had decided to rush off rather than remain and interrogate me. In the distance I could hear Violet's high-pitched voice, though I couldn't make out what she was saying. No doubt her father had further chastised her for being alone with a man in the barn.

Anton had moved a short distance from me and leaned against one of the barn poles. His lips were curved in a curious smile. "I see you care enough for me that you were willing to crawl around on the floor and listen to my conversation with Violet."

Did he feel so smug and secure that he thought he could joke about his recent conversation with Violet? Did he think I'd not heard what had been said? When she'd come to see him before, he'd denied any feelings for her, but now I knew he hadn't spoken the truth. I had vowed to guard my heart—but I hadn't. My stomach burned as hot as glowing coals in a firepit, and I wheeled around to face him. "You have no reason to smile at me, Anton Becker. I heard the two of you exchanging your words of love for each other. How dare you speak of love for me one week and do the same with that mean-spirited woman the next! How you could even consider marrying someone as callous and hurtful as Violet Nagel is beyond my imagination, but I suppose you deserve each other."

His eyes opened as wide as two of the kitchen saucers. "What does that mean? Are you saying I am hurtful and callous?"

I straightened my shoulders and gave a firm nod. "That is exactly what I am saying. One week you say you care for me, and then I hear you saying you care for Violet."

He jerked as though I had slapped him. "I did not say I loved Violet. Never! Not in my entire life have I said such a thing. I told you before that there was never anything beyond friendship between us. You are the only woman I have ever loved and the only one who has heard those words from my lips."

I ignored his denial and pointed my index finger at him. "And I heard you say that you would be returning to live in High. Why have you been telling me you wanted to remain in East and continue to work with the sheep? All the time you were saying those things you knew you were going to return to Violet as soon as the elders gave their permission."

"'The Lord is my shepherd; I shall not want. He maketh me to lie down in green pastures: he leadeth me beside the still waters. He restoreth my soul: he leadeth me in the paths of righteousness for his name's sake. Yea, though I walk through the valley of the shadow of death, I will fear no evil: for thou art with me; thy rod and thy staff they comfort me.'"

"Stop it, Anton. Quoting Scripture is not going to convince me."

"'Yea, though I walk through the valley of the shadow of death, I will fear no evil: for thou art with me; thy rod and thy staff they comfort me. Thou preparest a table before me in the presence of mine enemies: thou anointest my head with oil; my cup runneth over. Surely goodness and mercy shall follow me all the days of my life: and I will dwell in the house of the Lord for ever.'" As if on cue, one of the sheep bleated and several others joined in.

"Are you finished now?" I raised my voice to be heard above the noisy sheep.

He nodded. "Ja, I am finished, but you should not tell me to stop when you are the one who taught me to use that Scripture when I could feel my anger taking hold."

Shame washed over me. It was true that I'd been the one to encourage him to use Scripture—particularly the twenty-third

Psalm. But when the recitation interfered with my own anger, I wanted him to remain silent. "You're right. I apologize. I should never discourage you from reciting Scriptures. But you should not be telling me lies."

He stepped closer and took my hand. "I have not told you any lies. Sit down beside me. I am going to tell you everything, so there will be no secrets between us."

We sat on one of the large toolboxes not far from where I'd been crawling on the floor a short time ago. I folded my hands in my lap, determined to remain silent and carefully listen to what he said. I was sure I would catch him in a lie—probably several.

I tipped my head at an angle and forced a smile. "You may begin. I'm listening."

"You know about my temper and that because I was in several fights, the elders lost patience with me. I received a warning that if I was involved in any more fisticuffs, I would be sent to another village."

"Ja, and you were."

He nodded. "That's right. It was snowing one day and there were about ten or twelve of us that went sledding. Violet and her brother were among those who joined in. On that particular day, she was determined to have time alone with me. On many occasions she made it clear she expected me to marry her, but I never encouraged her and told her I did not have plans to marry anyone."

I arched my brows. "Well, that may turn out to be true enough if you—"

He held up his hand. "Please let me finish." He smiled, but I knew he didn't want my interruptions. "As I told you, we were sledding. Violet insisted that she ride down the hill with me. Her brother had gone down right before us. We were approaching the bottom of the hill but still moving pretty fast when she lunged to the side and we both rolled off of the sled. She ended up on top of me. Her brother was standing nearby. I tried to get her off, but she remained there and kissed me—all in front of her brother."

I gasped. "What did he do?"

"He grabbed my arm and pulled on me while screaming at Violet to get up. Once I was on my feet, he swung at me and landed a hard blow to my cheek." One corner of his mouth turned upward. "I didn't turn the other cheek. Instead, I knocked him to the ground and gave him the fight of his life." He massaged the knuckles of his right hand with his left palm. "By the time we finished that fight, the entire truth had been turned upside down. Violet said she hadn't intentionally caused us to roll off the sled. And though she didn't say I had been the cause, she denied that I had tried to get away from her. And her brother said I had struck the first blow. Not wanting to suffer the wrath of her father, Violet said her brother's story was closest to the truth."

"And you still called her your friend when she visited here the first time? And you were willing to be alone with her in the barn after all of that? Do you think she has changed and will not create more problems for you?"

"You are right, but she is a difficult woman to fend off when she sets her mind to something. I came into the barn with the sheep, and she was sitting in here waiting for me. Her father felt safe leaving her because I was out in the pasture. Your Vater was down here when she arrived and told her she would come to no harm."

Anton brushed a piece of straw from my hair. "Your Vater probably didn't think she would be here so long or that I would return while she was still here." He reached down and took my hand. "You do believe me, don't you? You are the only woman I have ever loved, Karlina. No matter what Violet may say, I do not have feelings for her. Please say you believe me."

Something deep in his eyes told me he was speaking the truth.

"I will take what you've told me as truth, Anton, but please don't disappoint me."

He gathered me in his arms and kissed away any misgivings I'd held on to. Within his arms, I fell under the spell of his tender kisses, and my suspicions evaporated as quickly as an early morning fog.

The supper bell rang, and as we walked toward the house, thoughts of Violet returned. Would she make further accusations against Anton? And if she did, would her father believe her? There was no doubt she was determined to have Anton as her husband. To what lengths might she go to ensnare him? A chill coursed down my spine as I considered the possibilities.

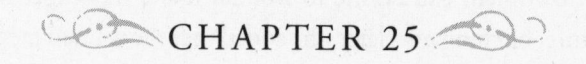

CHAPTER 25

May 1893
Dovie

During each of the many days that followed, Karlina and I returned to Jakub's home. Either together or separate, at least one of us would make a trek up the hill to the Sedlacek farm. Only once had Cousin Louise mentioned missing a portion of that day's broth. Fortunately for me, Sister Bertha had pointed at the stove and told Cousin Louise she was to blame for leaving the kettle on the stove and the broth had boiled down. Cousin Louise hadn't appeared convinced, but she didn't question it further. She did apologize for the scanty portions of gravy served that day, and I remained silent.

Although Sophia's weakness continued, the rest of the family had recovered and her mother and grandmother now were able to care for the girl. For that, I was most thankful, as the journeys to the farmhouse had proved both worrisome and exhilarating. Each time I had ventured to their home, I worried that someone would see me. Yet providing help to the family had given me a sense of fulfillment that I hadn't experienced since I had provided care to my mother. When I expressed those thoughts to Karlina, she said that unless I planned to marry, maybe I should consider training to become a midwife or nurse when I joined my father in Texas.

Her comment caused me to wonder if she was eager for my departure, but moments later, she added that she wanted me to live in East. I didn't confide that my desire to stay wavered back and forth. Once I discovered the truth about my mother's departure, I wasn't certain if I would want to remain. If I was Berndt's half sister, it would be an uncomfortable situation for both of us—and for his father. Not to mention the effect it would have on his stepmother, especially if she hadn't been told the truth. Increasingly certain he was my half brother, guilt overcame me. A half sister should not have the kinds of feelings for her brother that assailed me each time I was in his presence. I had feelings for Berndt, and my thoughts were those of a woman in love with a man she desired to marry—not the thoughts of a sister for her brother.

This morning when he had delivered the bread, I promised to meet Berndt at the pond later in the day. Since it appeared he knew nothing about a relationship between my mother and his father, I decided it would be best if we didn't meet alone again. Karlina and I hadn't departed immediately after the noonday meal. Sister Marta had taken ill, so I stayed to help clear the dishes. Karlina had helped, as well, and though she hadn't moved at her customary speed, it was good to have the extra set of hands. Cousin Louise had been thankful for our help, and my departure had been delayed by only a little over half an hour.

Karlina and I walked toward the barn at a quick pace. There had been another cold snap and we both bowed our heads against the chilly breeze. "Has your father decided when he will begin the shearing?" I had heard Karlina speak at length about the event, and I was curious to see how the shearers would handle the sheep. Karlina told me the experienced men had no problem and could accomplish the task with ease and speed. Though I didn't doubt her word, I couldn't imagine those large sheep holding still for the process.

"With the unexpected change in the weather, Vater has decided to wait until June to begin. Some of the other sheep farmers have already sheared, but Vater will not shear until he is certain the radical changes in temperature have ended. If it turns cold after they are sheared, it is too hard on the sheep." She smiled. "We wash the sheep before shearing so the wool will be cleaner for the mill. We don't want any possibility of cold weather at shearing time. Vater says that if a shepherd thinks first of his sheep's comfort and care, he will be rewarded with a healthy flock."

She had lowered her voice as she spoke, and I giggled. "You sound just like your father."

Karlina joined in my laughter and then pointed toward the barn, where Anton was leading the sheep out to pasture. He lifted his shepherd's crook toward us, and we waved. "What about Anton? Will he help with the shearing?"

"Ja. Vater will give him some lessons before the other shearers arrive. He won't be able to work as quickly as the seasoned shearers, but I think he will do fine. The sheep have learned to recognize his voice and trust him. That should help."

"Has your father asked Jakub to come and help, too?"

Karlina glanced at me. "Ja. I think Mr. Sedlacek would like Jakub to work at their farm, but he needs the extra money and has agreed Jakub should help with the shearing. Vater is pleased, because Jakub is pretty fast. Not like the professional shearers who go from farm to farm, but he is gut."

The thought of Mr. Sedlacek speaking to Cousin George was

enough to make my stomach drop to my ankles. "Jakub's father didn't tell that we had been there, did he?"

"Nein. Vater didn't talk to Mr. Sedlacek. Jakub came to the barn and spoke to Vater. He said they needed the extra income." Karlina grasped my hand and we continued onward, walking hand-in-hand like young schoolgirls. "Jakub told me that Sophia has now regained all of her strength and is doing very well." She drew a little closer as we walked. "He also asked about you. He said you hadn't been near the pond and he missed seeing you."

"Jakub is a nice young man."

"Ja, and I think he is as smitten with you as Berndt is." Karlina squeezed my hand. "You should discourage both of them before you break their hearts."

I stopped short and yanked on her hand. "I have not been encouraging either one of them. I am going to meet Berndt this afternoon and tell him that we should not see each other alone again."

"And Jakub? Will you tell him the same?" She shook her head and a lock of brown hair escaped from beneath her bonnet. "I am sure he thinks he might win your heart."

I sighed, frustrated by the complications. Berndt was the man who had won my heart, but I could not have him. With each passing day I was becoming more and more attracted to life in the colonies—the people, their way of life—and to Berndt. And though I enjoyed Jakub's company and thought him a fine man, I knew he could never be anything more than a friend. It would be unfair if I didn't tell him the truth.

"The next time I see Jakub, I will talk to him, but I hope that we can always be friends."

Karlina turned loose of my hand. "After you talk to Jakub, you should not meet alone again. If you accidentally cross paths, you should speak and continue on your way. To do otherwise would build false hope."

"I suppose you are right, but I shall miss his friendship."

"Better that you feel the loss of his friendship than to have him suffer heartbreak if you continue to see him." She arched her brows and stared at me. "Ja?"

"Yes, I will tell him." I had agreed, but in my heart I disliked the idea of terminating my friendship with Jakub, for I knew it would hurt his feelings—and those of his family, as well.

When we neared the barn, Karlina stopped beside me. "I know Berndt will be unhappy with your decision, but soon he will realize that it is best. If you decide to stay and live among us, who knows what the future will hold for the two of you?"

I smiled and gave a slight nod. If Karlina had known Berndt was my half brother, she would never have said such a thing. But she didn't. And neither did I—at least not for sure. Yet I did know my feelings for Berndt were not those of a sister for her brother, and to continue down this path would be treacherous for both of us.

I glanced toward the village. "Your father is coming down to help you this afternoon?"

"Nein. He needs to rest this afternoon, but I am accustomed to being here alone. You go on." Beads of perspiration dotted her forehead, and she wiped them away with the tips of her fingers.

"You are perspiring when it is this cold? Are you not feeling well?"

"I am fine." She lifted the corner of her cloak. "I wore my heavy winter cloak, and it is too warm."

I frowned at her, not sure if she was being completely truthful with me, for I was wearing a heavy coat and was thankful for the warmth. "You are sure you're not ill?"

"You should stop with your worrying. Go and meet Berndt, and when you've finished your talk with him, come back and tell me how it went."

After promising to return, I hurried toward the pond. I wasn't certain what time Berndt would arrive, but I didn't want to miss him. If he wasn't there when I arrived, I decided I would wait in a nearby grove of trees. If I didn't hide and Jakub should happen along the road above the hillside, he would see me and likely come down for a visit. To be sitting and talking with Jakub when Berndt arrived would not be good.

I was pleased to see Berndt sitting in our usual spot near the pond. I called to him as I approached. Several birds that had roosted on a nearby limb took wing when I shouted my greeting, and I glanced heavenward as they flew off. Berndt stood and waved. Even at this distance, I could see his broad smile. I doubted he'd be smiling when we parted. That thought caused me pain, but I remained determined.

When I'd drawn a bit closer, he ran to meet me, but when he attempted to kiss my cheek, I backed away. I saw the hurt in his eyes but continued to smile. "Come, let's sit down." Once he was seated beside me, all thoughts of how to begin the conversation escaped me. I should have rehearsed.

He reached for my hand, but I moved my arm before he could gain a hold. His eyebrows furrowed and confusion shone in his eyes. "Have I done something that has angered you? I thought you wanted to meet me this afternoon. I am on time, ja?"

I nodded. "You are on time and I wanted to meet you, but what I have to say is something that will make neither of us very happy."

He frowned, but then he tipped his head to the side and chuckled. "If it will make both of us unhappy, then I will talk instead."

"I wish it could be that easy, Berndt, but it will not." Tears burned the back of my eyes. I folded my hands together and placed them in my lap. I couldn't bear to look at him, so I stared at my hands resting atop my black woolen skirt. "It is better if we do not see each other anymore. I will still see you when you deliver the bread, but it is not wise for us to see each other like this in the future."

Mouth agape, he stared at me as if I had announced a recent death. And perhaps I had. The death of our relationship and what might have been. "You are teasing with me, ja? Why would you not be able to see me again? I have spoken of how much I care for you, Dovie. You know it is my wish that you remain in the colonies. I do not understand."

"I don't know what the future holds for me, and it isn't fair for us to continue to build hope and then have it end. It would be too painful."

"You are speaking in riddles. Why was it fine a week ago, but it is not today?"

"It never was all right, but I wanted to believe it could work."

He grabbed my hand. "It can work. Together we can make it work."

"There's so much you don't know and can't understand right now, Berndt." My voice broke as I spoke. "And I can't change any of it. I'm doing my best to unearth the truth, and when I do, I hope that you will remain my friend."

He shifted on the log and turned to face me. "You know that nothing you say is making any sense. If you came to me and said that you have decided to go and live with your father—this I can understand. I would not like it, but I would understand. But all of this talk that you are trying to dig up some truth—this I do not understand." He closed his eyes and then opened them wide. "Can you say you do not love me?"

His question shot through me like a sharp arrow, and I jumped to my feet. "I must go now. I am sorry it must be this way." Hiking my skirt above my ankles, I ran toward the barn. I couldn't answer any further questions. If I did, he would see my tears and ask even more questions. Questions I couldn't answer.

When I had almost reached the barn, I turned to glance over my shoulder. Berndt was nowhere in sight. I had expected him to run after me. A part of me had wanted him to, but I knew he'd made the right decision. The one that was best for both of us.

Once inside the barn, I wiped my damp cheeks with the back of my hand and waited for my eyes to adjust to the dim light before I went to seek out Karlina. She would be pleased to hear that I had been straightforward with Berndt. When I didn't hear any noise, I called out to her. After waiting a few moments and not hearing a reply, I started through the barn while continuing to call her name.

I'd gone halfway through when I stood still and listened. It was then I heard her. A soft, low groan from near where I stood. I peeked around the barn pole and caught sight of her. "Karlina! What's wrong?" She lay motionless on the floor and moaned my name.

I kneeled beside her, and it took only a quick look to see she was ill. Heat radiated from her body like a cast-iron cookstove. She coughed and rolled to her side, her eyes glazed with fever. I needed to get her back to the house, but she couldn't walk—and I couldn't carry her.

"I've got to go get help. I'll be back." I hesitated. "Do you hear me, Karlina? I'll be back to get you."

She whimpered, but I couldn't wait any longer. I raced to the door and had cleared the entrance when I saw Berndt. Head bowed low and shoulders slumped, he was walking toward the village, just now returning from the pond.

"Berndt!" I screamed as loud as I could. "Come help me! Karlina is ill."

He looked in my direction but didn't change course. Instead, he stood there staring at me.

I waved my arms overhead. "Berndt! Come and help Karlina."

My words finally seemed to register, and he loped toward me. "What is wrong?"

"In the barn. Karlina is very sick. Can you carry her back to the house?"

"Ja, of course I can."

I ran ahead of him and returned to where Karlina lay in the straw. I knelt down on one knee and brushed her damp hair from her forehead. "Berndt is going to carry you back to the house, Karlina." I turned my attention to Berndt. "Should I run ahead and tell Cousin Louise, or should I go to Main for the doctor?"

Berndt leaned down and carefully lifted Karlina into his arms. She moaned and her head fell back against his shoulder. "Go first to your cousin. The doctor may not be necessary. Let her decide." He settled Karlina in his arms and strode toward the doors. "Go on now. I will be fine."

The wind whipped at my coat, and I yanked it tight to my body. I silently prayed that God would heal Karlina. What if she'd contracted influenza? What if she should die? My mind raced as I ran toward home. If Karlina died, it would be my fault. I was the one who had taken her to the Sedlacek house. She hadn't wanted to go, but I'd finally persuaded her. If anyone was going to be ill, it should be me, not Karlina. "Please, Lord, don't let her die."

My feet clattered along the wooden sidewalk and up the porch steps. I pushed down on the metal door latch and flung open the door. "Cousin Louise!" All of the sisters had gone home for a few hours. No one was downstairs. I raced up the first few steps. My legs ached and I grabbed the banister for support. "Cousin Louise, are you up there?"

"Ja, I am changing the beds. I am in Anton's room."

I continued up the steps. "Berndt is carrying Karlina to the house. She's very sick. Do you want me to go to Main for the doctor?"

She met me in the hall, her eyes clear and her demeanor calm. "Nein. First you must tell me what is wrong with her."

I rattled off the symptoms I had observed. "I think she has influenza."

"Why would you think that? There has been no word of influenza in the colonies. We would have received word if there was an outbreak of some sort." She patted my cheek. "I'm sure it's because of your Mutter, but every little ailment will not end up as influenza."

Her words were brave, but I detected a glimmer of worry in her eyes. Was she thinking about her sons who had died of pneumonia and fearful she might lose her daughter? My stomach squeezed into a knot. In my haste to help the Sedlacek family, I had placed Karlina and her family in jeopardy.

This wasn't the time to tell Cousin Louise about the Sedlacek family, but once she'd seen Karlina and decided whether to call the doctor, I would have to tell her. There would be consequences for my behavior. And I deserved whatever the elders would mete out.

Cousin Louise gestured toward Anton's room. "Please finish dusting in Anton's room. I will go downstairs and wait for Karlina. Cousin George is asleep in our bedroom. He needs his rest, so we will try to avoid waking him." I heard Cousin Louise's retreating footsteps in the hallway. She was halfway down the steps when she called, "And please turn down Karlina's bedcovers."

"I'll do it right now." Doing my best to be quiet, I hurried down the narrow hall and pulled back the covers with the care of a mother preparing a perfect space for her newborn. The dusting could wait. Karlina's needs must come first. My fear and guilt mixed together and formed a hard knot that now resided in the pit of my stomach. Nothing I did for Karlina would erase the fact that I was the one who had influenced her to go to the Sedlacek farm. I was the reason she now suffered with some unknown illness—probably influenza. I bit back my tears. Losing control of my emotions would not help. If I was going to be of any help, I must keep my wits about me.

As the sound of Berndt's voice drifted up the stairs, I closed the distance between the bedroom and the top of the stairs in short order. I peered over the railing. Berndt still held Karlina in his arms. My heart ached at the sight of her head lolling against his chest. Berndt took the steps at a careful pace. Cousin Louise followed close on his heels with several towels draped over her arm and a basin of water balanced in her hands.

I motioned for Berndt to follow me. "Be careful when you place her on the bed."

Once he'd lowered her onto the bed, he exhaled a whoosh of air and massaged his upper arms. "That is a longer walk than I remembered."

Cousin Louise placed the basin on a small table. "That is because you didn't have to carry someone the entire distance until today. Thank you, Berndt. Your help has aided a great deal toward Karlina's recovery."

I glanced at Berndt. He nodded and backed from the room. "I am pleased I could help. I will be praying for Sister Karlina." He hesitated in the doorway. "You would like me to go and fetch Dr. Zimmer, Sister Louise?"

"If you would take a seat in the parlor until I have examined her a little further . . ."

I leaned over the end of the bed. "I can go if a doctor is needed. There's no need for Berndt to wait."

Cousin Louise didn't turn away from Karlina. "Even in a weary state, Berndt can get to the doctor much faster than you, Dovie." She motioned to Karlina's feet. "You can take off her shoes."

I didn't argue about going for the doctor. Instead, I deftly removed Karlina's shoes and awaited the older woman's next instruction. She wrung out towels and placed them on Karlina's forehead. As Cousin Louise ministered to her daughter, memories of caring for the Sedlacek women flashed through my mind.

A short time later Karlina coughed—a raspy, strangled sound from deep in her chest. Cousin Louise turned to me. "Ask Berndt to go for Dr. Zimmer." I was certain I saw fear lurking behind the tears that now rimmed her eyes.

Once advised the doctor was needed, Berndt didn't hesitate. He jumped up from the chair and flew down the stairs. He was out the door before I could catch my breath. Through it all, Cousin George continued to sleep. Cousin Louise said it was a blessing, for he would pace and worry if he knew what was happening a few doors away. I carried fresh water to Karlina's bedside and was relieved when Dr. Zimmer and Berndt finally returned.

I hovered near Karlina's bedside while the doctor examined her. Cousin Louise advised him of the few changes since Berndt had carried her upstairs. She mentioned the cool compresses she had used and the deep cough. He pressed his stethoscope to Karlina's chest and, with Cousin Louise's help, rolled her to one side so he could listen to her back.

"It could be pneumonia, it could be influenza, or it could be a bad case of catarrh. Hard to know for sure, but I'm going to rule out influenza unless I see some other symptoms. I'll have the pharmacist in Main prepare her medicine. Under your care, I'm certain she'll be out of bed in no time, Sister Louise."

I stepped near the side of the bed. "But if she has influenza, would her treatment be different? Would you order different medicines for her?"

The doctor turned, peered over his eyeglasses, and looked down his nose at me. "I do not believe we've met." Some of the kindness drained from his voice as he spoke to me.

"I'm Dovie Cates. A relative of the family." I leaned to one side, hoping to gain a look at Cousin Louise, but the doctor blocked my view.

"I see. And why are you concerned about the treatment of influenza?"

Cousin Louise immediately entered the conversation and explained that my mother's death had occurred due to influenza. The doctor gave me a sympathetic look and patted my arm. "We haven't had any influenza in the colonies for several years. There is no need to borrow trouble. With the two of you caring for Sister Karlina, I'm sure she will have a speedy recovery."

I forced a smile, uncertain if I should confide in Dr. Zimmer or wait and speak to Cousin Louise alone. By the time I had found the nerve to speak with him, the doctor was on his way downstairs. I called to him, but Cousin Louise shook her head and placed her index finger against her lips. She made my decision for me.

CHAPTER 26

Although I wanted to talk to Cousin Louise and clear my conscience, I didn't find an opportunity until the dishes had been washed after the evening meal. Drawing near as she hung a dish towel to dry, I gathered my courage. "I need to speak with you, Cousin Louise. It is important."

The older woman's shoulders sagged, but she poured a cup of coffee and followed me into the dining room. After settling on one of the long wooden benches, she stared at me. There was a hint of impatience in her eyes, a look that said she had no time to waste. I swallowed hard and folded my hands atop the table, not sure where to begin.

She swallowed a sip of coffee and gestured for me to speak. "What is it you need to tell me, Dovie?"

"My fear that Karlina may have influenza has nothing to do with my mother's illness. Karlina and I went to the Sedlacek farm to take medicine to them. I think Sophia and maybe some of the other family members may have had influenza."

"You are saying Karlina has been out of the village and has been around people with influenza?" Cousin Louise leaned toward me with her face wrinkled into a frown and a shimmer of disbelief in her eyes. "Tell me everything, because this is hard for me to believe."

I told her how I had been at the pond alone when Jakub arrived and pleaded with me to come to his home because his family was ill. Her complexion paled as I disclosed all that had happened.

"It is all my fault. Karlina didn't want to go, but I begged her. I didn't know how to help them. And now she has fallen ill, and it is because of me." Before I finished the story, I had worked myself into a tearful frenzy that I couldn't control.

Cousin Louise tenderly clasped my arm as I gasped for a breath of air. "All this sobbing will not help. Neither of us will be any gut to Karlina if we do not remain calm."

I sniffled and pulled a handkerchief from my pocket. "I know I've done a terrible thing, and I beg you to forgive me. I'll do whatever you ask, but I know nothing I can ever do will set things aright."

"So now the Sedlacek family has recovered from their illness, ja?" Instead of looking at me, Cousin Louise stared at her folded hands.

I nodded. "When Jakub's family returned to health, he came to the barn and told Karlina."

Her lips drooped into a frown. "How did you get the medicine?"

"I asked Karlina to take it from the cabinet."

The silence that followed was worse than a shouted reprimand. Finally Cousin Louise closed her eyes and nodded. "Well, it seems you both played an equal part in this. You and Karlina knew you were going against the rules. While I would not expect you to abide by the rules in all circumstances, I am surprised at Karlina's decision."

Cousin Louise rested her forehead in the palm of her hand before she slowly lifted her head and met my gaze. "I understand you were trying to help people in need, and that is gut. But instead of taking the matter into your own hands or going to Karlina, you should have come to me or Cousin George and asked for help. For several years, Jakub has helped with the shearing. I am sure he has a gut family. We would have provided help to them—but not by sending two single women to their home."

"I told him Dr. Zimmer would come, but his father didn't want a doctor."

She held up her hand. "There is no need to go on with this now. It changes nothing. What is done is done, and the elders will decide what should happen. I will speak to Cousin George, and he can speak to the elders and seek their opinion."

My hands trembled. I had hoped Cousin Louise might agree to forgo speaking to Cousin George or the elders. "Do you think they will tell me to leave the village?"

"I do not know what they will ask of you or Karlina, but you should be prepared to take your punishment without argument." She looked deep into my eyes. "Is that everything? You have left nothing out? There will be no more surprises?"

Should I tell her what I knew, or at least suspected, about Berndt? It would likely be better to go ahead and tell her now. Who could say if I would have another opportunity? With Karlina ill and Cousin George sure to go to the elders very soon, I might be on a train to Texas and never have resolution about my mother's past.

I inhaled a deep breath. "There is one more thing I should tell you."

Cousin Louise sighed. "I hope it is gut news and not something else that will cause me more gray hairs."

I peeked at her from beneath my thick eyelashes and shrugged. "I wanted to tell you that I read some of the letters you left out in your bedroom. The ones my mother wrote to you."

"Ja, I knew you did. They had been moved from where I left them. And so? What is it you want to tell me? Something about those letters of your mother's or something about you and Berndt? If you want to tell me you have been meeting him at the pond, I already know."

Heat climbed up my neck. I wanted to ask how she knew, but it was more important that I tell her what I'd learned about my mother. "It is about the letters and Berndt."

Cousin Louise gestured for me to continue.

"I know that Berndt is my half brother."

"You know what?" Cousin Louise stared at me as though I'd lost my senses. "What would make you believe such a thing?"

Cousin Louise wasn't going to make this easy. I had hoped she would simply tell me that I was correct and then answer the rest of my questions. But that would not be. She was going to test me before she revealed anything.

I spouted everything I had learned: "I read about the baby and the man she referred to as E in her letters. I read that she loved him and how much she regretted leaving the baby with his parents. And when Sister Elsa spoke of my mother being in love with someone, you interrupted her before she could finish speaking, but I heard her say Brother Er—. At first, I thought she was talking about Brother Erich, the schoolteacher."

A smile tipped one corner of Cousin Louise's lips. "That old man? He was as old as her Opa."

"That is what I discovered. Once I knew it wasn't the schoolteacher, I continued to look for anyone named Erich. It didn't take long to find out that Berndt's father was the man my mother loved. They had a baby, and I think my Oma and Opa left the colonies with her because they were ashamed. I think that, for all of her life, my mother continued to love Berndt's father, and that is why she never talked about her life here. She was afraid that if she spoke of the past, she might slip and tell more than she should." I inhaled a deep breath. "And I also think that is why you and Berndt's father have worked so hard to keep us apart. You knew if we fell in love, you would have to tell us the truth—that we are related."

Cousin Louise shook her head. "You think you have all the answers, but you have none that are correct. You have conceived a story that is beyond any imagination except your own."

I wasn't surprised by her reaction. Though I had hoped she would simply tell me I'd unveiled the truth, I had expected the long-held secrets would be protected. "If what I have said is no more than a fairy tale, please tell me the truth, Cousin Louise. That is what I have been seeking since the day I arrived."

"And from the day you arrived, I have told you there was no deep secret to your mother's leaving the village. Yes, she loved Erich Lehmann, but they did not have a child. Your Mutter never did anything to cause her parents embarrassment or shame. My heart is heavy that you should think so little—"

"I do not think little of her, but it was—"

Cousin Louise waved me to silence. "I will say this to you only one time, so you listen very carefully." She touched her finger to her ear. "The baby you read about in that letter was not Berndt. That little boy was the son of your Opa's cousin Johann. His wife died in childbirth, so your Oma and Mutter cared for the infant. Your Mutter became very attached to the baby, and it was very difficult for her to leave him. She wanted to stay in East because she loved Erich and also because of the baby, Wilhelm, but your Oma and Opa insisted that she leave with them."

I was trying hard to comprehend what Cousin Louise had said.

"I never heard my Mutter speak of any relatives named Johann or Wilhelm. Do they still live in the colonies?"

She shook her head. "They lived in East until Wilhelm was three and then they moved to Homestead, where Johann worked in the warehouse where they stock our woolen and other goods for shipment by railroad. After they had lived in Homestead for about five or six years, the two of them left."

"For where?"

"One of the elders in Homestead told Cousin George that Johann met some men who came to the warehouse to purchase goods. They told him he could have a gut life on the outside. I never heard where they went, but Johann took Wilhelm, and no one has heard from them since. At least not that I know of."

"So Berndt is not my half brother?"

She chuckled. "No. Berndt is not your half brother. Sister Anna and Brother Erich are Berndt's parents."

"Then why did you and Brother Erich work so hard to keep us apart?"

"Ach!" Cousin Louise waved a dismissive gesture. "Because we did not want the two of you to suffer the way your Mutter and Erich suffered when her family left the colonies. His heart was broken and so was hers. It took them both a long time before they healed."

"Why did my Oma and Opa leave here? And if my mother loved Erich, why couldn't she refuse to go with them, or come back later and marry him?"

Cousin Louise sighed. "You are so full of questions." She hesitated a moment. "Did you not find the answers in your Mutter's letters?"

Shame washed over me while I shook my head. "I did not have time to read all of them."

"I see. Well, I will answer the best I can, but I am not sure it is the best thing for you. I told you before that sometimes the past is best left behind. Some of what I tell you may cause disappointment and pain, but if you are determined . . ."

There was no doubt she wanted me to tell her I was satisfied to leave the past buried. But I wasn't. No matter how it would change my feelings, I wanted to hear everything. I folded my hands and nodded for her to continue.

She sighed. "Your Opa was a clockmaker here in East—a very fine clockmaker. The beautiful clock in our parlor was made by him. Did you know that?"

"No, but it is quite lovely." When I first arrived, I had noticed the intricately carved clock, but I'd had no idea my Opa had made it. My grandparents had died before I was born, and like everything else in her past, my mother had seldom mentioned them. My questions appeared to pain her, and I had ceased asking.

"Your Oma and your Mutter enjoyed living in the colonies, but your Opa always had a desire to live in the outside world. He was never content, and I think that is why he took matters into his own hands." She inhaled a deep breath. "I am telling you everything I know, so there is no need to ask questions once I finish. There will be nothing more I can tell you."

I nodded and scooted to the edge of my chair, eager to hear what else she would reveal.

"While they were living here in East, your Opa became friends with a farmer who lived nearby. The farmer and your Opa had an arrangement between them."

"What kind of arrangement?"

"For some of the clocks he made. Your Opa gave several clocks to the farmer, who made arrangements to sell them, and your Opa received money for the clocks."

"And he kept the money?"

"Ja. Somehow the elders discovered what he had done."

I couldn't believe my ears. My grandfather had kept money that didn't belong to him. Little wonder my mother hadn't told me any of this. "And they made him leave?"

"Nein. The Grossebruderrat asked him to repent. They decided if he would ask forgiveness, he would be banned from church for one year and all would be forgiven. He was never asked to leave the colonies."

"But he didn't want to do that?"

Cousin Louise took another sip of coffee. "Nein. He wanted to leave, and this gave him the opportunity to do so. They left for Covington a few weeks later."

"Why Covington?"

"There was a shop in Covington where your Opa secured work, but I do not know the particulars. I never heard how the arrangements were made—I doubt your Mutter ever knew, either. He had great talent, so I am sure he did not worry much about finding work."

"What about my grandmother? Did she want to stay?"

"Oh ja. She loved it here, but she knew she had to go with her husband. She never complained." Cousin Louise shrugged. "And your Mutter had no choice, either. Your Opa was strong-minded and determined to keep his family with him."

Hearing all of this caused me to think of the conversation with my own father last November. Even though he hadn't wanted to be alone when he moved to Texas, he had permitted me to come to the colonies—a vast difference from the way my mother's request had been handled many years ago. His desire to see me content had been greater than his own happiness.

I waited until Cousin Louise drank the remainder of her coffee and placed the cup on the table.

"From what you've said, I can see that my Opa would never have permitted my mother to stay in East, but couldn't she have returned later and married Erich?"

"Nein. Erich married Sister Anna two years after your Mutter left. Eventually she met your Vater, and she was mostly happy with him, I think." She reached across the table and lifted my chin with her index finger. "I know this is not the exciting story you imagined, but it is the truth, Dovie. There are no hidden secrets about other children in your Mutter's past."

My thoughts whipped around like cream in a butter churn. I was sure Cousin Louise was telling the truth, but after piecing together my own version of my mother's past, it was difficult to push aside my disbelief.

"I thought you would be pleased to have the answers you wanted. Instead, you look disappointed."

"What did you mean about my mother being mostly happy with my father, and why did the two of you cease writing to each other?"

"Questions, questions, and more questions. You are always wanting to hear more." She glanced longingly toward the stairway, likely wishing to escape, but she remained. "Your Mutter was always sickly and a bit melancholy." Her lips tilted in a slight smile. "But you already know that, ja?"

I nodded.

"After she and your Vater had been married for several years, she became very sad—after she lost the baby."

"What baby?"

Cousin Louise momentarily closed her eyes. "A son, who died in childbirth when you were maybe two or three years old. Your Mutter was very sad but determined to have another child. When that did not happen, she decided she wanted to return to the colonies to live. She did everything she could think of to convince your Vater to move here, but he would not."

Disbelief wrapped around me like a thick cord that threatened to cut off my breath. "My mother wanted to return?"

"Ja. It is in some of those letters I have upstairs."

"So when my father refused to move, she finally realized she had to be happy with her life in Cincinnati?"

Cousin Louise's frown deepened. "Not so much. She wrote and told me that she planned to come here without your Vater."

I gasped. "She was going to leave my father? Did she ever return?"

"Nein. I wrote to her and said I did not believe she should do such a thing. I told her she had made a commitment to her marriage and that unless your Vater was mistreating her, she had an obligation to work toward making her marriage stronger."

I reeled at the shocking news. Never had my father or mother mentioned that there was unhappiness in their marriage, but the news explained much about my mother and her unwillingness to speak of her life in the colonies. No doubt it caused her heartache.

"So my mother agreed with what you wrote to her."

"That is when she stopped writing to me, so I cannot say. I wrote to her several times after that, but she didn't respond. Finally, I wrote of my concern for her and asked that she write to let me know if she was well."

I leaned across the table. "And did she send you a letter?"

Cousin Louise shrugged. "I would not call it a letter. She wrote one sentence on a piece of paper that said she was fine and I should not worry about her. I was sad that she was angry with me and would not write, but there was nothing I could do." She motioned toward the stairs. "You may read the letters, if you like."

My thoughts swirled. Did I want to read them? Already the image of my parents' marriage had changed. Would reading those letters further shatter my memories? Cousin Louise could not answer that question and neither could I. My heart squeezed. I did not want to take the risk. "All these years and I knew nothing of this."

"God has made all of us different. Some talk about the painful problems in their life. It helps them to heal. Others do the opposite. Your Mutter was never one who talked a great deal when faced with obstacles. Even when she was forced to leave, she did not speak against her Vater or feel pity for herself. For sure, she was sad to leave Erich, but she believed God had a plan that was different from her own." Cousin Louise smiled. "And she was right."

Cousin Louise pushed up from the table. "Let's go and check on Karlina. If she remains the same, Cousin George and I will go to prayer meeting."

When we arrived at the top of the stairs, Cousin Louise turned toward her bedroom. "I must see to something and then I'll be in. You go on and look in on Karlina."

For a moment I stood in the doorway and gazed at Karlina's motionless form lying on the bed. What had I done? Fear and regret assailed me. This was my doing. I should be the one suffering, not Karlina. I pulled a chair close to her bedside and felt her forehead. She wasn't as warm now—a good sign. I was leaning close to whisper her name when Cousin Louise entered the room.

She held the packet of envelopes in her hand. I recognized them as the ones I'd seen in her bedroom. "These are all of your Mutter's letters. Take them and read them if you wish. If it will help you through your grief, then you may read them."

She handed me the letters and then moved to the other side of the bed. With a deft hand, she examined Karlina and gave a nod. "She is doing a little better. Call for me if there is a change for the worse." She pointed to the bottle on the table. "One teaspoon in an hour. Wake her if you must. She needs the medicine." She hesitated at the door. "I will send a note to Dr. Zimmer and explain that Karlina has had contact with someone who may have had influenza. He should know. And don't forget the medicine."

"I'll be sure she takes it," I murmured.

After Cousin Louise left the room, I stared at the stack of letters.

Once again the string had been carefully tied around them, but they no longer beckoned to me. I was sure Cousin Louise had spoken the truth. What would be gained by reading the letters? But one thing I knew for certain—if ever I had children of my own, I would not withhold my past from them. That way, once I departed this world, there would be no unanswered questions about my life.

Rather than open the letters, I bowed my head and prayed. I asked forgiveness for all of my misdeeds since coming to the colonies, but mostly I asked God to heal Karlina. I don't know how long I had been praying when I heard the bedsheets rustle.

"Water? Could I have a drink, please?" Karlina's voice was a croaking whisper. She attempted to smile, but the effort proved too great.

I was so eager to meet her request that I hit the pitcher handle. Had I not moved with lightning speed, the pitcher would have toppled and spilled water all over her. Once I regained control, I poured a little water in the glass, lifted her with one arm, and held the glass to her lips while she sipped.

"Thank you." Her eyes fluttered, but she forced them open. "What happened to me?"

I quickly recounted how I had found her lying in the barn. "Berndt carried you back home, and Dr. Zimmer has been here to examine you." I glanced at the clock and lifted the spoon from the wooden table. "It is time for you to take some more medicine."

"Does he think it is influenza?"

"No, but he did not know we had been around the Sedlacek family."

I held the spoon to her lips. She opened her mouth, swallowed, and wrinkled her nose. "Tastes bad."

I smiled and nodded. "After Dr. Zimmer left, I told your mother everything. She knows we went to Jakub's house and that the family was ill. She sent word to the doctor so he would know."

Karlina's eyelids drooped and soon she returned to a deep sleep. I heard the opening and closing of doors and the shuffle of feet as Cousin Louise and Cousin George walked downstairs.

"*Psst.* Dovie!" I turned to see Anton standing in the doorway. "What has happened to Karlina?" Fear clouded his eyes. "Brother George was at the barn when I brought the sheep back from the pasture. He said Karlina was very ill."

I nodded. Brother George had stood in the same doorway a short time ago. Cousin Louise, worried her ailing husband might contract the illness himself, asked that he not come near Karlina. Though he had expressed displeasure, he had abided by her request.

Anton attempted to edge around me. I held up my hand. "You know the rules, Anton. You cannot come into Karlina's bedroom."

His face remained awash with concern. "But what can I do to help her?"

"Pray, Anton. She is doing some better, but prayer is what is needed the most."

CHAPTER 27

Other than helping downstairs in the kitchen when needed, I had remained at Karlina's bedside since she'd taken ill. The doctor continued his daily visits, and though he assured me Karlina was on the road to recovery, I still worried. I had heard those exact words about my mother during her illness, but she had taken a turn for the worse and died. The doctor couldn't be certain—and neither could I. With each passing day my fear mounted regarding Karlina's health and about my future in the community.

Dr. Zimmer had been most unhappy when he learned I hadn't immediately told him of the illness at the Sedlacek home, and I had received a stern warning from him as well as from Cousin George. In the future he expected me to send word to him rather than take such things upon myself. I doubted I would have a future in the colonies, but I didn't voice that opinion to Dr. Zimmer. And I didn't try to explain Mr. Sedlacek's attitude toward doctors, for to argue would serve no purpose.

Though I had heard nothing further, I knew our visit to the Sedlacek farm would be reviewed by the elders. While caring for Karlina, I'd had ample opportunity to consider my actions and the influence I'd wielded upon her. Without my insistence, she would never have gone to the farm. Instead of lying in bed, she would be caring for the sheep and enjoying the arrival of spring. Thoughts of going before the elders to explain my actions caused a chill to course through my body. I could not expect them to grant me permission to remain in the colonies. They did not need the disruptions of an outsider—especially someone who willingly swayed one of their own to break rules.

As the days passed, my prayers became more earnest. I prayed for Karlina and I prayed for myself. Gradually she remained awake for longer periods. Her coughing and occasional nighttime moans decreased. During her waking hours we talked, and though she tired easily, her color returned. While she ate her meals, I regaled her with stories of life in Cincinnati, and I took heart in her progress.

Finally the doctor declared her well enough to be up and about for short periods of time. I decided it was our prayers that contributed to Karlina's progress, as well as her determination to be at the barn by the time the shearing began.

If any punishment had been decided upon by the elders, we hadn't been told, but both of us understood there would be consequences for our behavior. Yesterday I had asked Cousin George about the matter and was surprised when he said the problem had been turned over to the Grossebruderrat. He explained that the *Bruderrat*, the group of men consisting of the trustees and elders in East, was divided on their decision. The members of the Grossebruderrat consisted of men from each village, with the number of representatives being determined by population. Since East was the smallest of the colonies, Cousin George was the only member of the Grossebruderrat from our village. He patted my arm in a fatherly gesture. "I know the waiting is hard, but we meet only once a month."

In truth, I was pleased about that bit of news, for it would give me a little more time in East before the elders decided my future. And I feared the decision would not go in my favor, since even the elders in East could not agree about my punishment. There were those who thought I should leave and others who disagreed. It was when I heard of their inability to reach a decision that I had packed most of my belongings into my large trunk. I didn't shed any tears when I folded and carefully packed most of my belongings, but I knew that would not be the case if I waited until I received the final decision.

I continued to pray the Grossebruderrat would not force me to leave. I wanted to decide for myself where I would live. But that wasn't the way of things in the colonies: The decision would not be mine. I rejoiced for at least this bit of extra time, for I wanted to be the one who explained my actions to Berndt.

Cousin Louise never divulged how she knew I'd been meeting Berndt, but this morning she pulled me aside and gave me permission to meet him later today. Along with the permission, she gave me instructions. "You should get no ideas about a future in the colonies and make no promises to Berndt. It is not fair when you do not know what the elders will decide. In addition, you have not yet shown that you are able to follow the rules of the community."

I wanted to argue that many had difficulty following all of the rules, but to disparage another member of the community would not win favor. Besides, I didn't want to say anything that could be considered a condemnation of Karlina. I walked into the small room where we sorted the mail and emptied the contents onto the table. I had promised Cousin Louise I would complete the task before I went to meet Berndt.

I had almost finished sorting when my gaze fell upon my father's familiar script. It had been some time since he had written. I couldn't condemn him. My letters had been less frequent, too, but I was eager to see what news had prompted his letter. I slid my finger beneath the seal, although before I had finished opening the envelope, I stopped. Had Cousin Louise written to my father and told him of my misdeed? I attempted to calculate the number of days. If she had immediately written to him and he had wasted no time in responding, there likely would have been time for the exchange of letters, but I shook off the idea. Cousin Louise had been far too busy to write to my father. At least I hoped that would prove to be the case.

At the sound of approaching footsteps, my attention moved from my father's letter to the remaining mail. I quickly sorted and placed the envelopes in their proper slots. "The mail is sorted, Dovie?" Cousin Louise peeked around the doorjamb.

"Yes, I just finished." I picked up the letter from my father. "I received a letter from my father."

"That is gut. It has been a while since he has written, ja?"

I nodded. "Neither of us has been writing as often over the past two months."

"You will need to tell me what he has to say about his life in Texas. I hope he is finding some happiness. I am sure it is hard for him. Moving to a new city while he is still grieving your Mutter and not having you there, either—I am sure he is lonely."

I didn't comment, for I wasn't sure if my father and the lovely lady he'd mentioned in his earlier letter had continued to see each other. Cousin Louise removed the mail from her family's box and trundled off toward the other room.

With a thrust of my index finger, I finished opening the envelope and, leaning against the sorting table, scanned the pages. There it was—a reference to the lovely woman he had met. I slowed to a word-by-word examination of the contents.

In my last letter, I mentioned a lady I had met. Her name is Ardella Mitchell. I think you would like her. We have been seeing each other and have much in common.

How much could he have in common with the woman? My father worked for the railroad and traveled a great deal. Maybe she had traveled to the places he'd visited, or perhaps she enjoyed reading. My father did enjoy discussing the many books that he read. Or maybe she held a position with the railroad, though I doubted that idea. My father was never one to think women should work outside the home. Then again, if she was a widow, maybe she'd been forced to go to work and viewed my father as an opportunity to resume her former way of life. I forced myself to stop guessing and returned to the letter.

I know you may find this news disturbing, but once the proper mourning period has ended, I plan to marry Ardella. No doubt you will think my decision rash, but I am lonely and she has been an excellent companion to me. Please do not think that my haste to remarry means that I do not miss your dear mother. It was my desire to live out the remainder of my years as her husband, but since her death I find myself in need of love and companionship. I do not think she would have wished me to remain alone. I hope you will feel the same way.

I pressed a palm to my cheek. I should be pleased to learn that my father had found someone with whom to share his life. Instead, a clawing sense of betrayal inched its way from my feet to the top of my head. How could he? So soon. In a few more days, it would be only nine months since my mother's death. Could he not have waited longer before he pledged his love to another woman? Tears threatened as I continued to read.

Ardella is eager to meet you and has expressed a deep desire to build a friendship with you. She is a fine woman, and I believe you will like her very much. She is hopeful you will come to Dallas and live with us once we are married. Ardella has a lovely home and says there is more than adequate room for you. She is eager for you to make your home with us. I know this is a great deal for you to take in, but with an open mind and loving spirit, I know the two of you will become dear friends.

So they had already formed their plans—not only to marry but also where they would live. If the elders decided to send me from the colonies, I would be making my home with my father and his new bride. I tried to envision how all of this had happened so rapidly. My father had said he would be traveling a great deal, yet he'd had time to develop a committed relationship with Ardella. Still, I had to consider my part in all of this. Had I gone to Texas, my father wouldn't have been as likely to seek the companionship of a woman. I sighed and returned to the final paragraph.

Please write soon so I must not worry for too long. It is my deep desire to gain your understanding and to know you will embrace these decisions regarding ~~my~~ our future. I send my love and hope to hear from you by return mail. Love, Papa

I didn't miss the fact that he had crossed out the word *my* and inserted *our*. Nor did I miss his signature. He knew that signing *Papa* would touch my heart with greater force than if he'd signed *Father*. There was little doubt he wanted my approval. He had added a hasty postscript at the end, saying Ardella would like permission to write to me.

It seemed they were going to do everything they could to gain my acceptance. I pondered the letter for a brief time and then tucked it into my pocket. If I didn't leave right now for my meeting with Berndt, I'd miss him. I stepped to the doorway of the mail room and spied Cousin Louise in the kitchen. "I'm leaving, Cousin Louise."

She looked up from the worktable. "There was gut news from your Vater?"

"I suppose it depends upon how one interprets good news." I forced a smile. "I'll read it to you when I return."

"Ja, that would be nice." If my remark about good news confused her, she gave no indication. "Remember what I have told you about your talk with Berndt."

"I remember," I called before rushing out the door.

My thoughts were a jumble as I went to meet Berndt. There was so much I must explain to him, yet I wasn't certain I could control my emotions. I was pleased to discover we were not brother and sister, yet trying to accept the fact that we were not related and I could indeed let myself love him as a woman loves a man felt very strange. I could only hope that once he understood why my behavior toward him had changed, he would still care for me. Of course it would matter little if the Grossebruderrat insisted I leave. I'd have no choice but to go to Texas.

As I recalled the contents of my father's letter, my heart squeezed with sorrow at the thought of his replacing my dear mother. But I hadn't walked far when I remembered what Cousin Louise had told me about my Opa and how he hadn't let my mother follow her heart and remain in the colonies. My father had wanted me to move to Texas with him, but he gave me the opportunity to follow my own path.

If I'd gone with him, perhaps he wouldn't have met Ardella. But that's not what happened. I came to the colonies, and Papa met Ardella. We both traveled our own paths. How could I fault him for wanting to fill the void in his life? I wasn't required to find joy in his choice, but I needed to show him the same respect and kindness he'd shown me.

A bird cawed overhead and I turned toward the barn. Berndt said he would be there by two o'clock. Cousin Louise had given permission, but a young man and woman visiting alone was not looked upon with favor. Originally I had suggested we meet at the pond, but Cousin Louise said we could have our choice: the back porch or the barn. I quickly chose the barn, for on days when the weather was nice, several of the older sisters would sit on the back porch to clean and pare vegetables—and talk. I didn't want them to overhear my conversation with Berndt.

In the distance I could see Berndt walking toward the barn, so I quickened my pace. I didn't want him to think I wouldn't be there.

Berndt saw me as I rounded the corner of the barn, and he waved and strode toward me. "Would you like to walk, or would you rather stay here at the barn?"

I glanced toward the barn. I knew Karlina wasn't in there. Cousin Louise had insisted she rest after the noonday meal. She'd been unhappy because the shepherds and some hired hands had begun the sheep washing, and she'd wanted to be there during the process.

"Do you know where they're washing the sheep?"

Berndt grinned and nodded. "Ja, at the pond. I was thinking it was gut we didn't meet there, but if you want to go and watch, we can do that."

"I've heard Karlina talk about it, so I thought it would be fun to see how it is done, but first I think we should talk. I have a lot to tell you."

He motioned toward a tree a short distance from the barn. "I hope what you have to say will make me happy."

His smile was as bright as the sun-drenched afternoon. My

heart pounded a new beat as we walked to a large oak tree and stood beneath the towering branches. My voice quivered while I did my best to explain everything from my desire to learn of my mother's past to thinking he was my half brother, to the revelation that my assumptions had been completely incorrect.

Berndt listened intently and interrupted only once. When I had finally completed the tale, he rubbed his jaw. "So that is the reason you changed how you acted toward me? Because you thought we were brother and sister?"

"Yes." Though I knew it would embarrass me, I needed to tell Berndt the truth. "I . . . I had started to think of you as a man I could love." Heat spread across my cheeks, but I forced myself to continue. "But then I read those letters and began to investigate. Soon I came to believe you were my half brother, and I knew my feelings for you had to change."

Using the tips of his fingers, he gently lifted my chin until our eyes met. "And now that you know we are not relatives, have those earlier feelings returned?"

Discomfort assailed me. How could I answer such a question and maintain my modesty? A woman didn't declare her love for a man until she was certain of their future plans to wed. At least that's what Margaret Holmann told me back when we'd attended school together years ago. Margaret had adopted the role of authority on young men back then, as she was never without an escort at her side. And all of the girls had listened to her.

I finally gathered enough courage to speak. "I believe my feelings for you are equal to those you possess for me."

Berndt's serious look gave me pause. I wasn't certain what he was thinking. Had he expected a more direct response?

He leaned toward me. "In that case, I suggest that I go and speak with the elders tomorrow. I will tell them we love each other and seek permission to marry."

I gasped and pressed my hand to the bodice of my dress. "Oh no. You cannot speak to the elders. That is impossible."

He arched his brows. "And why is that? I know they may have some misgivings, but once you declare your desire to live in the colonies and embrace our faith, they will agree. I am sure of it. Your grandparents and Mutter lived here; you still have relatives here—there will be no problem."

I shook my head. "You don't understand. After they learned that Karlina and I visited the Sedlacek farm, the Bruderrat in East could not come to a decision about my future in the colonies. The matter has been passed on to the Grossebruderrat for determination. They may elect to have me leave. I didn't follow the rules, and I caused Karlina to go astray." I lowered my head. "I don't think they will look kindly upon my request to remain here."

Berndt squared his shoulders and inhaled a deep breath. "I will convince them! You are the woman I wish to marry. If you feel the same, then I will do everything in my power to influence the Grossebruderrat that they should give you another chance." One corner of his mouth tipped in a smile. "They were young men at one time, too. They will listen to my plea."

He looked deep into my eyes and stepped closer. When he wrapped his arms around my waist and drew me into an inviting embrace, I didn't resist. A flash of heat seared my cheeks as I met his ardent gaze, and my knees felt as though they might buckle. He lowered his head and covered my lips with a passionate kiss. A delightful tremble raced through my body as I responded to the warmth of his kiss. I belonged right here—in Berndt's arms.

"Say you wish to be with me always, Dovie."

"I do want to be with you forever and remain in East, but—"

He touched his finger to my lips. "Then with God's help, we will be together. Trust me." With a wink, he grasped my hand. "Let's go and see how much progress they have made washing the sheep."

I smiled and nodded. "Oh yes. Karlina will expect a report from me." I glanced at our clasped hands. "But I do not think holding hands is wise."

He chuckled. "We are safe for a little while."

We walked as far as we dared with our hands clasped, but once we caught a glimpse of the men at the pond, I pulled my hand away and put a little distance between us. There were a number of men standing in the water, as well as those who were moving the sheep toward the water. "Have you ever helped wash the sheep?"

"Nein. It is not something that appeals to me. Have you ever smelled a wet sheep?"

I laughed and shook my head.

"You'll soon discover that it's not a very pleasant odor."

As we approached, Cousin George motioned for us to stay at a distance. A short time later he walked toward us. "Sheep don't particularly like being washed, so they're a little skittish. You need to stay over here where we're washing them rather than with the ones on the hillside. The men are trying to keep them calm so that when they herd them down, they're easier to handle."

I glanced toward the rise. With all of the woolly sheep, it looked as if a snowstorm had descended upon the hillside. Karlina said the sheep preferred the closeness of their flock, so I thought they should be profoundly happy at the moment. The three of us walked toward the water, where the men had partitioned off a shallow section of the pond with wood slats that reminded me of a narrow corral. The sheep had been herded into a wagon, and one by one, they came down a ramp with protective sides and into the water. One of the men stood in the knee-high water and briefly submerged each animal, head and all, and then pushed it along to the next man, who sent the sheep up another wood ramp and into the bed of the wagon waiting at the opposite side. Once the wagon of dirty sheep had been emptied, the shepherds loaded another flock into the wagon and the process began anew. The clean sheep were taken back to the pasture, where the sun would help their wool dry before shearing took place.

"What do you think of our method?" Cousin George asked while he waited for another load of dirty sheep.

I wrinkled my nose. "It appears to be efficient, although wet sheep have an odor—and it isn't particularly pleasurable."

Cousin George tipped his head back and laughed. "You get used to it after a while." He pointed to the partitioned area in the water. "Before we started washing them this way, we used to take them one at a time into the water, and with one man at the head and one at the tail, we would grab hold of their hooves and swing them to and fro in the water to remove the excess yolk."

I arched my brows. The only yolk I knew about was the yolk inside an egg. Cousin George grinned. "Sheep yolk is the oily secretion that covers a sheep's wool. It protects the sheep from rain and keeps the wool from becoming matted. When some of that substance is removed, the sheep are easier to shear." He rested one palm on his opposing shoulder. "It was hard on the shoulders. This is better and we can wash more than seven hundred sheep in one day."

The thought of washing that many sheep in one day amazed me. I was certain the men would be exhausted by the time they had completed this chore. Another wagonload of sheep was positioned near the water, and Cousin George watched closely as the men set up the ramp. "You tell Karlina I do not want her to come down here. Being around the water and the wet sheep will not be gut for her. She needs to rest, and then she can be at the barn when we begin shearing."

"I'll tell her, but I know she won't be happy with your decision."

"It is for the best." He tipped his hat, turned, and strode off toward the wagon.

We watched a while longer, and I wasn't sure if I felt more sympathy for the sheep or for the men who washed them. The men sounded as though they were enjoying themselves, while the bleating sheep appeared far less happy.

I was afraid Karlina would feel more like one of the unhappy sheep when I delivered the message from her father. But even the thought of delivering unpleasant news to Karlina couldn't spoil my own happiness or squelch my excitement. The possibility of a future with Berndt burned warm in my heart.

CHAPTER 28

June 1893
Karlina

The decision had been made. Shearing would begin on Monday. At prayer meeting on Friday, Vater asked God for continued good weather. Since being washed, the sheep had regained the amount of yolk that provided their wool with excellent luster and softness, yet not so much as to cause matting. Extra shearers had been hired, and all was in readiness to begin shearing on Monday.

My father glanced around the group that gathered for prayer each evening. "I am asking all of you to join me in continued prayer that our sheep will not suffer from any effects of cold weather after we shear them."

Brother Herman elbowed my father and chuckled. "I do not think you need to worry the gut Lord about the weather, Brother George. June has arrived, and from what the traveling shearers tell me, our sheep are the only ones in all of Iowa still wearing wool coats."

"Ja, that may be true, but perhaps you should ask those shearers how many sheep were sick or died due to the cold weather that arrived after they sheared them so early. Like the others, I had planned to begin washing the sheep earlier, but I watched the barometer. It showed we would have a change in the weather. I was not willing to take any chance that our sheep would suffer from cold weather while their wool was wet or after they had been sheared."

There were murmurs of approval. "I was only joking with you, Brother George. We are all thankful for your gut care of the sheep," Brother Herman said. "You watch after your sheep just like the Father in heaven watches after us."

Anton scooted to the edge of his chair. "Ja. Brother George says that just like sheep need a gut shepherd to care for them, we need the Lord to care for us." He smiled at his mentor. "He also taught me that the sheep learn the voice of their shepherd and learn to trust him, and if we listen for God's voice, we will hear Him speak to our hearts. He even showed me in the Bible where Jesus says He is the Gut Shepherd and the sheep hear His voice and know Him." Anton tapped his chest. "I like that the Bible talks about us as sheep. Jesus said He would lay down His life for His sheep, and that meant He was willing to die for us. Isn't that right, Brother George?"

"Ja, that is right, Anton. Jesus died so we could live. In the book of John, Jesus uses a parable about sheep to refer to mankind." My father handed his Bible to Anton. "We have been talking about sheep, so why don't you read the tenth chapter of John for us? Then we will pray."

I was surprised by Anton's bold behavior during prayer meeting. He seldom spoke out, but tonight he appeared pleased when my father asked him to read from the Bible. Earlier in the year he would have refused to participate. With his shoulders squared, Anton read the entire chapter without faltering.

While my father led the prayer time, I opened my eyes a mere slit and peeked across the room at Anton. He sat with his eyes tightly closed and his hands folded. Great changes had taken place in his life since he'd arrived in East, and my heart swelled at the progress he'd made.

During the days while I'd been confined to bed, Anton had written notes and drawn sketches of the sheep for me. Though he wasn't permitted to enter my bedroom, he sent the messages with Dovie or slipped them beneath my door. On a few occasions, he'd stood in the doorway and talked to me. Worry had shone in his eyes, and his gentle concern touched my heart.

Although Dr. Zimmer had declared me completely recovered, Anton continued to watch after me as carefully as he would a newborn lamb. His caring behavior and words of endearment had dispelled my former doubts about him, and I had given more and more thought to his suggestion that we build a life together.

Tonight as we departed the prayer meeting, Anton moved to my side. I smiled, pleased to have him walk beside me. "You did a gut job with reading tonight."

"Danke. I feel more at ease now, and it is because of you. I always feel better when you are near me." His lips tilted in a bashful smile. "You will come to the barn tomorrow while your father is teaching me to shear, ja?"

Darkness had not yet descended, and I could see the shadow of apprehension lurking in his eyes. "I will be there, but you will do fine. The sheep know your voice, and they will respond well to you. After you shear a few of them, it will become easier for you."

He didn't appear totally convinced. "I was hoping there would be enough of the hired help that your Vater wouldn't think I needed to shear."

I smiled and shook my head. "A gut shepherd knows how to care for his sheep in every situation. You must learn so if outside help is not available in the future, you can perform the task yourself."

"I know you are right, but the shearing is one thing I would rather not learn."

I took hold of the banister on my way upstairs to bed. "I will pray that all goes well in the morning."

His smile didn't quite meet his eyes, but he thanked me. "You should also pray for the sheep that must tolerate my clumsy attempts."

I chuckled. "You can be sure I will be praying for them, as well."

The thought of Anton's concern over the sheep warmed me. He had developed the heart of a true shepherd. I understood his worries and had done my best to reassure him. Though he didn't appear swayed, I believed that the Lord would grant him the peace and skill to handle the shearing.

After breakfast the following morning, the three of us made our way to the barn, where Anton would begin his lessons. Father had made certain no one else would be around while Anton tried his hand with the shears.

My father walked toward one of the larger ewes. "I am going to shear this one while you watch, Anton. While I shear, I will do my best to explain, but you should ask me questions if you do not understand." He pointed to a spot nearby. "Move over there and stand beside the tarp. Karlina will gather the wool once it is off the sheep. Later today we will get all the spaces ready for the shearers. We want the sheep and shearers as comfortable as possible, and we want to keep the wool nice and clean."

After positioning the animal on its rump and resting its back against my father's thighs and lower legs, he held the shears aloft. "I like to talk a bit while I'm shearing so they hear my voice, but you'll soon discover the sheep are pretty cooperative when it comes to the process. We clip in a circular fashion, and if you keep their feet off the floor while you're working on them, you won't have any trouble."

Anton arched his brows. "I'm not so sure, but I hope you are right."

My father commenced clipping the underpart of the ewe's neck and moved around the top of the neck to the top of the shoulders. He pointed to the sheep's belly. "Now you clip from midbelly down to the hind legs and then move from midbelly to the thick portion of the forelegs, always shedding the wool back and forth from the right and left."

Moving with ease, my father clipped the thick part of the wool near the foreleg, continued in parallel rings over the shoulder, ribs, and loins, and then clipped up and along the top of the back before he gently dropped the sheep on its side. He talked to the sheep in a low voice while he continued the circular cuts over the hip and thighs until he had sheared up to the line of the backbone.

"Now we turn and do the same thing on the other side," he said to Anton.

"But how do you know how close to make the cuts and how close to the skin?"

My father moved the sheep into position and motioned to Anton. "Come closer and you will see my ring marks are about a half inch apart. You don't want them much more than a half or three-fourths of an inch apart." My father lifted the wool far enough for Anton to see where he had cut. "Put your hand beneath where I've cut so you will know how it should feel. You want to make your cuts about a third of an inch away from the skin."

Anton stepped back after he'd examined the sheep. "You are cutting pretty close to the skin."

"Ja, that is the idea. The sheep needs to be cool in the summer. We don't want to give them only half a haircut." My father chuckled.

"What if you nick them?"

"Sometimes it happens, but always we try to be careful. Place your free hand flat on the skin and draw it tight as you shear and you will have an easier time." He nodded toward the wool he had clipped and lifted along the sheep's body. "Always try to keep the wool collected together so the sheep does not break the fleece with its feet if it should kick."

"There is a lot to remember. I hope the shearers will move quickly, because I doubt I'll be able to finish more than two or three sheep in a day's time."

"Ach! You will do better than that. Most of the men can shear about thirty sheep in a day. Some a few more and some a few less."

"Ja, well I will be among the group who shear less. Much less."

"Do not become defeated before you begin. The Lord made you as capable of shearing a sheep as any other man."

"We will see," Anton said. He maintained a watchful eye while my father continued shearing the ewe, but his uneasiness increased as my father made the final cuts.

I swept the tarp with a besom and picked up the stray locks of wool before I carried the fleece to a large table. When work began in earnest on Monday, the sheared woolly coats would be piled in stacks and sent by wagons to the woolen mill, where they would be sorted, cleaned, spun, and woven into blankets.

My father waved Anton forward. "Now you can begin with that ewe over there. Remember to keep her feet off the floor, and you will do fine."

I wasn't certain if he would be more at ease if I didn't watch or if he wanted me to give him my attention, so I stood at a distance and kept my eyes trained on him. If he looked in my direction, he would know I hadn't left the barn. He pulled the ewe into position and hesitated.

"You cannot expect the sheep to remain in that position all day, Anton. You must begin to shear." My father opened and closed his hand in a rapid motion. "Put your shears to work for you."

Anton placed his hand on the sheep's belly and made his first cut, and then the next. His confidence increased, and while my father offered verbal instruction, Anton worked his way around the left side of the sheep. He turned her and had begun the second side when his shears went too deep.

Anton gasped. The sheep bleated, fought her way to her feet, and ran across the barn with the half-shorn portion of her coat dragging along one side of her body. Had the lower barn door been open, she would have run outside. Instead, she circled around the barn with Anton racing after her. As the ewe circled for the third time, my father managed to gain a hold on the animal, and Anton leaned forward to catch his breath. I did my best to squelch the laughter that threatened to escape.

His face turned the color of a beet and his features pinched in a tight frown. I expected him to lash out with an angry exclamation, but instead he looked up at me. "I do not think she is bleeding too much, since she made it around the barn three times."

My father chuckled and shook his head. "Not bad enough to need a stitch, but it could use a little tar." My father called for me to bring the small pot of hot tar. He quickly dabbed a little on the nick. "That should take care of it. She's fine. Now pick up your shears and finish the job."

"I thought maybe you'd want to finish up since—"

"That's not the way you learn. You're doing fine. A small nick on your first sheep is to be expected."

There was reluctance in Anton's step, but he settled the animal in position and set to work. Perspiration dotted his brow by the time he finished, but he smiled with delight when my father congratulated him on his accomplishment.

"Now you can set to work on those others over there." My father pointed to several sheep in a far stall.

Anton's smile slipped away as quickly as it had arrived. "Do you mean it? I have to shear those others?"

"If you're going to feel gut about working with the other men on Monday, you need to shear more than one sheep today. You have tomorrow to rest up." There was a gleam in my father's eyes. "You'll be suffering a few aches and pains in the morning, but by Monday you'll be eager to begin."

Anton didn't argue, but I could see that my father's remarks hadn't swayed him. If he could have his way, he would go out to the pasture or work on another invention, but I was pleased when he went and dutifully brought another sheep to the tarp. Anton was not the same man who'd first arrived in East.

Word had spread throughout the villages that we would begin shearing today. And though most of the men had to go out to the fields, there were visitors from the outside and a few from Main who arrived to observe the men perform their shearing. I understood the enthusiasm of those who came, for even after all these years, I still enjoyed watching the process.

We had prepared the shearing area in the shelter that adjoined the east side of the barn after Anton finished his lesson on Saturday. This morning my father and Anton had gone to the barn so they could prepare the sheep to be moved on and off the shearing floor in a quick and orderly fashion.

The shearing was moving along, with all of the hired shearers as well as our own shepherds working at a steady pace. I was pleased that Jakub had taken a position next to Anton. Already Jakub had given Anton several compliments on his shearing and had come to his aid when one of the sheep had become uncooperative.

The men had just begun when I arrived at the barn. I took my place on the floor where I would help sweep up the locks and carry off the fleece as the men finished each sheep. Visitors had gathered along the perimeter of the shelter. Their faces reflected escalating admiration as the shearers worked with speed and agility. I was carrying fleece to the stacking table when I heard someone call Anton's name. I turned toward the group of visitors, and my eyes were immediately drawn toward the voice. *Violet!* Her father was at her side. He directed a stern look at her and leaned toward her to say something I couldn't discern. Moments later, the two of them headed toward the shearing shelter. My stomach roiled and I thought I might faint.

CHAPTER 29

The weight of the fleece didn't permit me to delay any longer, but I kept my eyes trained on Violet and her father as I carried the pile of heavy wool to the stacking table. After placing the bundle on the table, I turned my full attention to the two visitors. Instead of going to where Anton was shearing, they stood near my father. Dr. Nagel's features twisted into a sour look as he motioned toward Anton and then looked at Violet. I couldn't imagine what they were saying, but I was sure it wasn't good.

Once Anton finished shearing his sheep, my father went to speak with him and then escorted him back to where Dr. Nagel and Violet were standing with their arms folded across their chests. Violet wore a look of triumph, while Dr. Nagel's features remained frozen in a disagreeable frown. What did they want? I knew it could be nothing good. My mouth felt as dry as the wool I'd carried to the stacking table only moments earlier.

Taking sidesteps across the straw, I drew closer. I wanted to hear what had caused Dr. Nagel to speak with my father. Whatever the reason, it must involve Violet, or she wouldn't be standing at her father's side. I watched as she rested her head on her father's shoulder and gazed up at him. She obviously was an old hand at using such tactics to gain her father's support.

Inching a few steps closer, I heard Violet confirm that she was telling the truth. "He did take advantage of me, Vater. Anton returned from the pasture right after you left for Main Amana. We were alone in the barn for almost an hour." She fluttered her lashes. "I told you all of this. Why must I repeat it?"

My father's face tightened. "Because you are making terrible accusations that can cause grave consequences for Anton. And because I am having some trouble believing he would conduct himself in such a manner."

Dr. Nagel squared his shoulders and glared at my father. "You think my daughter would lie about such a serious matter?"

"It would not be the first time." Anton glared at Violet. "Tell the truth, Violet. You came to the barn and tried to convince me to ask the elders for permission to marry you. When I refused and said I loved another, you became angry with me."

Violet shook her head. "That isn't true. You said you loved me and that I must prove my love for you. When I refused, you attempted to take advantage of me and didn't turn loose of me until you heard my father call for me."

I gasped. "Violet! How can you say those things?"

Violet and the three men all turned in my direction. I didn't know who was the most surprised by my unexpected intrusion. Violet's eyes flashed with anger, and I knew she wasn't going to easily admit the truth. I sensed a hint of fear in Anton's bearing, and my father and Dr. Nagel seemed taken aback that I had entered the fray.

Violet had shown no indication she planned to answer my question. Unwilling to let my question pass without hearing a response from her, I rested my hands on my hips. "And how did you convince your father such a story could be true? I was in the barn and heard portions of your conversation. You weren't attempting to get away from Anton. In fact, you were trying to convince him to marry you." I hadn't heard that portion of the conversation, but I did believe Anton had told me the truth. I also knew that Violet had no idea how long I'd been in the barn.

I inhaled a deep breath. "The only anger you exhibited that day was toward me. If Anton had attempted to take advantage of you, why didn't you say something when your father appeared? Your clothing showed no sign of a struggle, and you exhibited more anger toward me than toward Anton."

Dr. Nagel cast a stern look at his daughter. "Well? Can you answer Sister Karlina's questions? These are some of the same things I asked about when you came to me and made these accusations yesterday."

"Yesterday? She waited until yesterday to tell you something so terrible had happened to her more than a month ago? You cannot believe this story is true, Dr. Nagel. I know that there were times I got into fights while I lived in High, but never have I done anything to dishonor a woman. Violet, you need to tell your Vater the truth—about everything."

Although he spoke with passion, Anton held any sign of anger in check. I gave my father a sideways glance, hoping he had noticed. Had this confrontation occurred back in December, Anton would have lashed out at both Violet and her father. Today, he wasn't controlled by anger. Instead, he was letting reason prevail.

Violet's face turned crimson. She narrowed her eyes, and for a minute, I thought she would hold fast to her accusations. "I don't want to talk in front of all of you." Hatred flashed in her eyes when she turned to me. "I'll speak to my Vater when we are alone."

"Nein!" I hadn't expected Dr. Nagel to disagree, but he pointed at Violet and shook his head. "You will speak right here and right now for all of us to hear. If you spoke the truth, there should be no shame. If your words were not true, apologies are required and punishment will follow."

Speaking so quietly we were all required to lean closer, Violet reluctantly admitted nothing had happened in the barn. "Anton said he did not want to marry me." She whined the final sentence and shoved her lower lip into a pout.

My father arched his bushy brows. "And you would make such claims against a man you profess to love?"

"I thought that once we were married, he would learn to love me." She turned her attention to Anton. "She isn't as pretty as me, and you could come back to High if you married me."

The discomfort hanging over our little group increased by the minute, but my father maintained his calm demeanor.

"I do not intend on returning to High, but you also need to tell your Vater that the incident that happened while we were sledding was not of my doing. He needs to know the truth, Violet."

Violet stomped her left foot, and a small cloud of dust flurried from beneath the hem of her skirt. "Why do I have to do this? I want to go home." She sounded like one of the little children at Kinderschule instead of a grown woman. Folding her arms across her waist, she turned toward Anton. "If you came back to High, you could work on your inventions, and you wouldn't have to take care of these stupid sheep."

"The sheep are not stupid, and I have learned much while caring for them."

Violet snorted. "What can anyone learn from sheep?"

"The Bible talks about people being like sheep and says God

is the Gut Shepherd. When we go down the wrong path, He still loves and forgives us—He wants to protect us. That's how it is for shepherds when they care for their sheep. When a sheep runs off, we search for it and bring it back to the flock so it will not be harmed by wolves or wild dogs. Tending for sheep requires a calm and patient shepherd. I did not put those abilities to use before I came here, but during my time in East, I have learned the value of those qualities." He hesitated a moment. "I have learned much from my job as a shepherd."

"Ja, and you now exhibit those gut behaviors every day." My father patted Anton on the shoulder before he turned toward Violet. "It is my hope that you will conduct yourself in the same manner, Sister Violet. Let us clear all misunderstanding so that Anton and I may return to our work."

Dr. Nagel cleared his throat. "Well, Violet? What do you have to say?"

"The day when we went sledding, I told Frank I planned to do something that would force Anton to marry me. He said he would help, because he liked the idea of having Anton become a part of our family."

Dr. Nagel frowned. "If he wanted Anton to marry you, why did they fight?"

She focused on the ground. "After we rolled off the sled, Frank came over and confronted Anton. Frank thought he could get Anton to say he would marry me. Instead, Anton kept insisting he did nothing wrong and that I had caused the sled to turn and rolled on top of him."

Anton bobbed his head. "Ja, which is exactly what happened, except I did not know Frank was part of your plan."

My father motioned Anton to silence. "Let her finish, Anton."

Violet glanced at her father. "Everyone heard what Anton was saying. I didn't want them to think I had acted in an unsuitable manner, so I whispered to Frank that he must defend me against gossip."

Anton sighed. "Thank you for finally speaking the truth, Violet."

Several sheep bleated and two of the shearers called for another sheep while the visitors clapped for those who were working with great speed. All of the sounds that had faded into the background now pulled me back to our surroundings.

Violet nodded. "I am sorry for the trouble I caused you, Anton." Her lips curved into a feeble smile. "It was because I cared for you and wanted to marry you. I hope you will forgive me and that one day you will decide that you wish to live in High."

"Violet . . ." Her father's voice carried a warning tone.

She shrugged. "Just so you know, I will probably marry someone else."

Anton glanced toward the flock of sheep awaiting the clippers. "That is gut. I hope you will be very happy."

Dr. Nagel tugged on his vest. "I am thinking that maybe this could all stay between the four of us and that nothing needs to be said to anyone else."

My father rested his arm on the fence railing. "Violet is your daughter, and the problem with the sled happened in High, so I have no say over what should happen. But I do not think it is proper that the elders continue to think Anton was at fault for an incident caused by two of your children. I do not believe this was fair to Anton, and I do not believe your children benefit if they escape all punishment." My father pushed his hat to the back of his head. "We are taught that our children should be praised for gut behavior and suffer consequences for misconduct. That way they will grow in God's ways."

Dr. Nagel didn't argue. "You are right. I should not let Violet or Frank think they can act in such a manner without punishment." He looked at Violet. "I am pleased you finally told the truth, but I think it is best if you go to the Bruderrat in High and tell them the truth."

"But I'll have to return to children's church."

Violet's father frowned at her. "It could be worse than children's church. If the elders decide you should not go to church at all, there will be even more questions. Besides, that is a small punishment compared to what has happened to Anton."

She thrust her lips into another pout. "If you would just agree to marry me, everything would be fine, Anton."

Dr. Nagel shook his head. "You must forgive her, Brother George. She has always been a little slow to see the error of her ways."

"Come on, Vater. I am ready to go home." Violet grasped her father's arm and tugged.

"I hope you will be this eager when the time comes to face the elders." Dr. Nagel tipped his hat to my father. "I am sorry that I misjudged you, Anton. Please accept my apology."

"Vater! Come on! Anton knows I am sorry; Frank is sorry, you are sorry, we are all sorry. Now, let's go home. I want to get away from these smelly sheep."

CHAPTER 30

July 1893
Dovie

The time for our meeting with the Grossebruderrat arrived on a
sticky hot afternoon in July. I thought the weather might be an
advantage. "The meetinghouse will be so warm the men won't want
to sit there very long. It will mean fewer questions, don't you think?"
I finished combing my hair and turned to look at Karlina. Her
complexion had turned as pale as a summer cloud. "Are you ill?"

"Nein, but I am frightened to go before the Grossebruderrat." Karlina arranged her black Sunday shawl over her shoulders.
"Please check the point to see it is centered."

I stepped behind her and moved the shawl an inch to the right.
"There. That is better." Leaning over Karlina's shoulder, I kissed
her cheek. "Try not to worry. I have been praying that God will
open the eyes of the elders and they will make the right decision
for all of us."

Karlina turned around. "What the elders hear from God may not be the answer we want. I have been thinking of what could happen, and none of it is very gut. No matter what, there will be consequences for breaking the rules."

"I am sorry you must bear this, Karlina. When it is my turn to speak, I am going to explain that you would never have gone to the Sedlacek farm if I had not begged you to come with me. I think I am the one who should be punished, not you."

Directing a sad smile at me, Karlina shook her head. "It does not matter what you think or what I think, Dovie. The only thing that matters is what the elders think."

"But they will listen to what we have to say before they make their decision. I think I will be able to influence them that you should not be punished."

Karlina shrugged. "The truth is that I made the decision to go with you. I knew the rules, and I knew that I was breaking them. That is the issue before the elders—at least where I am concerned." She bowed her head. "I am willing to take my punishment."

"But you've already suffered through your illness. That should be enough punishment." I picked up my bonnet and followed Karlina into the parlor. "And that's what I'm going to tell them."

"I became ill because I was around others who had a sickness. It wasn't a punishment from God. It happened because of my foolish behavior."

I frowned, disappointed that Karlina didn't believe her illness should exclude her from further penalty. "But you still suffered, so that should be enough."

Cousin Louise stepped into the parlor. "We will depart in a few minutes." She turned to me. "I think it will be wise to guard your tongue when you go before the Grossebruderrat, Dovie. You should answer their questions with truth and honesty, but it would not be prudent to advise them what they should or should not do in regard to punishment." She tied the strings of her cap beneath her chin. "Sometimes less is more."

"What do you mean?"

"To say a few words with great meaning is better than to ramble on with nothing of value."

I nodded. "I'll try to remember that, Cousin Louise."

"If you hear me cough, you will know you are saying too much. If you truly want to remain in the colonies, I do not want you to jeopardize your future. Should you appear to be a young woman who is headstrong and will not take direction, I fear the elders will consider you a poor candidate to live here." Her lips curved in a generous smile. "Not that living with your Vater would be a terrible punishment. I would never want you or him to think such a thing."

"I know, Cousin Louise. You don't need to explain." I had read to Cousin Louise the recent letter from my father. Like me, she had been surprised to hear of his future plans, but she had been quick to mention he'd had to make many changes in his life. "To live alone after all the years he had with your Mutter and you would be very difficult." She'd smiled and quickly added, "I do not think he would choose a woman who would not be kind and loving to you."

I thought Cousin Louise had correctly assessed my father's situation. My feelings had softened toward my father's plans for a future with Ardella, but I still didn't want to leave the colonies. Today I would need to choose my words carefully and pray God would give the elders a clear directive to absolve Karlina and to let me remain here and marry Berndt. After Cousin Louise's warning, I doubted that all of my prayers would be answered in the affirmative.

"Where is Anton?" Cousin Louise folded her arms and tapped her foot.

"He has already gone downstairs, Mutter. He said he would wait for us outside."

The sound of Cousin George's heavy footsteps in the hallway brought all three of us to attention. "We do not want to be late. Let us go."

The four of us descended the stairs into the dining room. The women preparing the midafternoon coffee and cake busied themselves as we paraded through the kitchen. All except Sister Bertha, who hurried to Cousin Louise's side. "No need to worry about the Küche, Sister Louise. I will be pleased to oversee supper preparations."

Cousin Louise clamped her lips into a tight smile. "I knew you would offer, Sister Bertha, but there is little oversight needed. The other sisters know their duties and complete them without direction." She spoke loud enough for the other sisters to hear. They nodded and smiled a silent thank-you. The comment from Cousin Louise would prevent Sister Bertha from taking command during our absence.

Anton stood on the wooden sidewalk, pressing the brim of his dark felt hat between his fingers. The five of us hadn't gone far when Berndt joined us. Several weeks ago he had sent a letter and asked to meet with the Grossebruderrat while they were in East. His letter hadn't contained the reason for his request, but I knew he planned to ask permission to marry me. After the elders had heard all of the rules I had broken, I wasn't sure this was the best time for his request, but he said it must be today, since we didn't know what decision they might make regarding my future.

He smiled as he joined us. "It has been some time since I have seen so many gloomy faces."

The sadness in Cousin Louise's eyes deepened. "To go before the Grossebruderrat when the Bruderrat of your village has been unable to arrive at a decision is not something that creates great happiness."

Cousin George motioned for us to wait before entering the meetinghouse. "Before we go in, I want to pray that God will give the Grossebruderrat wisdom as they make their decisions." After he'd led us in prayer, he held up his finger. "One moment. The elder in charge of the meeting is Brother Michael Weizmann. He will ask most of the questions. When you speak to him, you should not address him as Brother Michael but as Brother Weizmann." He glanced at me. "As a sign of respect for his position."

The others likely knew the proper way to address the leader, but I was thankful for Brother George's words of advice.

Berndt looked in the opposite direction. "We better go or we'll be late. That would not be a gut way to begin."

Cousin George agreed. The three men turned and trod toward one end of the meetinghouse while Karlina, Cousin Louise, and I walked to the women's door at the opposite end. Just like at morning worship, the elders sat behind a long table. Although Cousin George was a member of the Grossebruderrat, his position in the group had been temporarily assigned to Brother Samuel, another member of the Bruderrat in East. Karlina had explained that her father didn't wish to sit in judgment when members of his family were involved. While I admired his integrity, I would have preferred to have Cousin George's vote.

My hands perspired as I took my seat beside Karlina. There were more than twenty members of the Grossebruderrat, and the only one I recognized was Brother Samuel. The rest were representatives from the other villages. I wondered if Anton knew the representatives from High—surely he did. I hoped they would look favorably on his request to marry Karlina. Then again, if they'd been the ones who had sent him to East, they might think such a decision premature. Would they expect to see further evidence that he'd learned to control his temper before they would consider his request?

I peeked across the aisle toward Berndt. Shoulders squared, he maintained a steady gaze on the group of elders. His air of confidence surprised me, but it helped to lessen my anxiety. I took a slow, deep breath and silently prayed that God would be with me when it was my turn to speak.

After folding my hands in my lap, I stared at a spot on the floor. I didn't have enough courage to look at the elders. The Grossebruderrat traveled from village to village one time each month, and although no one wanted to have a grievance brought before them, it was considered a privilege to have the elders eat at one's Küche. Rather than partake of the meal at our kitchen house, they had decided to take their evening meal at the Fuchs' Küche. I was certain Sister Martha had been delighted by the selection. And while Cousin Louise hadn't exhibited disappointment, I wondered if she felt slighted. I hoped their decision to eat at another kitchen didn't mean anything other than they wanted to be fair in all matters. They had, after all, eaten in Cousin Louise's Küche the last time they'd been in East.

Brother Weizmann sat in the center of the group and glanced at a sheet of paper before he looked toward the men's side of the room. "Today we are seeing many of the same names before us. We have been in High, where we heard from Sister Violet Nagel and Brother Frank Nagel." He turned a keen eye toward Anton. "Your name was involved in that conversation, Brother Anton." Then he looked at Sister Karlina. "And your name as well, Sister Karlina." He cleared his throat. "Even though the elders sent you to East, it appears trouble has followed you, Brother Anton."

I expected Anton to jump up and defend himself, but he remained silent.

The elder turned to our side of the room and shook his head.

"And we have young sisters who have decided to visit the home of outsiders." He tapped his finger on the piece of paper. "Not once, but several times, I believe." Heaving a sigh, he leaned back in his chair.

Blistering sunlight rippled across the glass windowpanes and heated the room to an insufferable temperature. Not a hint of a breeze drifted through the open windows to cool the room. Two of the elders used their large white handkerchiefs to mop perspiration from their foreheads while another fanned himself with a sheet of paper.

"Brother George, is there anything you would like to say before we begin?"

He stood. "Ja. There is mention of trouble following Brother Anton. I would like to point out that you have correctly stated what happened. He was not the cause of any trouble, but trouble pursued him in the form of Sister Violet. He was abiding by my instructions on that day—both out in the pasture and when he returned to the barn. Anton did not know Sister Violet was in the barn. I was the one who spoke to Dr. Nagel and gave permission for Sister Violet to wait while her father went to talk to Dr. Zimmer in Main Amana." Cousin George glanced down at Anton. "I had no idea Dr. Nagel would be gone for so long, or I would not have—"

Brother Weizmann held up his hand. "We know that Brother Anton was not at fault in this matter, Brother George. Sister Violet's Vater spoke in support of Brother Anton and his behavior, and when we came to a decision that both Sister Violet and her older brother, Frank, could not attend any church or prayer meetings for six weeks, Dr. Nagel asked that Sister Violet receive additional punishment."

I let my eyes stray toward Karlina. She did her best to hide it, but I saw a slight smile tug at the corner of her lips.

Brother Weizmann leaned forward and looked down the table at his fellow elders. "We decided Dr. Nagel knew his daughter best, so we obliged his request. Sister Violet has been assigned to work in the garden for the remainder of the summer. From her reaction, I do not believe she was particularly pleased with our decision."

Cousin George nodded. "Then I have nothing further to say except that Brother Anton has proved to be a gut worker and has become a gut shepherd to our sheep. He has learned that much more can be accomplished with a soft voice and calm spirit than with anger and raised fists."

The row of elders murmured their approval. I hoped Cousin George's compliments would be remembered when Anton asked for permission to marry Karlina. It suddenly seemed strange to me that the elders could now find more reason to deny the request due to Karlina's behavior than Anton's temper. And all because of me!

The senior elder turned a steely gaze in my direction. "Now I would like to learn more about these visits to the farm belonging to—" he hesitated and looked down at his notes—"to the Sedlacek family."

I didn't know if I should stand, but since Cousin George had done so, I followed his example. Fear assailed me. My legs threatened to buckle, and I grabbed the back of the wooden pew for support. "Thank you for giving me permission to speak."

One of the elders cupped a hand behind his ear. "Talk louder!"

His shouted command echoed off the walls like a shotgun blast. My lips trembled. I couldn't remember a time when I'd been so overcome. Standing before the Lord on Judgment Day would likely be thousands of times worse than this, but at the moment I couldn't imagine how anything could be more frightening.

In my loudest voice, I once again thanked the elders. The hard-of-hearing elder nodded his approval. I hoped that I wouldn't lose my voice before I finished, but I wanted to clearly detail what had happened so they would understand that Karlina hadn't initiated any of the visits. Three of the elders interrupted to ask questions, but mostly they remained silent and listened. At least most of them listened. From time to time, one of the older members nodded off until his chin dropped against his chest and jerked him awake. He would glance around, snort, and be back asleep a few minutes later.

When I'd finally explained everything to my own satisfaction, I added one final comment. "I hope that the Grossebruderrat will consider holding me alone responsible for the visits to the Sedlacek farm. Sister Karlina would not have given in to my requests if I had not placed undue pressure upon her by quoting Scriptures that command us to love our neighbors."

One of the elders near the end of the table shook his head. "Your neighbors live within the colonies, Sister Dovie."

The old elder who had fallen asleep through most of my recitation frowned and pursed his lips. "But we must remember the Gut Samaritan. Our Lord wants us to show compassion for those who do not believe the same as we do. We must show His love to others. I think that is what Sister Dovie and Sister Karlina were doing. They were instruments of God's love to a family in need."

More murmurs followed before Brother Weizmann waved the group to silence. "Sister Karlina, do you wish to add anything?" Once again, he wiped the perspiration from his brow. "If so, please do not repeat what Sister Dovie has already told us. The room is very warm, and we hope to finish within the hour."

Karlina shook her head. Remaining silent was probably the best choice, given Brother Weizmann's latest comment.

Tapping the page, Brother Weizmann sighed. "It appears both of the young men have petitioned the Grossebruderrat for permission to marry. Usually this would not take long, but since the two of you have asked to marry the two sisters who have strayed, we will need time to discuss this." He looked at me. "As well as the punishment we decide should be meted out. You may all wait outside. We'll advise you when we have a decision."

The six of us gathered beneath the branches of a large red oak. A warm breeze whipped at my hem, and I turned to catch the next puff of air that might move in our direction. Although Berndt continued to offer an optimistic view while we waited, the rest of us didn't express any opinion. I had no idea what the elders would decide, but I was thankful the old bald elder had mentioned the story of the Good Samaritan.

Not more than twenty minutes had passed before Brother Weizmann waved for us to return inside. We parted and entered our respective doors and then took our places on the hard pews. I folded my hands together and clenched them so tight, my fingers turned odd shades of red and white.

"We have come to our decisions. First, you should know that we do not condone leaving the boundaries of the colonies. In the future you should not do so." He stared directly at Karlina, and my stomach lurched. Next, was he going to tell me I must leave the colonies? "We are thankful that the Sedlacek family has returned to health and that your health has been restored, Sister Karlina."

I held my breath until I thought my lungs would burst. Earlier he had been in such a hurry, yet he now pondered every word before he spoke.

"We will grant permission to Brother Anton and Sister Karlina to marry in one year's time." Again he looked at Karlina. "Tell me, Sister Karlina, would you be willing to spend your year of separation working at a Küche in Middle?"

Karlina gasped and I reached for her hand. Did she love Anton enough to leave her home and working with the sheep? "I . . . I . . ."

Brother Weizmann turned toward Anton. "Since you are still learning your duties as a shepherd and because living in this village will benefit Brother George, we thought you should remain in East, Brother Anton."

He turned back to Karlina. "What say you, Sister Karlina? Do you wish to marry this man enough to leave your family for a year?"

"Ja." Karlina's response was no more than a whisper. My eyes filled with tears thinking about her working in a kitchen rather than spending most of her days with her beloved lambs.

"Gut." Brother Weizmann nodded. "And we have also decided that Sister Karlina should return to children's church for the next two weeks."

The demotion to children's church was a punishment that was more easily accepted. Although the rest of the village would know she'd been chastised, it would be nothing compared to the pain she would bear living away from East for a year. I tried to sneak a look at Anton, but I couldn't see his face. Surely he must know how much she loved him if she would agree to such a thing.

Brother Weizmann turned his attention to Berndt. "Brother Berndt, we will agree that you can marry Sister Dovie, but we have decided upon a stipulation. If either of you refuse the requirement, we will withdraw permission to marry."

I inhaled a ragged breath and clenched my hands so tight they lost all feeling. Brother Weizmann cleared his throat and looked at me. "We have decided Sister Dovie should leave the colonies and return to her family. If she desires to return one year from now, we will not object to her joining our faith or to the marriage." He tugged on his collar. "Let us see if your love will withstand the test of time and separation—and if the colonies are truly the place where Sister Dovie wants to live the remainder of her life."

The air whooshed from my lungs, and I thought I might faint. I would have to leave. What would I do without the direction of Cousin Louise and Cousin George? What would I do without Karlina? And how could I possibly leave Berndt, the man I loved?

Giving no thought to propriety, I stood. "How soon must I go?" My voice quaked, and a tear slipped down my cheek as I awaited the elder's answer.

"As soon as Brother George and Sister Louise can make proper arrangements, but do not try our patience by prolonging your time in East." He straightened his shoulders. "You must remember that the quicker you depart, the sooner you may return—if that is your ultimate choice."

None of the others said a word. I dropped back onto the bench. It seemed as though time stood still as we awaited permission to leave the room.

Instead of telling us we should leave, Brother Weizmann folded the sheet of paper and once again looked at Karlina. "Sister Karlina, we have tested you to see how you would answer regarding a move to another village. And while we prefer the year of separation for couples who ask to marry, we also know that your father depends upon you for recordkeeping in the sheep barn. Because you agreed to our condition and did not argue, we will permit you to remain at home."

Karlina clasped her hand to her bodice. "Danke, Brothers. I am grateful."

Brother Weizmann motioned to Anton. "I will make arrangements for you to live with another family. The two of you must have some separation during your year of waiting. I will speak to Sister Fuch when we are there for our evening meal. I believe she has a spare room."

He pushed up from his chair. "We are dismissed." The elders filed out of the room, with Anton, Berndt, and Cousin George following behind them. Tears rolled down my cheeks as I trailed behind Karlina and Cousin Louise.

"You should not cry, Dovie. The elders are wise in their ways, and this will be a gut test for you and Berndt. If your love is true, it will last." She drew me close and wrapped me in her arms. "You need to have time with your Vater and his lady friend. This will be a gut thing—you will see." She tipped her head back and looked into my eyes. "Trust God, Dovie. This is only a small interruption in your life. If this is what He wants for your future, it will happen."

I wanted to agree. In my head, I knew she was right. In my heart, I remained unconvinced.

EPILOGUE

July 14, 1894
Dovie

My father extended his hand and helped Ardella down the step from the train. She took her place beside him while he held out his hand to me. A full year had passed since I'd departed the colonies, but everything looked exactly as I remembered. "Don't forget what I've told you, Dovie. You can change your mind at any time."

I scanned the platform and sighed. Though I knew Berndt would be delivering bread in East Amana when we arrived at the train station in Main Amana, I had secretly hoped to see him waiting here when we arrived. I tried to hide my disappointment as I perched on my toes and kissed my father's cheek. "That's the same thing you said to me when we arrived at this train station a little more than a year and a half ago."

My father chuckled. "You have a good memory, but I want you to be absolutely sure before you commit the rest of your life to a man who plans to live his entire life in the colonies. I know you love him, but I hope you understand that the changes in your life will be enormous."

"I know, Papa. Remember, I lived here for eight months, and I am prepared to create a new life with Berndt here in East. In fact, I am probably as eager as you were to marry Ardella." I smiled at the radiant woman who had married my father only a few months ago.

I had expected the twosome to wed immediately after the one-year anniversary of my mother's death, but Ardella had insisted on waiting longer. Though I had assumed I would dislike Ardella, I had been surprised. She was nothing like my mother. Instead of a quiet, melancholy nature, Ardella, who'd lost her husband and both of her children in a train accident five years ago, discovered joy in most everything that touched her life.

When I'd asked how she managed to deal with the grief, she'd taken my hands in her own and said, "I have much for which to be thankful, Dovie. I refuse to let bitterness rule my life. After the death of my family, the Lord showed me that it is much better to rejoice in what I have than to dwell on what I've lost."

Ardella's explanation made perfect sense, and I decided that instead of dwelling on the loss of my mother, I would be pleased that my father had found a new wife who could make him happy—and that God had led me to a life in the colonies, where I could find my own happiness with Berndt.

My father went inside the depot to arrange for a buggy to East while Ardella and I remained on the platform with the baggage. She gazed around the village, and I did my best to answer her questions. Prior to our arrival, I'd tried to explain the different way of living and appearance of the villages. Now she was to see and experience the colonists' unique way of life for herself.

The conductor sounded two short blasts of the whistle as the train chugged out of the station. Moments later, my father strode to Ardella's side. A broad smile enhanced his good looks. Since meeting Ardella, he appeared ten years younger. There was no denying she'd had a good effect upon him. I glanced toward the station. "Is there a buggy to take us to East?" I'd been waiting a year to see Berndt, and I was more than ready to end our separation.

"Yes, but it will be a little while, so I said we would go over and get settled at the hotel." My father grinned when I sighed. "I'm afraid you'll have to wait a little longer before you see your intended. I thought we could unpack and the two of you could change clothes for Karlina's wedding. That way we won't need to return to the hotel prior to the ceremony. We'll have more than sufficient time to visit with the family before the wedding."

My heart warmed at my father's reference to Karlina and her parents as "family." During the past year, we had embraced the decisions of one another, and that acceptance had strengthened and enlarged our relationship. My father was eager for me to find happiness with Berndt, and I was thankful he'd begun a new life with Ardella.

After signing the register, he carried the baggage upstairs and gestured toward the door. "I believe it might be best if I remain out of the way while you and Ardella change and unpack."

After placing a fleeting kiss on Ardella's cheek, he hurried down the steps. "I'll let you know when the buggy arrives. No need to come down before then."

I arched my brows at his sudden decision to leave us to the unpacking, but Ardella waved him onward. Apparently she'd decided it would be easier to prepare for the wedding without my father pacing about. She lifted a pink day dress from the trunk and held it in front of her. "Now that we've arrived, I'm not certain this dress was the right choice. I don't want to offend anyone."

"No one will be offended by your choice of clothing, Ardella. Even though the people who live in the colonies choose to wear only dark clothing, they don't expect the same from outsiders." I smiled, lifted another dress from her trunk, and hung it in the wardrobe.

"Don't fuss with unpacking the clothes right now, Dovie. We both need to hurry and get dressed for the wedding. We don't want the buggy to arrive before we've changed."

Over an hour passed before my father tapped on the door and entered. "Don't you two look lovely." His gaze swept over both of us. Ardella in her pale pink dress and me in my plain dark calico—complete opposites on the outside, yet two women who cared deeply for this wonderful man. He turned to me and winked. "The buggy has arrived, but I need to speak to Ardella for a moment. Why don't you go downstairs and tell the driver we'll be there shortly?"

"Of course, Papa." I hurried down the steps and hoped they wouldn't take too long. I'd been waiting to see Berndt for a year, and the time since our arrival had seemed to drag on forever. The driver was standing near the window with his back toward me. My shoes clicked on the wood floor as I approached. He turned.

"Berndt!" My heart raced at the sight of him. Forgetting all decorum and proper behavior, I ran to his arms and reveled in the warmth of his embrace. "Oh, how I have missed you!"

He pressed a kiss to the top of my head, and I held tight to him, enjoying the strength of his arms around me until I heard a tapping sound across the room.

We continued to cling to each other, but the tapping grew louder and the hotel clerk finally cleared his voice. Berndt and I turned to the old man who stood behind the desk. He pointed his finger at us. "This is not a gut way to behave! You should know better."

At his strident reprimand, we jumped apart. I mumbled an apology and was thankful to see my father and Ardella descending the steps. A wide smile spread across my father's face. "Were you surprised to see who I hired as our driver?"

Berndt grinned. "I'm not the driver. Brother Ackermann wouldn't agree to let me take charge of his buggy, but he gave me permission to ride along."

I looked back and forth between my father and Berndt. "How did you arrange for Berndt to meet us?"

My father's eyes sparkled. "I can't tell you all of my secrets. If I did, I'd have no way to surprise you in the future."

His words had a soothing effect upon me, for I had worried that once I returned to Amana, he would completely withdraw from my life. I grasped his arm and smiled up at him. "Then in the years to come, I shall look forward to being surprised by you."

"Good. Now we best be on our way. We don't want to be late for Karlina's wedding."

❖

Karlina

I sat on the edge of the bed and traced my fingers over gray pin-stripes of my navy blue dress, which was carefully spread across the bed. Perhaps I should press the skirt one more time to assure myself that it was completely free of wrinkles. Even though my dress wasn't a white satin wedding gown like those worn by out-siders, I had created it with as much love and attention as any lace-laden white gown. Besides, in the colonies white was worn only for burial—as a symbol of purity for the soul that ascended to God—never for weddings or other ceremonies.

I pictured myself walking forward to meet Anton in my navy blue dress, and I knew that no matter what I wore, Anton would think me beautiful. Hadn't he repeated those very words to me throughout the past year? Still, I didn't want to look down and see a wrinkle in the skirt of my dress. It was my hope that everything would be perfect when I took my vows and during the large reception that would follow.

Mother had worked feverishly over the past weeks. She'd arranged for flowers to decorate the tables, and along with supervising the preparations in our Küche, she had enlisted the help of the other Küchehaases in East. There would be plenty of food, of that I had no doubt. Wedding ceremonies might be simple affairs in the colonies, but the reception that followed was always a party to be enjoyed by everyone.

"Karlina! What are you doing up there?" My mother's voice drifted up the stairs, and I jumped up from the bed. "I hear the wagon coming. You should be down here to welcome Dovie, ja?"

I pushed aside all thought of pressing my skirt and ran through the parlor and down the stairs. "My window was open, but I didn't even hear the train whistle."

My mother chuckled. "Because you spend all of your time lost in daydreaming. The train passed through Main Amana more than an hour ago." She grabbed my hand and together we walked outside.

After stepping down from the buggy, Brother Ackermann turned and tipped his hat. "Guten Tag, Sister Louise and Sister Karlina." He extended his hand to help Dovie out of the buggy. "Some of your wedding guests got here just in time, Sister Karlina." With a glance over his shoulder, he shot a grin in my direction.

"I thank you for bringing them, Brother Ackermann. Since you won't be here for the reception, perhaps you should step into the kitchen. One of the ladies will be pleased to cut you a piece of pie."

He chuckled and nodded. "I thought you would never ask."

I hurried forward to welcome Dovie. We had corresponded regularly since her departure last year, but it seemed forever since I had seen her. "You look wonderful. I'm so glad you've arrived." As I drew her into an embrace, I glanced up and met her father's gaze. I stepped back. "It is wonderful to see you, as well, Mr. Cates. And . . ." I hesitated as a lovely woman stepped to his side. I switched and spoke in English. "And I am pleased to make your acquaintance, Mrs. Cates."

Dovie hurried to introduce her stepmother and smiled with pride when the older woman answered in German. "She speaks quite well, don't you think?"

I could see the relief spread across my mother's face. Dovie's stepmother would feel more included if she could understand the language. My mother ushered us into the Küche and suggested we visit in the upstairs parlor. "With all the baking and decorating, there is too much activity down here."

Once upstairs, Dovie and I retreated to my bedroom. There wasn't a great deal of time before the wedding would take place, and I wanted her to help me with my dress. "What do you think?" I nodded toward my dress on the bed.

Dovie stepped closer and examined the fine lace I'd tatted and attached to the cuffs and collar. "It is beautiful, Karlina. Anton is a very lucky man."

I giggled. "He is wonderful, Dovie. I am so very happy that today has finally arrived, and we can soon begin our life together."

"The elders have assigned him to remain in East permanently?"

"Ja. We will live here with Mutter and Vater. There is enough space, and it will prove easier for Vater. The elders said that it would be best for all of us."

I hadn't been surprised by the decision. Our house had enough bedrooms. Still, most couples received housing that included a private parlor, but Anton had agreed it would be easier to remain in a house not far from the sheep barns. His choice had warmed my heart. Once my father was certain of the decision, he made plans to rearrange the rooms. Anton and I would share my bedroom and the current parlor, while Anton's former bedroom would become the new parlor for my parents.

I quickly explained the arrangement to Dovie. "I think it will be perfect for us." I didn't admit it, but I felt like a little girl who would soon begin to play house. "How are the rooms at the hotel?"

"The rooms are quite nice. We will be comfortable there."

In her recent letter, Dovie had told me she would stay at the hotel with her father and his wife until her wedding. "I wish you could stay here until the wedding, but soon you and Berndt will be living—" I clapped my hand over my mouth. Berndt had told me that he wanted to tell Dovie about their living arrangements.

Dovie inched closer. "We will be living where? Tell me, Karlina."

"I promised Berndt I would not say. He should be the one to tell you. But I can tell you that the elders assigned you to work with Mutter in the Küche. I hope that makes you happy."

Dovie sighed. "I was very worried they might assign me to Sister Fuch's Küche. I'm sure I could do so if I had to, but I have been praying they would assign me to work with Cousin Louise and the other sisters that I already know."

"Then your prayers have been answered." I gestured toward my dress. "Do you see any wrinkles in the skirt?"

Dovie lifted the dress from the bed and held it before her. "No wrinkles. It is perfect. And you must get dressed or you will be late for your own wedding."

"I don't think Anton would appreciate that, do you?"

We burst into laughter and soon my mother tapped on the door. "You need to stop chattering and get dressed, Karlina. This is not a day to be late. Elder Adler will not be happy if you keep him waiting in the July heat."

Dovie helped me into my dress and insisted upon combing and fashioning my hair in a delicate knot at the nape of my neck. After seeing that the point of my shawl was centered, she gave a firm nod. "Perfect. You look beautiful."

"Will your father and stepmother be shocked when they see me wearing a dark dress for my wedding?"

"I have explained everything to them. When I returned to Texas and told my father and Ardella that I planned to marry Berndt, she was eager to help me find fabric for the perfect wedding gown." Dovie chuckled. "I think she was disappointed, but she understands that I will be wearing a dark dress for my wedding and the ceremony won't be lavish."

"For sure, that is true." I leaned forward and kissed Dovie's cheek. "I am thankful you have returned to live here. We may not share the same house, but we will always be friends."

A tear glistened in Dovie's eyes and slowly rolled down her cheek. "You are the sister I never had, Karlina."

I wiped the tear from her cheek. "Ja, we will now be sisters in every way."

Anton smiled at me as we walked to the front of the meeting-house. I could see the joy that shone in his eyes as he pledged his love and stated his desire to marry me. He grasped my hand as Brother Adler bowed his head and prayed a blessing on our marriage. When the prayer ended, the elder declared our lives joined as husband and wife, but we knew there could be no kiss. Not in the meetinghouse, for that was forbidden. We returned down the aisle and exited through the doors at opposite sides of the meetinghouse.

Once outside, Anton raced toward me and scooped me into his arms. Twirling in a circle, he kissed me soundly and then lowered me back to the ground. "It is a wonderful day because I can now call you my wife."

My father shook Anton's hand and offered congratulations to both of us. "Now I think we should enjoy some of the gut food we left in the Küche." He patted his stomach. "I am ready to eat and celebrate."

Anton stole several kisses as we walked toward the Küchehaas, but I longed for time alone with him. Time when we could savor the presence of each other without interruption, but that wouldn't happen until much later.

By the time we returned, friends and neighbors had already arrived for the reception. The women had decorated the dining room of the Küche with flowers they'd cut from their gardens or wild flowers from the surrounding fields. The tables were laden with tortes, pies, and cakes of every shape and size. Many had been baked in the other Küchehaases and delivered for the party. The long wooden tables had been moved outdoors, pitchers of grape and cherry juice sat on the tables for the children, and a barrel of grape wine sat at the ready for the adults.

I motioned for Dovie and Berndt to join us at one of the tables. Dovie carried several pieces of cake to the table and placed them in front of us. "You need to have some of this good food."

I touched my hand to my stomach. "I am too excited to eat. In two weeks, you will know exactly how I feel."

A wide grin split Berndt's face. "It cannot come soon enough for me." He leaned closer to Dovie. "I hope she feels the same way."

Dovie giggled and rested her hand on Berndt's arm. "You know I do." She looked across the table and met my gaze. "Berndt has told me we will have the extra apartment in the house with his parents, but you already knew."

"Ja, but I did not tell." I arched my brows. "Does this make you happy?"

"Yes. I think it will be perfect. Berndt can bring me to the kitchen in the bread wagon each morning."

"It is a gut arrangement, and I think you both will be happy." I grinned. "Maybe not as happy as Anton and me, but you will be happy."

The four of us laughed and talked, but soon other guests sat down to visit. A short time later, Anton took my hand and we slipped away and found a secluded spot beneath one of the large cottonwood trees.

In the shade of the low-hanging branches, he drew me into his arms. His lips traveled down the length of my cheek, and I dragged in a quick breath. He lightly kissed my neck and then captured my lips with his own. As if perfectly fitted, our lips melded together. I leaned into him and gave myself fully to his kiss.

He inhaled a ragged breath as we drew apart. Cupping my cheek in his palm, he looked into my eyes. "You have helped me to become a better man, Karlina, and I want to do everything I can to make you happy. I hope you believe that I will always love you."

My heart fluttered at the sweetness and sincerity of his words. "It is God who has made you into a better man, Anton. I have thanked Him many times for bringing you into my life." I tenderly touched my hand to his cheek. "I love you more than you know."

His lips curved in a slow grin, and his eyes sparkled. "Then perhaps it is time for you to show me."

"Perhaps I should!" Pushing caution aside, I stood on my toes until our lips touched in a gentle caress. Slowly he took command and claimed my lips with another kiss that left me breathless.

He smiled down at me. "That is a gut beginning."

SPECIAL THANKS TO . . .

. . . My editor, Sharon Asmus, for her generous spirit, excellent eye for detail, and amazing ability to keep her eyes upon Jesus through all of life's adversities.

. . . My acquisitions editor, Charlene Patterson, for her enthusiastic encouragement to continue writing about the Amana Colonies.

. . . The entire staff of Bethany House Publishers, for their devotion to making each book they publish the best product possible. It is a privilege to work with all of you.

. . . Lanny Haldy and the staff of the Amana Heritage Society, for sharing history of the Amana Colonies.

. . . Peter Holhne, for answering my many questions about the Amana Colonies.

. . . Mary Greb-Hall for her ongoing encouragement, expertise, and sharp eye.

. . . Lori Seilstad, for her honest critiques.

. . . Mary Kay Woodford, my sister, my prayer warrior, my friend.

. . . Above all, thanks and praise to our Lord Jesus Christ for the opportunity to live my dream and share the wonder of His love through story.

Judith Miller is an award-winning author whose avid research and love for history are reflected in her bestselling novels. Judy makes her home in Topeka, Kansas.

More Tender Romance from Judith Miller

To learn more about Judith and her books, visit judithmccoymiller.com.

In the picturesque Amana Colonies, family secrets, hidden passions, and the bonds of friendship run deeper than outsiders know. As three young women come of age, must they choose between love and their beloved community?

DAUGHTERS OF AMANA: *Somewhere to Belong, More Than Words, A Bond Never Broken*

When greedy investors set their sights on Audrey's ancestral home on Bridal Veil Island, Marshall Graham is charged with protecting the fiery young woman who seems to disdain him. But her refusal to sell could cost more than they know.

To Have and to Hold
BRIDAL VEIL ISLAND

Melinda leaves her position as a lady's maid in order to return home to Bridal Veil Island after it is devastated by a hurricane. But when she overhears a dangerous plot, will she find reason to distrust the one she loves?

To Love and Cherish
BRIDAL VEIL ISLAND

If you enjoyed *A Hidden Truth*, you may also like...